The Three Monks of Tears

THE ROSE KNIGHT'S CRUCIFIXION #2

Being a Novel of Historical Adventure

and a Romance of Ideas

Strangely Contiguous to

Dumas's *The Three Musketeers*

LAWRENCE ELLSWORTH

The Three Monks of Tears
Copyright © 2018 Lawrence Schick

A WORD TO THE FORE

The Rose Knight's Crucifixion: A Novel of Historical Adventure and a Romance of Ideas stands on its own, but it's also a parallel novel to Alexandre Dumas's *The Three Musketeers*. It shares certain characters and plot elements with Dumas's classic work, the story of Louis d'Astarac interweaving with that of d'Artagnan, Athos, Porthos, and Aramis.

Here's how it works: *The Three Musketeers* has 67 chapters, and so does *The Rose Knight's Crucifixion,* though the latter is published in two parts, the first 29 chapters as *The Three Mystic Heirs,* and the final 38 in *The Three Monks of Tears.* You could read *Musketeers* and *Crucifixion* separately, simply enjoying the correspondences between the two works, or you could read them interleaved: chapter one of *Musketeers* followed by chapter one of *Crucifixion,* then back to *Musketeers* for chapter two, and so forth. Crazy!

If you do intend to read (or re-read) *The Three Musketeers,* then I recommend my own recent translation of Dumas's most famous novel, published by Pegasus Books of New York and London. It's a sparkling new translation for the contemporary reader, and I think you'd enjoy it.

Table of Contents

WHAT HAS GONE BEFORE

The Three Mystic Heirs, the first part of *The Rose Knight's Crucifixion,* introduces Louis d'Astarac, the Vicomte de Fontrailles, at his provincial home in Armagnac in the south of France, in the year 1626. Louis is a young French noble, witty, cultured, and trained in all the social graces of a 17th century courtier. But he's also a hunchback, stunted and deformed. Rejected by his lady-love, Isabeau, Louis, desperate, can see only one way to win her hand: cure his condition by using the Rosicrucian Brotherhood's secrets of spiritual alchemy. This esoteric and forbidden magic was compiled in *The Three Mystic Heirs,* a book eradicated by the Inquisition in 1620—except for one copy. And Louis thinks he knows where to find it.

The trail of the lost book leads to Paris; along the way Louis, expecting trouble, hires a rogue known as Cocodril to act as his bodyguard. In Paris, Louis contacts a young scholar named René des Cartes, who warns him against pursuing the Rosicrucian book, for the power of its secrets are being sought by the high and mighty of Europe, who will stop at nothing to get it—including murder. But Louis is determined, and becomes a player in a fast-moving game between agents of England's Duke of Buckingham, France's Cardinal Richelieu, the Jesuit Order of Rome ... and the shadowy Rosicrucians themselves. (And who is this noisy swordsman d'Artagnan, with his cronies the Three Musketeers, who keep popping up at every turn?)

Louis's investigations soon bring him to the attention of Cardinal Richelieu, who has him detained and presents him with a choice: disappear into prison, or join the Cardinal's Guards and hunt the Rosicrucian book on behalf of the minister. Louis reluctantly picks the latter option. Newly-made Ensign d'Astarac searches for a Rosy Cross mechanist named Salomon de Caus, and when he learns the man has been confined by the Jesuits in the horrific Paris insane asylum, he allies with the seductive Lucy Hay, Countess of Carlisle—herself an agent of Buckingham—to get him out. De Caus,

1

dying of his wounds from being put to the Question, reveals that the book has been sent to London in the effects of Ambassador Bassompierre, and Louis and Lucy set out separately for England to recover it.

In London Louis is drawn into the intrigues of another agent of the cardinal, the dangerous Milady de Winter. He burgles the ambassador's bedroom to get the book, only to find that Lucy has been there ahead of him. But now Milady de Winter is also aware of his quest; she subverts Cocodril, nearly kills both Louis and Lucy, and gets away with the book. D'Astarac and Lucy Hay pursue her back to France, but they are trailed by yet another agent of Buckingham: the wily Sir Percy Blakeney.

Back in Paris, Milady de Winter bargains with Richelieu for the book by letter, pretending to be Louis d'Astarac, so when the real Louis returns to the capital, he and Lucy are arrested and interrogated by Richelieu's spymaster, Father Joseph. They escape, and during a night of drunken passion Louis deduces what Milady is up to. Lucy leaves him yet again, but Louis finds refuge with Aramis and the other musketeers while planning his next move. To get *The Three Mystic Heirs* from Milady, he sets up a phony ransom-payment rendezvous, but Milady sees through his ploy and secretly brings Cocodril to the meeting. Louis spots him in time to run for it, but the rogue chases him down to the banks of the Seine, where he draws a long knife and attacks him.

CHARACTERS

An **asterisk*** indicates a person recorded in history.

The Vicomte de Fontrailles and Associates

Louis d'Astarac, Vicomte de **Fontrailles***: A young nobleman of Armagnac.

Vidou: His valet.

René **des Cartes***: A scholar.

Jean Reynon, known as **Cocodril**: A rogue.

Gitane: A smuggler.

Beaune: A jailer and inquisitor.

Sobriety **Breedlove**: An English sailor.

Nobility of France

Philippe de **Longvilliers**, *Seigneur de Poincy**: A Commander of the French Priory of the Knights of Malta.

Seigneur **de Bonnefont**: A nobleman of Armagnac.

Isabeau *de Bonnefont*: His daughter.

Éric *de Gimous*: A young nobleman of Armagnac.

Nobility of England

Lucy Percy Hay, Countess of **Carlisle***: A lady of the English Court.

George Villiers, Duke of **Buckingham***: Prime Minister of King Charles I.

Sir Percy **Blakeney**, *also known as "Diogenes"*: Amateur intelligencer for His Grace the Duke.

Enfield: Blakeney's valet.

Balthasar **Gerbier***: The duke's art agent and envoy.

Doctor John **Lambe***: The duke's astrologer and alchemist.

King's Musketeers and Comrades

Aramis: A musketeer, formerly trained as a priest.

Bazin: His valet.

Athos: A noble musketeer.

Porthos: A vainglorious musketeer.

The Chevalier **d'Artagnan***: A Gascon guardsman, later a musketeer.

Planchet: His lackey.

The Cardinal and His Fidèles

Armand-Jean du Plessis, Cardinal de **Richelieu***: Prime Minister of King Louis XIII.

François Leclerc du Tremblay, known as **Father Joseph***: A Capuchin monk, intimate of Richelieu and head of his intelligence service.

Comte de **Rochefort**: A cavalier, an agent of His Eminence the Cardinal.

Lady Clarice, Countess Winter, known as **Milady** *de Winter*: A lady of the French and English Courts, and an agent of His Eminence.

François d'Ogier, Sieur de **Cavois***: Captain of the Cardinal's Guard.

Jean de Baradat, Sieur de **Cahusac***: A Cardinal's Guard.

Claude de **Jussac***: A Cardinal's Guard.

Bernajoux: A Cardinal's Guard.

Marin **Boisloré***: Agent of Richelieu in England, an officer in the household of Queen Henriette.

The Society of Jesus

Athanasius **Kircher***: A Jesuit scholar of Mainz, in Germany.

Jean-Marie Crozat, known as Père **Mikmaq**: A Jesuit priest, recently recalled from the New World.

The Court of Miracles

Great **Caesar**: King of the Beggars of Paris.

Proserpine: His daughter.

Bronte: A beggar.

Montfaucon: A former solicitor, now a beggar, "Intendant" to Great Caesar.

With the exception of *The Three Mystical Heirs of Christian Rosencreutz*, all published works mentioned in this book are historical.

CHAPTER XXX
MIRACLES

Cocodril's mistake, Louis thought later, was probably assuming that a stunted hunchback must be a weakling. But Fontrailles's muscles had strained for many years against his own misshapen skeleton, and he was stronger than he looked. In Cocodril's last conscious moments, it must have seemed as if the smaller man simply exploded.

Fontrailles's right collarbone was broken, but his arm worked nonetheless; though it was agony to use it, when faced with death the pain simply didn't register. As Cocodril struck, Fontrailles's right hand flicked out and deflected Cocodril's knife-hand up and over, and then Fontrailles's left arm spun around like the wing of a windmill, whipping his weighty leather purse out of his belt and down on Cocodril's head. The purse hit hard and split at the seams, showering Fontrailles's ex-servant with the coins intended to ransom *The Three Mystic Heirs* from Milady.

Cocodril dropped his knife point-first into the sand, where it stuck, quivering. He put one hand to his head, staggered blindly to the water's edge, and then fell heavily into the Seine, whose current swiftly whisked him away.

Fontrailles watched Cocodril's body disappear into the river, then stared stupidly for several moments at his trembling dagger—that, and the man's footprints, were the only signs that Cocodril had ever been there. Then a motion to his left drew his eye along the riverbank, toward the piers supporting the nearby Pont du Bois, the temporary wooden bridge that had replaced the Pont du Change after that bridge had burned to the water in 1621.

Dark masses in the shadows under the bridge, mounds that Louis had initially taken for refuse, were rising, assuming human form, and moving. Toward him.

Fontrailles blinked and looked again, but they were still there: ragged figures, beggars, cripples, and mudlarks, lurching toward him, blinking themselves in the light of the open riverbank. Louis felt the hair rise on the back of his neck. He turned to stagger for the stairs up to the quay, crying out as the twist sent pain shooting down his right side, then limped sidewise in a gait as irregular as that of the shambling beggars boiling out from beneath the bridge.

When almost to the stairs Louis remembered Cocodril's knife, his only chance for a weapon. He looked back, but the beggars and mudlarks were already swarming over the site of the brief battle. Louis saw then that they weren't coming after him, but were all scrabbling after the money spilled from the burst purse. All, that is, except one gaunt figure, stooped like a vulture, who regarded Fontrailles speculatively for a moment and then reached down to pick up Cocodril's knife, spinning it between his fingers as if he knew how to use it.

The gaunt man looked at him hungrily—with, Louis noted with both dismay and a certain fatalistic resignation, only one eye, as he wore a patch over the other—and then started toward him. Fontrailles turned, immediately tripped over the bottom step, then scuttled up the stairs to the quay as fast as he could go on all-threes.

The gaunt man was right behind him as Fontrailles reached the top of the narrow stairs and reentered the bustling world of the Paris streets. Panting, clutching his right arm, emitting a low moaning wail, he scurried into the traffic on the Quai de la Mégisserie with no thought except to get away from the gaunt man. He stumbled over a loose cobblestone, fell to his knees, and was scrambling to his feet again when he heard a clatter of wheels and hooves and a loud, shrill whinny. He looked up: once again, a speeding carriage was hurtling toward him, an elegant white rig drawn by a team of matched grays—but this time, events seemed to accelerate rather than slow, and he had no chance to avoid the onrushing doom. He caught a glimpse of the horses' wide, rolling eyes, then their iron-shod hooves came down and the world went dark.

My aching head, Louis d'Astarac thought. *And shoulder. What happened?* He opened his eyes and looked up at the familiar arch of the trunk of the ancient plane tree on the hill behind Château de Fontrailles. It was spring, birds were singing, and sunlight flickered through the new green leaves.

Oh, right. I fell out of the tree.

"Are you hurt, Louis?" It was Isabeau, kneeling beside him in the leaf-loam, concern in her dark eyes. She was fifteen years old.

"I was trying to get you that spray of fuschia," Louis said, sitting up. "But the branch broke, and I fell out of the tree." He was still dizzy.

"And now I can reach it," said Éric de Gimous, plucking the flowers from the drooping vine. He presented them to Isabeau with a small bow. "For you, Demoiselle."

"Why, *thank* you, Éric!" she said, coloring.

"Hey!" Louis protested, but night seemed to be falling and the hillside was growing dim. Isabeau was singing, crooning wordlessly, which was strange because she never sang, always complained that she couldn't carry a tune. And her voice seemed higher, almost a soprano. "Isabeau?" Louis said, into the dark.

The song broke off with a little chuckle—not Isabeau's laugh at all. "Bronte, bring a lamp," said a voice, flutelike. "Your little lordling seems to be coming around."

There was a dancing light; Louis felt himself squint as a candle flame came into focus, its glow augmented by the radiance of an approaching oil lamp. He couldn't quite make out the tall figure carrying the lamp behind the glare from its silvered reflector, but the rest of the room emerged from the shadows. A lady's boudoir, by the look of it, but the furnishings, though sumptuous, were strangely mismatched: light contemporary furniture, painted and gilded, mixed with antique pieces from previous centuries, dark, heavy, and deeply incised. Behind tapestries of clashing colors the walls were peeling, and rodents scrabbled in the still-dark corners.

A large canopied bed dominated one side of the chamber, and lolling on it among mounds of oriental pillows was a broad-faced young woman in a gaudy embroidered robe. She smiled at Fontrailles, toyed with a curl of her abundant red hair, and said, "Welcome, Monsieur—I presume you *are* a gentleman?—to my *chambre de coucher*. Is there anything you'd like?"

"Uh," Fontrailles said, and licked his dry lips. "Water. If you please," he added, "Madame."

"Mademoi*selle*," she corrected. "Set the lamp on the table, Bronte, and go send for some water." The tall figure did as she bade, and once he was out from behind the lamp Louis started as he recognized the gaunt man who had pursued him on the riverbank. He surveyed Fontrailles intently with his one eye, then turned and sidled out of the room.

"We're somewhat informal here," said the woman on the bed, toying now with the frogging on the lapels of her robe, "so I'm afraid you'll have to introduce yourself." She smiled, appearing genuinely pleased, and her narrow eyes shrank above the ruddy globes of her cheeks until they almost disappeared.

Fontrailles was lying on a venerable claw-footed divan, his back propped up on more oriental cushions. He sat up straight, suppressing a gasp and wince as the edges of his broken collarbone ground together, and bowed his head toward his seeming hostess. "Louis d'Astarac, Vicomte de Fontrailles, at your service, Mademoiselle."

"I *knew* you were a nobleman." She nodded happily, red ringlets swaying. "I could tell by the scent of your clothes. You wear the perfume of rank!"

This was a surprise to Louis, who'd spent the previous night in a stable. "And with whom do I have the pleasure of conversing?" he asked.

"Proserpine." Her broad slippered feet thumped on the floor as she slid from the bed. She stood and sketched a brief curtsy.

She was tall, and built on a grand scale. If she were divided three ways and parceled out, Louis thought, one might make three Isabeaus of her. He said, "Proserpine de…?"

"Proserpine will do. Ah, here comes your water, Monsieur!" It was almost a song—she really had a remarkably musical voice. She gestured with a hand that glittered with rings; Fontrailles turned to see the vulturine Bronte stalk back into the room, bearing a pitcher and cracked goblet. He set them on a table near Fontrailles's divan and then stood looming, gazing at him hungrily.

"Gazes at you hungrily, doesn't he?" Proserpine said. "Bronte hopes to profit from you, Monsieur de Fontrailles, and he's wondering how much. Of course, Bronte gazes hungrily at everyone—even at me." She smiled again, dimpling. "What is it you want from me, Bronte? Shall I guess?" She laughed, a rising arpeggio, and preened a little. Bronte dropped his eyes.

Weird, thought Louis. He filled the goblet, pouring awkwardly with his left hand. As he set the pitcher down he noticed a slender knife thrust through Bronte's belt: Cocodril's knife. Louis's hand shook a bit as he drank; when he reached for his handkerchief to dry his chin he found it was missing from his sleeve, and was forced to blot his lips with his lace cuff.

Proserpine and Bronte watched the entire operation as intently as spectators at a royal ballet. The whole situation was absurd, and Louis began to find it annoying.

Worse than that was the realization of his utter failure to find a way to win Isabeau. His situation was a thorough and comprehensive mess: he was a fugitive from justice with no resources, he had a broken shoulder, and he'd bungled his last chance to get his hands on *The Three Mystic Heirs,* his only hope of redemption. He was a joke, and everything he did was a joke.

And on top of everything else, now he seemed to be in some sort of madhouse. He had nowhere to go, but he had a good idea that wherever this was, he'd be better off somewhere else. "I'd hate to be a burden on your household, Mademoiselle," he said. "To whom do I tender my thanks before I take my leave?"

The young woman seemed amused by this. "Why, as to that...."

"He's coming," the gaunt man interrupted, in a voice that sounded like it wasn't used very often.

"*Là!* There you are!" Proserpine clapped her hands delightedly, rings clicking together. "You can thank him personally, Monsieur de Fontrailles."

A rhythmic thump-thud-thump-thud approached from the next chamber, a sound Louis found hauntingly familiar, and then a man, stiffly erect and glittering in golden court raiment, stood in the doorway. A man with a wooden right leg, a patch over his right eye, and a hook where his right hand should be.

God's holy breeches! Louis thought. *At least old Sobriety Breedlove had both hands. This fellow goes him one better ... or worse.*

"So this is your latest find, Bronte?" the new arrival rasped. He put hand-and-hook on his hips and surveyed Fontrailles. Louis returned the compliment. The newcomer was past middle age, with features strong and regular but somehow worn, and the skin around his nose and eyes was webbed with a lacework of fine red capillaries. His eyebrows, mustache, and *royale* goatee mixed gray and white bristles, and Louis noticed without surprise that he was missing his right ear. He was dressed in a Court ensemble of gold and caramel, an outfit as splendid as any Louis had ever seen, marred only by an eight-inch run in the white hose that clad his left leg.

Gaunt Bronte thumped his heart with his right fist and then held his arm straight out toward the golden man, palm down. "Hail, Caesar," he croaked.

The man acknowledged the salute with minuscule nod, directed a more pronounced nod at the young woman while saying, "Proserpine," then stumped toward Fontrailles's divan.

Social superior, Louis thought reflexively. *Must stand.*

Fontrailles was still in the process of getting off the divan when the man stopped an arm's-length away, sniffed, and peered down at him. He reached up with his hook to his face and fumbled with its point at the rim of his eye-patch, then cursed, gripped the hook with his left hand and popped it off, wooden mount and all, from the end of his right arm.

Louis gulped but held his tongue as the man wiggled his right fingers—all five of them—then took the edge of his eye-patch twixt thumb and forefinger and flipped it up, revealing a perfectly sound eye. Full vision restored, he looked Fontrailles over again from top to toe, briefly fingered the stuff of Louis's collar with his pale right hand, and then nodded as if he'd made up his mind. He took a step back with his wooden leg, stumbled slightly, uttered a shockingly filthy curse, then reached behind him with both hands and fumbled for a moment behind the small of his back. There was a snap, and then he reached down, unstrapped the wooden leg from below his right knee, and unfolded his right leg from behind him. "Much better," he said, stamping his right foot to restore the circulation.

The man laughed harshly at Fontrailles. "You look as if you'd seen a miracle, young man. Well, so you have! This is the place where they happen."

"What place do you mean, Monsieur?" asked Fontrailles.

"Mean?" the man said gruffly. "There's no question about what I mean. I know exactly what I mean. Furthermore, I'll ask the questions, and you will answer when spoken to. That's logical! Now, what's your name, and who's your family?"

Fontrailles bowed slightly—he was afraid that if he bowed any more, he might not be able to straighten up—and said, "I am called Louis d'Astarac, and I am Viscount of Fontrailles, in Armagnac."

The man acknowledged Fontrailles's bow with a haughty nod and said, "And I am Great Caesar, Emperor of the Beggars and Vermin of Paris, *les Parasites Parisiens* ... but you recognized me, of course. Though you attempted to master your awe at finding yourself in my presence, it was detected nonetheless. How could it be otherwise? ...That was not a question you are required to answer. I shall sit."

Bronte quickly steered an upholstered chair into position behind him, getting it in place just as Great Caesar's fundament met the cushions. "You are no doubt asking yourself how you came to be here in my domain, the Court of Miracles," Great Caesar continued. "Well, leave off! I'm asking the questions. Don't make me remind you again. Now, this Fontrailles—is it a wealthy domain? What assets does your father command?"

"None, Mon... Monseigneur," Louis said, thinking, *I have no idea what's going on here, but this man is clearly a lunatic. Best be cautious.* "My father is dead, Your, uh, Majesty; I am the last of my family."

"Nonsense." Caesar's eyebrows bristled. "Your father must be alive, as he must pay your ransom. That's simple logic." A low growl of assent came from Bronte.

"One hesitates to contradict Monseigneur," Fontrailles said, as Caesar's eyes narrowed, "but even if my father was still alive, my domain is a small one, with no monetary assets to speak of. I'm afraid that if you're looking for a ransom, Great Caesar, you've got the wrong man."

"Hmph," Caesar said. "If you're the wrong man, then the wrong is yours and not mine. That goes without saying. If you've entered my domain under false pretenses, then you are an impostor and must be tried."

"Oh, no!" cried Proserpine. "No, father!"

"I'm afraid so, my dear. And logically, if he's found guilty, then he must pay the penalty," Caesar said majestically. "Which is, of course, death."

CHAPTER XXXI
CHEVALIER AND CAVALIER

"As soon as I heard about the absurd duel Winter had gotten himself into with that young lout d'Artagnan I knew you'd have to be one of the seconds," Sir Percy Blakeney said, raising his glass of burgundy.

"He's not a lout, you know; just unpolished," Aramis said, clinking his glass against Blakeney's. "*Santé.* Knowing Winter is one of Buckingham's men, I suspected I might encounter you as well, so I made certain you were my opponent when the eight of us squared off."

"Of course we had to make sure one of us didn't spit the other, but I still don't see, Monsieur le Chevalier d'Herblay, why *I* had to be the one to run away," Blakeney said, aggrieved.

"Call me Aramis, if you please. And you had to be the one to retreat, Sir Percy, because it was clear as soon as your compatriots drew their swords that our side was bound to win. Fine gentlemen, I'm sure, but I don't think they face blades every day like those of King's Musketeers."

"I imagine not—though we're not all duffers, you know," said Blakeney. "And I'd be obliged if you'd call me Monsieur Mouron."

"Fair is fair," said Aramis. "Next time I'll be the one who legs it." He held up his empty glass to signal the tavern wench for refills. They were seated in a corner of the Beehive, a low-but-not-too-low dive in the Marais a few streets from the Place Royale. It was a place Aramis had been patronizing since his days as a student. It wasn't frequented by the upper classes and seemed a good place to meet Blakeney on the sly.

"I imagine you know why I'm back in Paris," Blakeney, or "Mouron," said after the barmaid had left.

"You're after the whatever-it-is for Milord Buckingham," said Aramis. "The same thing my friend d'Astarac went to London for."

"It's because he's your friend that we're talking now," Blakeney said. "If he has the item I'll have to get it from him, and I'd hate to have to do him an injury. If you value Monsieur de Fontrailles, you'll help me find him and persuade him to give the thing up."

"My loyalties are to the Throne of France," Aramis said. "Why should I help this object go to England?"

"Because you're not the cardinal's man, you're the king's—or more precisely, the queen's," said Blakeney. "It's Richelieu who wants the item, and I know you're no friend of his."

"True enough," said Aramis. "The fact is, I don't care what happens to this thing—but I do care what happens to Louis d'Astarac. I haven't seen him since he left Paris, but I know his haunts and habits." Aramis smiled disarmingly. "Tell me what you know, and together we may be able to find him."

Blakeney frowned and drummed his fingers on the table. He said, "Very well. I have no reason to mistrust you, other than the fact that you're French. In London, your Fontrailles purported to believe that the object was here in Paris, in the hands of someone with the curious sobriquet of the Peregrine. I traced Fontrailles as far as Chantilly, but there the trail became confused and I lost him. So I came on to Paris to look for this Peregrine fellow."

He's left out Lady Carlisle's involvement, and who knows what else, Aramis thought. *But then I haven't mentioned finding d'Astarac at my house, or the deal I've made with the Jesuits. Fair, after all, is fair.* He asked, "Have you had any luck?"

"Of a sort," said Blakeney. "I made a few inquiries after this Peregrine in the usual places—and some unusual ones, too. I haven't found him yet, but somebody else found *me*." He cocked an eyebrow at Aramis.

"I quiver with suspense," said Aramis. "Who was it?"

"One of your distinguished French nobles, a Philippe de Longvilliers," Blakeney said with seeming nonchalance—but Aramis could tell the Englishman was watching closely for his reaction. The musketeer hoped he didn't supply any.

"I knew who Longvilliers was, by reputation," Blakeney continued, "but I'd never seen nor met him before; he keeps rather a low profile for a Commander of the Knights of Malta."

"What did he want?" Aramis asked. He was trying not to appear too interested, but his brain was racing. *The commander! How did he get involved with this? And since I had to inform Blakeney of my true name before that duel, how long before he finds out what Philippe de Longvilliers is to me?*

"It seems he's looking for this Peregrine as well," Blakeney said, "though he wouldn't say why, or how he'd learned about him. Demanded I tell him everything I knew without offering to give me anything in return. Damned impertinent, even in a Knight of Malta." Blakeney smiled his rather foolish smile. "So I just stuttered and played the silly ass, and neither of us learned anything. He made the usual vague-but-ominous threats and left. Slammed the door on the way out, too—terrible manners."

"Strange," Aramis said. "I wonder who put him onto this?"

"I've no idea," Blakeney said, "but I thought you might."

"Me? *Tête de Dieu*! I'm no Knight of Malta! But I will see if I can locate Louis d'Astarac. Shall we meet here again tomorrow evening?"

"Here?" Blakeney wrinkled his nose. "All right … if we must. I have some other appointments between now and then that may prove fruitful. This affair is getting complicated, and I'm afraid we have little time to waste."

"I'm afraid you're right," Aramis said. "Till tomorrow, then."

When he returned home Bazin was waiting at the door with news that he'd had a visitor while he was out. "It was that Superior of Amiens, Monsieur," Bazin said. "I was surprised to see him in Paris, but he said he had a message to pass on to you."

"Written?"

"No, Monsieur, spoken. He said, 'Tell your master that we trust he is wasting no time in the completion of his thesis. Another promising candidate is pursuing the same argument and may finish before him.' I don't understand—I thought you had given up on your thesis, Monsieur."

"Oh, I understand it, friend Bazin. I understand it perfectly," Aramis said, twisting his mustache thoughtfully. "And you should know by now, *mon ami,* that I never give up on anything I really want."

CHAPTER XXXII
PROSECUTION AT DINNER

The Court of Miracles: an outlaw society of beggars, paupers, and vagrants, presided over by a Beggar King, where at the end of a day of begging "miracles" occurred as the lame laid down their crutches and the blind regained their sight. Louis had heard of it, of course, but had always assumed it was just one more Paris legend, another story the Parisians liked to tell to reassure themselves that they lived in the most extraordinary city in the world. But it seemed the Court of Miracles was real—and even more bizarre than the legend.

Fontrailles, bound by his legs to a heavy bench in the middle of the Court, was in an ideal position to take it all in. And though he was more than a little preoccupied with his own predicament, his surroundings almost made him forget his personal peril.

The Court was in fact in a sort of courtyard, one of those nameless urban vacancies hidden behind rows of high houses, bounded by the blind backs of unkempt buildings. It was the end of the day, already dark at the bottom of this artificial ravine, and the beggars of Paris were gathering to pay their respects to their leader. They filed in through narrow alleys, entered through creaking back doors, even emerged from some sort of fissure in the ground.

The Court of Miracles began to fill with its citizens. One by one they walked, limped, or hopped past the Intendant, a waspish, wheezing old man in a ragged barrister's robe seated behind a trestle table. Before him they placed what Louis assumed were the proceeds of their day's work: coins, trinkets, buttons, some jewelry, a few purses with their leather belt-ties neatly cut through.

The Intendant kept up a steady derisive commentary on the paucity, tawdriness, and probable counterfeit nature of these offerings, but from the way the beggars grinned at these sallies Louis gathered that this was more in the nature of greeting than complaint. He could hear the Intendant clearly because he was seated right behind him, and occasionally the codger would turn to share some witticism with Fontrailles's guards, the vulture Bronte and a dim thug the Intendant called *Cervelle-de-Merde*: Shit-for-Brains.

A stranger stopped in front of Fontrailles and looked down at him: cloaked, hooded, and with a cloth over the bottom half of his face, only his deep-set eyes were visible. The man gave off such a powerful odor of rot that Louis almost sneezed. He prodded Fontrailles with heavy boots crusted with mud and mold. "What's the *bossu* here for?" he growled, face-cloth fluttering over his mouth.

"Trial," said Bronte.

"Huh," said the moldy man. "What happens to the body?"

"Auction," said Bronte.

"Huh," the moldy man repeated. "I got a buyer for a hunchback. I'll be back." And he slouched off toward one of the narrow alleys.

Louis's curiosity got the better of him. "I'm sure I'll be sorry I asked," he said, "but why is that man leaving when everyone else is coming in?"

"Hur-hur-hur!" laughed Shit-for-Brains. "Works at night. *Grave* robber. Hur!"

"Ah," said Fontrailles. "I'm sorry I asked."

Somewhere behind them a bonfire was lit with a whoosh and crackle, and everything in the forgotten courtyard was thrown into high, dancing relief. More trestle tables were set up, and a diverse assortment of food and drink was laid out and instantly laid into by the assembled dregs of the Paris streets. Some of the diners, Louis noted, appeared to be actually maimed or deformed, including two or three with backs as humped as his own.

"We give them whatever we're able to steal each day from the markets of Les Halles," said Proserpine, appearing out of the darkness dressed in a lavender linen gown that would have suited a royal lady-in-waiting—with, alas, a mismatched mantle of clashing turquoise. She tousled Fontrailles's hair affectionately with a many-ringed hand, which he found rather shocking; no one had tousled his hair since he was six years old. Smiling, she said, "In the markets, the mongers are wary and their produce is guarded; often we're not able to get enough. Sometimes, like tonight, there's plenty, and then we feast. My father's subjects will be well fed this evening, which is good for you: they won't be surly and demanding your blood."

"You mean they have a *say* in this so-called trial?" Fontrailles asked.

"In theory, they do not," said the Intendant, weighing in with a voice like sand. "But our Caesar is a canny ruler who likes to keep his subjects happy."

Proserpine nodded to acknowledge the Intendant. Louis caught an undertone of apprehension in her voice as she said, "Monsieur de Fontrailles, allow me to introduce Monsieur Montfaucon. Father has appointed him to serve as defense attorney in your trial."

The ancient man indicated his ragged solicitor's robes with a gesture that somehow evoked courtroom histrionics, then bowed and said, "Your servant, Monsieur."

Tied to the bench, Fontrailles was unable to bow, so he nodded to the Intendant. *His hands are shaking, and under that robe, so are his knees,* he thought. *He looks like he could keel over at any moment.* He asked, "You have experience in legal matters, Monsieur Montfaucon?"

The old man drew himself up. "I was full partner for over thirty years with Monsieur Coquenard, now chief prosecutor at the Grand Châtelet." He smiled wryly. "But Coquenard objected to my marriage, Monsieur, and forced me out of the firm."

"Why should he object to your marriage, Montfaucon?" asked Fontrailles. "Was your bride far beneath your station?"

"Indeed no: my bride's lineage is long and distinguished. What he objected to was her concupiscence—for it's Madame Vin I took to wife, and she'll share her delights with anyone." He produced a bottle from beneath his robes and gave Fontrailles a broad wink.

Oh, excellent—my attorney is a drunkard, Louis thought. "And who will be the prosecutor?" he asked.

"Great Caesar will prosecute. He is bringing the charges, after all," said Montfaucon.

"And who are my judges?" said Fontrailles.

"Great Caesar will judge, of course," said Montfaucon. "Who else?"

"Wait a minute…" Fontrailles began.

"Here he comes now!" said Proserpine. She leaned down and gave Fontrailles a peck on the cheek. "For luck," she whispered.

The great man entered the courtyard from the back door of one of the houses, flanked by two torchbearers clad in motley and preceded by a pair of toothless crones strewing straw on the muddy ground in his path. Caesar was clad in the same golden raiment Fontrailles had seen that morning, augmented now by a gilded hook on his right hand, a carved ebony wooden leg, and a black silk eye-patch with a round-cut ruby set in its center. He stumped majestically to the center of the courtyard, raised his arms and proclaimed, "Great Caesar is among you! Serve the ale and wine, and let joy be unconfined!"

This brief speech was greeted with ragged cheers and throaty cries of *"Vive* Caesar!" and "Hail Caesar!" As Caesar gravely condescended to accept the plaudits of his subjects, an upholstered chair was brought forward and placed on a makeshift dais of empty crates. A tall girandole was placed next to the dais, the linkboys fixed their torches into its sconces, and then carefully lifted Great Caesar and placed him on the chair, where he sat erect as a pike with the ebony leg projecting straight out in front of him—pointed, Louis thought, directly at him.

Caesar raised his arms again, which evoked a short cheer. "My subjects!"

21

he said loudly, in the voice of a practiced orator. "We have in our midst, as legitimate salvage, a personage brought among us in the character of a seigneur of the *noblesse*." (Cheers and cries of, "A ransom! A ransom!") "Yet though this personage bears a noble title, he disclaims the possession of the appropriate assets appertaining thereto." (Confused murmurs, cries of "What?" from the back.) "He says he *has no money*." (General outrage: hisses and boos.) "He has been accused, therefore, of entering our society under false pretenses—in short, of being an impostor!" (Shouts of "The dog!" "The pig!" "The rat!")

The beggars pounded the tables and waved their stumps angrily, both real and artificial. Great Caesar waited for his subjects' indignation to abate, then said gravely, "That's right, my children: an impostor. And what is the penalty for such a heinous crime? How must an impostor be punished?"

The crowd erupted with conflicting cries of "Flogging!" "Disfigurement!" "Transportation!" and "Attachment of income!" Caesar, annoyed, just kept shaking his head until a small, incredibly filthy girl standing on a table mewed, "Death?"

Caesar pointed at the gamine and thundered, "Yes! Death! Death to impostors!"

"Death!" repeated the assembled multitude. "Death!"

Fontrailles tugged urgently at the wine-stained sleeve of Montfaucon's robe. "I thought you were going to represent me! Isn't it irregular to announce the verdict before having the trial?"

"I can see you have little experience with matters of law," Montfaucon said dryly. "But I'll see what I can do." He shrugged. "It depends on Caesar's mood, really."

The aged solicitor stepped up to the makeshift throne where Caesar sat smiling beatifically as his subjects danced around arm-in-arm gaily chanting, "Death! Death! Death!"

Montfaucon caught his liege's attention and bowed, throwing his arms wide, then assumed a declamatory pose and said, "Great Caesar! Pursuant to your own dictum and in accordance with your express will, the impostor must be *tried* before he can be condemned. We must have a trial! Is that not logic?"

Caesar's white eyebrows rose as his face lit up. "*Vraiment!* Quite so, Monsieur Montfaucon. We must have a trial! Is that not logic?"

The beggars' dancing ground to a halt. "A trial?" one called. "What about death?"

"Trial first, death to follow. That's logic!" said Caesar. He added, "More wine!" and the resulting cheers drowned out the murmurs. "Let the accused be brought forward!"

Bronte and Shit-for-Brains picked up Fontrailles's bench, marched it forward until it was three paces from Caesar's throne and set it down with a thump that went straight to Louis's broken collarbone, making him gasp in spite of himself.

Caesar leaned forward and boomed, "Tremble now, miscreant, in the face of divine and righteous justice! I, Great Caesar, shall assume the roles of both prosecutor and judge, and will speak in both capacities."

Fontrailles swallowed and said, "How will I know which is which?"

"Silence! Defending counsel will speak on your behalf. That's logic." Caesar swiveled his eyebrows toward his Intendant. "Montfaucon! You may commence. What pathetic defense can you possibly hope to make to justify the manifest crimes of this sordid malefactor?"

"A defense, Your Revered Imperial Honor," Montfaucon announced, "so simple, elegant, and airtight that Your Magnificence will find it logically unassailable! I confidently predict that it will knock you onto your arse— solely in your role as prosecutor, of course." He turned and gave his client a broad, boozy wink that Louis did not find very reassuring.

"Ha! Such mendacious bombast will avail you nothing, you broken-down pettifogging old sot!" Caesar frothed, then added, "That was speaking as prosecutor, of course. As judge, I will naturally permit you to develop your case, despite the obvious hopelessness of your position."

"Ahem," said Montfaucon, squaring his narrow shoulders, then cracking all ten of his knuckles with a sound like a string of firecrackers going off. "Would the prosecutor please remind the court of what crime this poor innocent has been charged?"

23

Caesar sneered. "This 'poor innocent,' as you call him, has been charged with the capital crime of willful and malicious imposture!"

"Imposture!" Montfaucon cried gaily. "Exactly! Or, to put it another way, *false* posture. And yet, as Your Sagacity cannot help but notice, my client, like many of Your Imperial Majesty's subjects, is a hunchback. Nature herself has already sentenced him to a *lifetime* of im-posture."

Caesar flipped up his eye-patch, glared at his Intendant with both eyes and said, "What are you blathering about, Montfaucon?"

"Ah, the prosecutor pretends not to understand—but I'm sure the judge follows the inexorable logic of my argument!" The old solicitor paused to pull on his wine-bottle, then continued, "My client's spinal malformation demonstrates that he has already been *found* guilty of imposture, by the only court higher than this one. And, by the well-known legal principle of double jeopardy, no man may be tried twice for the same crime! That," he concluded with a flourish, "is logic!"

"Speaking as prosecutor, I object," said Caesar. "That principle obtains only in the traditions of English law."

But Montfaucon, without missing a beat, replied, "What? Is the prosecutor maintaining that His Sagacity the Judge-Emperor cannot try my client under any legal tradition he so wills? I will uphold with my dying breath the right of Great Caesar to adjudicate under the English legal tradition whenever he damn well pleases! The defense rests."

"Well said, Montfaucon!" cried Caesar with delight, clapping his hands in applause. "You have acquitted yourself nobly, and have upheld, nay, even broadened, my all-encompassing powers of Imperial jurisprudence! Monsieur," he said to Fontrailles, "I find you not guilty of imposture."

"Th-thank you, Monseigneur," Fontrailles said, still trying to sort out what had just happened.

"But attend, Monsieur!" said Caesar. "Logically, this ruling has several inevitable consequences. One: if you are not before me as an impostor, then you must be a legitimate subject of my realm, as is evidenced by your admitted malformation."

"Admitted?" said Fontrailles.

"*Chut!* My subjects speak to me when spoken to. Two: as one of *les Parasites Parisiens,* you will pull your weight like everyone else around here. And three: ...Bronte, untie this man. I will not have my loyal subjects gratuitously bound to benches."

"What about my salvage fee?" Bronte growled.

"That's a civil matter, Bronte, and may not be heard before a criminal court," Caesar said in a minatory tone. "If you choose, you may bring a civil suit against Monsieur, here, in small claims court."

"Small claims, my eye!" snarled Bronte.

"Hrrrh!" growled Caesar, flipping his patch back down and engaging Bronte in a monocular staring contest until the vulturine man dropped his gaze. Satisfied, Caesar nodded. He held out his arms and his motley-clad retainers lifted him down from his dais.

"Wait!" Fontrailles cried as Caesar turned to go. "Monseigneur, uh, Your Majesty. What was number three?"

"Ah, yes! Number three, Monsieur, is that tomorrow you start your new life as a beggar on the streets of Paris," said Caesar. "Montfaucon, see to his preparation. He's a novice, so pick one of the standard ensembles."

"Might I suggest the Necrotic Gnome, Your Magnificence?" Montfaucon said.

"Excellent!" said Caesar. "You may issue yourself another bottle of wine. So let it be done!"

CHAPTER XXXIII
MASTER AND MENDICANT

Without a doubt, Louis thought, the worst part of the Necrotic Gnome ensemble was the smell. But Montfaucon assured the former Vicomte de Fontrailles, now dubbed Monsieur Gobbo, that the appalling odor was an essential part of the overall effect. "One of the easiest ways for a beggar to induce a donation from a beggee is to be so viscerally offensive that the donor will disgorge his spare change just to get the beggar to go away," Montfaucon said, as if lecturing before the bar. "It's an approach often used by novice beggars who have not yet developed their own unique *persona mendica*. In your case it's doubly useful, since your right arm must be immobilized against your chest for several weeks to allow your shoulder to heal."

"*Merdieu!*" Fontrailles cursed as Bronte tightened the sling behind his back. "Does it have to be bound up *this* tight?"

"It does, if the prosthetic Bronte will affix to your arm is to carry anatomical conviction," Montfaucon said.

Somewhat more roughly than Louis thought necessary, Bronte next tied a false amputated arm, complete with half-sleeve, to Fontrailles's right shoulder. The arm, which ended short of the elbow, was made up to appear infected with gangrene. For maximum repugnance the stump ended in a gobbet of actual rotten meat that gave off a stench so putrid it almost made Louis gag. "Hold still, Gobbo, till I get it cranked down," Bronte rasped.

"*Monsieur* Gobbo to you, Bronte," Proserpine corrected, dressed once again in the gaudy boudoir robe that seemed to be her everyday attire, and standing back several paces with a clove-studded orange held to her nose. "He may be going begging, but our Louis is still a person of quality."

"Heh. Can't call nobody by a title what looks like *that*," Bronte said, standing back to admire his work.

Louis d'Astarac, eyes watering from the reek of rotting flesh, his skin twitching like a horse's hide under rags crawling with vermin, stood up as straight as he could within his bindings. "No, Bronte," he said, "I insist on the title. If I have to be Gobbo, and at the moment I don't see any way out of it, I'll be Monsieur Gobbo or nothing. And I'll out-beg you and the rest of your gang, no matter what you call me."

"That's the spirit, Monsieur!" said Montfaucon. "Keep that up and you'll do our little community proud."

"Hrmp. No way to make friends in the Court of Miracles," muttered Bronte, fingering the hilt of Cocodril's knife, which he still wore at his waist.

Fontrailles/Gobbo glared at him but made no reply. He said, "Where are we going, Montfaucon?"

"Left Bank, Quai des Augustins," the Intendant said. "Nobody else is doing the Necrotic Gnome in that quarter, and there's good traffic throughout the day."

"Stop up and see me after you come back," Proserpine simpered. "I'll want to hear all about your first day!"

Monsieur Gobbo's premiere in the theater of the Paris streets was, to put it bluntly, a flop. The day started out well enough, as far as Louis was concerned. Binding his arm had mitigated most of the pain from the broken collar bone, and shambling down the street doubled over to emphasize his humped back actually felt more natural than his usual practice of trying to stand up straight and stride.

It was one of those clear early-spring days with the first hints of the warmth of the summer to follow, and it was a relief for Louis to be able to pass through the city streets without constantly looking over his shoulder for Cardinal's Guards or other agents seeking Andreaeus's book of lost Rosicrucian secrets. *To hell with* The Three Mystic Heirs, Louis thought. *Chasing that book has bought me nothing but trouble. Isabeau, married, to a half-man like me? I must have been out of my mind.*

He'd been careful not to mention to anyone in the Court of Miracles that he was wanted by the cardinal. Even beggars would prefer to avoid that kind of trouble. Louis assumed that if they knew he was a fugitive, Great Caesar, or Bronte, for that matter, would instantly turn him over to Richelieu for whatever reward was available, and then it would be off to the Bastille for Louis d'Astarac. No, better by far to play the role of beggar for a while. It might even be amusing.

It was not amusing. Sidling up to prosperous-looking burghers or gentlemen on the Quai des Augustins and stuttering out a request for alms was degrading and humiliating. Worse, he wasn't even good at it, and was rewarded with cuffs more often than coins. This just made him angry and surly, which got him more cuffs.

After Montfaucon had observed half a morning's labor in which Fontrailles netted only one *denier*, a couple of *sous*, and a broken button, the Intendant took him aside into the shadow of the Convent of Grands-Augustins. "I've been observing your technique, Monsieur Gobbo," he said, "and though I hesitate to criticize the choices of one who is my social superior, I have been given the responsibility of assisting you in your new life and therefore feel some constructive commentary might be appropriate."

"To the devil with your legalisms. Get to the point," Fontrailles huffed, still wincing from a cane-thump he'd received from the last gentleman he'd approached. "What am I doing wrong?"

"You must grovel, Monsieur Gobbo," Montfaucon said. "You are approaching these bourgeois as if they had an obligation to give you alms, which is not begging but extortion—a different racket entirely, and already dominated by tax-farmers and the clergy. Your intended beggees are more repulsed by your effrontery than moved by your pitiful condition, and thus more inclined to strike you with whatever is handiest than to give you alms.

"No, Monsieur," the former solicitor said gravely, "it will not do. You must cultivate an aura of unworthiness; you must persuade your donors that though you know you are the lowest of the low, and you have no right to tread the same ground as your betters, without their help you won't survive even one more day. In short: grovel."

"It's just not natural to grovel to people such as master tanners and slaughterhouse owners," Fontrailles grumbled. "*Diable!* Half of them can't even write their names, and some of them smell nearly as bad as I do. In the past they've always deferred to *me*."

Montfaucon shrugged. "Then perhaps begging is simply not your *métier*. I suppose we could try you out in another line—maybe grave robbing. I understand there's a certain tradition of employing hunchbacks in the bodysnatching trade."

Fontrailles shuddered. "No thank you. I'd rather grovel. Gobbo the Groveler, that's me."

Groveling slavishly was hard work, but Monsieur Gobbo's alms-to-assault ratio improved somewhat. Montfaucon clued him in to a few more tricks of the trade, such as keeping a pebble in his mouth to enhance drool production, and cocking his head back and rolling his eyes to show the whites. "A touch of dementia never hurts," the old solicitor remarked.

By the end of the day Fontrailles was exhausted and aching, but he had a purse jingling with a handful of copper coins and even a few *billon* pieces. "Not bad for a first day," he said with a touch of pride.

"One hates to precipitate on Monsieur's procession," Montfaucon said, "but the average daily take of even a mediocre *mendigot* is about thrice what you earned today."

"But this is more than my vineyard hands make in a week!" Fontrailles protested.

"Perhaps so," said Montfaucon, "but they don't live in Paris, which is the most expensive city in the world—even for beggars."

"Can I at least dispose of this stinking prosthetic now?"

"Monsieur must be jesting!" cried Montfaucon. "Why, rotting meat has a thousand uses...."

"Spare me, Montfaucon," Fontrailles interrupted. "Some things I'm just not ready for yet."

They were approaching the Pont Neuf, the last rays of the sun backlighting the great bridge and painting the Seine with long rippling shadows of its arches. Most of the street vendors who cluttered the bridge and its approaches during the day had already shuttered their stalls or rolled away their carts, and respectable citizens were hurrying to reach their destinations before darkness fell and commerce gave way to crime. As Fontrailles limped onto the span, followed by Montfaucon, tottering as much from drink as from decrepitude, a burly youth stepped in front of the hunchback and blocked his way. "Toll," he said.

"What?" Fontrailles said. "The Pont Neuf isn't a toll bridge."

"It is for your kind, *bossu*," the youth said, thumping a big fist into a palm. "Gimme money."

"My arse," Fontrailles said. After a full day of knuckling under to tradesmen, this was too much. But Montfaucon was tugging at his good arm.

"Caution, Monsieur!" said the Intendant. "They're bridge bandits—Knights of the Short Sword. They shake us down almost every night."

"We ain't the Knights, those bastards, we're the Brothers of La Samaritaine," said the bully indignantly. "Pay up, beggars."

"But there's only one of him," Fontrailles said.

"There are three more behind me. Please, Monsieur," Montfaucon said. "My bones are old and brittle."

In the end, Fontrailles gave up half the coins in his purse to the grinning Brothers of La Samaritaine, who added insult to injury by jeering at his take. He returned to the Court of Miracles disgusted and fuming.

It was dark in the fetid alley that led in to the Court, almost as dark as Louis's mood. Proserpine was waiting at the far end, a thick shadow in dark brocade. "*Bon soir*, Louis," she fluted. "You don't mind if I call you that, do you? 'Monsieur de Fontrailles' seems so stiff."

"It's certainly better than most of the things I've been called today," he said, stopping several paces short of her. He was all too aware of his outfit's aroma.

"First day didn't go so well, I guess." She turned in toward the courtyard, beckoning, and he followed. "Bronte said it wouldn't," she continued. "He wagered you wouldn't come back at all, and that he'd have to go out and drag you back. So at least you won a bet for me. Doesn't that cheer you up a little?"

"What were the stakes?" Fontrailles growled.

She laughed in her rising arpeggio. "What, jealous already? Why, we hardly know each other." She swayed toward him.

"Beware, Mademoiselle." He held up his hand and backed away. "You don't want to get too close. Wait until I have a chance to put on some clean rags."

"All right, Louis. You know where my chamber is." And she disappeared into the gloom, light laugh, heavy tread.

A half-hour later, once he'd shucked the Necrotic Gnome and browsed the night's buffet on the trestle tables—black bread, salt herring, and last fall's wrinkled apples—he went in the back door of one of the largest houses that bordered the Court and slowly clumped up the steep stairs that led to Proserpine's gallimaufry room. Why was he going? *Well, who else am I going to pass the time with?* he thought acidly. *Shit-for-Brains?*

Proserpine was reclining on her broad bed, a brocade alp among foothills of Persian pillows in the light of three thick candles in a cracked candelabrum, tuning an Austrian rebec to the scale she hummed with perfect pitch. "Come in, Louis," she warbled. "You're looking a little less ready to kill someone. Pull up a divan and I'll sing for you."

He slumped down on the filigreed divan, and sank back into a pile of cushions whose welcoming softness began to drain him of all ability to move or even think. "What made you so sure I would visit you?" he said, fighting the urge to fall instantly asleep.

"I didn't think you had anywhere else to go," she said, picking up her bow. "Neither do I." She drew the bow slowly across the rebec's strings and it hummed a low, sweet song. At the fret, her thick, ringed fingers fluttered like birds.

"Proserpine," he said. *I'm so tired of fighting,* he thought. *I'm not made for it.* But what he said was, "Do you know 'My Love Lies A-Sleeping'?"

She smiled, her eyes almost disappearing into her cheeks. "Of course," she said, and began to sing.

A warm blanket of music tucked in around him. A rat skittered in the corner. Louis turned his face into the pillows and sank deep into the dark.

He kept at it. Almost every other day the Brothers of La Samaritaine or the Knights of the Short Sword waylaid Monsieur Gobbo on his way back to Court of Miracles and made him "pay toll," but by the end of the first week they quit mocking his daily take. Montfaucon declared him graduated from his novitiate; Fontrailles, ever more confident in his role as a mendicant, gave up the Necrotic Gnome and adopted a more jester-like persona, relying on wit and self-deprecatory humor to jolly the burghers out of their spare change. It was a much more comfortable act for him than pathetic groveling, and his income improved as he sharpened his routines.

He spent most of his evenings on the divan in Proserpine's chamber, listening to her sing and talking with her about Life and Philosophy. She was unread—indeed, could barely read at all—but had a nimble mind and a sharp and mordant sense of humor. In short, she was pleasant company, especially compared to the likes of dour Bronte or drunken Montfaucon.

Over several evenings, in dribs and drabs, he told Proserpine his brief life story, up to Isabeau's rejection of his proposal. She was sympathetic … to a point. "Poor dear! It must have hurt you terribly," she said. "But what did you expect? Did you really think you were destined to mate with some socially ambitious aristocrat? Preening popinjays, all of them!"

When Proserpine discovered Louis was a chess player she told her father, and the next evening Monsieur Gobbo's presence was required at the Imperial chessboard. So the former Vicomte de Fontrailles dressed in what remained of his doublet and hose and ascended the stairs past

Proserpine's room to the loft that served as Great Caesar's audience chamber. A mumbling crone opened the door for him, and Louis found himself in a garish parody of the kind of royal chambers he'd seen in the Louvre. The walls were hung with scores of paintings, many of them awful, and the ceiling beams overhead had been coated with gallons of gilt paint. The floor was covered with overlapping oriental rugs of various shapes, sizes, and contrasting colors, as many as three or four deep in some places, and Fontrailles had to step carefully to avoid tripping as he approached the Presence.

Great Caesar was seated in a high-backed armchair and dressed, *sans* prosthetics, in a simple outfit of fine cream-colored linen. Louis was unsure of the etiquette for approaching a beggar monarch, but Caesar seemed not to be in the mood for ceremony, and beckoned Fontrailles forward with an impatient, "Come along, come along, Monsieur Gobbo. We haven't had a decent game of chess since Montfaucon's wits began to wander."

The only other people present were Proserpine, standing behind her father's chair with an affectionate hand on his shoulder, and the toothless codger in livery of motley who served as Caesar's *valet de chambre*. Fontrailles stepped forward and gave his best Court bow to Great Caesar, who responded with a royal flicker of his hand. Louis then bowed, only slightly less deferentially, to Proserpine, who smiled and dipped him a courtesy in return.

"Welcome, Monsieur!" Caesar said heartily. "Ready to play? Let's get started." He leapt spryly from his chair. Fontrailles, who though half Caesar's age was feeling far from spry after a day on the streets, followed him to an inlaid chess table crowded with brightly-painted pieces too big for the squares they were set on. "Antiquo!" Caesar called to his valet. "Bring wine! Look alive, there!"

"Oh, aye, wine," grumbled the relic. "Live it up, live it up. I suppose you want the good stuff?"

"Sacred name! Of course I want the good stuff." Caesar grinned as the aged valet shuffled arthritically toward them with bottle and glasses. "Dodders a bit, doesn't he? I keep him around because he makes me feel young."

"You keep me around, you criminal loon, because I'm your father," Antiquo wheezed, and then pulled the cork from the bottle with the last two molars on the right side of his jaw. He spat out the cork and added, to Fontrailles, "Makes me follow him about the place and do his bidding, he does, and wear these foolish clothes to boot. Now I ask you, is that respect?"

"It beats pimping your three toothless old sisters, which is what you were doing when I found you," Caesar said pleasantly. Proserpine giggled.

"No respect from my granddaughter, neither," Antiquo griped, thumping the bottle down on the table and putting the glasses next to it. "Pour it yourself. I have to go lie down." And he turned and shuffled off.

"Dear old Papa," Caesar said fondly. "Proserpine, if you'll pour the wine, we men will get down to business. Now, as I am a sort of white king"—Caesar waved a hand at his attire—"I, of course, will play white. That's logic! You may sit, Monsieur Gobbo."

Louis flinched inside as he always did when he heard the ridiculous name, but as a French nobleman he'd had a great deal of experience in ignoring the eccentricities of his social superiors, which Great Caesar was by situation if not by birthright. He took his place behind the red pieces and said, "Thank you, Monseigneur. And thank you, Mademoiselle, for the wine."

"*De rien,* Monsieur," Proserpine said sweetly. "Be careful, father; I imagine our Monsieur Gobbo is a pretty sharp player."

"Yes, but I'll wager he's never played an emperor before. That ought to put the fear into him," Caesar said cheerfully. He moved his queen's pawn forward two spaces and said, "Check!"

"Check?" Fontrailles said. "I don't understand, Monseigneur; my king isn't threatened."

"Oh, I know," Caesar said. "I just like to say 'check' every time I move a piece. Makes the game more exciting. If I really put you in check, I'll say 'double check.' You should do the same."

"Ah," said Fontrailles carefully. Playing chess or cards with a higher-ranking noble was really an excuse for conversation between people who couldn't otherwise socialize, but Louis could already see that holding up his end was going to be a challenge. He decided to fall back on the age-old stratagem of encouraging the prince to talk about himself, always a favorite subject with princes. "Please tell me, Monseigneur, how Your Majesty got to be an emperor," he said, then pushed one of his own pawns forward. "Check?"

Caesar nodded. "How did I get to be Emperor? The usual way, of course. A leader must show respect for his people's traditions. Check."

"The usual way?" Fontrailles said. "Check. Would Monseigneur enlighten me as to what that was?" *Poison?* he thought. *Garrotting? A knife in the dark?*

"Apprenticeship," Caesar said. "Check. After I proved myself a capable beggar on the streets and an able organizer off them, the previous Caesar appointed me his Centurion. I spent fifteen years consolidating support among all the factions of Paris beggardom, and when Caesar passed on I was named his successor by acclamation. What could be more logical?"

"What, indeed?" Maybe the old man wasn't as crazy as he seemed. Fontrailles sipped his wine—it *was* good stuff. "And how many subjects does Your Majesty have? Um, check."

Caesar smiled. "I have millions of subjects, of course—so many I can't count them. That's why, logically, I'm an emperor, where your King Louis XIII is only a king. Check."

"M-millions, Monseigneur?" What was *in* this wine? "Would Your Majesty care to expand on the subject of, ah, subjects?"

Caesar cocked his head back so his white goatee pointed directly at Fontrailles and said, "It's your move."

"Oh! Yes. Right. Check."

Caesar nodded happily, drained his wine glass and said, "Yes, millions upon millions of subjects! That's because, as lord of all parasites in Paris, I must logically be master of not only our human beggars, but all rats, mice, roaches, and lice in the city as well! Who could count them all? Not I!" He moved forward his queen's rook. "Double check!"

Whoops! Louis thought. *I'd better start paying more attention to the game.* He pulled his queen's bishop back into a defensive position and said, "Check. Your Majesty plays a mean game of chess."

"Well, of course I do, lad! I may be frothing mad—as who should know better than I?—but I'm not stupid." His king's knight corkscrewed forward. "Check."

Fontrailles's game was in trouble. He temporized, "Monseigneur's clever move with the knight brings to mind the so-called Knights of the Short Sword, those rascals on the Pont Neuf who so regularly rob Your Majesty's subjects of their hard-won alms. Check."

"Whoreson pigs!" Caesar cried, clenching a fist. "Those bandit gangs have been a thorn in our foot for years. Even when I have my subjects vary their routes back to the Court of Miracles, the bandits always discover them. Which is only logical, as they know the streets as well as we do. Check."

"I suppose that must be true. And the river bridges are the natural choke points that your—*our*—people can't avoid." Louis thought about the city of Paris, itself a sort of chessboard with opposing pieces moving across it. "It's a problem indeed. Check. What about your Bully Boys? Can't they protect our people from the bandits?"

"A logical suggestion, but flawed," Caesar said. "Bronte's handful of strong-arm men are enough to maintain order and obedience within our numbers, but too few to challenge the bandit gangs." Head still angled down toward the game, he looked up at Fontrailles thoughtfully for a moment from under his bristling white brows, and then looked back down at the board, where the pieces were dwindling on both sides. He slid a rook sideways. "Check. You've seen the bandits at work, Monsieur. How much would you estimate we lose to them, on an average weekly basis?"

"Oh, two parts in ten, at least—perhaps as much as three," Fontrailles said without looking up. He slid one of his own rooks, not sideways but forward. "Double check."

"Indeed?" Great Caesar leaned over the board. Proserpine smiled, refilled their glasses, and tousled Louis's hair.

Fontrailles sipped his wine abstractedly. "Suppose, Monseigneur, that the Bully Boys were employed not to confront the bandits, but merely as escorts to bring in the take. There are enough of them for that, aren't there?"

"Eh? No, no, not at all. God's head, lad—when nightfall comes, they can't be in every quarter of the city at once, now, can they?"

"It's Your Majesty's move."

"I'm aware of that! No one more so than I!" Caesar's eyes flashed, and Louis realized that the wine was loosening both their tongues. He'd better be more careful. Caesar scowled. "Now, what's this codswallop about the Bully Boys? Where are you going with this, eh? These bandits are a genuine problem. Give me logic!"

Fontrailles took a deep breath. "Well, Monseigneur, I didn't mean to imply that there were enough Bully Boys for them to cover every quarter on a daily basis. But why collect every day? I know we have safe gathering-places, minor Courts of Miracles, if you will, in every quarter. Why not have the daily take collected in those places, and have the Bully Boys do one escort run from a different quarter every day?"

Caesar glared at him, then his features slowly relaxed into a smile. "Now that's logic! A brilliant idea, my lad! We'll do it!" He hopped his knight over Fontrailles's defenses and said, "Double check! Let's see you get out of that one." He grinned.

Louis felt almost giddy at the rush of unexpected praise from Great Caesar, even if he was a madman and a monarch only of beggars. Proserpine laughed and tousled his hair again, which Caesar didn't seem to mind. Then Louis remembered that he was playing chess, and spent several minutes trying to remember what he'd been planning. The wine was beginning to fog his thinking. Finally he said, "Well, Your Majesty, I think you have me. Unless I'm mistaken, it's mate in four moves."

"You're not mistaken," Caesar said proudly. "And I admire grace in defeat. Thank you for the excellent game, Monsieur Gobbo."

This time Louis couldn't completely hide the flinch. "So, you don't like your name?" Caesar said. "Well, since all names at the Court of Miracles are provisional, I'm sure we can find you another. Good night!" He stood suddenly. "I have a bellyful of wine, and to quote dear Papa, I have to go lie down. Take the boy downstairs, Proserpine."

"Yes, father," Proserpine said complacently. "Finish your wine, Louis, and come with me. I'll light the way."

"It was good wine," Louis said. It was all he could think of to say. His thoughts, which had seemed to be all flashing fireworks not long before, now seemed to flicker like a single, guttering candle. He was content to follow Proserpine slowly down the narrow stairs, carefully guiding himself by keeping his good hand on the wall. When they reached her familiar boudoir, it seemed the most natural thing in the world that they should both remove their clothes and crawl into the bed together. They made love; Proserpine was warm, and attentive, and despite the wine Louis le Petit rose to the occasion and performed quite well.

When they were finished, Proserpine folded Louis in her arms, cushioned his head on her abundant bosom and sighed.

"Was that all right?" Louis mumbled into her breast.

"Not bad," she said, tousling his hair, "for a preening popinjay."

CHAPTER XXXIV
CONCERNING THE ENGAGEMENT
OF ASTARAC AND PROSERPINE

The next day Great Caesar announced to his subjects that Gobbo would henceforth be known as Monsieur Hephaestus, which Louis found gratifying, and that Hephaestus would oversee a new decentralized collection scheme, which was surprising. Reaction was mixed; as a rule the beggar community was deeply distrustful of change. However, they were even more resentful of being shaken down by the bandit gangs, so they were willing, on balance, to give the new idea a try. The boss beggars congratulated the newly-dubbed Monsieur Hephaestus with a respect they hadn't previously shown him—while attempting, Louis suspected, to take the measure of the new fair-haired boy. Proserpine was proud of him, Antiquo smiled and called him a filthy name, and Montfaucon drank his health.

Bronte, on the other hand, was far from pleased, particularly when he found that he and his Bully Boys were an integral part of the new scheme, and that henceforth he would have to report to Hephaestus. The narrow man narrowed his one eye, growled, and stalked off for a private conference with Caesar. He apparently received a shock, for he emerged white-faced and in a mood to be more cooperative. But more than once over the next few days Louis turned to find Bronte glaring at him from the shadows and fingering Cocodril's dirk.

Organizing the new *quartier*-based collection and the rotating escort runs soon took up so much of Louis's time that he had to give up begging—which didn't bother him in the least. The first implementation collapsed into chaos, as various beggars forgot or misunderstood their instructions. But after another ten days of tweaking the kinks were worked out and the system was running smoothly.

The new system meant increased costs, as every quarter needed its own intendant to collect the daily take, as well as a Bully Boy to guard it until the next escort run, but the reduced loss of income from bandit depredations more than made up for the expense. With the increased revenue Caesar was able to supplement the beggars' evening fare with food that was actually purchased rather than stolen.

Monsieur Hephaestus became a regular guest at Great Caesar's dinner table, and frequently played chess with him in the evenings. He usually ended up in Proserpine's bed at night, and eventually, with Caesar's tacit approval, he moved out of the communal lean-to he shared with Shit-for-Brains and into her room.

Louis was fond of Proserpine, and once Monsieur Hephaestus had become a de facto member of Caesar's household, he found that she did much more than lounge about and play the astonishing array of musical instruments she'd mastered. As the ranking female member of the Court of Miracles Caesar had delegated to her what he termed "women's matters": health care for the sick, burial for the deceased, the protection of children, placement of orphans, and relations with the powerful Whores' Guild, who lodged complaints with the Court of Miracles when mendicants strayed into prostitution. She also adjudicated conflicts between female beggars. She performed these duties with wisdom and tact—which didn't stop her from cursing like a stevedore when some beggar-woman had to be put in her place. The beggars' world was a rough one, but Louis was surprised and moved by the care and respect Proserpine showed to its lowliest members.

Louis grew more attached to Proserpine daily. He enjoyed the attention she paid him, and he was bothered less and less by her rough edges and rather crude manners. He began to teach her to read; in return, she tried to teach him to sing, but it was hopeless: he couldn't carry a tune if his life depended on it, and his crooked hands just couldn't be persuaded to finger a lute properly. But he enjoyed the lessons nonetheless.

And so time passed in the Court of Miracles. Beggar society was utterly uncouth: filth and stench were commonplace, disease was rampant, and disagreements often ended in violence. But Monsieur Hephaestus, once he'd moved into Great Caesar's house, was out of the worst of it, and most days ate better food and drank better wine than the Vicomte de Fontrailles had. Caesar made a practice of consulting him when he had unusual problems to solve, and began giving him other administrative duties once Louis's collection system had become routine. Louis felt useful and engaged: Caesar appreciated his abilities, Proserpine lavished him with affection … and no one flinched when they looked at him, or seemed the least bit bothered that he was a stunted manikin with distorted features and a twisted spine.

Eventually Caesar officially appointed Monsieur Hephaestus to be his Centurion, his heir in all but name. It was a popular decision among the *mendigots*; the lowest layer of society was still sensitive to class distinctions, and having a centurion of noble birth made even toothless half-mad old cripples feel somehow more respectable. Everyone seemed happy about it.

Everyone, that is, but Bronte, who still scowled at Louis whenever he saw him, despite the fact Louis had gotten him appointed Intendant of one of the most prosperous quarters of the city. Bronte seemed even less happy when Great Caesar announced the inevitable engagement of his daughter and his centurion, a declaration that occasioned a wild, drunken celebration in the Court of Miracles that lasted until dawn. Louis drank and danced as much as anyone, whirling with Proserpine in the center of a spinning circle of Caesar's ragged subjects, but all the time he was aware that Bronte was grimly eying him from the shadow of a ruined portico, glaring like a gargoyle.

For his wedding suit, Louis returned to the same couturière in the Rue de la Pourpointerie he'd gone to for a new wardrobe when he was appointed an officer in the Cardinal's Guard. The clothier remembered him—of course—and was relieved when Louis told him he didn't want another outlandishly exaggerated cavalier's outfit, just a conservative gentleman's ensemble in the latest style. By this time his collarbone had healed, so stretching his arms to be measured caused him no discomfort. However, when the clothier asked him to stand up straight to take his height it felt strange, and Louis realized he'd gotten out of the habit of trying to force himself erect. In fact, it suddenly struck him that now, when he walked, his knuckles nearly grazed the ground.

With the couturier out of the fitting room for a moment, Louis considered himself in the shop's three-paneled full-length mirror. He looked leaner than he remembered; older, somehow. He needed a shave— Lord, how he needed a shave—and had his left eye always squinted like that? (Was he going one-eyed?)

You, Monsieur Hephaestus, he thought, *are being fitted out for a wedding suit. For marriage to a beggar chief's daughter. Who cannot read or write. And who once won a childhood contest to see who could kick a dead rat the farthest.*

He scowled. *I don't deserve better. I failed Isabeau. Failed myself.*

"Louis d'Astarac," he said aloud. "Vicomte de Fontrailles."

"Pardon, Monsieur?" said the clothier, coming in with a stack of fabric samples.

"Nothing," Louis said. "I like this, with the transverse stripes. Do you have it in green?"

Next, the hatter's. Then, the bootmaker. Tonight, a meeting with Great Caesar; the subject: what to do about a band of Romany who had camped outside the southeast city walls and were making inroads on the beggars in the Porte Saint-Marcel quarter.

Saturday, the wedding.

Well, why shouldn't he marry Proserpine? By now Isabeau must certainly have married Éric de Gimous. What else was he going to do? Go back to Fontrailles and spend the rest of his life a hunchbacked bachelor seigneur, with no one to talk to but ignorant rustics? What other option did he have? His tiny domain certainly didn't generate enough income for him to delegate its management and live as a dilettante noble-scholar in Paris. And behind everything still hovered the shadows of Richelieu and the Bastille. It was better by far to be the anointed heir to the King of the Beggars.

Wasn't it?

Yes, of course it was.

After visiting the bootmaker, Monsieur Hephaestus went back to the Court of Miracles, dragged a delighted Proserpine upstairs in the middle of the afternoon and made furious love to her for the rest of the day.

Saturday, April 17, 1627: the Wedding Day of Centurion Hephaestus and the Lady Proserpine in the Court of Miracles. "To be followed by Mindless Drunken Revelry and Obscene Jests at the Expense of the Bride and Groom," Louis said.

"Whazzat?" said Antiquo, who was helping him dress for the occasion. "You talk like a fool much of the time, you know that?"

"It has not escaped my attention," Louis said. "Careful with that jeweled stickpin; it was stolen for me at great personal risk by Shit-for-Brains."

"That toad-eater. Just sucking up to the centurion, he was. You want a shave?"

"What, allow you near my throat with a sharp implement? No, thanks— I'll shave myself."

"Good," said the ancient valet. "I have to go lie down."

The Honorable Centurion wished he could go lie down as well. Underneath his surface *sang froid* his stomach roiled with bile, his neck and shoulders were tense as iron, and he was afraid at any moment his hands would start to shake.

Proserpine's head appeared around the door. "Oh, Louis—you look wonderful!" she warbled. Her wild mass of red hair had been marshaled into ranks of careful curls, but the rest of her form was hidden by the door.

"So ... so do you—darling!" Louis said. "What are you wearing?"

"Nothing yet, so stay there!" she said. "I'm about to get into my gown." She pouted her lips into a kiss and then disappeared with a tinkling laugh.

The Good Lord preserve me! Better distract myself, Louis thought. *I'll go down and check on preparations in the courtyard.*

The Court of Miracles was thronged with the elite of Paris beggardom, including a number of disreputables from distant neighborhoods who rarely made it in to headquarters. The centurion's appearance was greeted with a ragged cheer, followed by some shockingly bawdy wedding-night jokes. Some of the "guests" seemed to have begun celebrating in advance, and Louis suspected that a keg or two of ale had already been broached.

Having become a politician of sorts, Louis began working the crowd, greeting those whose names he could remember, thumping hunchbacks on their humps and slapping giggling crones on their derrieres. There were a number of faces he hadn't seen before, all of whom certainly seemed to belong there—until he recognized, with a shock, a face at the edge of the crowd that was definitely out of place.

The One-Eyed Bruiser.

The last time Louis had seen him, the man just been clobbered outside the locked door of Father Joseph's inner sanctum. Now his single eye locked with Louis's, he gave a feral smile and nodded his head toward the entrance to an alley. Then he turned and casually strolled across the courtyard.

Louis followed. He had to.

Of course I should have known the cardinal would track me down eventually, he thought furiously. *Why didn't I prepare for this?*

He paused at the entrance to the dark *ruelle*, chewing his lip. *Because I shut off my brain and just refused to think about it, that's why.* "Devil take me for a fool!" he growled to himself. "I'm not even wearing a weapon."

He stepped into the shadowy alley where he found the One-Eyed Bruiser awaiting him, sitting casually on an empty stockfish barrel. "*Bonjour,* Monsieur de Fontrailles," the Bruiser said, his voice edged with mockery. "Busy today?"

"You might say so," Fontrailles answered warily. "What do you want?" One-Eye was big, even for a bruiser, and Louis could see a dagger at his waist and a pistol thrust through his belt. And that was only his visible armament.

"What *I* want is of little moment. I'm no lord, not even of beggars," the Bruiser sneered. "No, what matters is what *Father Joseph* wants. Though you seem to have forgotten that—or thought that you could."

"Then have done with insolence and tell me what he wants, *canaille.*" With a couple of pops from his spine, the Vicomte de Fontrailles stood more erect.

The Bruiser's expression hardened. "Don't play the *Grand* with me. I'm to bring you in to Father Joseph, but as long as you can still talk when you get there he doesn't care what condition you're in. And if you need persuasion, I'm to tell you this: we have your pretty little Bonnefont girl—and her father, too. If you don't give us what we want, the girl's going to have a nice quiet little trial for heresy, followed by a private execution." One-Eye grinned. "And I get to watch. Are you coming?"

"I… I…."

"Oh, good." One-Eye drew his dagger. "Resisting arrest."

Then suddenly he was collapsing to the ground, blood spraying from his throat, dagger flying from his hand. Bronte stepped from the shadows behind him as One-Eye flopped once on the ground and was still. Bronte knelt down and wiped Cocodril's dirk on One-Eye's jacket. Then he looked at Fontrailles with his own single orb and said, "That was probably a mistake." He spat on the ground. "I should have let him take you."

Louis gulped. "I'm glad you didn't," he said, breathing raggedly. "Thank you."

"Don't thank me," Bronte said. "I didn't do it for you. Just get out." He spat again. "I heard what he said—you've got another girl. All the time you were courting Proserpine, you had another girl. Nobleman! You make me sick."

"You'll tell her why I had to go?" Louis said. "And Caesar?"

"Oh, yes. They'll probably be all broken up about it—you took them in, all right, you and your nice manners. But I knew." He sheathed the knife. "I knew. And if they decide to send someone after you to make you pay for the way you've fooled them, I'll make sure I get the job."

One-Eye's fallen dagger, Fontrailles noted, was only an arm's-length away. "So why not kill me now?" he said.

"Because Proserpine would know," Bronte said. "Better hurry—they'll be looking for you. The wedding is supposed to start in less than an hour."

"All right," Fontrailles said. "However, first I'm going to take this man's weapons. I might need them."

But he was talking to himself. Bronte was gone.

CHAPTER XXXV
A CAT MAY LOOK AT A PRINCE

The Vicomte de Fontrailles walked as far as Rue Montorgueil, clanking a bit with all of One-Eye's hidden weaponry, then hailed a *vinaigrette* and told the porter to take him to Rue Serpente on the Left Bank. The porter looked askance at the passenger climbing onto the seat of the two-wheeled cab—an ugly *bossu*, but with a lofty demeanor that matched his gentleman's dress—so he shrugged, tucked the shafts beneath his armpits and began trotting toward Les Halles.

The bells of Saint-Eustache began sounding noon. Proserpine had planned to begin singing her wedding-song when the twelfth peal had died away, but by now Louis presumed the celebration had been canceled and that Great Caesar was making some sort of hurried excuses to the guests. He clenched his hands on the open cab's sidebars, shook his head, and tried to think of Isabeau.

The idea of Isabeau in the hands of Richelieu and Father Joseph was so terrifying he was almost nauseous. Where would she be held? Not the Bastille—the cardinal would have to get a *lettre de cachet* from the king for that, and a mere hostage wouldn't be worth the trouble. No matter: wherever she was imprisoned, it would be secure enough to keep out a lone hunchback. He needed help—which was why he'd asked the porter to carry him to Rue Serpente, where he knew Beaune and Gitane had had lodgings. They'd stood by him in the past, and he didn't know where else to turn now.

Narrow Rue Serpente, on the edge of the Latin Quarter, was a typical Left-Bank mix of disparate buildings, with hôtels and hovels side-by-side. The last Louis knew, Beaune and Gitane had been sharing a room above an apothecary's shop in a tall, narrow half-timbered house. He found the house, paid off the *vinaigrette* porter, and stepped down in front of the door that opened on the stairway to the upper stories. There was no concierge; he opened the door and began climbing the steep, narrow stairs.

At his knock, the door to the third floor was opened by bulky Beaune, who squeaked with surprise when he saw Fontrailles. He shook his head violently, raised his big hands and made a *go away* gesture in front of his broad chest.

But an authoritative voice from within called, "Who's there, Beaune? Why are you dithering? Open the door!" Beaune sighed, stepped back out of the way, and Fontrailles resolutely entered the room. He might have fled at the sight of Beaune's unambiguous signals, but he simply wasn't in the mood to run, and he wanted to see whom the bossy voice belonged to.

The voice belonged to a strikingly handsome man in his late forties, dark-eyed and with a nose even more like a beak than Bronte's, though on this fellow it looked distinguished. He stood, an erect and commanding presence, in the center of the room, wearing slashed doublet and breeches of shimmering indigo satin ornamented with a fortune in Mechlin lace. He looked as out of place in the humble walk-up as a peacock in a chicken coop, but his manner suggested that any discord with the world around him was the fault of the world.

He looked Fontrailles up and down, nodded curtly, and said, "Excellent. Close the door, Beaune, and block it. Apparently my bad fortune has turned to the good. Welcome, Monsieur de Fontrailles—or perhaps I should say, Monsieur Peregrine. I've been looking forward to meeting you."

Smug bastard, Louis thought. *And he obviously means me no good.* "You have the advantage of me, Monsieur," he said, deliberately addressing the man as an equal. "With whom do I have the pleasure of speaking?"

The dandy's nostrils flared slightly with displeasure, but he maintained his composure and bowed—slightly. "I am Philippe de Longvilliers, Commander of the Knights of Malta," he said, as if that were all the explanation required.

Louis started slightly at the name, which seemed to gratify the man and restore some of his good humor. The Knights of Malta were an order of chivalry at once religious, political, and military, a power throughout Christendom, and a commander ranked with dukes and peers of the realm. And this grandee had been looking for *him!*

Dark Gitane now stepped out of the background and said warily to Longvilliers, "What do you intend to do with him, Monseigneur?" Which made clear to Fontrailles what he'd already guessed: Beaune and Gitane were now in the pay of the commander.

"Don't concern yourself about that, Gitane," Longvilliers said, without taking his eyes off Louis. "I'm sure Monsieur de Fontrailles will be quite reasonable—since he has no other option. And thus all trouble will be avoided."

Since he was clearly in big trouble, Louis wondered why he wasn't panicked. He glanced around the room. The door: blocked by Beaune, who looked rather embarrassed. The window: blocked by Gitane, also looking doubtful, but nonetheless loading his pistol. (And the window, in any event, must open on a three-story drop.) Furnishings: a pair of pallet beds, a table, some chairs, a wardrobe. A fireplace, with a couple of pigeons on a spit hissing over a low fire. And that was all. "Why did you address me as Monsieur Peregrine?" he asked, while taking this inventory.

"Oh, Monsieur, don't be disingenuous," Longvilliers said. "Play fair with me, and upon my honor, I'll play fair with you." He was wearing, Louis noted, a silver-studded baldric of tooled Spanish leather, a beautiful piece of work, but hanging from the end of it was a very serviceable rapier with a well-worn hilt. Longvilliers fingered the pommel as he continued, "Calling yourself the Peregrine, you have engaged in a protracted correspondence through intermediaries in an attempt to draw Cardinal Richelieu and the Duke of Buckingham into a bidding war for *The Three Mystic Heirs*. You have not been successful because both still hope to acquire the book through more, shall we say, *direct* means. But where they have failed, I will now succeed."

Fontrailles glanced at Beaune, who shrugged apologetically. He looked at Gitane, who coolly returned his gaze, meanwhile setting his powder-pouch on a table and dropping a ball into the barrel of his pistol. Fontrailles looked back at Longvilliers and said, "And who are you allied with, Commander?"

"Well, I am Commander of the French Priory of the Order," Longvilliers said with a half-smile, "and would hate to see that book go to our enemies the English. On the other hand, I could give the book to Richelieu and Joseph, but clergy though they are, I'm not sure they have the best interest of Mother Church at heart. So on balance, I think that heretical work would be best placed in the hands of my friends in the Society of Jesus. I'm sure they'll be quite grateful to me—and to you as well."

"So you're offering me a way out from between the cardinal and the duke," Fontrailles said. "I might find it tempting, if I didn't have another concern. I've learned that Richelieu has kidnapped a young woman named de Bonnefont and is holding her hostage for my good behavior. Do you, or your Jesuit friends, know where she is being held—and will you help me set her free?"

"Liberate a prisoner of the cardinal?" Longvilliers said. "*Zut!* That is a tall order. And it would be an offense the cardinal would not be quick to forgive. No," he shook his head, "I'm afraid I can't see it."

Fontrailles glanced again at Beaune, who no longer looked so uneasy, and whose eyes flickered toward Gitane. Fontrailles cast a fleeting look toward the dark man; he took a moment from checking his pistol's priming to glance at his powder-pouch and the fireplace. He locked eyes with Louis briefly, then dropped his own back to his pistol.

"That puts me in a dilemma, Monseigneur," Fontrailles said to Longvilliers, finally according him the title due his rank. "The Jesuits may, as you say, be grateful—but if I give them the book, the cardinal, as you also point out, is not likely to be forgiving." He put his hands behind his back and looked down at the floor, as if deep in thought, and took a slow step toward Gitane's table. "I'm afraid Richelieu will take out his anger on Mademoiselle de Bonnefont ... and as a man of honor, Monseigneur, I'm sure you'd agree that I can hardly allow an innocent young woman to suffer on my account."

"Hmm. Yes, I see the problem," Longvilliers said thoughtfully. "As a matter of honor, you can't give up the book if you would thereby be responsible for mademoiselle coming to harm." He brightened. "I have it! We'll turn you over to the Jesuits, and they can put you to the Question. Then, when you tell us where to find the book after a bit of torture, it will have been done under duress. Your honor will not have been compromised!"

Fontrailles shook his head. "That still leaves Isabeau likely to suffer at the hands of her captors."

"Nonetheless, Monsieur, that is the situation you are in," Longvilliers said darkly. "You will cooperate with me, or else it will go hard for you."

Fontrailles snorted. "Spare me, *Monseigneur*. In the last twelvemonth I have been threatened more times than I can count, by bravos, bullies, guardsmen, haughty cavaliers, mad priests, sinister agents of foreign powers, even Cardinal Richelieu himself. I've been threatened so often that I've become a sort of connoisseur of intimidation. So believe me, as threats go, yours is a featherweight. It's not even the direst threat I've received *today*. No, Monseigneur." Fontrailles crossed his arms and shook his head. "*Merdieu!* You're talking to a man who spent an entire year in his own personal Iron Maiden, so don't wave your Jesuitical torturers at me and expect me to tremble and beg for mercy."

He took another casual step toward the table. "But listen," he said, "if you're trying to impress the Society of Jesus, this isn't the way to go about it. Moreover, from what I've seen of them, they're just not your kind of people. If I may be so bold as to offer advice, Commander, you should find another pursuit that better accords with your considerable gifts. A man of your charm, personality, and military reputation, a man of honor and faith but rather modest intellectual attainments, would be far better off sticking with the Knights of Malta, where you're sure to eventually rise to the top. Reconsider, Monseigneur!"

Longvilliers seemed taken aback at this verbal avalanche, but set his jaw resolutely. "You are very, ah, *forthright* in your opinions, Monsieur de Fontrailles. But I am committed to my current course."

"Then I have a further suggestion, Monseigneur," Fontrailles said.

The commander actually rolled his eyes. "Oh, very well, Monsieur. Really, you are most exhausting. What is your further suggestion?"

"It's actually better demonstrated than explained," Fontrailles said, now standing next to the table. "And it goes like *this*!"

He turned, scooped up Gitane's powder-pouch, and tossed it into the heart of the fire. Then he dropped to the ground, upending the table as he fell so that it was between him and the hearth. There was a second's pause, filled with the sound of bodies diving for corners, followed by a deafening *Boom!* Objects went flying about the room; something hit the other side of Louis's table, hit it hard, driving it against his knees. Then it was all over but the curses.

Fontrailles removed his hands from his ears and looked around. The roasting spit from the fireplace, with two blackened pigeon carcasses still impaled on it, was quivering on the other side of the table, its point driven deep into the wood just opposite where Louis's head had been. Most of the rest of the furniture was now firewood. The room was rapidly filling with black smoke, so Louis decided to rush for the door while he could still see where it was. The commander and Beaune both dove for him as he passed, but Beaune somehow got in the commander's way and the two went down in a tangle. Fontrailles pulled open the door, cried, "*Au revoir, Monseigneur!*" and dashed down the stairs, followed by a blistering volley of knightly oaths.

Fontrailles hurtled down the narrow stairway and tripped on the last step. He crashed into the street door, which gave way and tumbled him out into dusty Rue Serpente, where he scrambled to his feet, laughing uncontrollably. He staggered around a corner, gradually getting hold of himself, then darted around three more, left-right-left, until he was sure no one was after him. Then he leaned into a handy doorway and gave way once more to helpless laughter.

What a bunch of fatuous nincompoops these intriguers and intelligencers were! And to think he'd been running scared of these mallet-heads for months, even hiding among the dregs of society for fear of them! Well, the Vicomte de Fontrailles had taken their measure … and found them wanting. Let them play their silly games among themselves. By threatening Isabeau de Bonnefont they'd gone too far, and now they'd get their comeuppance.

Fontrailles dusted himself off, squared his shoulders (insofar as possible), and smiled confidently. The tide had turned! Let the new era begin.

A whisper, a thump, and a whirr, and for the second time in an hour Louis was looking at a sharp metal shaft buried in wood an inch from his face: a long, narrow knife quivering in the oak of the door he'd been leaning against. He turned to run, but escape to the street was blocked by a tall, slim figure in a feathered cap.

Cocodril.

CHAPTER XXXVI
SCHEMES OF DELIVERANCE

"But you're dead!" Fontrailles cried. "I saw you disappear into the river!"

Cocodril grinned his alarming grin. "Oh, Your Lordship—I'm disappointed in you. Surely a man as well-educated as Monseigneur would know that cocodrils can swim!"

"What do you want?" Fontrailles said, searching in vain for the confidence he'd felt moments before. "Are you going to kill me?"

"Tut-tut, Your Lordship. If I were going to kill you, you'd already be dead." Cocodril reached one long arm past Fontrailles and pulled his knife from the panel. "No, it will benefit my career advancement far better to take you for an interview with my mistress, Milady de Winter. She's just burning to see you! Besides," he said, cocking his head at a jaunty angle, "we can't have two Peregrines flitting about Paris, now can we?"

"So you know about that?" Fontrailles said, right hand drifting down. *I have One-Eye's pistol in my belt....*

"Oh, no, no, no!" Cocodril chided, slamming Fontrailles back against the door and snatching the pistol from his belt. "Naughty! No more pistols in the face, *merci beaucoup*." He shook his head sadly. "You continue to disappoint me, Your Lordship. It occurs to me that we had better continue this conversation elsewhere. Come along, Monseigneur."

Cocodril gripped Fontrailles firmly just below his right elbow—and something happened that surprised them both. When Fontrailles had appropriated One-Eye's weaponry, under the dead man's right sleeve, strapped to his forearm, he'd found a dagger in a curious sheath. Fontrailles, in a hurry, hadn't looked very closely at the weapon; he'd simply rolled up own his sleeve and strapped it to his arm, copying One-Eye's placement. Now Cocodril's sudden grip popped the release on the arm-sheath, a release Louis hadn't even known was there, and One-Eye's dagger dropped, neat as you please, into the palm of Louis's hand.

And Louis, his hand doing his thinking for him, instantly stabbed Cocodril in the left leg just above the knee.

"Name of a *pig!*" Cocodril cried, staggering back and clapping his hands to his leg. "You cut me, by God!"

Heart thumping, Fontrailles darted into the street and ran for his life. Glancing behind as he turned a corner he saw that Cocodril, leg streaming blood, was coming after him. And despite the wound, the rogue, whose legs were twice as long as Fontrailles's, was gaining.

The turn had put Fontrailles on Rue Saint-André-des-Arcs, a busy thoroughfare leading to Porte de Bussy, and he had to weave between pedestrians, street vendors, carts and riders, one of whom, a mounted *ritter* cursing in German, nearly rode Fontrailles down when he dashed in front of the horse's hooves.

That's what I need, Louis thought. *A horse. Aha! There's one.*

A spavined nag of a bizarre yellow color was near at hand, standing harnessed to a wagon full of onions while its owner haggled with a grocer. Fontrailles, who usually had trouble mounting a horse, somehow vaulted right up onto this one's back. He then slashed at the harness and traces with the knife he still had in his hand, envisioning that in one bold stroke he could free the horse from the wagon and gallop away.

Only it didn't work. The knife was a stiletto, all point and no edge, and the blade just slid along the leather traces and jerked up the bridle. This got the attention of the horse, which had been dozing when the something-or-other had landed on its back. It turned its ugly yellow head to look behind, so both horse and rider saw the snarling Cocodril clamber onto the back of the wagon and stalk forward through the onions. Louis read death in his eyes, the horse smelled blood, and both decided they would prefer to be somewhere else.

Horses, even spavined yellow nags, are designed by Nature to put such thoughts into instant action. The yellow horse bounded forward, nearly throwing Fontrailles off its bare back, jerking the wagon so that Cocodril fell heavily back into the onions. He tried to scramble to his feet, but onions make for uncertain footing under the best of circumstances, and in a bouncing wagon even the nimble Cocodril found progress impossible. So he dropped to all fours and began to crawl, snarling in fury.

The yellow horse heard Cocodril seemingly gaining on him. Its eyes rolled in panic and it broke into what passed, given its unusual gait, for a gallop. Citizenry scattered left and right as the runaway wagon clattered toward the Porte de Bussy, trailing a wake of rolling onions.

Fontrailles desperately gripped traces and mane and tried to figure out what to do. If he jumped or fell from the horse he would likely go under the wheels of the wagon, but if he stayed where he was Cocodril would eventually get close enough to stick a knife into him. He hoped the guards at the gate might halt the runaway and disarm the mad Cocodril, but they seemed to regard the show as a jolly entertainment staged for their amusement and merely cheered the ensemble on as it passed under the portcullis. Hooves and wheels drummed across the drawbridge and then they were in the Faubourg Saint-Germain, plunging into the crowded market of curving Rue de Bussy.

It was there, among the butcher shops and produce stands, that the sheer press of traffic forced the horse to a sudden halt, sending Fontrailles flying over its withers and landing with a mucky splash in the street's central gutter.

Before he could clear his head Cocodril had grabbed him by the collar and hauled him to his feet. "This is *it* for you, *bossu!*" the red-faced rogue cried. "You've humiliated me for the last time!"

Thump! Cocodril closed his eyes and collapsed to the ground like a suit of empty clothes, followed by his jaunty feather which, separated from his hat, drifted lazily down in a series of short arcs to come to rest on his face. Behind him stood a stout man clutching a shovel, a figure with a familiar face: Planchet.

D'Artagnan's lackey handed the shovel back to the street-worker who had been using it to unclog the gutter. "Allow me, Monsieur," he said, and helped Fontrailles to his feet. "This way." He urged the viscount away from the scene of the crime, where the yellow nag was gazing placidly at the fallen Cocodril among a gathering crowd of marketgoers. "Is there anyone else after you, Monsieur de Fontrailles?"

"I ... I don't think so," Fontrailles said, trying to catch his breath. "No, he was the only one."

"Good. Then we needn't run," said Planchet. "I prefer to save my strength, for in this city one never knows what's around the next corner."

"But how...?" Fontrailles asked. "That is to say, why...?"

"I recognized the yellow horse first," Planchet said. "It once belonged to my master, d'Artagnan. Next I recognized Monseigneur and decided you must be in trouble, or you would never be seen riding an animal such as that one. Then, when I saw you were pursued by that cur of Milady's, I knew what I had to do. This way, Monsieur." They turned up the Rue des Canettes.

"How did you know Cocodril was one of Milady's creatures?" Fontrailles asked.

"That horrible woman!" Planchet said. "*Hélas*, my master is infatuated with her. He's taken me with him several times when he's gone to call on her at her house in the Place Royale. That's where I saw that grinning dog; he was chasing around Milady's pretty maid, Kitty, trying to get her to kiss him."

The bells of Saint-Sulpice were just ringing two o'clock. "Where are we going, Planchet?" asked Fontrailles.

"To my master's rooms, in the Rue des Fossoyeurs. Monseigneur is looking a bit of a mess, if I may say so, and we should get you cleaned up.

And I imagine," Planchet added, "that Monsieur would like a drink."

"You are wise, Planchet," Fontrailles said. "Lead on. And thank you."

D'Artagnan was on guard duty, so Fontrailles and Planchet had his place to themselves. It was a modest pair of rooms on the second floor of a mercer's house, and the paucity of its furnishings told Fontrailles all he needed to know about the young guardsman's financial status. Planchet sponged off his clothes and sewed up a tear in Fontrailles's collar, while the viscount sat in the only half-comfortable chair sipping cheap wine and listening to Planchet's tale of woe.

D'Artagnan, it seemed, had fallen deeply in love—or in lust—with the delectable Milady. He was determined to get into Milady's bed, and had come up with some sort of duplicitous scheme to do so. But Planchet was convinced that Milady was poison and d'Artagnan was only getting himself deeply into trouble.

"I daresay you're right, Master Planchet," said Fontrailles. "I've had several distinctly unpleasant experiences with Milady de Winter, and would keep a good safe distance from her myself if she didn't have something I urgently need. And no," he said, in reply to Planchet's surprised look, "it's not the same thing your d'Artagnan wants so badly!"

Louis mused a minute, sipping wine. "Planchet," he said thoughtfully, "when is the next time your master intends to call on Milady?"

"Tonight, alas! And I think he hopes to stay the night through. Oh, Monsieur! If only you could persuade him to stay away from that woman. He'd listen to you!"

Fontrailles shook his head ruefully. "Oh, no, he wouldn't. I've seen Milady at work, on no less a personage than the Duke of Buckingham. If she wants d'Artagnan for some reason of her own, she'll get him. But with Milady distracted by d'Artagnan, this could be an opportunity for me to get what *I* want, and keep an eye on your master at the same time."

"I'm not following Monsieur," Planchet said.

"Allow me to explain…."

Ten hours later, in the dark of an alley behind the Place Royale, Planchet helped Fontrailles up onto the wall that enclosed the small garden at the back of Milady's mansion. Once over, Fontrailles hung for a moment from the top, then dropped quietly into a bed of daffodils, the dark cloak he'd borrowed from d'Artagnan's small wardrobe flaring for a moment. He wrapped it around him again and crouched in the dark for a time, listening. No one shouted or came running.

Until he had joined the Court of Miracles, it had never occurred to Louis d'Astarac to wonder what the average street beggar had done before he'd become too old or crippled to continue doing it. In fact, many beggars had been thieves and burglars in their nimbler days, and having little else to do at the Court of Miracles in the evening hours, they reminisced about their former criminal careers. Listening to those old codgers quarreling irascibly about the finer points of breaking and entering, Louis had learned a great deal about the art of burglary.

The theory of it, anyway. Now that he was faced with actual practice, he wished he'd asked more questions. Such as, how were you supposed to see what you were doing when it was so cursed *dark*?

By moving so absurdly slowly that he thought the sun would come up before he got anywhere, he finally managed to reach the back of the mansion without kicking over any crockery or stepping on any sleeping cats. He jimmied open a rear window with another of One-Eye's knives, a blade which he suspected had been made for exactly that purpose, and let himself quietly into what proved to be a kitchen.

Though the lights in the upper windows showed that Milady and her immediate servants were still up, most of her household was asleep. Following the basic precepts of guard-and-dog-avoidance as advocated by the old codgers, Fontrailles slowly made his way upstairs, flitting cautiously from one temporary hiding place to another.

Finally he reached the antechamber of Milady's private suite of rooms, a dangerous area because there all lamps were still lit. But their wicks had been trimmed to burn low—probably, Louis thought, to create a more romantic atmosphere—and there was an abundance of large potted plants a small hunchback could hide behind. He waited a while, counting servants, listening to their remarks, and noting the patterns of their movement—and then, picking his moment, he took a deep breath and darted through the doorway into Milady's chambers.

Milady, Louis reasoned, wasn't the sort of person to trust anyone else to keep something as valuable as *The Three Mystic Heirs* for her. As long as she wasn't suspected of being the Peregrine—and everyone assumed, of course, that the Peregrine was Fontrailles—she'd be sure to keep the book near her, almost certainly in her most private chamber. In fact, Louis figured it could be nowhere but in Milady's boudoir.

He cat-footed across a sumptuously furnished drawing room to the entrance to Milady's parlor and peeked in. It was even more opulent than the drawing room; across the chamber a painted door stood half-open, revealing beyond it a sliver of Milady's bedchamber. The goal! But to the left light streamed into the parlor from the only brightly-lit chamber in the house: Milady's dressing room. Fontrailles couldn't see the Comtesse de Winter, but he knew she was within because he could hear the liquid sounds of bathing. He also heard her voice as she addressed cutting remarks to her maid, Kitty, who *was* visible, framed in the doorway, and turned only half-away from the parlor so that Fontrailles didn't dare enter the room for fear she'd see him.

So he waited, crouched at the parlor door, each heartbeat a rush in his ears, each breath on the edge of a gasp, while Milady took eons to finish her bath, dress, and apply her make-up. Every time Kitty disappeared from the dressing-room door he prepared to dash across the parlor, but she would reappear a moment later and he would be forced to draw back. It was maddening. And Fontrailles knew that at some point a footman was going to come in behind him to announce the Chevalier d'Artagnan, and he'd be caught like a beetle in a bowl.

Finally Louis heard someone approaching from the antechamber, just as Kitty disappeared again from the dressing-room door. He swallowed, put his head down, and made his dash. And, to his utter surprise, he made it into Milady's boudoir without triggering alarums and excursions.

He took a deep breath and looked around. Louis had thought the outer chambers luxurious, but Milady's bedchamber was beyond extravagant. Gilt wallpaper, tapestries, statuary, chandeliers, carpets—clearly, the lady had plenty of money to spend. So why, Louis wondered, would she engage in something as risky as trying to extort *more* money from both Richelieu and Buckingham? What kind of person was she to play dangerous games with heads of state for something she didn't need?

And if she still had *The Three Mystic Heirs,* where, in this Byzantine harem, was it hidden? Louis thought again about Isabeau in the hands of Father Joseph's men and his hands twitched. He *had* to find it, and he didn't have much time.

And then, suddenly, he had no time at all, as he heard Milady's quick steps crossing the parlor and approaching her boudoir—which Fontrailles was standing square in the middle of, foolish look on his face. With Milady almost at the door, there was only one place to go.

He dropped to the floor and rolled under the bed.

CHAPTER XXXVII
MILADY'S OTHER SECRET

For Fontrailles, the next two hours were excruciating, far worse than when he'd hidden under the seat in Milady's carriage to steal Buckingham's diamond studs. At least the tryst with Buckingham had been brief. But with the energetic d'Artagnan, Milady's lovemaking went on and on.

For a fact, the lad's vigor and enthusiasm were impressive; if he was the same man with a blade, Louis could understand his burgeoning reputation as a swordsman. And he had to admit that Milady was up to the challenge and met him, bout for bout. Though at times he couldn't tell exactly *what* was happening on the top side of the mattress, at other times it was shockingly obvious—and Louis, below, couldn't help but imagine what it would be like with Isabeau, doing the same things.

And what was there to stop a man like Rochefort from...?

No, best not to take that line of thought too far.

The worst part about being stuck under Milady's bed while she and d'Artagnan romped abovedecks was that all the time Louis was certain he *knew* where she'd hidden the book ... and yet he couldn't get at it. Shortly after he'd rolled under the bed he'd found a gap in the dust ruffle that allowed him to see out. When Milady had come in the lamps had still been burning, albeit dimly, affording him an unobstructed view of her *prie-dieu*, the elaborately-carved padded stool where Milady would kneel to say her prayers (though Louis was willing to wager it didn't see a lot of use). It had a small lectern to support a prayer book, and a little cabinet beneath for storage of holy works.

As soon as he saw it, Louis had no doubt but that he was looking at the place where Milady de Winter kept *The Three Mystic Heirs*.

As the gymnastics upstairs dragged on he considered simply sliding out from under the bed, standing and bowing to Madame and Monsieur, then taking the book and leaving, relying on shock and sheer audacity to carry it off. But considering d'Artagnan and Milady de Winter were probably the two people in Paris least vulnerable to shock and audacity, he vetoed the idea and decided to wait it out.

But, my God! Couldn't they just take a break and go have breakfast or something?

Finally, as dawn was starting to filter through the curtains, the acrobatics reached their end, and Louis heard the two bodies drop limply onto the sheets. D'Artagnan fell for a few minutes into a light snore; Louis had almost dropped off as well when he heard Milady nudge the youth awake. Then, to Louis's amazement, the pair began to argue, at first jocularly, then seriously.

Apparently Milady wanted d'Artagnan to murder somebody named de Wardes, but the young guardsman kept trying to change the subject, which infuriated Milady. Then d'Artagnan made some sort of admission Louis didn't quite catch, Milady shrieked in rage, and the two of them began to struggle. Louis saw Milady's bare feet hit the floor outside his gap in the dust ruffle as she slid off the bed. There was a tearing sound from above, both d'Artagnan and Milady gasped, and for a moment everything froze.

Then hell broke loose.

Milady cried something like, "You wretch! Now you know my secret! For that, you die!" Louis slid his head closer to the gap just as Milady, nude, turned to her vanity table, jerked open a drawer and pulled out a golden-hilted stiletto. She spun back toward the bed, and Louis saw with a shock that on one perfect shoulder she was branded with a *fleur de lys*: the mark of a condemned criminal. Then, face distorted by fury, Milady lunged across the mattress and the battle was joined.

In the confusing clamor that followed Louis heard one clearly recognizable sound: that of a rapier hissing from its sheath. More furious shouting followed, but with a three-foot blade in his hand d'Artagnan seemed able to keep Milady at bay, until he suddenly slipped out through the closet door from which he'd entered the room two hours earlier.

Milady went wild and tried to hack through the door with her stiletto, but it was the wrong tool for the job. Finally she turned and ran howling from the bedchamber, calling for her retainers to arise and bar the doors.

Fontrailles slid from under the bed, stretched prodigiously, and then opened the door of the little cabinet in the prie-dieu. Within he found a little-used missal, a prettily-embroidered purse filled with coins, and *The Three Mystical Heirs of Christian Rosencreutz*. Leaving the missal, he took the purse and the big leather-bound book.

The entire household had been roused to catch d'Artagnan, who despite Milady's orders managed somehow to escape from the house into the Place Royale. The pursuit became general and went off down the street, so Fontrailles simply walked out of Milady's chambers, down the main stairs of her mansion, and out the front door.

It looked like it was going to be a nice day.

CHAPTER XXXVIII
HOW ASTARAC, WITHOUT THE INCONVENIENCE OF BEING MENACED OR PURSUED THROUGH THE STREETS, ACHIEVED SETTING A RENDEZVOUS FOR THE EXCHANGE OF THE HOSTAGES FOR *THE THREE MYSTIC HEIRS*

Fontrailles dipped his quill in the ink and began, "Monseigneur Father Joseph: Rejoice!"

CHAPTER XXXIX
A FIASCO

Other than in front of the pumphouse of La Samaritaine, there were no lights on the Pont Neuf at night, and halfway across the great bridge, at the streaming tip of the Île de la Cité, it was dark in the little *place* that surrounded the statue of Henri IV. At midnight, Louis d'Astarac thought, it was even rather peaceful—if one didn't have to worry about having one's throat cut. He had forestalled that probability by paying off the Brothers of La Samaritaine to avoid the middle of the bridge that night, and to keep away all rival gangs and freelance cutthroats. But the Brothers were only to prevent obvious criminals from using the bridge and allow respectable citizens to pass, for Fontrailles's planned exchange wouldn't work if his customers couldn't get to market.

He was fairly confident that the exchange would actually take place. Louis presumed the cardinal's whole purpose in holding the de Bonnefonts hostage was to trade them for *The Three Mystic Heirs*; to continue holding them afterwards would be a liability that the ever-efficient Richelieu simply wouldn't care to assume. Of course, there was always the possibility of treachery ... but Fontrailles had taken precautions.

A heavy coach-and-six clattered onto the bridge from the Quai des

Augustins on the Left Bank. It almost certainly contained the cardinal's party, which meant that Isabeau hadn't been held in the Bastille or any of the other official prisons, which were on the Right Bank or the Île itself. So Richelieu, Louis thought, hadn't troubled the king for a *lettre de cachet,* but had detained the de Bonnefonts on his own authority.

The coach slowed, stopping as it came abreast of Place Henri IV, where Fontrailles stood waiting in front of the late king's statue. Behind him the bronze effigy of Louis XIII's father smiled down on his subjects, mounted on his favorite Béarnese cob, high on a stone pedestal engraved *Henrico Magno*—Henri the Great. Louis almost felt as if the jovial, fatherly King Henri was backing him up in his lone game against his royal son's prime minister.

The driver hopped down from his seat, opened the door of the coach, and out oozed Father Joseph, Richelieu's master of intelligence. Barefoot and cowled as always, he somehow seemed less sinister in the dark than in the daylight, as if the night were his natural habitat. He took two steps toward Fontrailles and stopped, his pop-eyes in a thoughtful stare.

Behind him the Comte de Rochefort issued from the coach, then helped the hostages down. First came the old Seigneur de Bonnefont, awkward and stiff, his hands bound before him. Then petite Isabeau—Louis's heart bounded in his chest—her hair mussed, her face pale but its features composed. And finally, to Louis's surprise, the slim form of Éric de Gimous. Louis's boyhood friend (and now rival) was wild-eyed and trembling a little, his hands, like de Bonnefont's, bound in front of him.

Somehow, in his preparations for this meeting, Louis hadn't considered what it would be like for him to see Isabeau again, and he was rocked by gusts of emotion. For one moment, Louis and Isabeau looked across the space between them and into each other's eyes, and Isabeau silently mouthed his name.

"Louis."

Then he was forced to turn his attention to the Capuchin. "God keep you, my son," Joseph said, in a voice barely audible over the hiss of the river. "As you see, we have come to make the exchange you proposed, and in good faith. It grieves me to see that our trust in you is not entirely reciprocated."

Fontrailles grinned. "Monseigneur is perceptive, as always. You immediately noticed that I hold a rope in my left hand, a rope that extends behind me, under some tension, up over King Henri's raised right arm and thence off into the darkness toward the river. As you've already divined, that book everyone wants so badly is in a weighted sack on the end of my rope, dangling from a pole over a deep spot in the rushing waters. If I let go, *The Three Mystic Heirs* goes for a fatal dive. Entirely unnecessary, of course, as I expect no double-dealing," he concluded pleasantly, "but I value your good opinion, Father Joseph, and want you to think of me as a man of prudence." Fontrailles smiled, though to his annoyance the hand holding the rope was visibly shaking.

"Insolence," the Comte de Rochefort growled from his position next to the hostages. "I'll see that you pay for it."

"But not tonight, if you please," Fontrailles said. "Father Joseph? Shall we proceed?"

"Indeed we shall, Monsieur de Fontrailles," interrupted a distinctly English voice, "but not quite the way you had in mind." Sir Percy Blakeney stepped out from behind the coach, holding a tall English longbow at full stretch, arrow aimed at Rochefort. He was followed by a slim, athletic masked man who held a pistol. "Oblige me by raising your hands, won't you, Monsieur de Rochefort?" Blakeney said, in a cheerful voice with steel behind it. "You, too," he said to the driver. "I assure you, I know how to use this weapon, and it reloads much faster than a pistol."

"Don't do anything rash with that rope, d'Astarac," the masked man said, in Aramis's voice. "This will all be over in a moment, and you're going to come out of it just fine. We get the book, and you get your fiancée."

"You mean *m-my* fiancée!" Éric de Gimous said loudly—to everyone's surprise, including his own. He clapped his mouth shut, but stood, trembling but upright, next to Isabeau.

"Be that as it may," said Blakeney. "Monsieur de Fontrailles, be so kind as to draw that book up from the brink. Once we have it, you may take these persons and be on your way."

"But that leaves France with nothing!" objected Father Joseph, forgetting his ominous whisper.

"No way around it, I'm afraid," said Blakeney. "We have only two objects of desire here, and three parties to satisfy."

"Four, actually, *mein Herr*," said Athanasius Kircher, appearing from the shadows behind Blakeney and Aramis. He was accompanied by Père Míkmaq, who placed a wide-mouthed blunderbuss on a forked support and swiveled it to cover all and sundry. Kircher said, "Let no one do anything reckless, or my associate will discharge his firearm, and as it is loaded with scatter-shot, more than one of you will be badly hurt. Monsieur Peregrine, I believe?" he continued, addressing Fontrailles. "Let us have that book. But pray, be careful! The wisdom it contains is incalculable. *Incalculable!*"

In a tick, Blakeney spun forty-five degrees to his left, and his bow, still drawn, was aimed at Fontrailles. "Check, I believe," Blakeney said. "I don't know who you are, my German friend, but if you don't withdraw immediately I'll put a shaft through your Peregrine, and that book, with its 'incalculable' wisdom, will be lost to everybody."

"Louis!" Isabeau cried.

Fontrailles looked along the shaft of the arrow to Blakeney's unwinking eye, gulped, and said, "Can I say something?"

"No, d'Astarac. It's my turn," Aramis said from behind his mask. He took a step back, out of Blakeney's peripheral vision, then gripped his pistol by the barrel and clouted the Englishman hard over the head with the butt. As Blakeney dropped Fontrailles flinched to the right, and the arrow, loosed, whistled past his left ear and broke against the stone pedestal behind him.

Aramis reversed his pistol again and said, "Hold it, Rochefort. Get your hands off your weapons and back up in the air. That's right."

"Ara ... I mean, whoever you are," Fontrailles said. "What's going on here?"

"Nothing bad, d'Astarac," Aramis said. "Just haul in that book and give it to Father Kircher, here."

"Lord bless you, *mein Herr*," Kircher said. "This will ensure your admittance to the Society."

"So it's the Jesuits you represent!" Father Joseph hissed, having recovered his sinister whisper. Everyone looked at the Capuchin, who continued, "Then you must be Athanasius Kircher. I have heard of you— but here you are in Paris, not Rome. You would be wise to come to an accommodation with the Gallican Church, Herr Kircher, or you may not survive to bring that book of wisdom back to your masters."

There was a sudden ominous *click* from behind Herr Kircher, and everyone turned to see Milady de Winter holding a dainty gold-chased pistol to the wide-eyed Jesuit's head. "You are right, Monseigneur Joseph," Milady said in her honeyed tones. "It is we who serve the cardinal who will be taking that book with us tonight. And I am confident that he will be appropriately grateful. Don't you agree?"

"Stop! Halt! Cease!" cried Père Míkmaq, swiveling his blunderbuss toward Milady. "Has everyone forgotten me? *I* have the biggest firearm, and *I* am in charge here!"

"Don't be an idiot!" Aramis said. "She has the drop on Kircher—and besides, if you shoot her, you'll probably shoot him too. Are you trying to get your master killed?"

"Shut up!" Míkmaq shouted raggedly. "*I* am in charge here. Everyone will do what *I say*!"

"All right. You're in charge here," Aramis said. He started to turn away, then spun completely around and neatly drop-kicked the blunderbuss from the priest's hands. Weapon and support when clattering across the cobbles as Míkmaq watched in helpless disbelief. Aramis then carefully placed his own pistol on the ground and said, "Very well, Milady. There's no need for anyone to get shot tonight."

"Thank you, Monsieur-in-the-mask," Milady said sweetly. "Now if Monsieur de Fontrailles will show the same good sense and draw up the book, we can conclude this farce."

"Now, just a minute," Fontrailles said, head swimming.

"Oh, foolish me, I forgot!" Milady said. "I'm pointing my pistol at the *wrong person.*" And she turned its muzzle on Isabeau de Bonnefont, who gasped and paled.

"Madame—Milady—whoever you are, please!" Éric de Gimous said. "Don't shoot! Louis, Louis—give her the book!"

"If I give you the book," Fontrailles said to Milady, "will you let the hostages go free?"

"I am not *bargaining* with you, Fontrailles," Milady said, in a voice with no sweetness in it whatsoever. "Give me the book, *now*, or the girl dies."

Fontrailles took a deep breath and said, "Very well, Milady. Don't shoot." He put both hands on the rope and began to haul it in hand-over-hand.

And that was when the horde of beggars launched their attack.

How they got past the Brothers of La Samaritaine Louis never knew, though when he thought about it later he decided the beggars must have somehow come across *under* the bridge. However they did it, the swarm of mendicants appeared suddenly out of the darkness from every direction, howling and swinging crutches, knives and heavy crockery.

Fontrailles's eyes were riveted on Milady despite the distraction; he saw the look of sudden fury contort her features and cried *"No!"* as she pulled the trigger. The Seigneur de Bonnefont darted forward as the pistol cracked—and the ball, intercepted, buried itself in his chest.

"*Father!*" cried Isabeau as de Bonnefont fell back in her arms. Without a second thought, Fontrailles rushed toward her—and the rope, forgotten, whistled from his hands. The end flickered as it whipped over Henri the Great's ever-upraised arm and disappeared into the darkness.

Fontrailles's attempt to get to Isabeau was foiled by the rising tide of beggars assailing all the parties around Father Joseph's coach. Spurred on by Isabeau's screams, Louis nonetheless made pretty good progress through the brawl, until his legs were suddenly kicked out from under him and he fell flat on the flagstones. He rolled over to find himself straddled by the long gaunt form of Bronte, who grabbed him by the front of his doublet and hoisted him, kicking, above the throng. "I've got him, Great Caesar!" Bronte shouted hoarsely, shaking Fontrailles like a rag. "I've got him!"

Fontrailles was helpless in the grip of Bronte's maniacal strength, especially when the man drew Cocodril's long knife and held it to Fontrailles's throat; he instantly went limp and gave up any idea of kicking himself free. In any event, from his vantage above the crowd, he could see that though Aramis and Rochefort were still struggling, the fight was basically over. At least Isabeau, sobbing over her father's body, didn't seem to have been harmed.

The mob of beggars parted as Great Caesar, dressed in full imperial splendor, thumped into its midst—followed by Proserpine, who glared at Louis with death in her eyes. "Well done, good Bronte," Caesar cried. "Do not fear, Mesdames and Messieurs," he said to his new captives. "We have no quarrel with you, and will hold you only so long as we must to enable you to witness Great Caesar's justice. Our business here," he roared, pointing at Louis with his golden hook, "is with him!"

"Fontrailles?" said Joseph.

"D'Astarac?" said Aramis.

"The Peregrine?" said Kircher.

"My Louis?" said Isabeau.

"*My* Centurion Hephaestus!" thundered Caesar.

"But what do you want with him?" Isabeau cried.

"His life!" cried Proserpine. "For what he's done to me, *he must die!*"

The sudden silence was broken by Milady de Winter's delighted chuckle. "Why, Monsieur de Fontrailles!" she said. "Have you led this poor woman astray? I have an entirely new respect for you!"

"Silence!" the Beggar King said majestically. "Great Caesar has tried this miscreant *in absentia*, found him guilty, and passed sentence. And so, Bronte, without further delay—you may execute the condemned."

Bronte's knife flicked at Fontrailles. He shut his eyes and felt a searing pain as the blade went into his neck. When he heard the simultaneous gunshot, he thought, *They're shooting me too!* But then, amid screaming, he tumbled to the ground ... alive.

He opened his eyes to chaos. Bronte staggered above him, holding bloody hands to his gouting face. More guns were going off and beggars were scattering in every direction. Fontrailles put his hand to his throat; his fingers came away bloody, but his head still seemed to be attached to his neck.

Fontrailles scrambled to his feet. Bronte, the left side of his face a ruin, fixed him with his remaining eye and let loose a savage roar. Fontrailles slipped on a puddle of blood and fell back on the cobbles; Bronte reached for him with red hands like claws, and then stopped in surprise as six inches of shiny steel emerged from his chest. The blade paused for less than a second before it was withdrawn, and Louis watched, transfixed, as Bronte closed his eye and collapsed with a piteous moan onto Louis's legs.

Behind the fallen Bronte, sword dripping, stood Philippe de Longvilliers, Knight of Malta, clad in a gleaming suit of full plate armor. Bizarrely, Longvilliers raised his sword to the vertical and formally saluted the man he'd impaled. Then he turned to face the rest of the fray.

Louis, losing blood from and beginning to feel faint, tried to pull himself out from under Bronte's body ... and found that he was being helped by the Countess of Carlisle. "Lucy!" he cried. It hurt.

"Don't move, Louis—that wound doesn't look well at all," said Lucy Hay. "Don't worry, sweetheart, we'll get you out of here."

"*Sweet*heart!" bugled Proserpine, looming suddenly above them. "So *you're* the one he left me for! I'll have your guts, you high-class whore!" Lady Carlisle raised her arms to try to fend her off but went down under an avalanche of Proserpine. Tearing at each other, Lucy and Proserpine rolled on the cobbles, screeching—while beyond them Isabeau watched in horror.

Louis stood up, dizzy, and tried to figure out what was going on. Longvilliers and Lady Carlisle had clearly arrived with a number of allies. Beaune and Éric de Gimous, his hands freed, were keeping the angry beggars away from Isabeau, who was still cradling her dead father's body. Aramis, Blakeney, and Gitane were holding back the horde on one side of the coach, with Rochefort, Míkmaq, and Longvilliers on the other, while Kircher and Father Joseph scrambled into the vehicle. Milady de Winter was nowhere to be seen.

"*He's* looked better, and no mistake," muttered a familiar voice at

Louis's side. He turned and gave a wordless cry of joy: Vidou! And looking dyspeptic as ever. "Here, Monsieur," said the Vicomte de Fontrailles's valet. "Found this lying on the cobbles. Thought maybe you could use it."

It was Rochefort's big double-barreled Spät. Fontrailles grabbed the heavy pistol eagerly and checked it: both barrels were loaded, both pans primed. He turned toward the mêlée, pointed the Spät toward the sky, and let off one barrel with a gratifying *boom!*

Everyone paused to look toward him. "*Merdieu!* That's enough!" he shouted, tearing his throat. "I have another barrel, and if anybody…."

Then he realized that everyone was looking *past* him, and that from behind him came the sound of a struggle. He turned to see what they were all looking at.

There, in front of the statue of Henri the Great, a sort of duel was taking place, a fight so desperate that the combatants hadn't even noticed the detonation of the Spät. It was a battle royale—literally, if one assumed a King of the Beggars was royalty—between Great Caesar and that tough old sailor, Sobriety Breedlove.

The two wiry old men were locked in a clinch, toe to toe, wooden leg to wooden leg—though Breedlove, Louis saw with surprise, seemed to be supported by a new limb, one made of wood rather than spiral horn. Furthermore, he now seemed to be missing his right hand; it had been replaced with a steel hook, which was locked above his head with Caesar's own golden sickle.

The pair swayed back and forth, seeking advantage. As the crowd watched, holding its collective breath, their wooden legs suddenly slipped on the flagstones and both men lost their balance, their hooks disengaging as they stumbled a half step away from each other. Then with a shout both men swung their hooks in roundhouse rights, and each buried his point in his opponent's neck. Blood fountained, both men gurgled hollowly, and the pair fell together to the flagstones.

With a mournful howl, the assembled beggary burst past the cavaliers and descended on the bleeding carcasses. As the others watched, open-mouthed, the mob hoisted the bodies—Caesar, Breedlove, and Bronte—to their ragged shoulders and carried them rapidly away across the bridge, followed by a wailing Proserpine. After a few moments the darkness had swallowed them, and all they could hear was the dwindling wail of Caesar's daughter.

Fontrailles suddenly slapped his forehead. "The book! Lucy, Longvilliers, this way, quick!" He staggered to the edge of the parapet, where his forked pole still jutted out over the Seine, hoping that somehow the weighted bag containing *The Three Mystic Heirs* had hung up and not gone plunging into the river. He leaned over the edge and peered down into the swirling waters, but could see nothing.

But he could *hear* something from downstream to his left: the thump of oars in oarlocks. He ran, followed by Lady Carlisle and Longvilliers, to the western parapet that overlooked the narrow spit of land at the point of the Île de la Cité. A ladder leaned against the parapet from the muddy strand below, and beyond a rowboat was just putting out into the swift current. Plying the oars, his grin unmistakable through the gloom, was Cocodril. In front of him, holding a lantern, sat Milady de Winter—and by the lantern's light they could see clearly that she had a burlap sack on her lap. The sack that contained *The Three Mystic Heirs*.

Milady's silvery laugh swirled up from the dark as the boat disappeared downstream. Longvilliers began to climb over the parapet and onto the ladder, but Fontrailles put his hand on his arm and said, "No, Commander, you'll never catch them now. And besides, I don't think you'll swim very far in that heavy armor."

"But Louis, how did they get it?" Lady Carlisle asked.

"I think Milady arrived by boat, rowed by Cocodril," Fontrailles said, wheezing. "She probably saw the bag dangling over the drink and had Cocodril station himself beneath it. When I let go, it fell right into his arms. In fact, Milady shot at Isabeau to *make* me let go. Then Cocodril just rowed back and picked her up when she came down the ladder during the fracas."

There was a whip-crack and clatter from the bridge as the coach got under way. "There goes Father Joseph—and Kircher with him," said Longvilliers. "If those two get together, it will give us a glorious challenge."

75

"To the devil with both of them," Fontrailles said thickly. "Milady shot Isabeau's father; we have to get him to a surgeon."

But when they returned to the *place*, they found the de Bonnefonts gone. "They went that way, Monsieur, toward where we used to live," said Vidou, pointing toward the shadows of Place Dauphine. "The Seigneur de Bonnefont—he's dead, Monsieur. I'm sorry. Monsieur de Gimous and mademoiselle ran off, the lady weeping. Beaune went with them, carrying the seigneur's body."

"The devil! Now why would Beaune do that?" said Fontrailles.

"He seemed quite taken with Mademoiselle," said Vidou.

Fontrailles looked around Place Henri IV, recently so crowded. He was alone with his rescuers: Lucy, Longvilliers, Vidou, and the dour Gitane. "*Nom de Dieu,*" he said, and sat down suddenly on the flagstones. "Her father—dead. Isabeau will never forgive me. *I'll* never forgive me."

Philippe de Longvilliers said to Lady Carlisle, "What do we do now, my love?"

"Damned if I know," she said in English. Then, in French, "It's up to the master mind." She turned to Fontrailles and said, "All right, centurion—what's the plan?"

Louis d'Astarac looked dizzily up at Lady Carlisle, with lecherous old Henri the Great leering down over her shoulder. He blinked twice, opened his mouth, and passed out.

CHAPTER XL
THE CONCLAVE

"Careful!" Lady Carlisle said to Vidou, who was changing the dressing on Fontrailles's neck. "That filthy beggar's knife just missed the big blood-vessel in his throat."

"Bah," said Fontrailles. "I've cut myself worse shaving."

"So *that's* what happened to your face!" she said.

"Ha. Ha. Ha."

They were sitting on the so-called "rear veranda" of the modest Bois-Tracy hunting lodge, deep in the forest of the same name a few miles east of the king's own hunting lodge of Versailles. The sun was disappearing through the tops of the trees beyond the small meadow to the west of the lodge; Fontrailles, Lady Carlisle, and Philippe de Longvilliers were sitting on rustic chairs around a rustic table while Longvilliers's several servants brought them refreshing drinks. It was, Louis reflected, a much more civilized approach to being a fugitive than the manner in which he'd formerly gone about it. There was something to be said for consorting with the high nobility.

"So tell me again, Madame," Fontrailles said, when Vidou had finished fussing at his throat, "how you learned about the exchange on the Pont

77

Neuf. I'm still trying to work out how everyone I know in northern France showed up for what was supposed to be a secret meeting."

Lady Carlisle, still wearing the dove-gray riding habit in which she'd ridden from Paris, sipped her *aperitif.* "I assume," she said, "that the Jesuits must have an informant among Father Joseph's intelligencers, because the commander, here, learned about the meeting from Herr Kircher."

"That's right," said Longvilliers. He sat in a chair quite close to hers, looking splendid in an ermine-trimmed hunting jack, legs extended on the white gravel in a pair of magnificent Spanish riding boots. "Kircher, who knows I've long wanted to be admitted to the upper levels of the Society, tried to recruit me to assist him in interrupting your *tête-à-tête* with Father Joseph. Naturally I turned him down flat."

"But why, Commander?" Fontrailles said. "I got the impression you *wanted* to help him get the book."

"Oh, I did. But that was before I met you in Gitane's humble abode. When I saw how you stood up to me, Monsieur le Vicomte, refusing to be cowed despite my manifest superiority, I knew that you were a true man of honor and I would far rather be with you than against you. Then, when my darling Lucy"—he paused to gaze adoringly at Lady Carlisle, who dimpled—"confirmed my impression by telling me what a wonderful fellow you really are—and that she had her own reasons for wanting that book— well, I knew which side I had to be on.

"And then there's your reputation as a planner," Longvilliers continued. "If there's one thing I learned from the Grand Master of the Order, it's to be aware of one's strengths and weaknesses. Plotting is not one of my strengths, I know that, and it seemed to me I could use an able advisor in that regard."

"Really?" said Fontrailles, somewhat nonplussed. "And which of my plans to date has so favorably impressed you?"

"Oh, none of them," the Commander of the Order said pleasantly. "But if there's anything else I learned from the grand master, it's that one learns only from failure, so I assumed you...."

"Very well, very well, I get it," Fontrailles said hastily. "And I'm flattered, of course."

"Isn't he a dear?" Lady Carlisle beamed at Longvilliers, who beamed back, basking in her admiration. She leaned forward, riding habit rustling, to whisper in Louis's ear: "Such potential! I can *make* something of this one, Louis."

God help him, Louis thought, discovering that he wasn't jealous of Longvilliers's good luck. Especially since the image of Isabeau, cradling her dying father in her arms, was now never far from his mind. "You said you'd been in England?" he continued.

"All winter and spring," Lady Carlisle replied. "After what Joseph said about my father, which you deduced was a lie, dear Louis"—she favored him with a warm smile—"I knew there were things I needed to tell him while he was still alive. But once I was back in England I fell once more into Buckingham's net, and had no choice but to return to doing his bidding."

"The dog!" erupted Longvilliers. "Have you heard of the outrages he perpetrated on her?"

"There, now, my eagle," Lady Carlisle said. "Once we get that book I'll have my revenge on Milord Duke. At any event, Buckingham got me appointed lady-of-the-bedchamber to Queen Henriette, which is really quite an honor, and I couldn't get away from the English Court for the longest time. But when the warm weather came around it got to be plague season again and everyone left Court for the country, so I hurried across the Channel to France—bringing with me your man Breedlove, whom I'd found in London. In Paris I located Vidou, and then right away I found dear Philippe here, who was making the most indiscreet inquiries after the Peregrine in that adorably direct way he has."

"You are too good, my darling," Longvilliers said. "I know now how clumsy I was. I've learned so much from you already about this business of intrigue."

"And you learn so *quickly*, Philippe!"

"Ahem. Yes," said Fontrailles. "By the way, what happened to Breedlove's leg? And his hand, for that matter?"

"After you left London, Breedlove was imprisoned for a while by Buckingham," Lady Carlisle said. "Apparently he was interrogated, rather harshly, by Doctor Lambe, the duke's astrologer."

"Another black mark against that dog Buckingham!" Longvilliers burst out. "He made your sailor pay for his loyalty to you. And then the man gave his life to protect you, attacking that beggar-king when he was about to fall on you from behind."

"So that's what happened," Fontrailles said. "All right, you've explained what you two were doing at my meeting, and also Kircher, with that maniac Míkmaq. But what about the Englishman, Blakeney?"

"That's my fault, I'm afraid," Lady Carlisle said. "Since I knew that he knew that I'd gone back to Buckingham—before I left him again, of course—I thought I might get Blakeney to throw in with us and help make sure things went our way. He is awfully clever, you know. He promised to join us, but then he made his own play. By the way, who was that masked man assisting him? He seemed familiar, somehow."

"I have no idea," Louis lied. He didn't really want to mention Aramis in front of the excitable Longvilliers, and in any event he preferred to square accounts with his friend the musketeer on his own ... though he wasn't quite sure at this point who owed what to whom. "Very well, that covers Blakeney. I assume Milady de Winter, as a cardinal's agent, learned about the meeting from Joseph or Rochefort, and took the opportunity to attend on her own account."

"But what about the beggars?" Lady Carlisle asked.

"That's easy enough to explain: they have eyes everywhere," Fontrailles said. "I was probably spotted going onto the bridge that night and a report was carried back to Great Caesar, who was hunting for me."

"On account of that ample daughter of his, I gather, who seems to have developed such *feelings* for you," Lucy Hay said sweetly. "When *are* you going to tell us about her, Louis darling?"

"She's ... not important right now," Fontrailles said, shifting uncomfortably in his chair. "What is important is that we can't stay here, pleasant as it is. Father Joseph knows you've been using the name Bois-

Tracy and will be sure to send someone to search this place."

"You're right, of course," Lady Carlisle said. "You're always thinking, Louis—that's what I like about you. They'll track down the Comte de Bois-Tracy at his city address, he'll confess that I've been paying him to pretend I'm his wife (who's actually a madwoman in a provincial cloister, poor dear), and then they'll be on our trail. But where do you suggest we go?"

"Oh, I know that already," said Fontrailles. "You're going to adopt another name and go back to Paris, while I go to La Rochelle."

"The city of the Huguenots?" said Longvilliers. "But why?"

"Because I'm certain Isabeau and Éric will head for La Rochelle. They're both Huguenots themselves, and they have relatives there. Isn't that right, Vidou?" His valet, who'd been listening discreetly to their conversation, nodded in confirmation. "Besides," Fontrailles continued, "it's the only place they can go in France that's still out of Richelieu's reach."

"Meanwhile, we go back to Paris to keep an eye on Milady Winter," said Lady Carlisle. "I can certainly approve of that. Better Paris than that dump La Rochelle."

"Oh, you'll be joining me there soon enough," Fontrailles said. "The king and his army are leaving any day to besiege the city—it's the last stronghold of the Protestants in France, and Buckingham is planning to support them. Where King Louis goes, so goes his prime minister, and where Richelieu goes, so goes Milady—especially since she will be trying once again to find a way to sell him *The Three Mystic Heirs*."

"If she's the cardinal's agent," said Longvilliers, "why doesn't he just order her to give it to him?"

"Because we're the only ones who know she has it, remember?" Fontrailles said. "Everyone else thinks it was lost in the river during the mêlée. That's why you need to watch her, in case there's an opportunity to get the book from her before she sells it to the cardinal."

And maybe, he added to himself, *once I get to La Rochelle, I can find a way to get Isabeau and Éric out of the city before its inevitable fall to the king.*

"Well, you've convinced me," Lady Carlisle said, "and I'm sure Philippe agrees—don't you, my dear? It's Paris for us, and you're off to La Rochelle.

I knew I could count on that fine, scheming mind of yours to come up with a plan, Centurion."

"I do wish you'd stop calling me that," Fontrailles said.

"But, darling," she replied, "that's why I *do* it!"

CHAPTER XLI
THE DREAM OF LA BONNEFONT

The town: Surgères, in Aunis; the inn: l'Auberge de Quatre Vents; the season: Autumn, 1627. Louis d'Astarac, clad in the dun wool and leather of a traveling merchant, stood just inside the front gate, staring at—nothing.

Yes, they were here: a young, married couple on their way to La Rochelle...

...a young, married couple...

...married....

"Of course, they would have to *travel* as married, even if they weren't," Louis said to the gatepost. "It's not like this hadn't occurred to me before."

It's not like I haven't thought about it every cursed day, all the way from Paris.

He sighed: enough. Time to see how his drover, Dindon, was making out in the stables. With the royal army devouring everything within a day's travel of its line of march to La Rochelle, Fontrailles had ridden ahead to Surgères to find food and livestock—and, hopefully, word of Isabeau and Éric. At the whitewashed grange behind the stables Fontrailles found Dindon loading his wagon with hay, oats, bottles of Pineau, and wheels of cheese. Helping Dindon was a big man who lifted sacks of oats as if they were feather pillows.

"Beaune!" cried Fontrailles. "Is that you?"

Beaune turned, smiled broadly, then looked down with embarrassment. "*Oui,* Monseigneur," he said in his incongruous tenor.

"But I thought you were with Mademoiselle de Bonnefont!"

"I was, Monseigneur, to protect her. But I wouldn't accept the Reformed religion, so I couldn't follow her into La Rochelle." Beaune's face clouded. "That was hard."

"I'm sure it was. But was she well, when you parted?"

"Yes, Monseigneur, though still grieving for her father."

Louis couldn't ask about what he really wanted to know, so instead he said, "And how is it I find you here loading my wagon?"

Beaune's broad forehead furrowed, and he turned to Dindon. "You said this wagon was owned by Monsieur Nouveau the *munitionnaire,*" he said accusingly.

Fontrailles smiled. "But, you see, Beaune, I *am* Monsieur Nouveau the *munitionnaire.* I needed a way to travel with the king and cardinal to La Rochelle without attracting attention, so I bought out an army supply merchant: stock, horses, and wagons. I kept on the teamsters and field cook, increased their wages"—Dindon smiled—"and started another new career."

"Monseigneur is going to La Rochelle?"

"I am. I intend to get Mademoiselle de Bonnefont out of there before the town falls to Richelieu's army. Will you come with me?"

Beaune smiled so broadly Louis thought his face would split. "Yes, indeed, Monseigneur! Just give me a few moments to collect my things and tell the hostler I'm quitting."

"*Trés bien!*" Fontrailles said, smiling himself for the first time in a week. "But, Beaune, you must call me 'Monsieur' now that I'm merely a humble bourgeois."

Fontrailles hadn't mentioned his other reason for traveling with the royal army: so he could stay near the cardinal in case his agent, Milady de Winter, turned up with *The Three Mystic Heirs.* The more Louis thought about Isabeau with Éric, the more he cursed his twisted spine—and the more he burned to get his hands on that book of Rosicrucian secrets. No matter how much trouble she was in, and no matter what Louis did to get her out of it, he knew Isabeau would still reject him so long as he was a distorted monster. Andreaeus's arcane tome was his last hope.

One week later Louis the King, trailed by Louis the *munitionnaire*, reached the camp at La Rochelle. Advance elements of the army had already placed the fortified Protestant city under siege, and warships had blockaded the harbor. But a more immediate problem for the French was that the Isle of Ré, just offshore from La Rochelle, had been invaded and largely overrun by English troops under the command of the Duke of Buckingham. This had heartened the Rochelois and strengthened their determination to withstand the siege; if reinforced, the English might even break the blockade and raise the siege entirely.

But Cardinal Richelieu, a surprisingly martial churchman, engineered a counter-invasion of Ré that routed Buckingham's troops, forcing them to take ship back to England in ignominious defeat. Nonetheless, the English were expected to return with an even greater fleet, so the French settled in to a siege designed to bring the Rochelois to their knees before help could arrive.

The lines of the besiegers extended in a leagues-long near-circle surrounding the city, from one shore of the harbor to the other—and Richelieu was having a dyke built across the harbor mouth to seal that entrance as well.

Monsieur Nouveau's team of sutlers was part of a secondary army of non-combatants supplying the vast camp of besiegers. Fontrailles delegated most of the supply business to his men and spent the bulk of his time on his personal concerns, scouting the Protestant defenses, trying to puzzle out how to get into La Rochelle and get Isabeau out. But the besiegers were alert, the cardinal's eyes were everywhere, and the gallows where captured Huguenot spies and messengers were hanged were nearly always full. So Fontrailles bided his time: by day he practiced his marksmanship with the big double-barreled Spät, and in the evenings he resumed his correspondence with Leeghwater in Amsterdam, Calderón in Madrid, and des Cartes, now once more in Paris.

By night he dreamed of Isabeau, and the look she'd given him that night on the Pont Neuf.

The winter storms began to blow in from the Gulf of Gascony, or the Bay of Biscay, as the English called it, and still there was no sign of Milady de Winter, and no word of *The Three Mystic Heirs*. Fontrailles had heard nothing from Longvilliers or Lady Carlisle, and had no way to communicate with them.

The weary siege dragged on—so weary that the king, fed up with its tedium, returned to Paris for a while, leaving matters in the hands of his prime minister, who continued to tighten his grip on the city. With little for the besiegers to do but gamble, drink, and gossip, their camps buzzed with rumors, and as spring turned to summer speculation was rife that *something* was about to change their situation. So when, one early summer morning, Fontrailles heard the sound of drums and the reports of cannon, he wasn't sure whether it augured attack or retreat, victory or defeat.

He hurried toward the drums, mounted, in his capacity as a bourgeois, on a humble Poitevin mare, along with a crowd of curious soldiers, servants, and camp followers. Fontrailles soon found that the commotion was the regimental artillery welcoming back His Majesty Louis XIII, returned to La Rochelle for the summer siege season. The king rode majestically into camp, followed by the usual swarm of guards, courtiers, and retainers—among whom was Philippe de Longvilliers, with Lady Carlisle riding next to him. Though they rode in with the middling nobility and both wore kerchiefs across their faces to keep out the dust, Fontrailles recognized them immediately and turned his mare to intercept them.

"Now isn't this a pleasant surprise," he said, bowing in the saddle. "Welcome, Commander and Madame, to our little siege. To what do we owe the honor?"

"Not so loud, Louis, Philippe is here *incognito*," said Lady Carlisle, but with a smile behind the kerchief. She lowered her voice. "For that matter, so am I. In fact, being English, you might say I'm *extra*-incognito. Is there someplace private we can go to talk?"

"Follow me to *chez* Nouveau, the little shack thrown together for me by the ever-efficient Gitane," Fontrailles said. "It's not much, but it's an improvement over the open tent I had when we first arrived; nobody likes to see a hunchback in his underclothes in the morning." He turned his horse and beckoned them to follow— Longvilliers had only four retainers, a modest entourage for him—and a few minutes later Fontrailles and his guests were seated on stools in his tiny cabin. The open door admitted the warm summer sun and the bustling sounds of the great camp around them.

"This will do," said the Maltese Commander, beating the dust from his clothes with his riding gloves. "Upon my oath, it's better than some of the places we've slept in during our two weeks' ride from Paris. I swear, some nights our horses were better bedded than we were. Do you have anything to drink?"

"Vidou, bring the Anjou wine," Fontrailles called. Once Longvilliers and Lady Carlisle had had a chance to wash some of the dust from their throats, he said, "All right, Madame and Monseigneur, I can wait no longer. What's the news? I'm certain you didn't travel to this arse-end of France for your health."

"No, indeed!" said Lady Carlisle, loosing her glorious dark hair from under her hat. "God's teeth, what a mess I am! And you're right, dear Louis, we're not here for pleasure." She gave him a smile that nearly knocked him off his stool, reminding him both of dear Isabeau and of the night spent with Lucy in Aramis's bed. "Here's your news," she said. "You didn't see her, because she didn't want to be seen—but Milady Winter also rode into camp this morning. And she has the you-know-what with her."

"She *does*?" Fontrailles was more excited than he'd been in months. "How can you be certain?"

"We have a reliable informer," Longvilliers said, with a certain smugness. "Come in, my friend," he called out the door, "and introduce yourself!"

A tall man wearing a dust-mask entered the shack, louted low, and then removed the kerchief from his face. "Jean Reynon, once again at your service, Your Lordship," said Cocodril, with his preposterous grin. "I can only imagine how happy you are to see me!"

CHAPTER XLII
THE VIDOU WHINE

"Oh, *no*, Monsieur! Not him!" moaned Vidou. "Take him! Bind him! Beat him!"

"I'm delighted to see you, too, Vidou," said Cocodril. "Another glass, my man, and we'll drink a toast to the reunion of old friends!"

Fontrailles, swallowing his astonishment, summoned Gitane. "As you see, the rogue Cocodril has returned," he told the ex-smuggler. "Go back outside and keep a sharp lookout; he may already have betrayed our location to some accomplice, and trouble may be on the way."

"What kind of trouble should I watch for, Monsieur?" asked Gitane, eying the grinning Cocodril.

"Soldiers; assassins; sheep bearing petards with fuses already lit; anything!" Fontrailles said. "Just be alert."

"Oh, Your Lordship, such suspicion!" said Cocodril. "You wound my sensitive nature!"

"I couldn't wound your sensitive nature with an axe," said Fontrailles.

"For a fact, Viscount, I think you *are* over-reacting," said Longvilliers. "Personally, I find friend Cocodril's good-natured candor quite refreshing."

"We'll see how refreshing you find it once friend Cocodril's tried to cut your throat a time or two," Fontrailles said. "If he found you, Commander, you can be sure Milady already knows you're here, and why."

"Now you're being unfair, Louis. Just hear us out," said Lady Carlisle. "Your former manservant didn't find us—we went to him. We made him an offer to join the commander's services, and he accepted."

"It was Lucy's idea," Longvilliers said proudly.

"And it was a most *generous* offer," said Cocodril, "fully consonant with my own assessment of my talents and skills. And tomorrow night, it will pay off for you all quite handsomely."

"What happens tomorrow night?" Fontrailles asked, intrigued in spite of his suspicions.

"According to Cocodril here, that's when Milady meets with the cardinal to present him with the Book, and to receive her next assignment," Longvilliers said.

"Where?" asked Fontrailles.

"At an inn at a crossroads called Colombier-Rouge," said Cocodril. "It's all arranged."

"I know the place—I've been through there," said Fontrailles. "So, you know when and where Milady will be, and with *The Three Mystic Heirs*. What's your plan for getting it? The cardinal will be well-protected, you know."

"Oh, we don't have a *plan*, dear Louis," said Lady Carlisle. "That's where *you* come in."

"God's holy breeches," Fontrailles said, sitting down on a camp stool. He took off his hat and pushed his crooked fingers through his hair. "All right. Fine. Give me some time to think."

"Take four or five hours," said Longvilliers. "The lady and I need some time to catch up on our rest, and this little bungalow will do nicely."

"Where am I supposed to go?" said Fontrailles.

"Didn't you say you had a tent, darling?" said Lady Carlisle.

It took more than four or five hours, since Fontrailles decided he needed to visit Colombier-Rouge to refresh his memory of the inn and its surrounding terrain, but by the following morning Louis had come up with a working plan. And it didn't involve hiding under any beds.

His noble guests were waiting for him when Fontrailles returned from his reconnaissance. Lucy and Longvilliers were in high spirits, apparently rejuvenated after a night of rest, though Louis also noted that they'd gone through his Anjou wine and started on his champagne, which might have something to do with their mood. He called in Gitane and Cocodril, whom the gypsy had been detailed to watch, and outlined his plan.

"It's a small coaching inn, with a common room downstairs and a single private room above," Fontrailles said, when his audience was assembled, "so any secret meeting between Milady and the cardinal must take place upstairs. Cocodril, you told me Milady is to arrive first."

"Quite so, Your Lordship!"

"So we will have an opportunity to get the book from her before the heavy security arrives with the cardinal," Fontrailles said. "Presumably she will await him in the upstairs room. Besides its door to the stairs, the room has a single window that opens onto a small wooden balcony over the stable yard. An active person could easily reach the balcony from the stable roof, which is low and should be easy to climb."

"I volunteer, Monseigneur!" said Cocodril. "An active person: that describes me perfectly!"

"Not so fast, *friend* Cocodril," Fontrailles said. "Gitane and I will climb the roof and conceal ourselves on the balcony on either side of the window. Then Vidou and Beaune, with two of our teamsters, will enter the inn, pretending to be drunk. They will loudly announce that they've heard there's a woman upstairs and intend to have their way with her. ...Now, don't look so scandalized, Vidou. It's only play-acting. You and the teamsters will climb the stairs and rush the door. Milady will retreat out the window and Gitane and I will relieve her of the book with a minimum of fuss."

"But where do I fit in?" said Cocodril.

"You will be in the trees nearby, holding the horses with His Lordship the Commander, who must maintain his incognito. You're too familiar to

Milady and her servants, Cocodril, they'd recognize you in an instant."

"I can wear a disguise!" said Cocodril. "A false beard! Or an eye patch!"

Fontrailles shook his head. "I like you better holding the horses."

"And me, Louis?" Lady Carlisle said. "You're not expecting me to stay out of this, are you? I still owe Milady Winter for trying to broil me in that barge on the Thames."

"You would be even harder to disguise than Cocodril, Madame," said Fontrailles. "I'd be obliged if you'd stay with the commander, who I'm sure will be glad of your company. Besides," he added, *sotto voce,* "I need you to watch over His Lordship, or Cocodril will talk him out of his sword, pistols, and knightly garter."

Everyone (except Cocodril, who wanted a greater role, and Vidou, who wanted less) agreed that it was a reasonable plan, with the virtue of simplicity. And it would have worked, Louis was certain, if it hadn't been for the Three Musketeers.

By nine o'clock it was fully dark, and Fontrailles's crew were in their positions around the lonely inn at Colombier-Rouge. After waiting for the stable boy to go into the kitchen for his supper, Fontrailles managed, with Gitane's help, to scramble up the stable's thatched roof. From where the stable roof met the wall of the inn, they then climbed quietly onto the little balcony outside the upstairs room. When he and Gitane were in position Fontrailles waved to Vidou, Beaune, and a pair of burly teamsters, who were looking forward to their charade, and had been passing a bottle between them in order to more credibly simulate a state of intoxication. Now they headed for the door of the inn, the teamsters cheerful, Beaune watchful, Vidou shaking his head gloomily.

Fontrailles leaned against the inn's outside wall to wait. Then he heard voices from within the upstairs room, and realized that Milady had a visitor. This was something Louis hadn't anticipated. He slid closer to the window to listen.

"Your fears are exaggerated, Monsieur de Rochefort," said the voice of Milady de Winter—the woman, Louis thought grimly, who had murdered Isabeau's father. "I'm sure the disappearance of Cocodril has a simple explanation," she continued. "He's probably chasing some camp slut, or lying drunk in a tavern. I reported it only because His Eminence insisted I report everything."

"He has reasons for his prudence, Milady," the Comte de Rochefort said coolly. "There have been several attempts on his life during the siege. Overconfidence is a mistake that could prove fatal."

"There is nothing to be concerned about. The matter is simple: I have acquired *The Three Mystic Heirs*; His Eminence has agreed to reward me appropriately for presenting it to him, and wishes to provide me with a new opportunity to serve him. There is no reason why there should be any trouble."

"Nonetheless," said Rochefort. "Tell me again how this book, which we'd thought lost, found its way into your hands."

"You are tiresome, Rochefort," said Milady. "It was never in that bag Fontrailles dropped into the river—he never intended to give it to Father Joseph, and had it hidden elsewhere. I suborned his manservant Cocodril, and he brought me the book when he defected to my service."

"Cocodril again. All the more reason to be suspicious of his disappearance," Rochefort said. "What is that infernal racket?"

It was Vidou and the teamsters going into their act. Fontrailles was proud of them: they sounded genuinely drunk as they stomped up the stairs, pounded on the door, and loudly demanded the woman inside let them in to slake their beastly desires.

Rochefort and Milady were genuinely alarmed. "You see, Milady?" the Comte de Rochefort hissed. "No trouble, you said! It's as well the cardinal sent me ahead to ensure his safety!"

"Get hold of yourself, Rochefort," said Milady. "It's just a few drunken louts."

"Even so, the way they're pounding on that door, it may not hold."

"Afraid, Count? Of a few drunken louts?"

"It may be a ruse, and they may not be drunk."

"You may be right—they sound determined. Stand by the door while I go out the window."

"*Bien.*"

Fontrailles nodded to Gitane, who nodded back with a tight smile. Over the pounding from the door they could hear Milady gathering a few things, then a rustling as she approached the window. Her fingernails ticked on the latch, then were removed, as the uproar from within changed its character. New voices were heard, demanding that the teamsters step away from the door and leave the lady alone, followed immediately by the sounds of a fray. Fontrailles started as the window beneath the balcony suddenly shattered outward and one of his teamsters hurtled into the stable yard. He landed, hard; Louis winced.

There was more noise from inside, seemingly involving furniture, and then Fontrailles heard the inn's front door bang open. He leaned out around the corner of the wall to see the rest of his men hustle hastily out of the inn, Beaune limping and streaming blood, a teamster leaning on a whining Vidou. They were followed by a cavalier with a naked rapier in his hand, who stopped to lean lithely against the door and laugh at them.

Aramis—damn him.

Voices inside the window drew Louis's attention back to the upstairs room. "Are they gone?" asked Milady.

"I think so. It sounds like someone chased them out," Rochefort said. "Hand me my cloak so I can conceal my face and I'll take a look."

Fontrailles heard the room's inner door open and close. A few moments later the sound was repeated, and Rochefort said, chuckling, "*Incroyable!* You have the luck of the devil, Milady. Your saviors were none other than those musketeer comrades of your young friend d'Artagnan!"

"Don't mention the name of that swine!" she hissed. "But as you see, I was right—it was just a few drunken ruffians, and His Eminence has nothing to fear by coming here."

"Perhaps. But I think I'd better have a look around the inn and its grounds. You'll be safe enough, I think. After all," Rochefort chuckled again, "you have the musketeers to protect you. If you feel threatened, just give them a call."

"You are not amusing, Rochefort."

Once again, the door opened and closed. Fontrailles caught Gitane's eye and pointed down toward the stable yard. Gitane nodded, and they climbed carefully down from the balcony and across the roof. The teamster who'd been thrown out the window was still lying in the stable yard, moaning; they picked him up, big as he was, and staggered off toward the copse where the others would be waiting.

"Bad luck, Monsieur." Gitane was a man of few words. "Back to the camp?"

"That's right. There's nothing we can achieve by brute force so long as those musketeers are here," said Fontrailles. "So, that's it for tonight; everyone back to the camp.

"Except for me," he added, looking back toward the solitary inn, silhouetted against the rising moon. "I'm not done yet."

CHAPTER XLIII
OUTSIDE THE INN AT COLOMBIER-ROUGE

The Vicomte de Fontrailles, alone, crouched in the shadows of the copse behind the inn at Colombier-Rouge, staring at the yellow light glowing from the window of the upstairs room.

He was in just the mood to do something reckless, but he couldn't quite justify putting any of his allies at risk, so he'd sent them all back to camp. If this attempt failed, they had lives to go back to, families. What did he have? Nothing and nobody. He was on his own.

In that little room with the flickering lamp, Milady de Winter awaited the cardinal. She had everything the world valued: wealth, beauty, brains, high position. Yet somehow she wanted more, and seemed willing to risk everything she had to get it. Moreover, beneath her calm and lovely surface, she boiled with hatred—Louis had heard the vicious way she'd spoken about d'Artagnan. He shook his head. What was he doing, mixed up with such people? How could it be that they ran the world instead of decent folk like him, or Isabeau, or René des Cartes?

A noise from the stable yard drew his attention, the sound of boots on broken window glass. It was the Comte de Rochefort, coming around the side of the inn, scouting the area. He walked slowly, listening, peering into shadows and scanning the horizon. He approached the copse, and Fontrailles crouched lower into the bushes. If the tall cavalier actually entered the grove, in the dark he might not see the trampled ferns and underbrush where Fontrailles's little band had waited, but he couldn't help but smell the fresh horse dung. Rochefort stopped at the edge of the trees, close enough that Louis could count his buttons in the moonlight. He stood still, listening, while Louis held his breath, and then turned, headed back around the other side of the inn.

Fontrailles waited until he was well out of sight, then made his own slow, cautious way back to the stable yard. Without Gitane's help it was a tough scramble for the short Louis d'Astarac to get atop the stable roof, but he finally made it with the aid of a handy water barrel. Then he crawled across the thatched roofline to the wall of the inn, stood, grabbed the wooden slats of the upstairs balcony, and hauled himself quietly onto it.

He resumed his place on the balcony, next to the window where he could hear everything said within. Inside, the Comte de Rochefort was just returning from his patrol. "All clear, Milady," he said. "I think those drunken louts were exactly what they appeared to be."

"As I told you," Milady said. "What did you expect to find?"

"Nothing in particular—though I shouldn't be surprised to see that little Vicomte de Fontrailles show up to make some kind of trouble. He can't have been very pleased about losing *The Three Mystic Heirs* to you."

"You give him too much credit," Milady said, her beautiful voice quivering with contempt. "You assume that he must have brains to make up for his ugliness. He's not as clever as you—or he—thinks."

"I'm not so sure of that," said Rochefort. "I don't think he's done badly at all, considering his limitations."

Well, God bless you, Comte de Rochefort, Louis thought.

"Do we have anything else to discuss before the cardinal arrives?" Milady asked.

"We do," Rochefort replied. But before he could continue the sound of hoofbeats came from the front of the inn. Fontrailles leaned out around the corner for a look: it was those three musketeers, riding off down the road toward camp. *Of course,* Louis thought. *Now that I've sent my attackers home, the defenders leave.*

But there was still Rochefort. "The window, Rochefort!" said Milady. "See who that is!"

"No need, Madame," the count replied. "It's just those meddling musketeers leaving; I heard them call for their bill as I came up the stairs. Now we're quite alone."

"At last! I've been waiting for this, Monsieur le Comte," Milady said, with a little purr. "Confess that you've been waiting for it too!"

"I have neither time nor inclination to afford you amusement, Milady," Rochefort said, dismissively, "especially at my own expense. I have a long ride ahead of me after the cardinal arrives—and so, for that matter, do you."

"You know what this new mission is, then?"

"I'm not to speak of it; that's His Eminence's prerogative. But I can tell you where we're to meet, once our missions are completed: at the Carmelite convent outside Béthune, in Artois. New orders will await us there."

The sound of horses again, from the front of the inn. Fontrailles peered around the corner in time to see five riders arriving, three of them the same musketeers who'd left the inn only a few minutes before.

"Ah! That will be His Eminence," Rochefort said. "I must go down to report. Wait for him here."

"Very well," said Milady, suddenly all business.

The inside door opened and closed, and a cold sweat broke out on Louis's brow. His Eminence! He felt a sudden urge to make sure of the charging of the pistol in his belt—Rochefort's big Spät—but the way his hands were shaking, he was afraid he'd make a noise. Besides, he'd checked it down in the stable yard. Still....

The door opened and closed again; he heard the sound of a chair pushing back as Milady stood, then the swish as she courtesied. "Good evening, Milady Winter," said an iron voice that Louis remembered well.

"Good Evening, Monseigneur," said Milady. "Won't you sit down?"

"I will. It has been a long day, Milady, and I am not as young as I was. So we must make this quick, before my vigor deserts me."

"I am at Your Eminence's service."

"That you are. So: do you have this book, this treasure of Rosicrucian secrets we'd thought lost?"

"I do, Your Eminence."

"Show it to me."

There was a pause—incredibly, Milady seemed to be hesitating in the face of a direct command from the cardinal—but then there were rustling noises, followed by the sound of something heavy thumping on a table. Louis's heart thumped in response.

"*Pardieu*," said Richelieu. "So here it is, at last. Father Joseph will be so very pleased. You have done well, Milady."

"And...?"

"Your payment? A letter of credit on the royal funds, in the amount you specified, has already been forwarded to your banker in Antwerp. And why Antwerp, Milady? Don't you trust the bankers in Paris?"

"Ask your own Antwerp banker, Your Eminence!" Milady said. "Now, I understand you have another mission for me?"

"Listen, Milady," said the cardinal, "this is an important matter. Sit down, and we'll discuss it."

But Louis had heard enough. *The Three Mystic Heirs* had changed hands yet again; he had missed his chance to get it from Milady. But he was still determined to have it, even at the risk of his life.

Only now he had to steal it from Cardinal Richelieu himself.

CHAPTER XLIV
OF THE FUTILITY OF PIPE-
DREAMS

Fontrailles worked his way on foot across the abandoned fields northeast of the crossroads of Colombier-Rouge, relying on keeping the rising moon on his right hand to ensure that he didn't lose his way. He checked on the moon once too often, looking up when he should have looked down, and tumbled over the edge of a drainage channel, landing face-first in a gorse bush. Quelling the urge to curse, he detached himself from the bush's thorns. *Well, at least I landed on my face,* he thought, scrambling up the other side of the gully. *Can't hurt that much.*

The besiegers' lines of circumvallation around La Rochelle ran for fully three leagues, curving in almost a full circle from Fort Louis, on the north shore of the harbor, to Fort d'Orléans, on the south. Between the trenches of the besiegers and the walls of the city, under the artillery of both, was a broad no-man's-land of marshes, salt pans, and abandoned fields, a debatable land that was actually far from deserted—especially at night, when patrols from both sides sought to intercept spies and messengers, and outlying bastions were stealthily occupied or abandoned.

The crossroads of Colombier-Rouge was in this debatable land, but closer to the royal lines than the city walls and separated from La Rochelle by a broad marsh. At the center of the marsh was a deep but sluggish stream that wound its way southwest between the opposing lines before losing itself in the moat that was part of La Rochelle's defenses. Despite being between the lines, the road that passed through Colombier-Rouge saw a fair amount of traffic from the besiegers, because it cut a chord between Bassompierre's command on the northern lines and the Duc d'Angoulême's command on the east. For most of its length the road was protected from Protestant sorties by the long, deep marsh, so Fontrailles wasn't worried—much—about running into Huguenot patrols as he cut across the fields more-or-less parallel to the road.

On the other hand, the possibility of encountering elements of the royal army was very real, and Louis was aware that, dressed in the sober outfit of a bourgeois *munitionnaire,* he looked very much like a Huguenot spy. Already he could see to his left, bristling with cannon in the moonlight, the scarps of Fort Saint-Marie, the royal bastion that marked the eastern limit of Bassompierre's one-third of the siege lines. He was nearing where he planned to wait for the cardinal to pass.

He still wasn't entirely sure what he was going to do if he was successful in intercepting the cardinal before he reached the royal lines. When Richelieu had arrived at Colombier-Rouge, he'd had an escort of four—but three of them were the musketeers who'd just left the inn, and must have met up with him on the way. So perhaps he'd return with just one man to guard him. If so, those odds weren't too bad.

Louis had to hope that threats would suffice to get the cardinal to give him the book; he wasn't really prepared to assassinate anyone. He was a small man, but he had a really big pistol. Maybe that would do it.

If he was successful at playing highwayman, he wasn't all that clear on what his next step would be. By now it was certainly after midnight, so the password he'd used when clearing the the checkpoint on the way to the inn, and which his people would have used on their return, would no longer be valid, and he didn't know the new one. This made crossing back through the royal lines a risky prospect.

Going the other way, into La Rochelle, would be even more difficult, despite the magnetic draw of Isabeau's presence there. He didn't know the Huguenots' passwords either, and by the time he could slosh his way across the marsh to the gates of the city it would be broad daylight. He supposed he'd just have to make the cardinal give him the royal password along with that damned book.

To be candid, with himself at least, Louis wasn't even sure he believed anymore in the wisdom hidden within the Rosicrucian tome. What had seemed enticingly possible, dreaming in his château in far-off Armagnac, seemed patently ridiculous in the here and now. After some experience of the rough-and-tumble of life, he now felt he had a better grip on its reality. Those cannon, frowning at him from Fort Saint-Marie, for example: they were real. The pistol in his belt was real. The gorse bush he'd fallen into was real. In the face of these things, the Rosicrucians' spiritual alchemy was beginning to seem as silly as … well, as the differences over transubstantiation and "justification by faith" that separated the Catholics and Protestants.

So why was he preparing to risk his life for that book if he no longer believed in its promise? He shrugged lopsidedly. At this point, getting hold of *The Three Mystic Heirs* was just something he had to do. The quest was too deeply entwined with his love for Isabeau, and his definition of himself, to give it up now.

His love for Isabeau: he supposed that was the one abstract principle that still drove him.

It seemed to be enough.

A sudden thrumming of hooves sounded from behind him. *Idiot*—he'd been woolgathering when he should have been alert! He dove under another gorse bush, collecting another series of scratches to crosshatch the first, and braced himself for the heavy impact of the hooves that thundered toward him. At the last moment the hoofbeats paused, there was a heartbeat of near-silence, and then their thunder resumed … on the other side of the gorse, which the horse had leapt clean over. Fontrailles emerged from hiding just in time to see horse and rider vanish over a rise to the north, the same direction he was heading.

Fontrailles picked out a few of the more troublesome thorns, dusted himself off, and set out after the rider, quickly but rather more carefully than before. As he topped the rise he saw that he'd finally returned to the road. It was right where he expected it to be, curving back toward the royal lines, now only a few hundred paces distant. He also saw the rider who'd almost brained him, stopped by the side of that road. Louis knew him: Athos the musketeer.

As Athos dismounted and began rubbing his horse down with leaves and grass, Fontrailles crept as close as he dared, then crouched behind yet another gorse bush to watch and wait. The noble Athos, it was clear, was up to something, and it might provide Louis with an opportunity of some sort.

He—and Athos—had waited no more than a couple of minutes before riders could be heard approaching up the road. Athos took a stand blocking the way, calling out, "Who goes there?"

"That is our brave musketeer, I believe," said one of the riders in the unmistakable voice of the cardinal. He was accompanied by three other mounted men: presumably his original escort, plus Aramis and Porthos. *Too many guards,* Louis thought. *So much for the idea of robbing Richelieu at pistol-point. It's probably just as well.*

"Yes, Monseigneur, it's me," said Athos.

"Monsieur Athos," Richelieu said, "accept my thanks for the excellent guard you've kept. Messieurs, we have arrived. Take the gate on the left; the password is, 'Roi et Ré'."

With these words, the cardinal saluted the three friends with a nod and took the path to the right, followed by his escort. The musketeers gathered into a knot and exchanged a few quiet words before riding off to the left. This didn't clear up for Louis what Athos had been doing on his solitary gallop, but he didn't particularly care: it was the cardinal he was after.

And now he knew the password.

CHAPTER XLV
A CONJURAL SCENE

In the hour after midnight, the royal army camp at Fetille, just east of Fort Sainte-Marie, was mostly quiet and peaceful. The exception was the vicinity of Cardinal Richelieu's pavilion, where the guards were alert, couriers still came and went, and the light glowing from within showed that the cardinal was still awake and at work.

Fontrailles, pretending to be asleep where he was slumped against a caisson a hundred paces from the entrance of the cardinal's big tent, watched the guards and couriers through eyes narrowed to slits and chewed his lower lip in frustration. He burned with impatience, and felt like a mine whose fuse was already lit. *Diable!* He was tired of being on the outside looking in to where *The Three Mystic Heirs* was in the hands of another—sick and tired of being teased, tantalized, and mocked by Fate.

It was time to grab Fate by the short hairs and make it pay attention to him.

The royal couriers, he noted, seemed to have easy entrée to Richelieu's pavilion. They had the password, and they had document satchels. Fontrailles already knew the password, so if he sought to impersonate a courier all he needed was a satchel.

At that moment a man with just such a satchel left the door of the pavilion, marching away with that appearance of zeal and activity that all the servants of the cardinal showed in his immediate vicinity. He strode past the caisson against which Fontrailles reclined; the hunchback yawned, stretched, rose, and sauntered off after him.

The courier went to a stable; Fontrailles, after making sure he was unobserved, slipped in behind him, and found the courier saddling a horse. Fontrailles allowed him to finish his preparations—he hoped to use the horse himself, later on—then approached him from behind and clouted him hard over the head with the heavy Spät. The courier dropped without a sound, though the horse shied a bit before quieting again. Fontrailles bound the courier with rope, gagged him, hid him under a pile of hay, then took the man's satchel and headed back toward Richelieu's pavilion.

He looped the satchel over his shoulder in the manner of the other couriers he'd observed, but on his diminutive form it nearly dragged on the ground, so halfway to the cardinal's tent he stopped to shorten the strap. Then he marched determinedly up to the door of the tent and said to the guard, "*Roi et Ré.*"

The sentinel, a broad man in a crisp new red tabard denoting membership in the Cardinal's Guard, said, "That's correct, Monsieur—but I must say, I've never before seen a ... well, a *hunchbacked* royal courier."

"It's a *disguise*," Fontrailles said. "And are you *authorized* to ask such questions? What is your name, Monsieur le Garde?"

"I am the Seigneur de Saint-Georges," the guard huffed back, "and as a matter of fact, I *am* authorized to ask such questions."

"Listen," Fontrailles said confidentially. He beckoned the guard closer and said, in a low voice with the accent of Castile, "As you have so alertly divined, I am not who I seem. I am from, shall we say, a more *southern* climate than this; you may address me as Your Excellency. His Eminence knows of my mission and awaits me."

"Ah! Very well, Mon ... Your Excellency," the guard said, trying not to look too impressed. "You may pass—since you know the password, of course."

"I will mention your vigilance to His Eminence," Fontrailles said, and entered the pavilion.

Louis had no idea whether Richelieu would be by himself or surrounded by a throng of advisors, but for once, Fate seemed to be on his side. The cardinal, having dismissed his secretaries for the night, was working alone by lamplight at a long trestle table covered with maps, paper, and parchment. His Eminence, dressed in an elegant embroidered *robe de chambre,* ignored Fontrailles as he approached the table, preferring to finish his memorandum before deigning to acknowledge his visitor. When he finally looked up, he found himself peering down both barrels of Fontrailles's big German pistol. His eyes widened, then narrowed again as he recognized his visitor.

"Monsieur de Fontrailles," Richelieu said, his voice controlled despite the threat of the Spät. "I had thought you an intelligent man. I see I must revise my opinion. What is the meaning of this arrant folly? Have you sunk to the level of assassin?"

"I hope not, Your Eminence," Fontrailles said, his voice markedly less steady than the cardinal's. "It's not your life I'm after, but something else you have. Though if I have to take your life to get it, I'll do so."

Richelieu nodded and sat back in his camp chair. "Of course. That book of the Rosicrucians'. I spent a few minutes looking through it when first I arrived here tonight, and I must say, if it does contain mystical secrets, its greatest power must be to make wise men do foolish things." The Cardinal steepled his fingers. "Are you really prepared to shoot me—for *that?*"

"That's right, Your Eminence," Fontrailles said, steadying the pistol. "Give it to me."

"You know," the cardinal said, with a little smile, "I don't believe I shall."

Fontrailles blinked, opened his mouth, closed it again, then said, "Monsieur le Cardinal must be aware that, having threatened him with bodily harm, I already know my life is forfeit. So I have nothing to lose by killing you."

"And nothing to gain, as you have no chance of escape, and won't find the book before you're taken by my guards," Richelieu said in a friendly tone, though Louis thought that beneath the nonchalance he could detect an edge of tension. "You are clearly a man of persistence and resourcefulness, valuable traits in perilous times like these. I hate to see such a life cut short before its promise can be realized. Take my advice, Monsieur de Fontrailles: put down that absurd firearm and place yourself in the custody of my guards, that proud unit to which you yourself once belonged. I will see that you are treated with clemency. After a nominal period of imprisonment, you may even be restored to favor and returned to the service of the Crown."

The pistol wavered. Fontrailles said, "Your Eminence is persuasive, and your offer is an attractive one. However, as the proud blood of the French nobility flows through us both, Monseigneur must recognize that honor allows neither of us to retreat in the face of a threat." He took a deep breath. "However, there is another debt of honor, equally sacred, which may give us a way to resolve this impasse. I speak, Your Eminence, of a wager."

"A *wager*, Monsieur?" Richelieu said. "You'd be willing to bet that book against your *life*?"

"And yours, Your Eminence, if I may make so bold as to remind you," Fontrailles said, waggling the pistol significantly.

"What do you have in mind, Monsieur?" asked the cardinal.

"We'll keep it simple," Fontrailles said. "A coin toss. If I win, you give me the book, and with it your oath not to call for your guards until I've had ten minutes' grace to make my escape. If Your Eminence wins, I'll give you this admittedly absurd firearm and will submit to the king's justice."

Richelieu smiled tightly. "Monsieur le Vicomte, I believe I will accept your offer. Not because of the menace of your pistol—as you say, the honor of a nobleman requires me to take no notice of such threats—but because having finally seen that benighted book, I don't believe it's worth a single drop of Frenchmen's blood. Furthermore, I think your reasons for wanting it are personal, and that you have no intention of allowing it to fall into the hands of our enemies the English. So if you win this wager, you may have it."

"Thank you, Your Eminence. One can see why Monseigneur has achieved his high position." Fontrailles laid the Spät on the edge of the table—Richelieu glanced at it, but made no move—and hunted through his pockets until he found a coin. "Here we are. A Spanish gold piece, Your Eminence, four *escudos*, the coin commonly called the double *pistole*. Monseigneur won't mind if I use a coin of foreign mintage?"

"Not at all," said Richelieu. "A king's minister can't afford to be so narrow-minded."

"Monseigneur's supreme practicality is renowned. Like all *pistoles*, this coin is struck with a cross on one side and a shield with the arms of Spain on the other." Fontrailles held it up to glitter in the lamplight. "I'll let Your Eminence choose his face."

"*Merci*, Monsieur. As a Prince of the Church, I choose the cross, of course."

"Of course," said Fontrailles. He paused a moment, then said, "Here we go," and tossed the coin lightly upward. It flickered in the air and came down; Fontrailles caught it and slapped it on the table. Then he slowly withdrew his hand.

Shield.

Fontrailles snatched up the pistol. "The honors are mine, Your Eminence. The book, if you please."

The Prime Minister of France shrugged. "A wager is a sacred debt of honor. It's right here, Monsieur, under this map of Saintonge. Take it."

Louis d'Astarac, breathing hard but still holding the Spät relatively steady in his right hand, reached out with his left and scrabbled under the cardinal's papers until he came up with the big leather-bound book. He drew it across the table to his side, opened the flap of his courier's satchel, slid the heavy volume into it, and looped the satchel over his shoulder. Then, keeping close watch on Richelieu, he backed toward the door. When he reached it he thrust the pistol back into his belt and said, "Remember your oath, Monseigneur: ten minutes' grace period."

Then he vanished into the night.

Cardinal Richelieu, still seated, placed his hands flat on the table and willed the tension to drain out of him. What a ridiculous melodrama! *Pardieu*, the things he had to do in service to God and the Crown! He smiled slightly, shook his head, and chuckled. Then he looked at Fontrailles's double *pistole*, glinting in the lamplight on the far side of the table.

A sudden suspicion crossed his mind, and he frowned. He reached for the coin and flipped it over.

Another shield. He'd been deceived, and by a trick so old not even a charlatan on the Pont Neuf would stoop to it.

"Cavois!" shouted Cardinal Richelieu, clenching his fist on the wretched coin. "*Capitaine de Cavois!*"

CHAPTER XLVI
THE GRILLE OF PORTE MAUBEC

Dark or no dark, Louis thought, if it weren't for the fog he'd be there by now. But with the moon shrouded by the mists rising from the salt marshes it was as black as the inside of an oven, and all Louis could do was try to feel his way forward and hope he was still heading west. He considered striking a light, but decided he was better off just cursing the darkness. He knew that somewhere in the fog was a large force of French soldiers: men edgy, armed to the teeth, and all bound for the same place he was.

This was not the route Louis d'Astarac had intended to take upon leaving the cardinal's command tent near Fetille. There, giddy with victory spiced by fear, he'd given the Cardinal's Guard at the door a jaunty salute as he passed, and trotted back to the stable to retrieve the horse of the courier whose satchel he'd stolen. Finding the unconscious courier still safely stowed away under his pile of straw, he'd mounted the horse and ridden out of camp.

Beyond the line of sentries he came upon the great ring road that had been built around the outside of the trenches encircling La Rochelle. That's where his plans, such as they were, started to change. Louis knew that the main road to Paris, the only way to ride dryfoot to the interior, led east through Surgères. He assumed that the pursuers who would soon be after him would concentrate on the Surgères route, so he'd decided to ride clockwise around the ring road, then strike out south for the town of Saintes; from there he would make his way east into Angoumois.

But he found the ring road thronged with French troops, all marching without torches and as quietly as they could manage to the south and east. Fontrailles recognized them as regiments under Bassompierre's command, and realized that he'd stumbled into a secret redeployment from the north side of the siege to the east or south, probably heralding an assault of some sort. The troops completely jammed the road in both directions, but since they were moving, albeit slowly, in the direction Fontrailles wanted to go, he joined their march.

Cardinal Richelieu was not known to have much of a sense of humor, particularly concerning himself, and Louis knew that he would not be amused to find himself the butt of the jest with the two-headed coin. Fontrailles had discovered it among the newly-minted double *pistoles* he'd appropriated from Milady de Winter and kept it as a curiosity; he'd had no idea it would turn out to be so useful. But he knew that, wounded in his *amour-propre,* the cardinal would now be after his head, and he could only hope that merging with the troops would afford him some camouflage until he could reach a point where he could break out toward the south.

The march, like all military movements, was plagued by inexplicable halts, when for no apparent reason the troops would all come to a full stop and have nothing to do for a while but complain about it. As one such halt dragged on, Louis occupied himself by reviewing his recent face-to-face triumph over Richelieu and congratulating himself on his cleverness and audacity. But then it occurred to him that, after all, perhaps his victory had been *too* easy—perhaps *he* was the one who'd been fooled! Was the heavy book in his satchel really the one he'd sought for so long?

He had to know. He rode to a sentry post, dismounted, and in the light of the sentry's fire opened the satchel. With trembling hands, he drew forth the book.

There could be no mistake: it was *The Three Mystic Heirs,* the same copy with the torn binding he'd briefly had in Paris.

Fontrailles sighed in relief and wiped the sudden sweat from his brow. Then he noticed something else in the satchel besides the book. Of course: the courier had been leaving Richelieu's tent with a message to convey. It was a letter of four or five sheets, folded and sealed. The sentry was looking at him curiously, so in the unlikely event that the man could read Fontrailles turned his body to conceal the letter, then cracked the seal and unfolded it.

The letter was from Cardinal Richelieu to the Duc d'Angoulême, commander of the central third of the siege lines around La Rochelle, a memorandum conveying final details of an intended assault on the city, a surprise attack scheduled for the pre-dawn hours of this very night. A diversion, a night attack on the Bastion of Saint-Gervais by des Essart's unit of Royal Guards, would cover the attackers' approach. An advance force of picked soldiers under Maréchal de Marillac was to enter the city by blowing a hole in a sewer grille near Porte Maubec. They were then to capture the nearby gate and throw open the doors to admit an assault force of French troops. Once Porte Maubec was in Marillac's hands two of Bassompierre's regiments, shifted south and east for the purpose, would pour into the city; Angoulême was to hold his troops in readiness to support them and, if they succeeded, follow them in.

A major attempt to take La Rochelle by surprise: no wonder Richelieu had been burning his midnight oil. Such ploys had been tried before, and failed; but suppose this attempt succeeded? By the prevailing code of siege warfare, a town that resisted its lawful liege could expect no quarter when it was sacked. Suppose Marillac caught the Rochelois napping and the city was taken by storm? Thousands of French troops would fan out through the streets in an orgy of murder, rape, and robbery.

Isabeau.

Louis's plan of escaping Richelieu's revenge by fleeing south was instantly forgotten. If a sack of the city was imminent, he had to find a way inside so he could protect Isabeau and, if possible, get her out alive and unharmed. And this surprise attack, even if it failed, could be his opportunity to do that.

Killing time on the ring road, waiting for the army to move, was suddenly intolerable, but thankfully just at that moment the troops began once more to shuffle forward. Whereas previously Louis had been reluctant to push ahead, unwilling to draw attention to himself, now he abandoned caution and began to force his way through, making enemies and attracting angry remarks. When anyone seemed disposed to actually block his progress, Fontrailles simply slapped his satchel, snapped, "Royal courier!" and he was reluctantly granted passage.

He was, of course, leaving a clear trail for his pursuers—everyone would remember the pushy *bossu* with the courier satchel—but if his new plan worked it shouldn't make any difference. Now, speed was all-important. And luck seemed to be on his side, for the road cleared up as inexplicably as it had jammed, and the soldiers marched forward at double-time, in an open formation that Fontrailles could ride through with relative ease. Soon he passed Fort Lafon, the stronghold that held down the center of Angoulême's lines; just beyond the fort he left the road and turned back into the camp, toward the line of trenches—and the city within.

Here, he knew, an old road extended through the lines to the city, a main trade route before it was cut by the siege. It ran up to Porte de Congrés, with a fork extending into the salt marshes in front of Porte Maubec. Louis knew from the cardinal's memo that the assault troops were to continue around the lines to Beaulieu, where they could approach the city through the marshes using the tall reeds as cover. Louis planned to use this drier, more exposed route as a shortcut, hopefully arriving at Porte Maubec ahead of the soldiers.

"*Roi et Ré,*" he said to the sentries at the checkpoint, who waved him through with barely a glance, preoccupied as they were with watching the flashes from the night-action where the Royal Guards were assaulting the Bastion of Saint-Gervais. So for the second time that night, Fontrailles entered the no-man's-land between the royal lines and the walls of the city.

The diversion at the bastion served Fontrailles's purposes as well as the cardinal's, for he encountered no one from either side as he rode down the long slope toward La Rochelle. When he reached the fork where the main road continued toward Porte de Congrés, he took the lesser left-hand path toward the marshes, dismounting and leading his horse; he was now too near the walls to ride without attracting attention, despite the diversion at the bastion.

The road entered the marshes and became a raised causeway, and soon Fontrailles was into the mist and blind as any bat. He'd scouted this area earlier in the season, when the reeds were only knee-high, but in the pitch-blackness with the reeds now waving above his head, nothing looked as it did before. The road dwindled to a path, and then a mere trail—and it must have been high tide, because the trail soon vanished under several inches of brackish water, becoming a twisting lane through the reeds.

This was bad. For a while Fontrailles was able to steer by keeping the sound of the bastion battle to his right rear, but then the firing abruptly halted as one side, or both, gave it up for the night. Fontrailles went slower, then slower yet. Where the devil was he, exactly? If he went too far to the right he'd pitch into the moat outside the city walls, and if he went too far to the left, he'd either slog around lost until daybreak or run smack into the advancing French troops. Neither prospect was attractive.

He took to sloshing forward ten steps, then listening for ten breaths, then sloshing forward again. During one of his pauses, he heard a splash from ahead. A fish? A large frog? He drew the Spät from his belt and moved cautiously forward.

Abruptly it seemed there were reeds to neither his right nor his left, and a subtle difference in the acoustics told him he had moved into an open area. He stopped: dark; fog; a trickle of water. He swallowed, and stepped forward.

"*Halt!*"

Startled, Fontrailles lost his footing and slid down the bank of the trail into waist-deep water. His horse neighed in alarm, jerked the reins from his hand, turned and splashed back the way they'd come.

The lurch as he lost the reins spun Fontrailles in a half-turn—and the heavy Spät flew from his hand and disappeared into the marsh.

As Fontrailles hissed an oath, flint struck steel and kindled a tiny flame, revealing a cavalier in a mud-flecked red tabard threatening him with a naked rapier. Other dark figures crowded out of the fog behind him.

"Well, well! The Vicomte de Fontrailles, formerly of the Cardinal's Guard!" the cavalier said quietly. "Not quite what we were after, but I suppose we must take what the Good Lord sends us."

"Blood of *Christ,* Cahusac!" Fontrailles said, scrambling back up onto the submerged causeway. "You scared the piss out of me, and made me lose my pistol to boot!"

"And what are you doing out here, eh, Fontrailles?" said the Seigneur de Cahusac in a low voice. "Spying for the Rochelois, I shouldn't wonder."

"So you believed that little story the cardinal and I cooked up, about me betraying the service?" Fontrailles said, trying to count the heads behind Cahusac. He still had a dagger in his belt, but that wasn't going to be any help in this situation. "The Rochelois believed it too," he continued, keeping his voice low. "That's how I got out the information that enabled tonight's little entertainment."

"What? Are you the guide who's supposed to lead us to the sewer grille?" Cahusac said. "Where in hell have you been?"

"Looking for you, Cahusac—looking for you," Fontrailles said. "You're late, you know."

"Damned right I know," Cahusac snarled. "Maréchal de Marillac's just behind us with the petard men, and so furious I swear most of this fog is steam that's boiled out of him. If we don't reach the grille soon we'll have Bassompierre marching right up our arses. But we couldn't find you, and our map is shit."

"Let me see it," Fontrailles said.

"The map, Perón," Cahusac said to one of the shadows behind him, who handed him a roll of soggy parchment.

"You see?" said Cahusac, holding the lit taper close to the sheet. "Utter shit."

The map showed the route Marillac's men were to take from the Pont des Salines through the marshes to the grille near Porte Maubec. Seeing it brought back Fontrailles's scouting survey of the same area, and suddenly everything clicked into place.

"*Croix et cœur, croix et cœur,*" Cahusac muttered.

"What's that?" said Fontrailles.

"The Huguenots' password for tonight; weren't you briefed on it?" Cahusac asked, suddenly suspicious.

"No, I mean what's *that?*" Fontrailles pointed to the compass rose on the map.

"Oh," said Cahusac. "That's the, uh, direction thing, tells you which way's north."

"Well, there's your problem," Fontrailles said, taking the map. "You're facing it the wrong way. Look, we're here, at this sort of crossroads. You can see, if you turn the map *this* way, that your route is the way I just came."

"Are you sure?"

"Of course I'm sure! I was waiting for you up ahead, and when you didn't show I came looking for you. That's your route, absolutely."

"Well, that's a relief," said Cahusac. "All right, Monsieur Guide—lead the way."

"Can't," Fontrailles said. "I have business off to the left here."

"Business? What business?"

"Now that I've set you on the right course, I have to see to the diversion."

"But I thought the attack on the bastion was the diversion!"

"That was just the *first* diversion, Cahusac," Fontrailles said. "Weren't you briefed? Believe me, you don't want to try to blow that grille without a diversion."

"But what about us?"

"Just follow that road. Can't go wrong," Fontrailles said. "But hurry! The operation's running late, you know." And with a final salute, he sloshed away into the dark, at a right angle to his original line of march.

But now he knew where he was, and where he was going.

Not fifteen minutes later Fontrailles was looking up out of the reeds at the walls of La Rochelle. Just to his right, looming out of the fog, was the fortified gate of Porte Maubec, its drawbridge drawn tightly up against its ramparts as it had been since the beginning of the siege.

And directly across the moat from Fontrailles, in the base of the high wall, was the sewer grille the Maréchal de Marillac's men planned to blow open and use as their entry into the city.

Louis considered the twenty paces of open water between him and the grille. Few northern Europeans knew how to swim; even among sailors the skill was uncommon. Immersion in water was regarded as dangerously unhealthy, and swimming was a practice confined to queer Mediterranean folk who dived after pearls or sponges. In fact, Louis reflected, Marillac's troop of picked men had probably been chosen for exactly that reason: because they could swim.

And fortunately, Louis thought, *so can I.*

At the age of six, when his brother Raoul had thrown him into the garden pond, he'd learned that when he was in the water, his back didn't hurt. While floating, his twisted spine was relieved of the pull of gravity, and he could, like other people, move without pain. And so, despite the scorn of his elder brother, he'd spent many an afternoon paddling about the garden pond, and over time he'd become quite a decent swimmer.

Peering up at the parapet atop the wall, he could see no helmeted heads except for those of a few guards at the gate. Of course, it was foggy, and he was at a bad angle for seeing up onto the wall, but that worked both ways. He slipped down the bank into the water, carefully holding his courier's satchel up over his head, then rolled onto his back and frog-kicked across the moat, keeping himself stable with broad, slow strokes from his off hand. No cries came from above; no shots or crossbow bolts; and in a few moments, he was at the grille.

The opening was about as wide as a man is tall, and half as high; at low tide it might be above the water level, but now noisome sewage flowed out of the city directly into the moat. The smell was truly awful, but wearing rotting meat as the Necrotic Gnome had permanently suppressed Louis's gag reflex, and he supposed the odor wouldn't kill him. The grille itself was made of wood rather than iron, but the bars were thick enough that it would take many minutes to hack through them with axes, even if the wielders could find purchase for their feet. Clearly, blowing it up was the only quick way to make a hole in the grille large enough for soldiers to pass through.

But Fontrailles was much smaller than the average soldier, and the wood of the grille, where it met the water, had rotted in several places. There was, on the right-hand side, a place where he thought he could just about squeeze through....

He looped the satchel over one of the upper bars so that it hung well above the water, then pushed his way into the gap. A half-minute of squirming, and he was through.

He retrieved the satchel, then slogged up a dark, stinking tunnel until he'd passed under the wall and into an open gutter beyond. This was it: after months of waiting and uncounted fruitless plans, he was finally inside the besieged city of La Rochelle. It almost made crawling through a sewer worthwhile.

Looking up from the gutter, he could see the inside of the towering city wall, while to his left and right were the backs of three-story houses. Upstream the rows of houses were split by an alley where the sewer was crossed by a plank footbridge. He waded up the slippery channel to the base of the bridge and climbed as quietly as he could to the level of the alley.

Two gaunt figures immediately stepped from the shadows: figures armed with halberds. "Why, look what we have here, Christophe," the first one said. "a spy, sure as hellfire! And we thought guarding the sewer outlet would be dull work!"

"Shut up, Leo," the second figure said, lowering his halberd toward Fontrailles. "Hands up, you."

Fontrailles was not entirely surprised by this development and had his reply ready. "*Croix et cœur*," he said. "I *am* a spy, but for our side. The True Religion."

"Sort of runty for a spy, aren't you?" said the first man, imitating his companion and holding his halberd at port-arms.

"Well, if I were as big as you, I couldn't get in and out through the grille, now could I?" said Fontrailles. "Weren't you briefed?"

"No," said the second man.

"Aye, why take the trouble to brief us?" said the first man. "We're only guarding a key entrance to the city. Waste of time to tell *us* what's going on."

"Shut up, Leo," said the second man. "What's your name, you?"

"You haven't been briefed, so if I told you, you wouldn't recognize it, would you?" Fontrailles said reasonably. "But you can tell your superiors that you welcomed the Peregrine back into the city. Now, I have important dispatches to deliver to headquarters. Are you *authorized* to question someone who knows the password?"

"Well … no," said the second man, putting up his halberd. "All right, go ahead. I don't guess you'd swim up a river of shit if you wasn't on an important mission."

"*Merdieu*! Exactly right!" said Fontrailles. "But I'm glad to see you're alert. Keep up the good work."

Hiding a smile, he hustled off down the alley, emerging shortly onto a main street that led, on his right, to the inside of Porte Maubec. A sudden heavy wave of fatigue rolled over him. He had no real idea where to go next, other than to put distance between himself and Porte Maubec. Marillac's men might yet find the right path through the marshes and unleash their surprise attack, and Louis didn't want to get caught in the ensuing chaos. So he turned left, away from the gate, and plodded toward the center of town.

La Rochelle was … eerie. The streets were entirely deserted. Dawn was not far off, but no cock crowed in the distance; no dog barked as Fontrailles passed; no rats scurried in the shadows. No lights shown between the slats of the shutters in any of the houses, and he had the impression of walking through a vast cemetery between rows of tall mausoleums.

So it was true. La Rochelle, sealed off by the king's army and the cardinal's dyke, was starving.

Fontrailles was exhausted. He found a public fountain on a street corner, where water trickled from a lead pipe into a stone basin, and tried to wash off the worst of the filth from the sewer, but he seemed to succeed only in fouling the water of the fountain. He shook the water from his eyes, trying to put an edge back on his dulled senses, but he was reeling, barely able to stay upright. He squelched on for another block and a half, then sat down at the base of the front stairs of a tall dark house, leaned back against the stones, and fell fast asleep.

A kick in the ribs, none too gentle, brought him back to life. It was early morning, the rising sun's light flaring behind a blunt brown silhouette with a droop-plumed hat. "On your feet," a voice from beneath the hat growled with a pronounced Teutonic accent. "I'm still two men short, so you're volunteering to join me."

"Uh …whuh … I am?" Fontrailles hoisted himself to his feet. He was surrounded by a dozen or more ragged men, scarecrows toting picks and shovels, apparently commanded by the man with the plumed hat, who bore the half-pike of an officer.

The men looked at him dully, except for the officer, who seemed all too alert. "My God, look at the flesh on you," the officer said. "You've been eating well, and no mistake. Been hoarding food?" The scarecrows looked at Fontrailles hungrily. "We know what to do with food hoarders," the officer said.

"No, sir! Really!" Fontrailles said. "You wouldn't believe the weight I've lost! Why, before the siege, the neighborhood children used to call me Monsieur Butterball!"

"Hmpf," said the officer. "Know how to use a shovel?"

"Never touched one in my life."

"Nonsense!" the officer said with a predatory grin. "You're a pioneer now, and who ever heard of a pioneer who didn't know how to use a shovel? Now take a shovel, shut up, and fall in."

"But … but…."

The officer spun around, hand on his sword hilt. "Are you disobeying an order, soldier?"

Fontrailles gulped. "No, *mon Officier.*"

"I didn't think so. Now, march."

The officer strode off down the street, the scarecrows shuffling after him, Fontrailles pumping his short legs to keep up. "May I ask where we're going, *mon Officier?*" he wheezed.

"No," said the officer. "But I'll tell you anyway. The Papists, damn their souls, damaged one of our bastions last night with a mine they brought in." He smiled a humorless brown smile. "And we, brave volunteers that we are, are going outside the walls to repair it."

CHAPTER XLVII
THE PERIL OF THE PIONEERS

The troop of pioneers under command of the Dutchman marched in the long shadows of the silent houses through what had once been a thriving commercial district. Now most of the shopfronts were shuttered, their useless trade signs creaking in the morning breeze from the sea. A few civilians were beginning to stir from their houses, and Fontrailles saw with a shock that they were even more emaciated than the men he marched with.

He saw two children, their limbs like sticks, wrestle feebly in the gutter over something that looked like a scrap of skin, while an old man sat nearby and watched apathetically.

He saw a woman stride blindly down the street clutching a dead infant in her arms.

Dear God, Louis thought. *They're all dying. What sort of fanatics are running this city? Why haven't they surrendered?*

He had to find Isabeau and get her out of here. Now that he'd been shocked to attention, it was time that he was on his way; he had no intention of joining some hare-brained Huguenot sortie into no-man's-land. If he made a break for it he didn't doubt that, even with his short legs, he could outrun the shambling wrecks that surrounded him.

They were passing a little *ruelle* that looked like a promising avenue of escape, but just as Louis was preparing to bolt the officer, apparently able to read his mind, turned and fixed him with a glare. Smiling like a wolf, he fingered his sword-hilt and said, "It occurs to me, my former butterball, that I have not hanged a deserter in almost a week. Are you going to provide me with an example to encourage the others?"

"N-no, *mon Officier.*"

The officer shrugged. "Either way. Whether you serve God at the end of a rope or the end of a shovel, you will still serve His purposes. *I* will see to that. Now come: we are almost to the Porte de Congrés."

Louis was beginning to feel frantic. Somehow, this hawk-eyed Dutchman had transformed him from cunning infiltrator into shovel-bearing stooge with a single kick in the ribs, and he could see no immediate way out. Trapped as he was, how in God's name was he ever going to find Isabeau?

He turned the corner and almost walked into her.

"Louis?" she cried. "Is that you? *Mon Dieu*, it is! Éric, look—it's Louis!"

He stopped, stunned. It was, indeed, Isabeau de Bonnefont—though not the girl Louis remembered from their youth in the hills of Armagnac, or even the woman of the midnight chaos on the Pont Neuf. Isabeau had always been unfashionably slim, but now she seemed to Louis to have waned to nearly nothing but skin and skeleton. She wore a worn black dress that was frayed and torn in places, and her once-shining hair was flat, dry, and brittle. Her cheeks were hollow beneath now-prominent cheekbones, her delicate fingers like fleshy twigs. To see her like this struck Louis to the heart—he thought it would seize up and kill him on the spot. But her brown eyes, though large and sunken in their orbits, were still clear and alert, and her lips, though cracked, still showed the little upcurve at their ends that he loved so dearly.

"So you know him, Mademoiselle?" It was the Dutchman, looming suddenly beside them. "That is all right, then. I suspected him of being a Papist spy, and was just waiting for him to prove it so I could spit him on my pike."

"We know him, Monsieur," said Éric de Gimous, speaking in a voice lower and rougher than Louis remembered. "Mademoiselle and I would be obliged if you would keep your pike separate from his guts, at least until we've had a chance to chat with him."

The Éric of former times had never been partial to black humor, and Fontrailles looked at him wonderingly. Though still slight, he was taller, thinner, and harder than Louis remembered. He wore the sword that denoted rank but otherwise was attired as a simple Huguenot soldier, in tan buffcoat and brown breeches. "Give us a minute, will you, Captain Ruyter?" Éric said. "We'll try not to be long."

The Dutchman grunted. "See that you aren't. We have a timetable, you know—not that you French ever seem to care about such things." He stalked away toward the square before the gate, herding his sad shovelers before him.

Isabeau bubbled over. "Louis! What are you *doing* here? How can you just suddenly *appear*, like Grigrigredin in a puff of smoke?"

Éric wrinkled his nose. "That's not sulfur you smell, Isabeau. Did you come in through the sewer, Louis?"

Fontrailles nodded ruefully. "I'm afraid so, and apparently it's no secret to anyone."

"But why?" said Isabeau. "You're … not spying for the Catholic army, are you? Ruyter will *hang* you!"

"No, no—if they caught me, king and cardinal would hang me even quicker." Fontrailles made a face. "It may sound foolish, but I came to get you—both of you—out of La Rochelle before the city falls."

Éric gave a short laugh. "It *does* sound foolish. La Rochelle isn't going to fall; Buckingham's fleet will be here any day, and with England's help we can hold out forever, if we have to."

"Éric," Fontrailles said, "you're wrong. The English aren't coming, and the city *will* fall."

"Nonsense," said Éric. "We *know* they're coming, we've had word. I'm leaving right now with a return dispatch."

"What do you mean?"

123

"Éric has volunteered to carry a message to the English," Isabeau said unhappily. "He's going out with the sortie."

"While the pioneers are retaking the bastion, I'll sneak through the lines," Éric said.

"That's *insane*," Fontrailles said. "They catch spies trying to slip out of La Rochelle every day. The gallows are groaning with them!"

Éric shrugged. He looked resolute. "It's my turn," he said.

"Listen: I know what I'm talking about," Fontrailles said. "The cardinal has this place sewn up tight. You haven't a chance."

"Oh? Then how were you planning to get *us* out?"

"I ... that is to say...."

"Ensign de Gimous? We're leaving." The Dutchman, Ruyter, was back. He turned his hawk eye on Fontrailles. "So, which is it? Do I gut this fellow? Or does he come with us?"

"Are you a party to this mad scheme, Captain?" Fontrailles said. "Do you know the Ensign is planning to get himself killed while you retake that bastion?"

Ruyter snorted. "It was my idea. And we're leaving now."

Fontrailles sighed. "Then I suppose," he said, "I'm going with you."

"No, Louis!" Isabeau said. "This isn't your fight."

"It is now," Ruyter said grimly. "March, soldier."

Fontrailles shouldered his shovel and followed Éric and the Dutchman toward the gate, his mind working feverishly. He had to find a way to persuade his childhood friend to give up this futile plan of trying to sneak through the French lines in broad daylight. The Éric de Gimous he knew had been a pleasant enough fellow, well-mannered and well-read, but utterly lacking the sort of cunning and determination required by military espionage. This was suicide, pure and simple.

The Porte de Congrés, like all of La Rochelle's fortified gates, had been shut up tight since the beginning of the siege, but a small sally port to the side of the towering gate enabled sorties like this one, and it was before this small door that Ruyter drew up his men.

A company of citizen-soldiers manned the gate, and their commander came out of the guard chamber in the base of one of the towers to address the small troop of pioneers. He bore a pronounced resemblance to the officer Éric had called Captain Ruyter, and when he spoke in the same harsh accent Louis knew he had to be a close relation. "Good morning, soldiers," he said, surveying the ragged pioneers without seeming to see much to approve of. "Last night the Bastion of Saint-Gervais was damaged by a gang of rascally French Guards. You are going to reconnoiter it and, hopefully, repair the damage. Four of my musketeers will join you to keep watch while you work. Be certain that God, who supports the righteous, will protect you." He gave them a final, skeptical look, then turned and marched back into the guard tower.

A pair of soldiers unbarred the sally port and pulled the door open. "All right, you rabbits, hop for me," said Captain Ruyter. "Out we go. Lively, now."

The little troop formed into an irregular column and shuffled forward. Fontrailles fell in next to Éric, then some instinct made him turn to see that Isabeau had drawn near. Biting her lip, she raised one hand nervously, palm toward them, and said, "Oh, please be careful!"

"I will," Fontrailles and Éric said as one, then looked at each other in surprise.

A narrow footbridge, easily drawn up in the event of an assault, spanned the moat from the sally port. At a distance of a couple of bowshots stood the outwork known as the Bastion of Saint-Gervais, and a quarter-league beyond that waved the banners of the royal army. Though just above the horizon, the sun was already hot, and here the sea breeze couldn't seem to find its way past the walls of the city. On this side of La Rochelle the land between the lines, once green with serried vineyards, was scarred by trenches, plowed up by cannon, and abandoned to the dead.

The troop of twenty hustled across the footbridge, gaping at the too-near enemy lines, in which individual cannon were clearly visible, then dropped one by one into a deep trench beyond the bridge. Instantly they lost sight of the enemy—and, even better, the enemy lost sight of them.

"Feel safer now, rabbits?" Ruyter said with a wicked grin. "We can march nearly all the way to the bastion by staying in the trenches, but we'll have to go back and forth quite a bit. Stay close to me or you'll lose yourselves. Follow orders, and we may yet get back to the city alive."

Ruyter strode off down the trench, the pioneers scurrying after him. Fontrailles caught Éric by the elbow and held him back until the rest of the troop had passed so they could talk out of earshot of the officer. "Éric, you must see how crazy this is," he said. "You're going to get yourself hanged or shot, and then who will protect Isabeau when the city falls?" *And,* he wanted to add, *what* is *Isabeau to you now? Friend? Lover? …Wife?*

"The city's not going to fall," Éric said stubbornly. "The English are bringing soldiers and food. …By the way, Louis, you wouldn't happen to have anything like a crust of bread about you, would you?"

"I'm afraid not," Fontrailles said, picking his way carefully over a pile of earth and planks where an errant cannonball had collapsed the side of the trench. "When did you last eat?"

"Yesterday morning," Éric said. The trench zigged, then zagged. "The soldiers on the walls still get almost-daily rations. They're meager enough, but the civilians get nothing at all, and have to shift for themselves." His air of resolution vanished, and he suddenly looked wan and tired. "I've been giving half my food to Isabeau … I'm a little dizzy, Louis. You're *sure* you don't have anything? Some cheese, maybe? Christ's wounds, what I wouldn't give for a little cheese."

"No, I've nothing to eat. And what is Isabeau going to eat if you're not there to give her part of your rations?" Fontrailles said. *"Think,* Éric."

"The English will come," he said. "I have to get this message to them. Isabeau will be all right, somehow. Besides, I can't just abandon my mission. What am I supposed to say to Captain Ruyter?"

"I don't know. Who is he? Tell me about him."

"He and his elder brother are Dutch Protestants from Utrecht. They spent years fighting the Spanish in the Lowlands, then came here after the Twelve Years' Truce was declared. No one can pronounce their real Hollandish names, so we just call them Old Ruyter and Young Ruyter. They're stiff old dogs, but they know their business." He stumbled, seeming to trip over his own feet. "No cheese, you said?"

"Éric." Fontrailles took him by the arm. "Look at me. When you got to the Catholic lines, and they asked you for the password, what were you planning to do?"

"I don't know. It's hard to think." Éric said. "They'd be distracted, diverted by our men at the bastion."

"Not likely. You must see you're in no condition to try something like this."

"What, then?"

"We must go back to the city, find Isabeau, and think of something else."

"Quiet, there!" It was Young Ruyter. They'd come to the end of the trench; the pioneers clustered in a knot behind the officer and the four soldiers. "Spread out!" snapped the Dutchman. "Do you want to all be killed by a single cannonball? You four," he said to the soldiers, "light the matches of your muskets while I take a look."

Ruyter scrambled up the bank of the trench and peered cautiously over the edge. Fontrailles imitated him, hauling himself up over stones and retaining planks. After a moment, Éric followed.

The trench ended within a hundred paces of the bastion. They were gazing directly into the sun, which stood a handspan above the bastion's center, so the outwork was mainly in silhouette, but they could see nonetheless that the little fort had been badly damaged in the previous night's action. A mine had been blown up under one of the corner barbettes, making a sizeable breach and leaving one stretch of wall leaning dangerously outward.

No one was visible but the dead.

Young Ruyter, Fontrailles, and Éric all slid back down into the trench. "All right, rabbits," Ruyter said. "Let's go."

One of the soldiers spoke up—something that would never happen in a Catholic army, reflected Louis. "What if the guards left hidden snipers behind?" he said.

Ruyter glared at him, but said, "Finding that out is one of the reasons we're here. And you have just earned yourself the honor of being first man out of the trench. Now," he gestured with his half-pike, which despite its name was still taller than he was, "up and over!"

The little troop clambered out of the trench and reluctantly marched toward the bastion. Fontrailles was no expert on fortifications, but it seemed to him that whoever had dug a trench that ended short of the bastion it served was guilty of a gross dereliction of duty. He stayed near Éric, who was looking a little light-headed. The soldiers scanned the walls of the bastion as they approached it; the pioneers all hunched over slightly, as if expecting to be shot at any moment.

Suddenly a figure appeared on the bastion, mounted into the breach and waved at them: a figure wearing the distinctive blue tabard of the King's Musketeers. "Messieurs!" it shouted. "My friends and I are taking breakfast in this bastion. Now, nothing is more disagreeable than being disturbed during breakfast, so we must request, if you absolutely must come up here, to please come back later—or at least wait till we've finished our meal."

"It's Athos," Fontrailles said. "He must be mad."

"What?" said Éric.

The pioneers gazed, astounded. The soldiers raised their muskets, but the man in the breach continued to address them in a friendly tone: "Unless, that is, you'd rather renounce the party of rebellion and come drink with us to the health of the King of France."

Fontrailles flinched as the four Huguenot soldiers fired together. The balls ricocheted from the stones of the breach, but all four missed; Athos calmly raised his own musket and fired back. Three other muskets, previously unnoticed, fired at the same time from loopholes along the parapet. A pioneer and three soldiers dropped, the pioneer wounded, but the soldiers stone dead.

Despite Captain Ruyter's order to charge, the pioneers and the surviving soldier immediately turned and ran for the trench. Fontrailles went with them, towing Éric, whose face was etched with dismay. The Dutchman cursed them, but then the four muskets rang out again from the bastion and the officer fell, along with two of the slower, more emaciated pioneers. The rest slid pell-mell into the trench and pelted back toward the city.

Fontrailles, less panicked than the others, followed at a more deliberate pace with Éric. After a few turns of the trench, Éric shook his head back and forth, and then said, quite lucidly, "You know, Louis, I think you're right. We have to get Isabeau out. Next time, we're taking her with us."

"*Next* time? Take her *with* us? What are you talking about? Éric, that's even worse than your previous plan!"

Éric shrugged. "I have to get my message out."

"But…" Fontrailles stuttered. "But…."

But then they were at the other end of the trench, following the terrified pioneers back across the footbridge and into the sally port—where Old Ruyter was waiting, a storm in his eyes. "You *left* him out there?" he exploded. "Back! Back!"

"But, *mon Officier*," began the last of the soldiers.

"I don't want your miserable excuses!" cried Old Ruyter, face black with fury. "Did you count the enemy, at least?"

"Four, I think," said Ensign de Gimous.

"And I believe I can guess their names," Fontrailles murmured.

"Only *four*?" Old Ruyter's voice trembled with rage and contempt. "Back out! Back, I say! I'll lead you myself!"

But the morale of the pioneers was utterly broken, so Old Ruyter turned to his own troops. "I want twenty-four men, half with pikes, half muskets, ready to go in three minutes," he snapped to his lieutenant. "If those damned Papists have killed my brother, I want their heads!"

"I don't see Isabeau," Fontrailles said. "I thought she'd be here. Where would she be?"

"She's not here?" Éric cried. "But she must be—she has to go with us!"

"We'll just have to go find her," Fontrailles said. "We can't go back out now."

"What did I hear you say?" Old Ruyter snarled at them. "Ensign de Gimous, my brother wasn't shot so you could back out of your mission. And who's this ugly, ill-smelling blot?" He glared at Fontrailles, who unconsciously recoiled from the Dutchman's fury.

"H-he's one of ours," Éric said.

"Intelligence, from headquarters," Fontrailles said, "They call me the Peregrine. I'm supposed to go with Ensign de Gimous, but the orders have been changed: we're not to leave before nightfall."

"We're going now—and *you're* going with us. I don't trust your looks, *bultenaar,* and you stink of treachery. So fall in with the others, and stay where I can see you."

There was nothing else they could do. Muskets were thrust into their hands, and a few moments later they were hustling back out the sally port and into the trenches, this time not with shambling pioneers, but among regular soldiers who, though starving like everyone in La Rochelle, still maintained a certain pride in their discipline. Old Ruyter led them, turning frequently to glare at Louis and Éric, whom he seemed to blame for his brother's misfortune.

When they reached the end of the trench, Old Ruyter unsheathed his sword and paused to address his men. "Attention, soldiers," he said. "You will climb out of the trench, form skirmish line in good order, and advance on the bastion. When the Papists begin to fire, I'll give the signal to charge. There will be no quarter given. You two," he pointed his sword at Fontrailles and Éric, "will collect my brother, alive or dead, and take him back to the city. If you do not, I will personally choke you with your own entrails. Now, up! And forward!"

"Stay with me," Fontrailles whispered to Éric as they climbed out of the trench. "Isabeau's safety depends on us not getting killed."

"But if we don't follow Old Ruyter's orders...."

"Things aren't going to go as he plans," Fontrailles said, as the soldiers formed their skirmish line. "I know the men in that bastion."

It was, as Louis had feared, a massacre. As the soldiers began to march toward the bastion, four shots rang out from the parapet, and four of the Rochelois fell. Old Ruyter immediately ordered the charge, but in the hundred paces before they reached the wall eight more soldiers fell. "Get down!" Fontrailles said to Éric, pulling him behind a boulder. "They must have a stack of pre-loaded muskets!"

With Old Ruyter at their head, the surviving soldiers charged into the dry fosse below the wall and began to climb into the breach. But then the damaged wall above them, already leaning dangerously outward, began to lean further, and with a sudden grinding roar collapsed onto the Rochelois below.

Most died instantly in that rain of heavy stone. A few, horribly mangled, limped or crawled away. Obscured by the cloud of dust thrown up by the avalanche, Fontrailles and Éric darted from behind their boulder and helped the walking wounded back into the trench, Éric muttering, *"Horreur! Horreur!"* over and over.

When they returned once again through the sally port into the city, it was to find the better part of a regiment forming up behind the Porte de Congrés for a sortie. But more importantly, Isabeau de Bonnefont was waiting for them, dressed in men's attire of breeches and doublet. At the sight of Fontrailles and Éric she cried, "Oh, thank God! Thank God!" and ran toward them.

Both Fontrailles and Éric instinctively opened their arms, but Isabeau stopped short of them and clasped her hands in front of her, weeping openly. "How I prayed! I feared you both were dead!"

"We live, as you see," Fontrailles said gently, "though barely. What, dear heart, is the meaning of these clothes?"

"And where had you gone when we came back before?" asked Éric.

"When I heard the shooting, and didn't see you returning right away, I was afraid you'd been shot and were wounded … or killed!" Isabeau said, the words tumbling out. "I ran to change my clothes so I could go outside, if I had to, and find you!"

Louis stared. This determined young woman was not the Isabeau he'd known in Armagnac—she'd changed, if anything, even more than Éric.

"Good," Éric was saying. "The clothes will help. When the regiment sorties to retake the bastion we'll follow them, and in the confusion we'll get out through the Catholic lines. And you're going with us, Isabeau."

"*What?*" Fontrailles erupted. "Now see here, Éric! I didn't save your fool head so you could come back and arrange for Isabeau to lose hers! I say we wait for nightfall and do it my way."

Éric turned bleak eyes on Fontrailles. "I can't wait, Louis. I can't stand any more. You were right. I have to get out, and get Isabeau out, before any more horrors happen. We have to go now."

"He's right, Louis," Isabeau said quietly. "Éric's been manning the walls for months. Look at him: he's at the end of his strength. Now that you're with us, I'm sure we'll make it." She looked him in the eye and gave him the little private smile he remembered so well.

He melted. "All right, all right. *Merdieu*, what an idiot I am. Here's what we'll do. There are only four King's Musketeers defending that bastion, and while they're holy terrors, I don't believe they'll commit suicide by taking on this many men. They'll retreat, but there's going to be an awful lot of shooting in the process, and shooting means smoke. The sea breeze is slight this morning, but it's blowing toward the French lines; we'll try to stay in the smoke, and sneak through while all eyes are on the musketeers."

Isabeau, once again to Louis's surprise, was skeptical. "The plan is to sneak toward the enemy in the smoke? Can't you do better than that, Louis?"

He adopted what he hoped was a confident smile, though with his face he could never be sure how such an expression would turn out. "It's the plan of the Peregrine," he said, "renowned master mind and man of mystery, so you may trust it implicitly! ...All right, it *is* rather lame, but it wasn't my idea to try to get out of La Rochelle in broad daylight. Do I hear any better ideas? No? Than that, by God, is what we'll do."

Fontrailles was more surprised than anyone when the scheme actually worked ... more or less. Once across the moat, the Rochelois soldiers formed columns and, eschewing the trenches, marched directly toward the bastion, though they refrained from beating their drums in hopes of catching the defenders unprepared. In this they were thwarted by the hundreds of French soldiers who had gathered behind their lines to watch the show and cheer on the musketeers, and who sent up such a shout at the sight of the approaching Rochelois that surprise was out of the question.

Fontrailles, Isabeau, and Éric followed immediately behind the troops, who halted about two hundred paces from the bastion once they could see that the outwork appeared to have been reinforced; there were now many more than four heads lining the parapet. The troop evolved from column into line, marched forward another hundred paces, and opened fire on the bastion. The smoke of a hundred black-powder muskets firing repeatedly was all Louis had hoped for, and the three friends detached themselves from the Rochelois and followed the low-hanging gray cloud toward the Catholic lines.

As they drifted forward a ridiculous farce played itself out behind them. The Rochelois continued firing as they advanced on the bastion, the four musketeers retreated, leaving only propped-up dead bodies behind, and the French army cheered its lungs out. As Louis had hoped, all eyes were on Athos, Porthos, Aramis, and d'Artagnan as they marched triumphantly back to their lines. His own little group had nearly made it to the Catholic trenches, and he was congratulating himself on his cleverness, when a sea-born gust abruptly dissipated their concealing cloud. They found themselves facing a French sentry at a distance of no more than ten paces.

The soldier, who had been watching the exploits of the musketeers like everyone else, started at the sudden appearance of the three apparitions and pointed his musket toward them. "Halt!" he cried. "State the password, your names and units!"

"*Roi et Ré,*" Fontrailles said. "*Régiment de Ribérac.*"

"That's last night's password," the sentry said, "and the Ribérac regiment is leagues from here."

Fontrailles noticed that another soldier was coming forward to join the sentry, apparently attracted by the commotion. They were deep in the shit this time. "No, no, *Monsieur la Sentinelle,* you misunderstand," he said, trying not to sound desperate. "*Régiment de Ribérac* is the password—the *special* password for the Cardinal's *Corps d'Espion.* Weren't you briefed?"

It wasn't working. He was dead tired, and Éric was in even worse shape, so rushing the sentry was out of the question—and now the second soldier was arriving. A hellish vision of Isabeau dangling from a gallows swam before his eyes. "Let me explain," he said frantically. "It's like this...."

The sentry's eyes narrowed as he sighted along the barrel of his weapon. "Put your hands above your heads," he said, "and come slowly toward me. You're under arrest."

Meanwhile the second soldier walked up, calmly lifted a musket from where it leaned against a stile, and raised it into the air. The sentry, sensing something wrong, turned, but too late: the butt of the upraised musket came down on his head with a sickening crunch. He dropped without a cry.

Louis stared. "Welcome back, Monsieur de Fontrailles," said Sir Percy Blakeney. "Did you have a pleasant morning walk?"

CHAPTER XLVIII
A FAMILIAR AFFRAY

Isabeau was safe.

That was the overriding concern for Louis, the issue that trumped all others. He kept returning to the central fact of Isabeau's safety, partly because he was too exhausted to wrestle with other matters. Such as the nature of her relationship with Éric de Gimous.

And the fact that, after "rescuing" them, Sir Percy Blakeney had immediately relieved Fontrailles of the satchel containing *The Three Mystic Heirs.*

It hung now over the back of Blakeney's chair as he lounged in his tent deep within the French camp. "Not so quickly, Mademoiselle," he said to Isabeau, who was inhaling a bowl of fish soup on the other side of a folding table. "After prolonged inanition, one mustn't eat too much, too soon. Isn't that so, Enfield?"

"So I have always heard, Sir," replied Blakeney's smoothly efficient manservant in perfect French. The balding, compact Enfield was engaged in altering some excess articles of His Lordship's wardrobe so they would fit the Vicomte de Fontrailles, whose clothes had been taken away at Blakeney's command to be burned.

When they'd reached the concealment of Blakeney's tent, and Éric de Gimous had heard that the Englishman was an agent of the Duke of Buckingham, Éric had gratefully delivered up his secret despatch to him and then tumbled onto a cot, where he still lay, snoring raggedly. Fontrailles, sitting on an adjacent cot and clad only in a set of Blakeney's clean linens, decided he wasn't yet ready for sleep himself, if only because he wasn't done looking at Isabeau; and the only way to stay awake was to talk. "What are you doing here, Blakeney," he asked, "and in middle of the French royal army?"

"Spying, of course," Blakeney said. "One of your infantry colonels had a run of very bad luck at a Parisian gambling establishment that we secretly own. In order to cancel his impressive debts, he was induced to take on a previously unknown nephew of his as aide-de-camp for the Rochelle campaign. *I* am that nephew, known here as the Chevalier de l'Estrange.

"And why not?" he continued. "I was at loose ends anyway after you— seemingly—lost that blasted book into the Seine. So I've been camped out here for the last eight months attached to a French regimental staff, sending regular reports back to London ... and growing thoroughly bored." He smiled engagingly. "Sieges are so tiresome; it's no wonder your King Louis keeps escaping to Paris every chance he gets. So when I saw my old friend Aramis this morning at the Heretic Inn with his comrades, I did a little discreet eavesdropping, hoping it might put me onto something interesting. Not quite the act of a gentleman, I suppose," he shrugged, "but when one is spying for one's country, such scruples tragically wither."

"And I suppose you did hear something interesting or we wouldn't be enjoying your hospitality now," Fontrailles said.

"Oh, indeed!" Blakeney's tawny eyebrows arched humorously. "One of Aramis's friends, a Monsieur Athos, made an absurd wager about breakfasting in the Bastion of Saint-Gervais. I knew immediately that Aramis and his comrades were up to something, and it would profit me to follow along. I was even drawn into the wager as the fourth bettor on the other side, though I can assure you I was careful not to let Aramis get a look at my face, lest he recognize me." Blakeney chuckled. "In any event, I knew that this extravagant folly of the bastion must have an ulterior motivation. I assumed it to be a diversion while someone went either into La Rochelle or came out. If it was to cover an infiltration, of course, there was nothing much I could do about it—but if somebody was coming out, all I had to do was to follow along, keep my eyes open, then either interfere or assist depending on what was in the best interest of King Charles."

"So you clobbered the sentry," Fontrailles said. "Was that interference or assistance?"

Blakeney laughed. "In the case of mademoiselle, here, I would sincerely hope it may be counted as assistance." Isabeau smiled, but said nothing. She had finished eating and was barely staying awake herself. She blinked sleepily and, to Louis's eyes, adorably.

He blinked sleepily himself. *Back to business, or I'll drop off,* he thought. *In my case, of course, whether Blakeney's meddling was assistance or not has yet to be determined.* "And how, exactly, did you know I'd be carrying *The Three Mystic Heirs?*" he asked.

"Must I reveal *all* my secrets?" said Blakeney. "After all, I haven't asked you how you managed to get it from Cardinal Richelieu."

"You do get around," Fontrailles said. "So now what? Where do we go from here?"

"Where?" said Blakeney. "Why, to London, of course. Where else?"

The three escapees slept the clock around, but next morning Fontrailles found no opportunity for a private conversation with Isabeau, especially with Éric sticking to her like a limpet. They left camp at midday in a coach-and-four that Blakeney had magicked up from somewhere; the Duke of Buckingham seemed to have a well-funded espionage network. Enfield drove. When they reached the exit checkpoint on the road to Surgères they were asked for the password; Blakeney leaned out and said, *"Guerre et gloire,"* and they were waved through.

Blakeney, in his French captain's uniform, chatted amiably with Isabeau, now attired in a fashionable gray and burgundy riding-gown that Enfield had laid out for her that morning. Where he'd gotten it was a mystery to

Louis. He noted that Éric, for his part, was just sitting in his corner of the cab, looking at Isabeau and Blakeney and brooding. It occurred unpleasantly to Louis that he was doing exactly the same thing. He thought *Enough*, and said, "I know why you're taking *me* to London: because of the book. Why do Isabeau and Éric need to go?"

"It's quite the safest place for them, don't you think?" said Blakeney. "At least until your King Louis stops making war on his Protestant subjects."

"But they're not hostages for my good behavior."

"My dear fellow! Of course not."

"So, now that we're out of immediate danger, they're free to depart and return to Armagnac," Fontrailles said. "Isn't that so?"

"No ... I don't think I could approve of that; wouldn't be prudent at this juncture," Blakeney said, shaking his head. "Definitely not in the lady's and gentleman's best interests."

"Yes, I completely understand," Fontrailles said, not entirely able to keep the irony out of his voice.

Before he could say more they heard Enfield reining in the horses as the coach came to a rather sudden stop. Blakeney thrust his head out the window, took a look, and said, "Damn, hell, and blast!"

Fontrailles put his own head out the opposite window and saw another carriage blocking the road ahead. It was canted over sideways, and one of its wheels was off and lying in the road; its mate on the same side still spun slowly on its axle, and the horses were still in their traces. Two men, their backs to Blakeney's coach, stood looking ruefully down at the detached wheel.

Blakeney hopped out of the coach and strode toward them, asking in rapid French what had happened and if there was anything he and his man could do to help them on their way, or at least *out* of the way. The men didn't turn immediately, which Louis thought was curious. In fact there was something strangely familiar about them, especially the tall one with the peaked hat....

Before Louis could decide whether he ought to say something, the two men spun and pounced on Blakeney. The big Englishman fought back shrewdly, but Commander Philippe de Longvilliers and Cocodril were both strong men, and when Beaune, Vidou, and Gitane came out of the underbrush it was clear that he hadn't a chance. Gitane pointed a pistol at Enfield, who had leapt down to come to the aid of his master, while Beaune waded into the mêlée with a truncheon. Soon Blakeney was lying unconscious in the roadway.

"Louis, darling!" cried the Countess of Carlisle, stepping across Blakeney's prostrate form and approaching the coach. She wore a sky-blue gown with a contrasting underskirt of cream, and looked as if she were on her way to the theater. "We were worried *sick* about you! But now you're rescued; you may thank me."

"I may?" Fontrailles said.

"But of course!" She kissed Fontrailles on either cheek, then looked inside the coach and smiled at Isabeau and Éric, who were only just beginning to figure out what was going on. "You have the book, I trust?"

Fontrailles sighed. "Yes ... in a manner of speaking. It's right here." He climbed out of the coach. "How's Blakeney?"

Longvilliers was just preventing Cocodril from giving the Englishman another vicious kick in the kidneys. "That will do, friend Cocodril," he said.

"But the whoreson tore my pourpoint!" Cocodril snarled. "Aren't we going to kill him, Your Lordship?"

"No, we're not going to kill him. Not today, anyway," Longvilliers said. "We've got what we want; we'll leave him for his man to take care of."

"Why?" said Lady Carlisle.

"It would scarcely be honorable to cut his throat when he's down."

"Now, darling," Lady Carlisle said reasonably, "you know that if we don't kill him now we'll only be sorry later. Your ideas of honor, *chéri*, too often clash with good sense."

Longvilliers laughed. "My dear Lucy," he said, "there's no point in *having* a code of honor unless you choose what's honorable over what's sensible." He nodded at Louis. "Ah, there you are, Monsieur de Fontrailles! And probably wondering what this is all about, eh? Well, when the alarm went through the camp to arrest a hunchbacked man bearing a courier's satchel, we knew you'd somehow gotten the book from Richelieu. So we prepared this little bit of theater and have spent the morning waylaying every likely traveler on the way to Surgères. And lucky for you that we did, as you seem to have fallen into the hands of the perfidious English! ...Present company excepted, of course." He bowed to Lady Carlisle.

"So now what?" Fontrailles said. *And didn't I just have this conversation?*

"Now we leave the area as fast as we can," Lady Carlisle replied, "before we run afoul of the cardinal's agents. Better get that wheel back on, Beaune—with this crowd, we're going to need both carriages."

"And where do we go from here?" said Fontrailles.

"Where?" said Lady Carlisle. "Why, to Paris, of course. Where else?"

CHAPTER XLIX
DESTINY

To Paris. Where else?

Because now, at last, they had the Book and were free to make use of its secrets. Louis d'Astarac would employ it to make himself a whole man, and win back his Isabeau; Lucy Hay would employ it to make the Duke of Buckingham a dead man, for revenge and restoration of her father's stolen honor.

However, now that Fontrailles finally had the opportunity to delve into *The Three Mystic Heirs,* poring over its pages in the jouncing carriage, he learned that the rituals of Rosicrucian spiritual alchemy required physical components: slivered metals, rare earths, and semi-precious stones; powdered bones of diverse animals, infusions of assorted herbs, and blood of varying humors. But in Paris these things could be found, and at last they would test the power of spiritual alchemy.

But getting to Paris was not easy. The cardinal's agents were soon in pursuit of Commander de Longvilliers and his party, and before reaching Poitiers they'd had to leave the main road to avoid imminent capture. After that, their journey had become a flight. At Moncontour they'd abandoned the carriages, transferring to horseback so they could ride across country when necessary.

Despite these precautions, on a country byway near l'Isle Bouchard they stumbled right into an ambush, and might have been caught if Longvilliers hadn't charged the *gens d'armes* and unhorsed their officer, leaving him wounded or dead—they hadn't stayed around to learn which.

That evening, in the barnyard of the lonely farmstead where they'd purchased shelter for the night, the noble-born members of the party gathered around an outdoor fire to review their options. Vidou fretted that by sitting outside the ladies were exposing themselves to a case of the Falling Damps. The ladies laughed him off. "After starving nearly to death in a filthy, disease-ridden city," Isabeau said, "I could happily stand unclad in a cloudburst."

And for a fact, regular food and the air of liberty were restoring the bloom to Isabeau's cheeks, despite the hard riding of the past three days. Louis just wished she would smile more often; her laugh at Vidou had been the first of that day. He felt a desperate need to speak with her alone, to find out what she thought, how she felt—but Éric never left her side.

Beaune and Gitane brought chairs and stools from the farmhouse, which had been deemed too low, dark, and smoky for the meeting; Cocodril, as usual when there was physical labor at hand, was not in view. Fontrailles and Éric both proffered a chair to Isabeau, but the commander had the precedence, and sat first.

Longvilliers surveyed his audience: Fontrailles, Éric, Isabeau, and Lady Carlisle. "We had a narrow escape today," he said, "and it won't be the last, so long as we continue making for Paris. It's our obvious destination, and the cardinal will only have more snares set for us as we approach it."

"But today *you* got us out of trouble so *handily*, my dear," Lady Carlisle said. "We *must* get to Paris. It will be far easier to hide from Richelieu's agents inside the city than out of it."

"So you said before, and so I've been persuaded," Longvilliers said. "I defer to Your Ladyship in matters of intrigue. But in military matters you must defer to me, and this has become a campaign. As long as we ride toward Paris, the odds against us increase with every league."

"I don't think you'd care for the life of a fugitive in the countryside, always on the move," Lady Carlisle said. "It wouldn't suit you at *all*, darling."

"Can we get over the border into Flanders?" asked Éric de Gimous. "From there, perhaps we could cross into the United Provinces."

Longvilliers gave a short laugh. "I would think you'd have been cured of taking refuge among the Protestants, Monsieur. But crossing into Flanders, or even Lorraine, is worth considering."

Lady Carlisle shook her head. "Now that France is at open war with England and her allies, the border crossings will be watched. Our only hope is to go to ground in Paris until some new crisis draws off Richelieu's attention. Paris is the most populous city in Christendom, and once we're inside its walls, we can drop wholly out of sight—I'll answer for it!"

Fontrailles said, "I agree with Her Ladyship. Paris is closer than the borders, and we'll be safer there."

Longvilliers shrugged. "Then we shall continue to Paris. However, that leaves us with the question of where to cross the Loire." With a stick he drew a wavy line in the dirt to represent the river, and crossed it with four short hashmarks. Then, adopting the manner of a colonel addressing his staff, he said, "The options are few: the bridges at Saumur, Tours, Amboise, and Blois."

"If we hope to find allies, we should cross at Saumur," said Éric. "Though the king has appointed a Catholic as its governor, Saumur is still a Huguenot city."

"That's why they'll expect us to go there," Fontrailles said. "Saumur will be closely watched—and Amboise and Blois are under the eye of royal fortresses. I'd elect the crossing at Tours. It's an old city on the south bank of the river; once we're within its maze of streets, we'll be concealed until we're practically on the bridge."

"Then Tours it is, Monsieur de Fontrailles." Longvilliers stood, ending the debate. "Your sage advice once again vindicates my decision to ally with you. And now," he said, with a glance at Lucy Hay, "to bed."

Gitane, who had the first watch, went to take up his position as sentry where the lane from the farm met the road. Everyone else retired to their makeshift straw pallets in the farmhouse, except for Éric de Gimous, who strolled off into the dark toward a nearby stream, and Fontrailles, who followed him. He watched from a little distance as Éric relieved himself against the trunk of a young hornbeam; when Éric returned toward the farm, Louis intercepted him.

"Éric," he said, in a low voice. "We must talk."

Éric stopped. "Louis. Yes, you're right. Of course."

Fontrailles took a deep breath, then said, "Éric, I must know: what is your relationship with Mademoiselle de Bonnefont?"

Éric squared his narrow shoulders, and in the light of the dying fire Louis could see his slight, proud smile. "We have not yet generally announced it," he said, "but Mademoiselle de Bonnefont is no more. Isabeau—*my* Isabeau—is now Madame de Gimous. I should have told you before."

"Ah," Fontrailles said. It was all he could say, and he almost choked saying it.

"And I should also have found the time to say ... thank you, Louis," Éric continued. "Thank you for saving her—and me."

Louis knew he should respond to this, though he couldn't think what to say. He drew in a breath, but it got stuck inside somehow and wouldn't come out as words.

"And now, I think we'd all better get some rest," Éric said. "Good night, old friend." He moved off toward the farmhouse.

Fontrailles just stood staring after him, his mind a blank, and his heart a stone in his chest.

Everyone knew that getting into Tours wouldn't be without risk, as the single bridge across the Cher River, which bounded the city on the south, was a natural chokepoint. But they were lucky: it was a market-day in Tours, and they simply merged with the throngs of merchants, produce-carts and pedlars surging across the bridge. Beyond, the gates of the city were flung wide, and though an officer of the guard looked at them suspiciously as they rode past, he made no effort to stop them. Cocodril waved gaily and tipped his feathered cap, and then they were inside the walls.

Tours was the biggest city on the Loire, and as Fontrailles had predicted, they had no trouble losing themselves in its crowded streets lined with tall, narrow half-timbered houses. They had their dinner under the blue-slate roof of an ancient inn packed with a crowd of chattering silk merchants, Commander de Longvilliers looking over his shoulder and growing more nervous as the meal went on. "We'd better be on our way," he said, as they finished the wine. "I didn't care for the look that officer gave us when we entered the city; I won't feel secure until we're outside the river gate."

Infected by Longvilliers's anxiety, the entire troop was tense as the band approached the towering Loire gate. But despite the commander's qualms, there was no trouble, and with little more than a nod they rode through and out onto the stone flags of the long Pont Saint-Edmé. As they crossed the first arch over the Loire the tension drained from the group, and Longvilliers actually laughed aloud. Cocodril cantered, and put his cob through a little caracole.

The sense of relief was palpable. The party strung out as they crossed the long, many-arched span over the broad, slow river. Longvilliers and Lady Carlisle lagged behind, the commander finding himself moved to recite romantic poetry, and Lucy in just the mood to indulge him. Éric was far ahead, talking over old times with Vidou, whom he'd known since childhood. Louis suddenly found himself riding, in relative isolation, next to Isabeau.

"Well, Monsieur l'Intrigant," Isabeau said, smiling at Louis in the way he knew so well, "it seems the commander was right to take your advice about crossing at Tours. You've become quite an expert at this game of hide-and-seek."

"I learned everything I know about hide-and-seek from you, Madame," he said, stumbling a bit over the word, "in the gardens of the Château de Bonnefont."

She laughed lightly, and it wrung his heart. Then her brow contracted and she said, "But why did you call me Madame?" She took her lower lip between her small white teeth and looked at him searchingly. "Have you been speaking to Éric?"

"Yes," he said. "Last night. He said you were … married."

She frowned, lines appearing around her mouth that hadn't been there before La Rochelle. "And so we are … in Éric's mind. Wait," she said, to Fontrailles's attempted interruption. "Let me tell this.

"When the cardinal's men came to Armagnac to take father and me back to Paris, Éric followed. Once he reached the capital he made such a noise that he was taken into custody, too. After that night on the Pont Neuf, when father … died, Éric took charge. He thought we'd be safe in La Rochelle, and I let him take me there." Isabeau sighed. "For a while after father's death, I didn't care much about anything. Éric thought we might be pursued, so we traveled under a false name as husband and wife. It didn't bother me then; it was necessary, and Éric was honorable and didn't presume—though he did, once again, ask me to marry him. I told him I would … but later."

"Why did you put him off?" Fontrailles asked. *Say it, Isabeau: Because of you, Louis. Say it.*

She reined in her horse and looked down at the paving stones. They were three-quarters of the way across the river, but everyone in their party seemed to have stopped wherever they were, engrossed in their private conversations.

Isabeau looked up, her eyes brimming with tears. "I know what you want me to say, Louis—but I can't. I don't want to hurt you, of all the people in the world, but…."

"But you couldn't spend your life married to a monster. Of course," he said rapidly. "But what if it didn't have to be like that? What if I could be made like a normal man, cured of my condition? It may be possible. That's what I've been seeking so desperately, Isabeau."

She looked at him sadly, and shook her head. A tear grew too heavy for her eye to contain and escaped down her cheek. "Not even then," she said, her lips barely moving. "I'd want … *children*, Louis. And how would we know…?"

"Dear God." He looked away, down at the broad sheets of brown water sliding under the bridge. "Not even then."

All for nothing. His quest, that had cost so much, that had cost Isabeau's father his life—had been for nothing. It had all been a fantasy, a childish self-indulgence. He was … pathetic.

Isabeau was talking again, trying to explain. He decided he should listen, if only out of courtesy. *Good manners,* he thought bitterly, *is about all I have left to recommend me.*

"In La Rochelle, Éric and I lived in the same house, but in separate rooms," she said. "When the siege came … it was horrible, Louis. You can have no idea what it was like once the food began to run out. The sound of the cannon day and night drove people mad. Éric, of course, joined the defenders on the walls, but he was young: nothing had prepared him for the killing. All that death, from the guns, from disease, from starvation...."

"He began to carry a psalm-book, and to pray, for hours every night. I joined him. He needed my strength, Louis, or I think he would have simply died. Every night I prayed with him, clasping one of his hands in mine, until he passed out from sheer exhaustion. One morning he awoke, face shining, and said that he'd had a vision. An angel had visited him in his sleep and said that his prayers were granted; he said that in the eyes of the Lord, he and I were henceforth … husband and wife."

She drew a handkerchief from her sleeve and dabbed at her eyes. "He was so happy, Louis, but I … I was scared. He was becoming somebody I didn't know any more. Then, one night...." She took a deep breath, almost a sob. "He had been spending time with the other junior officers—drinking wine. And you know, Louis, Éric never did drink very much, never learned how to keep his head. He came back very drunk, and said that … that the marriage had to be consummated. And," she said in a whisper, "he forced himself upon me."

"He *raped* you?" Fontrailles cried.

"Hush, Louis! Don't say it that way. You don't know … you *can't* know, what it was like."

"He *raped* you!" Fontrailles repeated. He turned to look at Éric, stopped ahead of them, almost at the north bank of the river. Then he dug in his spurs and his horse leapt forward.

"Louis, stop!" Isabeau cried. "*Listen* to me!"

Éric and Vidou had drawn up their horses, as if waiting for him. But they were looking ahead, not behind. He charged up, reined in next to them, and snapped, "Gimous!"

"Fontrailles," Éric said without turning. "Look—at the end of the bridge. This doesn't look good."

Louis glared furiously at Éric for a moment, but finding himself ignored, he looked where Éric was looking. His former friend was right: it didn't look good at all. A heavy coach had appeared from behind a gatehouse and drawn up across the north end of the bridge, accompanied by a squad of mounted men-at-arms; the afternoon sun glinted from their helmets, crested Spanish-style morions.

The door of the coach opened and out stepped two figures in the austere black robes of the Society of Jesus. "Kircher," spat Fontrailles, "and Père Míkmaq."

"Those black crows from the Pont Neuf," Éric said, "with soldiers this time. Do they mean to kill us?"

"By God's blood, whether they mean to kill us or not," Fontrailles cried, "*somebody's* going to die." Because no gentleman should ever go unarmed, Longvilliers had lent Fontrailles a spare sword. He drew it now, and once again dug his spurs into his horse's flanks.

"*No!*" Vidou cried. As Fontrailles's horse leapt forward, Vidou's horse did the same. The old valet grabbed his master's bridle, and was pulled instantly from his saddle; he hit the ground hard with a cry of pain, but he still had hold of Fontrailles's horse; Louis had to rein in, or drag his kicking servant down the bridge.

He stopped, reached down and helped the shaken Vidou to his feet. "I'm sorry, old friend," he said.

"*De rien,* Monsieur," Vidou gasped.

The rest of the party rode up from behind. Longvilliers and Lady Carlisle had donned domino masks. "The Jesuits again," the commander said. "And more to the point, with eight or ten mounted mercenaries. We can't ride through *them*."

"Then we'll have to go back," Fontrailles said.

"Look behind us," said Lady Carlisle.

Fontrailles looked. A dozen mounted men, royal cavalry, were approaching from Tours, followed by another carriage, this one built lightly, for speed. "Sacred name of a blue pig!" he cried. "That's the final straw!"

"Very nearly," said Longvilliers. "We can't fight, so we'll have to talk."

"That means *you*, Louis," said Lady Carlisle. "*We* have to maintain our incognito."

What have I ever done so right that you keep turning to me *in a crisis?* he wanted to snarl. But he looked at Isabeau, now visibly frightened, and said, "All right. I'll talk to them."

The royal cavalry drew up fifty paces short of Fontrailles's party and separated, six to a side, to allow the carriage to pass between them. Beyond the soldiers it halted, a door opened, and Father Joseph slid out, his bare feet slapping as they hit the flagstones. He walked serenely toward Fontrailles, hands in his sleeves, pop eyes blinking in the bright sunlight.

Fontrailles dismounted and went to meet him. "God's blessings upon you, Monseigneur," he said, with an edge in his voice. He gestured at the carriage. "I thought you Capuchins were forbidden to travel except by foot." It was dangerous to be sarcastic with Father Joseph, but Louis was in a dangerous mood.

Father Joseph actually smiled, his whiskers bristling. "That is true, my son. But we Capuchins do not withdraw from life, like Carthusians—we are called to take an active role in the world. I have a dispensation from walking if the need is urgent. But I shall do penance for it, nonetheless."

"Nothing is free but free will," Fontrailles said.

Joseph's smile broadened. "I will enjoy debating theology with you another time, Monsieur de Fontrailles." The smile disappeared. "But today we must defer to a more secular business. I have an order to take you and your accomplices into custody. I assume," he said in his quiet voice, "that you will not be so unwise as to believe you have any alternative but to cooperate."

"You may have such an order," declared Longvilliers, "but it cannot apply to me and my companion." He and Lady Carlisle, still mounted, had walked their horses forward to where they could overhear the conversation.

Joseph looked up at Longvilliers and Lady Carlisle and said, in a mild hiss, "The order is signed by His Eminence the Cardinal himself, and does not grant exceptions to accomplices just because they choose to mask their features."

"I say again: your order cannot apply to me." Longvilliers removed his mask and stared haughtily down at the Capuchin in his frayed and spotted robe. "I am Philippe de Longvilliers, Seigneur de Poincy, Commander of the French Priory of the Holy Order of the Knights of Malta. You have no authority to detain me."

Joseph was unabashed. "His Eminence might have such authority...."

"I dispute that!"

"...But, as you say, *I* do not. You may pass, Commander de Longvilliers." Joseph bowed. "Go, with God's blessings."

Longvilliers's moustache twitched, as if he'd been ready to say more, but decided in favor of a dignified silence. He gave a majestic nod and spurred his horse forward, followed by Lady Carlisle and, a moment later, by Cocodril, who assumed a demeanor as haughty as the prince's in the event that someone might try to stop him. No one did. Longvilliers stared down his nose at the royal cavalry, and as he passed between them, one by one, they saluted. When beyond the soldiers Longvilliers paused, removed his hat and waved it to Fontrailles, as if to say, *I shall not forget you.* Then, he and his companions trotted back to Tours.

"*His* life is a never-ending pageant," Fontrailles said.

"Do not succumb to bitterness, Monsieur de Fontrailles," Joseph said quietly. "It avails nothing, and leads to the sin of despair. A knight of high rank must play at politics or he feels he's been denied his proper honors. And perhaps he will learn something from his games, for who knows? God may have an important role for him yet. As you have an important part to play now."

"Me?" Fontrailles patted the courier's satchel that hung from his saddlebow. "What you want is in here. Once you have that, what do you need me for?"

"You underestimate yourself. The book is nothing without you."

"I don't pretend to understand that—but if you want me, here I am." Fontrailles gestured at Isabeau and the others. "What about my ... accomplices? If you let Longvilliers go, why not them?"

"They will come to no harm, if you cooperate. You *will* cooperate, will you not?"

Fontrailles glanced around at the cavalry, and at the mercenaries of the Jesuits, who had closed up behind his party. They were fingering their weapons and looking appraisingly at Beaune and Gitane. Fontrailles sighed. "You needn't ask. You know very well that you leave me no choice."

Joseph gave a matter-of-fact nod. "Very well then. Let us be on our way—we still have a long journey ahead of us."

"Where are you taking me?"

"We are taking you," Father Joseph said, without the least accent of irony, "to the Column of Destiny."

CHAPTER L
A CONVERSATION BETWEEN TWO BROTHERS

A brief colloquy between Father Joseph and Athanasius Kircher decided that Fontrailles would join the Jesuits in their coach, while Isabeau and Éric would ride with the Capuchin. Louis started to protest, but at a look from Joseph, he thought better of it.

The Jesuits' coach was so crowded with books that Fontrailles was at a loss as to where to sit. Père Míkmaq made room for him by sliding a stack of Rosicrucian volumes to the floor—a pile in which Fontrailles thought he recognized the *Famous Fraternity* and the *Confession of the Fraternity of the Rosy Cross*—with a lack of care for the works that made Herr Kircher wince.

As the coach bounced into motion, Kircher reached across, grasped Fontrailles's hand, and pumped it in welcome. "Greetings, Monsieur de Fontrailles, greetings! So, we are done with chasing about and all together at last, eh? The book—may I see it?"

"It's in here," Fontrailles said, handing over the battered satchel. "May it bring you as much happiness as it's brought me."

Kircher ignored him. Fingers fumbling, he opened the satchel and drew forth the heavy tome. "Ah! *The Three Mystical Heirs of Christian Rosencreutz*," he said, drawing out every syllable in tones of deepest satisfaction. He opened the book and paged through it quickly, his face lit with enthusiasm. "This is it, indeed. To finally hold it in my hands! Almost certainly this is the last copy in existence. Now we can set this proxy aside and apply ourselves to the genuine article."

To make room for the heavy book, Kircher slid a slim volume onto the stack on the floor—a folio Fontrailles recognized. "*Ohé!* That's my introduction to *The Three Mystic Heirs,* stolen from me by Balthasar Gerbier!" he said. "I thought he took it to England! How did you get it?"

Kircher, rapt in contemplation of the complete work, seemed not to hear him. It was Père Míkmaq who answered: "Doctor Lambe brought it to us."

"Lambe? I've heard that name, somewhere," Fontrailles said.

"He was the Duke of Buckingham's astrologer and font of esoteric knowledge." Míkmaq smiled sourly. "Now he performs the same services for us."

"And he's told us many interesting things, Monsieur de Fontrailles," said Kircher, looking up, "many interesting things indeed. The court of Frederick, Elector of Palatine, was the intellectual center of Rosicrucianism, you know. When the Palatinate fell to the Catholic forces, many of the Brotherhood fled to England. As Elizabeth, the Elector Frederick's wife, was the daughter of the English King James, they expected to find sanctuary there."

"So this Doctor Lambe claims to have spoken with actual Rosy Cross Brothers?" Fontrailles said, interested in spite of himself. "And they were more forthcoming with him than Salomon de Caus was with you?"

Père Míkmaq frowned at this gibe, but Kircher looked a little embarrassed. "Apparently so, Monsieur. Through his conversations with exiles of the Brotherhood, Doctor Lambe claims to have gained significant insight into the Rosicrucian mindset. He believes that with the rubrics in this book, augmented by his astrological knowledge and my studies of Hermetic wisdom, we shall be able to actually invoke the powers of spiritual alchemy!"

"Does he?"

"He does! His confidence is really most inspiring. It was Doctor Lambe who suggested that it would be most felicitous to conduct our researches on the Column of Destiny."

"The Column of Destiny?" Fontrailles said. "Father Joseph mentioned that, but I thought he was just being allegorical."

"It is no allegory, but a real place, a tower built specifically for the pursuit of astral wisdom," said Kircher. "I'm told it was given that name by the astrologer Ruggieri, for whom it was built in the last century by your Queen Catherine de Médicis."

"Ah, *bien sûr.*" Fontrailles nodded. "It's in Paris; we call it the Colonne Astrologique. I thought it was abandoned; it's reputed to be haunted by spirits of evil. And Father Joseph has agreed to these, ah, researches?"

"In principle," Kircher said, "in principle. We are to discuss it with him later, after he has a talk with your Huguenot friends."

"Whom I'm more than a little worried about," Fontrailles said. "How much influence do you have with the Capuchin, Père Kircher?"

"*Frère* Kircher, if you please, for the time being—I'm to be ordained after the conclusion of this affair. So for now, I'm still a Brother. And I hope, because of your background, to be able to speak to you as one brother to another. I'm told you were educated at the Oratorian seminary in Paris, and as the Oratorians are inclined to mysticism, Father Joseph has more sympathy for them than for our worldly Society of Jesus. I believe that is why he has such a soft spot for you."

"He has a curious way of showing it!" Fontrailles said. "Whenever I speak with him, he never fails to threaten me and everyone I know."

"Nonetheless, I believe you may have more influence with him than you realize," Kircher said owlishly, "and therein may lie the best hope for your friends."

With this, conversation ended for a time. Louis mulled the situation over, Kircher studied *The Three Mystic Heirs,* and Père Míkmaq stared out the window at the countryside of the Touraine. Eventually Fontrailles, fatigued by the stress of the past few days, began to doze off. He was roused by Kircher saying, "Remarkable! Absolutely remarkable!"

"What?"

Kircher tapped the page in front of him. "You know, Monsieur de Fontrailles, the more I read of the Rosicrucian texts, the more correspondence I find between the Jesuitical worldview and the thinking of the Brotherhood."

Père Míkmaq snorted. "Except that the Rosicrucians were damned heretics who called the Pope the Antichrist."

"They had fallen deep into mortal error, of course," Kircher continued, undeterred. "But that aside, there is nothing erroneous about their core belief that the order and pattern of God's macrocosm is reflected in the microcosm of the world in which we live, and that by identifying and invoking these patterns we worship and glorify the Creator. Indeed, the Rosicrucians' respect for classical verities reflects the same principles upon which our own order was founded."

Père Míkmaq pulled at his long nose, still red above the V-shaped scar where Cocodril had nearly sliced it from his face. "I don't think," he said, "that our superiors in Rome are quite ready to agree with you on that, Frère Kircher."

"Ah, but they will," Kircher replied. "We will show them."

At a pause just short of Blois they were joined by Father Joseph, who sat next to Fontrailles once more books were removed to the stack on the floor. "It is always good to breathe the air of the Touraine again," the Capuchin said. "For many years I was Provincial of my order for Touraine and Poitou, and spent uncounted days crossing and re-crossing the land on foot, spreading the word of our Lord, enjoining rigorous devotion and admonishing weakness."

"This countryside must be dear to you, then," Fontrailles said.

"Oh, no—I never saw any of it. My eyes are weak, and I preferred to employ my time in deep contemplation upon the sufferings of Christ on Calvary." Father Joseph sighed, his eyes misty with nostalgia. "Alas! Those days are past, and such opportunities have become rare, with heresy such an ever-present threat to the body politic."

"I hope you're not referring to my friends Gimous and Mademoiselle de Bonnefont," Fontrailles said, trying to keep his voice light.

"They do persist in the error of adherence to the Reformed religion," Joseph said, "though otherwise, the youthful naïveté of your friends is quite charming."

Despite his words, Father Joseph did not appear the least bit charmed. He seemed as cool and composed as ever, enveloped in his coarse woolen robe like a turtle in its shell. Kircher had said Louis had influence with the Capuchin; he decided to see how much. "I don't want to see them harmed, Monseigneur," he said. "They're guilty of nothing but friendship for me."

"I wish, for their sake, that that was true," Joseph said. "But the young man freely admits that he bore arms at La Rochelle against his lawful monarch. He is an enemy combatant, and will be held as such. Oh, do not worry too much, Viscount—Monsieur de Gimous is a nobleman, after all, so perhaps he can be exchanged to the English for Frenchmen they hold prisoner."

"But ... what about Mademoiselle de Bonnefont?"

"Or Madame de Gimous," Joseph said, almost wry. "There seems to be some disagreement about her proper appellation. I believe it will be best for the present if we hold mademoiselle—or madame—as surety for your cooperation. We will treat her in accordance with her rank, of course: she can have that valet of yours to wait upon her, and I'm sure we can find a maidservant to attend her as well."

"What of Beaune and Gitane?"

"Those two rough fellows who so ill-treated me in my house in Paris? Men such as they are always useful; we will find new employment for them, far from the capital where they will not be tempted to misbehave by any lingering loyalty to you. Who knows?" He shrugged. "In the service of the Lord they may even find some measure of redemption."

"Such clemency is the mark of greatness, Monseigneur," Fontrailles said. Joseph didn't even bother to acknowledge the remark; he seemed completely immune to flattery. "But I'm completely in your power, Father, and I've promised to cooperate; why do you need to continue to hold mademoiselle as a guarantee?"

"Because you do not know yet with what you have agreed to cooperate, my son," Joseph said quietly. "What we intend to ask of you will not be easy."

"I don't understand, Monseigneur."

"We had deduced, of course, why you went to such lengths to acquire *The Three Mystic Heirs*—and having spoken with mademoiselle, even I can understand her power to distract. Ardor burns so bright in the heart of youth. So rejoice, my son," Joseph said, placing a hand on Fontrailles's arm, "for we are going to grant your dearest desire."

Louis looked at him uncomprehendingly. "Don't you see?" Kircher said helpfully. "We're going to prove the power of spiritual alchemy by using it to cure your sad condition! Some excruciation may be involved, of course—but the results, should you survive, will be worth it!"

Louis's eyes widened. "You can't mean it."

"But we do, Monsieur de Fontrailles," Kircher declared. "We are taking you to the Column of Destiny to straighten your spine!"

CHAPTER LI
"INTRUDER!"

"It's as if the Vicomte de Fontrailles had vanished from the face of the earth!"

The Commander of the French Priory of the Knights of Malta reached the limit of the narrow parlor, turned on his spurred heel and paced back in the other direction, a scowl on his hawk-handsome face. Lady Carlisle watched him through half-lidded eyes from where she reclined decoratively on an overstuffed divan. "I told you that Paris was the best place in the world for a person to hide—or be hidden," she said. "Wherever the Capuchin has him, he's as much out of sight there as we are here."

"Oh, *here*," Longvilliers said disdainfully, as he reached the opposite wall and turned again. "When you said we would 'go to ground' in Paris I had no idea you meant we would be staying in an actual *hole*. A knight needs esquires, you know! But where, in this hovel, are we to put them? There's barely room to house that devil Cocodril."

"Did you call, Your Knighthood?" came the voice of Jean Reynon from the next room.

"I did not, Cocodril! Remain on watch by the door, if you please."

"I am the soul of alertness, Monseigneur!"

"As far as I'm concerned," Lady Carlisle said, "if you want some servants, you can trade that rascal in for a real valet, and get me a tiring-woman while you're at it. I don't trust him, and worse, he wears on my nerves."

"He is loyal," said Longvilliers, "and I consider loyalty the first of virtues."

"Then be loyal to me, Philippe!" Lucy Hay sat up, lifting her chin to gaze imperiously at Longvilliers. "You swore to help me avenge myself on the Duke of Buckingham. Well, now that the Rosicrucian spell-book is lost to us, we're just going to have to go to England and deal with him ourselves. I've had enough of indirect methods."

"And I have had enough of lurking about in shadows like a thief. Direct methods, indeed! What, Madame—do you take me for an assassin? Am I to *sneak*—to *skulk*? If I meet Buckingham on the field of battle I may cross swords with him, but I shall not stoop to the dagger in the dark. No, Madame—this 'espionage' of yours is not to my taste."

"No, you prefer gadding about the countryside like some colonel of cavalry, forever on campaign, living out of tents and consorting with peasant farmers. Why don't you go back and play soldier with the other boys, if that's what you want?"

"Now, Lucy, you know perfectly well that's not what I meant," Longvilliers said, in the same soothing tone he used with horses and hounds. "It's just that I'm fed up with hiding in obscure corners of the city, waiting day after day for news from your 'network.' You can see that, can't you?"

Lady Carlisle refused to be mollified. "Yes, it would suit you to go back to your soldiers and sailors to clash with Moorish pirates on the bounding main. But how am I to go anywhere, with what's left of my wardrobe? I've barely a dress to my name!"

"Don't start in about the *money* again," Longvilliers fumed. "You know very well that, despite my rank, my estate is a modest one, and my finances are at their limit. You're the daughter of an earl, and married to another! Why should you need *me* to buy you gewgaws and tinsel?"

"Because...."

"Intruder!" hissed Cocodril from the foyer. "I hear voices outside the door, Your Knighthood!"

Longvilliers went for his sword, which hung from its baldric over the half-open door to the foyer, but his hand was barely on the hilt when a key rattled in the lock and the street door was pushed open. And there, tawny eyebrows arched in mild surprise, stood Sir Percy Blakeney.

He sketched a little bow. "Monsieur de Longvilliers, is it not? I do beg your pardon, but I was under the impression that this unassuming abode had been reserved for the use of agents of His Majesty King Charles."

"Idiot," Lady Carlisle said. "Come in, Percy, and shut the door, before someone sees you making an ass of yourself in the street."

"Thank you, Madame—I believe I will come in, if only out of curiosity." Blakeney opened his cloak to put the key into a belt pouch, revealing as he did so that he was fully armed with sword, dagger, and two pistols. "You don't mind if Enfield comes in as well, do you?" he said cheerfully. "Since we met you on the road to Surgères, he's been most eager to get reacquainted with that toothy manservant of yours."

Blakeney's compact servant stepped warily into the foyer, locked eyes with Cocodril, and closed the door behind himself.

"If it pleases Milord, your man and I could step outside to further pursue our acquaintance," Cocodril said pleasantly.

"That will do, Cocodril," said the commander, but before he could continue he was once again pre-empted by Lady Carlisle.

"If you're after that spell-book for Buckingham, Blakeney, you may as well know right now that it isn't here," she said. "Father Joseph has it."

"As well as the Vicomte de Fontrailles and those Huguenot friends of his," Longvilliers added.

"Does he?" said Blakeney. "Hard luck. But I'm here on another matter entirely, negotiating a *sub rosa* prisoner exchange between Buckingham and the cardinal. Officially I'm not in Paris at all, and would much prefer to remain unnoticed until I return to Béthune. I rather thought I might stay here—but if you're in residence, Lady Carlisle, I shall have to find other lodgings." He looked around at the faded wallpaper, low ceilings, and cracked floorboards of the shabby little house, and didn't seem to think staying elsewhere would be much of an inconvenience. "By the way, Madame," he added, "His Grace the Duke might not be best pleased to find you making free with his intelligence assets after opposing his interests."

"Are you going to tell him?" Lucy asked.

"I hadn't decided," said Blakeney. "But I think that, if you cause me no further trouble, I can see no reason to cause you any. Good night, Commander," he said to Longvilliers, with a more formal bow than previously. "If you don't mind, I'll be taking my leave. It grows late—and as I lack the, ah, *felicity* of your sleeping situation," he flicked an eyebrow at Lucy, "I must make my own arrangements. *Au revoir.*"

With that, Blakeney and his man backed out into the street and were gone.

"Damn him!" said Lady Carlisle. "No one is simultaneously so well-mannered and so insolent as Blakeney."

"Despite his promise, he will certainly inform the duke of your whereabouts," said Longvilliers.

"I know it; we must leave immediately," she said. "If we're going to give Buckingham what he deserves, we have to get to him before Blakeney does."

"But, *chérie*, I thought I'd made it clear," Longvilliers said. "Going to England with the idea of doing in the Duke of Buckingham is completely out of the question. For one thing, I'm no assassin—and I don't believe you are, either. For another, we owe it to the Vicomte de Fontrailles to find him and rescue him."

"Philippe," she said through her teeth, "for the last time, do you hold loyalty to your boy's club above your commitment to *me?*"

"But my dear, honor…."

"*Shove* your honor sideways up your arsehole," she snarled, in English. "I've had enough." She pushed past Longvilliers, opened the door and stamped out into the street.

"Lucy!" he cried. "Where are you going? It's after dark!"

"Maybe I can still catch up with Blakeney," she called over her shoulder.

"But Blakeney's an agent of your deadliest enemy!"

"Yes—but at least," came her voice out of the gloom, "he's *not French!*"

"Shall I go after her, Your Knighthood?" asked Cocodril.

"No." Longvilliers sighed. "Just shut the door."

"But what will we do now, Monseigneur?"

"First of all," Longvilliers said, looking around with distaste, "we will find more suitable lodgings."

"But naturally! Shall we retire to Monseigneur's country estate, where he can take consolation for his loss among more salubrious surroundings?"

"No. Fontrailles is here, somewhere, in Paris—so here we stay until we find him."

"Is that not a task best left to such low people as tipstaffs and informers?" asked Cocodril. "Delegate the task to me, Your Commandery, and I will see to it that you are not demeaned by association with such scum."

"Thank you, friend Cocodril, but I'm the one who owes the debt of honor to the viscount, so I must see this through personally. But you're right," Longvilliers mused, "we will need help: men we can trust. I think we'd better track down our old friends Beaune and Gitane. And we'd best be quick about it," he added. "I fear Monsieur de Fontrailles is in terrible danger."

CHAPTER LII
THE FIRST DAY OF CATHARSIS

Father Joseph's small caravan reached the outskirts of Paris at midday on August 16, 1628, but the Capuchin insisted they wait for nightfall before entering the city. The party installed itself in an auberge in the village of Vaugirard, where Fontrailles, Kircher, Isabeau, and Éric sat, with a few guards, in the inn's common room. There they engaged in desultory conversation, and watched the steady stream of messengers and couriers that came and went from the private room in the rear occupied by Father Joseph.

Some of Joseph's visitors wore monastic robes; some were cavaliers, a few in military regalia; most were utterly nondescript, the kind of people who never look one in the eye and whom one forgets as soon as they pass. One visitor in particular attracted their attention, a tall, martial-looking man wearing a white friar's habit. He emerged from his conference with Joseph and marched directly to the table of Fontrailles's party, where he announced that Monsieur de Gimous had been remanded into his custody and was to go with him immediately. When he saw the party casting doubtful looks at his monk's habit, he let the cloak fall open to show that underneath he wore a leather jack, and in his belt were both pistol and dagger.

At this, Éric nodded and stood up. He put on a brave face, but he was pale as he took his leave of Isabeau; Louis, remembering what he had done to her in La Rochelle, suppressed his feelings of sympathy for the man who had been his childhood friend.

Éric's ominous departure brought conversation to a halt. It was a long wait thereafter—darkness comes late to Paris in August—but eventually, when shadows filled the common room and the host was lighting the tapers, Father Joseph emerged from his lair and declared that it was time to go. They re-entered the coaches, drove less than a league to the Porte de Bussy, and passed into the capital. Torches lighting their way through the gloom, the little cavalcade made its way across the river, negotiated the maze of dark and malodorous streets surrounding Les Halles, and pulled up before the ornate Italianate gates of the Hôtel de Soissons.

It was an imposing mansion, constructed in the middle of the previous century to serve as the royal Parisian residence of Queen Mother Catherine de Médicis. The hôtel had been built in the form of a hollow square, with the tall fluted Colonne Astrologique, or Column of Destiny, rising from its empty center.

When the Valois dynasty had died out with Henri III, and the throne, under Henri IV, had passed to the Bourbons, Catherine's mansion had devolved upon the Soissons family, cousins of the new king. However, at the doors of the grand hôtel they were met, not by footmen in Soissons livery, but by Bernajoux, Fontrailles's former subordinate in the Cardinal's Guard. He bowed to Fontrailles, saluted Father Joseph, and opened the heavy door.

Fontrailles, Isabeau, and Vidou followed Father Joseph into the entry hall and found it dark, deserted, and almost entirely unfurnished. Three more guards entered behind them. "Where is His Highness the Comte de Soissons?" asked Fontailles, his voice echoing harshly in the empty hall. "I'm surprised he would agree to lend you his Column of Destiny for your experiments."

"Monsieur le Comte knows nothing about it," Father Joseph said, in a penetrating whisper that evoked no echoes, even from bare marble.

"Having been implicated in the recent conspiracy against His Majesty, he is presently in voluntary exile at the Court of Savoy. We are ... borrowing his abode in his absence."

"Won't it be embarrassing for you if he returns suddenly?" Fontrailles asked, as they followed the Capuchin into a dark and empty antechamber.

"He is watched, and can make no such move without our knowing of it immediately. Ah, here we are, Mademoiselle." Joseph stopped before a tall double door of carved oak. "Monsieur le Comte's own bedchamber. The appointments are somewhat austere, the count having removed most of the furnishings to his château at Soissons, but I do not think you will be uncomfortable."

Bernajoux opened the door to reveal a candlelit room, where a sumptuous bed was already turned down; while they were waiting outside the city, someone had come ahead and prepared for their arrival.

Isabeau turned uncertainly toward Fontrailles. "Louis?" she said. "I...."

"Don't worry," he replied. "I won't be far ... will I?"

This last remark had been directed at Father Joseph, who said, "No, Monsieur—not in distance."

With this equivocal reply the pair had to be satisfied. Fontrailles said, "*Bon soir,* Isabeau," as she vanished behind a pair of guards into the Comte de Soisson's bedchamber.

Father Joseph led them through two more chambers, halting at the door of a third. "You, Monsieur de Fontrailles, will have the honor of staying in what was once Queen Catherine's own bedchamber. It lacks windows, as the old queen had a fear of assassination that was not, perhaps, unjustified, but it makes up for that by having a most convenient private passage that leads directly to the base of the Column."

"Made to order," Fontrailles said.

"Very nearly so," said Athanasius Kircher, his moonlike face appearing out of the gloom with the glowering Père Míkmaq at his elbow. "There are no coincidences, only congruities. Rest well, Monsieur de Fontrailles, for we rise early to begin the catharsis."

"The catharsis. Right," Fontrailles said. "And what will be the first step of this process?"

"You'll know soon enough," Père Míkmaq said. "Just be thankful you have a bed to sleep in. I was left bound to a stake the night before the savages of the New World tortured *me*." Bernajoux snorted, opened the door and slid Fontrailles within, and then locked it behind him.

Louis turned to inspect his new abode, a large, mostlly empty chamber, and then realized he wasn't alone in it. A dark-haired, dark-eyed man was sitting on Queen Catherine's immense old bed where he had been reading by the light of a small candelabrum.

"Monsieur des Cartes!" Fontrailles cried. "I'm astounded! What in the name of all the devils are *you* doing here?"

"A question I've been asking myself, Monsieur de Fontrailles." Des Cartes rose from the bed to bow to Louis and shake his hand. "I had developed a chain of inferences, but your appearance means I shall have to revise them."

"So you think, if I'm here, it must be because of...."

Des Cartes held up a hand. "I do not know yet quite what I think."

"Then let's compare what we know. Did you...?"

"Monsieur de Fontrailles!" des Cartes interrupted. "Have you hurt your hand? Let me see it."

"Why ... no." Fontrailles looked in surprise at both his hands which, though crook-fingered, were quite whole. But des Cartes gestured peremptorily, so Fontrailles offered him his right hand.

"*Merci*," des Cartes said. "No, you're quite right—I was mistaken." However, instead of releasing Fontrailles's hand, he began drawing lines across the palm with his index finger, lines that Fontrailles quickly realized were meant for letters.

I—L—S—E—C—O—U—T—E—N—T. *Ils ecoutent.*

They listen.

Fontrailles nodded slowly to des Cartes to indicate that he understood. "Let me just tell you, Monsieur des Cartes, *some* of the circumstances that brought me here." And he proceeded to relate his recent history, confining himself to what he was sure was already known to the agents of the cardinal. That would still be enough, he thought, to convey the gist of the situation.

Des Cartes took it all in without comment or change of expression. "And Father Joseph has agreed to allow the Jesuit to test these theories, with you as his subject?" he said, when Fontrailles was finished. "That, I confess, does not make sense to me. Some important factor is unknown to us."

"But, you, Monsieur," Fontrailles said. "How did you come to be in Cardinalist custody?"

"I believe someone made the mistake of trying to do me a favor," des Cartes said—a remark which might have been wry coming from someone else, but from him was entirely humorless. "You know Monsieur Mersenne, the mathematician?"

"The Minim friar? Yes, we've met."

"I had shared some notes with him that I'd made for an essay to be titled *Rules for the Direction of the Mind*. He was so impressed with them that he recommended me to Père de Bérulle."

"The founder of the Oratorians?"

"The same. Perhaps you know him from your days in the Oratorian seminary?"

Fontrailles smiled. "Only from a distance. He came to address the students two or three times a year."

"Well, since Bérulle was made a cardinal he sits on the King's Council, so when he summoned me for an interview, I thought it wise not to refuse. He questioned me about what he called my 'thought-provoking' ideas, and I replied in such terms as I thought he would find acceptable. Did you know he and Father Joseph were childhood friends?"

"Not at all! Are they still close?"

"Less so—Bérulle, you know, is a leader of the Devout party, and opposes Richelieu's anti-Spanish foreign policy. But Bérulle, like Joseph, is a Catholic mystic, and apparently he thought there was something in my ideas that ought to be brought to the Capuchin's attention. Three days ago I received an 'invitation' from Father Joseph"—des Cartes shrugged—"and here I am."

"But why have we been lodged together?" Fontrailles asked.

"As to that," des Cartes replied, "I could not say." But he nodded toward the wall, and casually pulled on his ear.

Fontrailles nodded. *That's* why *they listen: in hopes des Cartes will say something unguarded and revealing to his friend Fontrailles—and vice versa.*

It was too much to sort out right then: he needed sleep. Except for the table, which bore the candelabrum, a bowl and a pitcher, Queen Catherine's massive canopied bed was the only furniture in the room. "It looks like we're sharing a bed," Fontrailles said.

"It's certainly big enough," said des Cartes. "I've fallen out of the habit of sleeping with others, but I snore only lightly and will do my best not to disturb you."

"You needn't worry," Fontrailles said. "Tired as I am, nothing could keep me awake."

But he was wrong. Long after des Cartes had dropped off, snoring, as he'd promised, lightly, Louis lay awake, eyes staring into a swirl of ominous mental images. Éric, a confessed enemy heretic, had vanished into the nameless limbo of political incarceration. Isabeau, guilty of nothing but association with Éric and Fontrailles, and of being witness to events it was dangerous to know about, was imprisoned a few rooms away, and probably staring into the dark herself, uncertain and afraid. And her only guarantee of freedom was Louis's cooperation in a risky attempt to unkink the very bones inside him.

And even if it works, he thought, *she has promised still to reject me.*

Fontrailles awoke to another ominous image: the face of Père Míkmaq staring into his, while the Jesuit priest shook his shoulder roughly. "*Vous réveillez,* Viscount," he said, a sour smile below his red-scarred nose. "This is your big day, no?"

"The first of five, actually," said Athanasius Kircher, holding up a lamp behind him. "The Catharsis will be a pentapartite process, culminating, we hope, in the complete restoration of your ideal human form."

"Hrn?" said Fontrailles, who had just been dreaming of a banquet in the Court of Miracles at which Isabeau, Lucy Hay, and Proserpine had been quarreling over who was more erect and manly, Cocodril or the Commander de Longvilliers. He sat up and shook his head to clear it. "Very well, Messieurs. Just give me a moment to wash up."

"That will not be necessary," said Kircher, "as you are about to undergo a ritual of purification anyway. Just don this vesture of white linen, as we have, and follow us."

Wiping the sleep from his eyes, Fontrailles saw that Míkmaq and Kircher were, in fact, both garbed neck to ankle in flowing white robes. Father Joseph stood quietly behind them, clad as always in his habit of coarse wool, hands buried in its sleeves, his face in shadow. "Good morning, Monseigneur," Fontrailles called. "Where are your pure white vestments? Didn't they have enough?"

"I need none, my son; I will leave the experimentation to Doctors Kircher and Lambe," the Capuchin whispered. "I shall stay here and have an exchange of views with Monsieur des Cartes. I am told that his opinions are most stimulating."

Fontrailles glanced at des Cartes, now sitting up on his side of the bed, and their eyes met briefly; des Cartes's gaze was calm, as always. *He'll be all right,* Louis thought. *Let's see if I can match his composure.* He took the proffered white robe from Míkmaq and pulled it over his head, only to find that the sleeves overlapped his hands by several inches and the trailing hem buried his feet in a pile of snowy linen.

Kircher made a rueful face. "We'll adjust the length for tomorrow, Monsieur, but for now, if you'd just pick up the hem ... thank you. This way, if you please."

Herr Kircher unlocked a black oaken door in a niche at the rear of the bedchamber, which opened to reveal a windowless passage. They passed through, and Père Míkmaq bolted the door behind them; Kircher then led them down a short corridor of whitewashed stone walls painted with faded astrological symbols.

At the other end of the passage were two doors, a black door ahead and a brown one to the left. The door on the left had a small grilled window set in it through which Fontrailles could see daylight infiltrating the center courtyard of the Hôtel de Soissons; the other door, set in a wall of square stone blocks, presumably led into the Column of Destiny. The door to the courtyard wasn't barred, and neither Kircher nor Míkmaq appeared to be armed, but Louis put thoughts of escape out of his mind. He had to think of Isabeau.

Kircher opened the black door and Fontrailles was ushered into the base of the Column, a square chamber perhaps six paces by six. Ahead was the foot of a staircase that mounted to the top of the pedestal before turning to spiral up the inside of the column. Light penetrated the interior of the tower from small windows that lined the staircase, and looking straight up from the center of the pedestal Fontrailles could see the stairs spiraling up around the gradually tapering column in seven revolutions.

"One hundred forty-seven steps," Kircher said. "I'm sure that is numerologically significant, though I have not yet worked out its full meaning. It is obviously seven, the number of the Heptarchs, plus seven again, times ten, the number of the Sephiroth, plus a final seven—but there must be more to it than that."

"No doubt," Fontrailles said, looking around the pedestal chamber. Everywhere were carved crowns and the letters C and H interlaced; on each wall was a tall gilt-framed mirror surmounted by a cornucopia; but the glass of each was cracked. "Who broke the mirrors?" he asked.

"Queen Catherine herself." It was Père Míkmaq who replied. "It was one of the symbols of her eternal grief over the death of her husband, Henri II." He smiled sourly. "You seem surprised that I would know such a thing—but I'm learned in more than religion, Monsieur le Vicomte. I studied at La Flèche too, just like your friend des Cartes."

Kircher, ignoring him, began to ascend the staircase. "*Materia, Spiritus, Intellectus*," he declaimed, his voice ringing in the tower like a bell. "Such, all true scholars have agreed since the time of Hermes, are the three levels of the cosmos. We inhabit the material world; above us the stars and planets orbit in the celestial world of light and spirit; and beyond that is the

Empyrean, the world of pure divine intellect where reside the ideal forms of which all in the material world are mere shadows. ...Take care where it begins to spiral, Monsieur de Fontrailles; the steps are steep, and there is no inner railing.

"We have fallen far from the days of the ancients. They were closer to the time of creation, and had perfect knowledge of how to invoke the astral powers of the celestial world. You have studied some of the sources of esoteric knowledge, Monsieur de Fontrailles, and you know their value: the mighty tools of Number, and of computation; the invocative power of Hebrew, the holy language God spoke when he spake the Word that created the world; and of Christian Cabala, the art that reveals the names and ordination of the angels, and how they may be addressed and approached.

"And now, at last, with *The Three Mystic Heirs,* we have the instrumentality once granted to the ancients," Kircher said, wheezing a bit; they were nearing the top of the stairs, which ended below a trap door in the circular ceiling. "Now we will prove the utility of spiritual alchemy, demonstrating the direct descent of divine knowledge to our modern theocracy—and the Church of Rome will be restored to pre-eminence."

Kircher pushed up on the door in the ceiling to open it, admitting a bright bar of sunlight that blazed back from his white robe. He looked down, the fringe of hair around his tonsure glowing like a halo. "That is why we are counting on your cooperation, Monsieur de Fontrailles, in the rites we will perform on the platform above. This could be a turning point in the history of mankind!"

I wonder if he practiced that speech, Louis thought. He followed Kircher up, emerging into fresh air on the square stone platform, about five paces to a side, that topped the tall column. They were within a circular cage of wrought iron bars that enclosed most of the area of the platform: a tall cylinder of seventeen iron stanchions rising from a ring set into the flagstones and curving into a dome above, the whole surmounted by a smaller, finial dome of curving wrought iron with a celestial globe at its crest.

Fontrailles looked out between the vertical bars. Below, beyond the hollow square of the Hôtel de Soissons, Paris spread out like a perspective map, smoke rising at a slant from ten thousand chimneys. The morning breeze wafted up the street cries, the odors and aromas of the stalls of nearby Les Halles. Just to the northeast bulked the dark shape of the great Church of Saint-Eustache; slightly farther, in the opposite direction, rose the blunt steeple of Saint-Germain-l'Auxerrois and the sprawl of the Louvre.

And standing between Louis and the Louvre was an unfamiliar broad-shouldered figure in yet another white robe. "Monsieur de Fontrailles," Kircher said, "allow me to introduce our colleague, Doctor John Lambe."

"*Enchanté,* Monsieur," Lambe said in a pronounced English accent, stepping forward and thrusting out his hand. Reflexively, Fontrailles shook it: the palm was clammy, but the grip was firm. Lambe had a round face crowned by a shock of dark hair, but he had the focused eyes of a politician rather than the vague gaze of a pedant. With an unctuous smile, the English astrologer said, "I apologize for not attending your levee, Monsieur," a remark that Louis assumed was meant for a joke, "but I was occupied in setting up our apparatus and instruments."

He gestured toward the center of the platform. The area under the tall iron cage was cluttered with a bizarrely eclectic array of items: lamps, books on bookstands, rolls of parchment, tall candles, colored bottles, bells, alchemic crucibles and mortars, rolls of silk, even a golden harp. There were also mechanisms such as ropes, block, and tackle whose purpose Fontrailles understood, and other, more obscure devices he did not.

In the center, under the apex of the dome, was a rectangular table, its top ornamented with an elaborate painted sigil. In its basic outline, Fontrailles recognized the *monas hieroglyphica* of Doctor John Dee: a circle with a cross below it like the symbol for Venus, with an upturned crescent intersecting the top of the circle, and two smaller downturned crescents springing from the foot of the cross. But this grand *monas* was glorified with colorful detail, the cross covered with Egyptian hieroglyphics, the circle containing the orbits of the seven planets around a central sun, and the upper crescent broadened into a sickle moon.

"You recognize this symbol, of course. I have added some decorative enhancements," Kircher said proudly, "to encourage positive celestial influences and to endorse the holy sanctity of our blessed purpose. You will lie with your head upon the center of the circle, here, with your arms upon the limbs of the cross, and your feet upon the double crescent at the base."

Louis was alarmed. "Are you planning to *crucify* me?"

"*Himmel!* No, indeed!" said Kircher, horrified. "Such a procedure would not subject your material form to the appropriate stresses! ...Plus, of course, it would be blasphemous."

"Allow me to explain," Doctor Lambe interjected smoothly. "We propose to subject your *corpus* to a process of materio-spiritual catharsis that will drive out the malign influences that have distorted your skeleton into variance from the ideal. By combining divine mathesistical incantations with a progressive lengthening of your limbs and realignment of your joints, your body will be prepared to receive a sympathetic reorganization that will emulate its ideal form in the Empyrean."

Louis paused for a moment to parse this. "*Merdieu*," he said. "You're planning to *rack* me."

"In part, in part." Kircher nodded energetically. "There will be other procedures of disjunction as well that I'm afraid will be somewhat unavoidably disagreeable. By themselves, of course, such operations would only serve to injure you, perhaps even fatally. However, by following the prescriptions in *The Three Mystic Heirs,* and combining my theoretical knowledge with Doctor Lambe's practical experience, we shall perform a series of operations that should both alleviate your body and elevate your soul!"

"If he lives," said Père Míkmaq.

"The success of the catharsis and the survival of the subject are not necessarily related," said Kircher. "Though we shall attempt to achieve *both* goals," he added brightly.

Willing himself to remain calm Louis considered his three would-be tormentors: Doctor Lambe wore the same oily smile Louis had once seen on a horse-dealer trying to sell a nag ready for the knacker's yard; Kircher looked hopeful and vaguely embarrassed; Père Míkmaq was almost openly skeptical. Was there something he could make of these contrasts?

"Let me see if I understand this," he said. "You intend to pull me apart, and then implore the divine celestial powers to put me back together in an improved form."

"One that will reflect its platonic ideal in the mind of God!" said Kircher. "*Ja,* that is it."

"And then Father Joseph will let Mademoiselle de Bonnefont go free?"

Míkmaq shrugged. "That's what he says."

"*Bien.*" Fontrailles raised his arms. "Tie me up; let's start the excruciation."

"Your zeal is commendable," said Kircher, "but this is only the first day, the Day of Purification. We must cleanse your *corpus,* inside and out, in accordance with the rites sacred to the holy angel Balabel, who rules Tuesday (that is, today) and whose power is in the bowels of the waters. You must be bathed in what Symphorien Champier calls the 'intelligible splendor' of the rays of the sun, and consecrate yourself to the reconstruction of the higher image in your degenerate corporeal form."

Fontrailles raised his eyebrows. "It sounds like you're going to be busy."

"Oh, not half so busy as *you,* Monsieur de Fontrailles," Doctor Lambe said. "Was it not explained that the catharsis requires your full cooperation and willing participation? We are here only to lead you through the procedures and provide you with the necessary materials. The actual transformation of your material person must be accomplished by you."

"Oh," Fontrailles said. "And what about the later, ah, procedures of disjunction?"

"The catalysis of disassembly must come from within, of course," said Kircher. "The will of the subject must be fully engaged. In short, Monsieur de Fontrailles, you must perform the tortures … on *yourself.*"

CHAPTER LIII
THE SECOND DAY OF CATHARSIS

Fontrailles staggered down the stairs of the Column of Destiny, blinking in the rays of the setting sun that penetrated the west-facing windows of the tower. It had been a long day.

Louis had stripped and bathed in consecrated water, naked before the entire citizenry of Paris (none of whom, it must be said, had appeared to notice the strange show in the iron cage atop the Colonne Astrologique). He had swallowed purgatives and emetics, and then exploded repeatedly into a silver chamberpot. He had laid spread-eagled on the *monas*-table, squinting up into the sun and imploring the angel Rahimmin to draw out the evil humors of his body, the errors of his thoughts, and the sins on his soul. He had repeated the names of the seventy-two angels through whom the higher Sephiroth may be approached, each name in forty-nine versions anagrammatized through the Cabbalistic system of Notarikon. Doctor Lambe had showed him how to press a lancet into the vein inside his elbow to bleed three inches of his own blood into a broad silver bowl. Finally Père Míkmaq had led them all, kneeling, in an hour-long series of prayers from a well-thumbed copy of Canisius's Jesuit prayer book. By the end of it Louis thought even Kircher looked a little impatient.

Through it all Fontrailles had been given nothing to eat and very little to drink: just a few fingers of barley-water when the sun had reached its zenith. Now, clutching the overlong white robe above his knees, he was more than a little dizzy as he trailed Père Míkmaq down the spiraling stairs, which after the third turn seemed to spin before his eyes, their circle expanding and contracting. He stumbled, gave a wordless cry—and Père Míkmaq turned just in time to prevent him slipping over the edge and plummeting five stories to the flagstones below.

Fontrailles sat down on the stairs and took his spinning head in his hands. "Thank you, Father," he finally managed to say.

"*De rien*," said Míkmaq. "Can you go on?"

"I think so." Fontrailles put a hand to the wall and levered himself to his feet. "But perhaps we could go more slowly."

"As you wish."

"That was ... a fine prayer session you led," Fontrailles said, placing one foot carefully on each stair. "Truly inspirational." Père Míkmaq grunted skeptically. Louis said tentatively, "Repeating the words of our Lord restored my spirits—it helped wash out the taste of all that heretical gibberish Lambe and Kircher had me say." This time Míkmaq's grunted reply was more affirmative. That was enough for Louis: he decided not to push it further.

Fontrailles was returned to Queen Catherine's bedchamber through the door in the rear wall. Pausing only to nod politely to Father Joseph and Monsieur des Cartes—he was afraid he'd fall over if he tried to bow—he marched directly, if shakily, to the big bed and plunged into it.

"Surely, my son, you're not going to deprive us of your company so abruptly," Father Joseph said quietly, in a tone that admitted of no alternative. "There are matters of which we must speak."

Fontrailles stifled a groan and forced himself to sit up. Father Joseph held the keys to his freedom—and Isabeau's. "Pardon me, Monseigneur," he said thickly. "A momentary weakness of the flesh."

"And yet your greatest trials are still ahead of you," Father Joseph said. He looked exactly the same as he had that morning; in fact, he always looked exactly the same. Des Cartes, on the other hand, was wan and looked like he'd been perspiring. It seemed that while Fontrailles had been being dosed and bled on top of the Column, the scholar had been through an ordeal of his own.

"I trust you had a pleasant conversation with Monsieur des Cartes," Fontrailles said tentatively.

"Tolerably pleasant," said Father Joseph, with a twitch of the black bristles around his mouth that was almost a smile. "Your friend was not, at first, disposed to be very forthcoming about his 'rules for the direction of the mind,' but eventually I was able to discern at least the outlines of his theory. While I would not call it actively heterodox, I fear it is nonetheless completely erroneous. The idea that man can use reductive logic to prove the existence of God by first proving the existence of himself is sadly backwards."

"Begging your pardon, Monseigneur," said des Cartes, "but I would not characterize my approach in that way at all."

"No, *you* would not," Joseph said, not unkindly. "But your approach is nonetheless utterly wrong. *Hélas,* such errors are only to be expected from one trained in a Jesuit college. Those Spiritual Exercises of theirs are entirely too active, based as they are on analytic thought." The Capuchin shook his head and sighed. "They have always failed to understand that divinity cannot be understood rationally, only intuitively, through an act of will and love."

"I wouldn't say that what we did today was particularly rational," Fontrailles remarked. He gave a brief account of the day's activities atop the column.

"Frère Kircher would disagree with you," said Joseph. "He contends that his procedures are entirely rational, based on close reasoning from received wisdom and observed phenomena."

"An example of how logic goes wrong when founded on unprovable bases," said des Cartes.

"An example of how logic is the wrong tool entirely for attaining knowledge of the divine," replied Joseph calmly.

"I am confused, Monseigneur," said Fontrailles. "If you think Kircher cannot succeed, why provide him with materials and a venue? And why compel me to be subjected to them?"

"Because, Monsieur de Fontrailles, this is not about Kircher and his futile ambitions. This is about *you*." The cowl turned and Father Joseph gazed as Fontrailles, his pop-eyes lambent with inner fire. "You have shown yourself a man of wit, of courage, and of persistence. Despite the forces arrayed against you, you have repeatedly succeeded in baffling your opponents. You have even frustrated efforts personally cherished by His Eminence the Cardinal ... and myself."

"I, Monseigneur?" Louis didn't think he had any fluids left in him, but now he broke out into a sweat. *"Merdieu!* How have I offended you?"

"At La Rochelle, my son. The idea of infiltrating the city at Porte Maubec and carrying the gate by surprise was mine. My agents had reported to me the suffering of the citizens within, and I had hoped to end their pain by taking the city through a *coup de main*. But you sent Cahusac astray—yes, he told me of your involvement—and the plan failed. My influence over military affairs was thereafter greatly diminished." He shrugged. "But unlike the cardinal, I do not hold grudges. It merely increased my esteem for you ... and my hopes.

"A man like you, Monsieur, who has studied mystic orison under the Oratorians; a man mentally acute, but with the unparalleled advantage of a lifetime of physical suffering and mortification—such a man might go far indeed." Joseph closed his eyes, tilted back his head. "I confess, I have envied you your condition, Monsieur de Fontrailles—yes, I have committed that sin. And scourged myself all the more, in penance. What I must do every day with the hair shirt and the lash, to mortify my flesh and turn my thoughts to higher things, God has granted you in perpetuity with a form that is a constant reminder of the vile corruption of the physical world."

Joseph's eyes popped open and locked again onto Louis's. "But the *soul*—the *mind*—is immaculate! By turning away from the world, it can consecrate itself to our true purpose, which is the exaltation of our Creator. Each man is but a part of which Jesus is the whole. It is not enough for a man to subordinated; he must be disarticulated, disassembled, annihilated, and appropriated to Jesus—subsisting in Jesus, grafted in Jesus, living and operating in Jesus!

"I, Monsieur, was once as you were: a blithe young nobleman, the Baron de Maffliers, proud of my lineage and the unearned privileges it afforded me. I even, long ago, fell prey to the ... attractions ... of a woman." Joseph's vision turned inward for a moment, and his lips moved silently, shaping a word that might have been *Antoinette*. "But God lent me strength, and I turned from the horror of that path. I was called to worship, to do God's work in this world that has fallen under the shadow of Satan. And every day I renew my purpose through prayer and contemplation, deep contemplation of the agonies of the crucifixion, of the horrors suffered on my behalf by our Lord made flesh. Sometimes it is almost ... as if I were *there....*"

Sweat beaded Joseph's broad forehead. He passed one hand, trembling, across his brow. "So you see ... my son ... this ordeal you are about to undergo is a *gift*. As you suffer, turn your mind and heart to the Lord and reflect on what He suffered on Calvary for you. *Use* the pain to help you put aside the vain pursuits of the world and the flesh; consecrate your entire will and purpose to the service of God! And then," Father Joseph reached out and rested his hands on Fontrailles's misshapen shoulders, "come and join me, and we will do the Lord's work together."

Fontrailles placed a hand on his heart. "Monseigneur, I ... I don't know what to say." *Though I know well enough that I'd better not say what I really think.* He looked down modestly. "You do me too much honor. You seem to hold an elevated opinion of me that I assure you is undeserved."

This time Father Joseph really did smile. "Don't be too sure, my son. There is greatness in you, if you can find the will to follow the proper path."

"It's so much to think about, Father ... and I'm so tired. I must sleep. But I do have one small request to make."

"Ask."

"May I ... see Isabeau tomorrow?"

Joseph's face hardened. "She is a distraction. You know she is not for you, my son. She is a Huguenot, and is contracted to another."

"But I ... feel responsible for her, Monseigneur. It is a family thing: she is the last of her name, and the Bonnefonts and the d'Astaracs have ancient ties."

"Promise me you will think about what I have said, my son, and a brief visit might, perhaps, be arranged."

"I swear, Monseigneur, to give your words all the consideration they are due."

Beyond Joseph, des Cartes raised an ironic eyebrow. *Damn him for a smart-arse*, Louis thought. But Father Joseph nodded his agreement.

Once the guard had opened the door to let Father Joseph out, Fontrailles groaned and collapsed once more onto the bed. Des Cartes sat next to him and said, "At least now we know Father Joseph's motive in staging this piece of theater."

"In part," Fontrailles said wearily. "I doubt if he ever has fewer than three purposes behind any action."

"A point I was going to make if you did not," des Cartes replied. "Do you want to hear about my interview with him? It was not without moments of interest."

But Fontrailles was already snoring.

"*Réveillez*! Rise and greet the day!" Père Míkmaq's voice brimmed with false heartiness.

"Bowels of Christ!" snarled Fontrailles, sitting up and grabbing for Míkmaq's throat, but the priest stepped nimbly out of range, smiling sardonically. "Pardon me, Doctor Kircher," Fontrailles said, seeing the Jesuit's shocked expression. "I had been having a nightmare." He ran a hand through his hair. "What have I to look forward to today?"

"Today is the second stage of catharsis, the phase of Purgation," Kircher said. He and Míkmaq were again clad in white robes, and he handed Fontrailles another. "Here is another vestment, more suited to your stature."

"My *current* stature." Fontrailles hopped to the floor; the tiles were cold on his bare feet. "Save that taller one for when we're finished."

"Heh, heh. It's good to see that you retain your sense of humor, Monsieur de Fontrailles."

Fontrailles wriggled into the white robe. "Purgation, eh? Wasn't I purged enough yesterday? I feel like an emptied wine sack."

"Yesterday you were merely cleared of your darker physical humors. Today we begin the real work of driving out those moral effluents lodged in the deepest penetralia of mind and body."

"But first we have breakfast, no?"

"No." Kircher appeared almost amused. "After cleansing the vessel, it must not once again be soiled. Fasting will maintain the purification, and encourage a mental state of visionary ecstasy."

"Visionary ecstasy—got it. You can count on me."

They returned to the Column of Destiny. By the time they reached the top of the spiral staircase, Fontrailles was out of breath. The previous day's rites had left him physically weak, but in fact his mind did seem sharp, his senses acute. He emerged onto the platform into moving air, the sky roofed with low clouds driving ahead of a damp wind from the west. "We won't stay dry today," he said. "I assume we postpone if it rains?"

"No need for that," said Doctor Lambe, hurriedly brushing crumbs from his white robe. Clearly *he* wasn't fasting. "I've brought a length of oilcloth to cover the books in the event of rain. As detailed in the Second Legacy of *The Three Mystic Heirs*, we have synchronized our rites to the wheeling of the stars and planets, so it's critical that we stick to our timetable." He tapped a whirring, multi-faced astronomical clock that Louis hadn't noticed before.

"*Ohé!*" Fontrailles said. "That's from my collection of Salomon de Caus automata!"

"Yes," said Kircher. "The cardinal confiscated the items after you left his service, and Father Joseph had them turned over to me. They've been very useful in helping to understand the First Legacy, and we will be employing several of them in our rituals."

"I wondered what had happened to them. Another mystery solved," Fontrailles said. "*À propos* of mysteries, what are we doing today?"

"Today we purge!" Kircher announced. "We will drive out the *nox* and the *tenebrae activa* with the Quintessence of Four, the Ternary of Two, and the Tetract of One."

"With a hey-nonny-nonny, a slap and a tickle!" Fontrailles hopped through a little jig. "Very well, let's get on with it: soonest begun, soonest done."

Père Mikmaq frowned, the lines around his mouth drawing down his ruined nose. "No mockery, Monsieur. These are holy matters."

Fontrailles bowed. He was a little light-headed, perhaps from lack of food. "No mockery intended, Father. I'm just trying to keep my spirits up. You'd do the same, if the first thing you saw in the morning was *that* little joy-rig waiting for you."

He pointed: from the center of the wrought iron dome hung a contrivance of ropes, pulleys, and weights. "Ah, yes," said Kircher. "The, er, strappado. We will have recourse to that later in the day, when we begin the process of disassembly. But for now," he glanced at the whirring clock, "we really must commence our orisons. We will begin by beseeching the blessing of the angel Bnaspol."

"Who rules Wednesday, and of whom it is said 'the earth with all her secrets are delivered and through whom what thou art, there I may know'," Fontrailles recited. "You see? I studied this stuff."

"You are a scholar, Monsieur." Kircher favored him with a curt bow. "Let us begin."

The orison to Bnaspol was followed by a mind-numbing series of invocations in Latin, Greek, Hebrew, and quasi-Hebrew, culminating in a long sequence of equations using values derived through the Cabalistic method of Gematria. Next the values were re-calculated using the Arabian art of *al-Jebra* within the symbolic logic syntax of Thomas Harriot. The resulting numbers were rendered back into verbal form, creating strings of barely-pronounceable Hebraic syllables that Fontrailles had to intone solemnly while Père Mikmaq plucked out the same note, over and over, on the golden harp.

And all the while Louis's gaze kept drifting back to the waiting strappado. The word beat in his brain: *strappado; strappado; strappado.* More than once he almost inserted *strappado* into the series of syllables Kircher was reciting for him to repeat.

At last they were finished. Fontrailles was allowed to wet his lips and mouth with a little pure water, and then he was turned over to Doctor Lambe, who had been preparing his alchemical paraphernalia for the next phase. "*Very* well done, Monsieur de Fontrailles," effused Lambe. "Now we proceed to genuine spiritual alchemy from the Third Legacy of *The Three Mystic Heirs*: the concoction of a Saphiric medicine of the Sun and Moon that will infiltrate your abscesses of corruption, moral and physical, and drive out the *materia vilis,* much as pus is expressed from a festering wound."

"Charming," Fontrailles said dizzily. The mental acuity of the morning was long gone, leached out of him by Kircher's linguistic gymnastics. Now, it seemed, he had to play alchemist. The *monas*-table was cluttered with the tools of the alchemist's trade, and to Lambe's alarm Fontrailles stumbled as he approached it, nearly knocking over one of the tall angled glass beakers known as pelicans.

"Be careful, damn you!" Lambe snapped in English, then added, in milder-toned French, "Your pardon, Monsieur. I spent many years collecting this array of implements, and much of it cannot be replaced this side of Venice. You are up to continuing, I hope?"

"Oh, yes—zeal and persistence are my watchwords," Fontrailles said. "Father Joseph was telling me so just last night. Show me what to do."

"Excellent," said Doctor Lambe. "If you maintain that frame of mind, you may find this procedure quite gratifying. In the composition of our elixir we shall draw upon the grand mysteries of the astrobolisms of metals, as this potion's most active ingredient is the Mineral Liquor, or *argent vive.*"

Fontrailles stared. "Wait a moment: you want me to drink an elixir of *quicksilver?* I'm a hunchback, not a syphilitic!"

Lambe gave a patronizing chuckle. "The idea that quicksilver is solely useful as a treatment for venereal pox is a common misapprehension. Believe me, the purposes to which mercury can be put are miraculous and manifold. And in this case, its effects will be buffered by a tincture of sulphur. Mercury cannot be coagulated without sulphur, you know, for *Draco non moritur sine suo compare* ... that is, the Dragon dies not without his companion."

"Well, that goes without saying," Fontrailles remarked dryly. "By the way, I can follow the Latin, so you needn't translate it."

"Of course, of course. I got into that habit in the service of Milord Buckingham, who lacked a classical education. Which was another reason to find a different patron."

"Was Buckingham a difficult master?" Fontrailles asked, in no hurry to drink a cocktail of quicksilver.

Lambe made a gesture that might have meant *no more than most*. "The duke could be demanding, but he gave me broad scope for my experiments, and a ready supply of subjects. But over time his policies and personality grew increasingly unpopular among the ill-bred, and being his mage became a dangerous occupation. In fact, after I left him my apprentice assumed my position, and was so unwise as to allow himself to be seen abroad in the London streets. He was mistaken for me by a mob of angry Puritans, murdered and literally torn apart." He shook his head ruefully.

"The timetable," Père Míkmaq said, nodding at the astronomical clock. "I didn't pluck that cursed harp all morning so you could throw us off schedule with nostalgia."

"Quite right, quite right," said Lambe, turning back to Fontrailles. "We begin by heating this alembic containing the inert solution that will serve as the base of our miscegenation...."

And so, under Lambe's close direction, Fontrailles followed the alchemical recipe. At step twenty-six of the procedure the wind blew a band of rain across the platform, and there was a sudden panic as the doctors scrambled to cover vulnerable objects. Fontrailles took the opportunity to pause, close his eyes and turn his face up to the rain, hoping the brief shower would revive him somewhat. But when he opened his eyes he was looking at the apparatus of the strappado, and his breath suddenly caught in his throat.

When they were ready to resume the procedure, Fontrailles's hands shook so badly as he dripped a solution of clarified salt into the elixir that the Englishman was forced to help steady them with his own. Fontrailles placed the beaker on the *monas*-table and looked at his trembling hand. "How many more steps are there?" he asked.

"Not many," said Lambe. "We must skim off the dross, leaving the salubrious liquor behind, and then add a tincture of cockspur of rye."

"What's that for?"

"It's a most potent galenical herb," Lambe said, "that has, for us, two beneficial effects: it induces a sort of delirium that opens the mind to celestial influences, and stimulates spasmodic convulsions that purge deeply-ingrained effluents." He handed Fontrailles a glass tube half-full of a thick blackish fluid. "Here we are: add eight drops to the elixir. Gingerly, now."

Fontrailles slowly raised the tube to the lip of the beaker and began to tip it. As he did, the clouds parted, and the sun cast the shadow of the strappado across the *monas*-table. Fontrailles's hand trembled, glass struck glass with a sharp *clink*, and a hefty dollop of the thick black tincture plopped into the shiny elixir.

"Drops, I said!" cried Lambe in dismay. "Drops, not great globs!"

"Was that too much?" said Fontrailles.

"Shit!" said Lambe. "It was twenty drops, at least."

"Is ... is it ruined?" asked Kircher.

"Probably not. No ... no, I don't think so," said Lambe.

"Maybe we should call the whole operation off," said Père Míkmaq, to Louis's intense gratitude. "There's no point in pouring that stuff into him if it wasn't mixed right."

Fontrailles looked at Lambe hopefully, but the Englishman said, "No, I'm certain all will be well. It's the metallic liquor, after all, that is the *primum mobile*. A stronger dose of cockspur might even be a good idea. In fact, I'm sure of it."

"Hrmm," said Míkmaq.

"We must defer to Doctor Lambe's years of experience in this area, Père Crozat," said Kircher. "What remains to be done, Doctor?"

"I will complete the operation myself, if no one minds," Lambe said. "All I need do is stir the elixir with this glass rod, then decant it into the Solar Goblet. Do you have it, Doctor?"

"Right here, Doctor." Kircher handed Lambe a cut-glass goblet chased with gold filigree depicting Sol in glowing magnificence. Lambe poured the nacreous elixir from beaker into goblet, and then offered it to Fontrailles. "Drink it all, quickly," he said, "then repeat after me: *Filius Solis, filia Lunæ.*"

Fontrailles did as he was told. The elixir slipped down his throat like a silver snake and coiled in his stomach. It tasted like coins he had bitten to test their validity. He spoke the Latin phrases, then suddenly felt an overpowering urge to vomit.

"Keep it down! Keep it down!" cried Lambe, clapping a hand over his mouth and nose. The English mage was a large, powerful man, and in Fontrailles's weakened state he was like a child in his hands. He felt his insides ripple as his body tried to eject the elixir, but his mouth and nose were stopped and it had nowhere to go.

The eruption subsided; Louis felt utterly limp. Doctor Lambe cautiously uncovered his mouth and nose to allow him to breathe. "Uh," Fontrailles said. "Gloig." He looked up at the trio of tall white-robed men, and they seemed to elongate, growing taller still. He blinked. "All right, that's done," he said weakly. "Now what?"

As if I didn't know.

Suddenly the Column of Destiny began to sway like an inverted pendulum. Alarmed, all Louis could do was fall to his hands and knees, wedge his fingers into the gaps between the flagstones and try to hold on, hoping the column wouldn't topple into the streets of Paris, like a tower of blocks flung down by a malicious child. But his fingers couldn't keep their grip because, to his horror, they were growing, extruding monstrously, changing into headless silver snakes that extended from his stomach down his arms and out his hands and writhed and slithered....

He screamed.

He knew they were picking him up, stripping off his robe, and tying him into the loops of the strappado. He knew he was under the wrought iron dome atop the Column of Destiny, but at the same time he was strapped into a saddle atop the neck of a great marble snake that swayed high in the air. He looked down and saw Paris, but he also saw the City of Dis from the Inferno of Dante, and it teemed with dancing devils and the tormented damned.

They pulled his hands behind him and tied them together, then they lifted them up behind his misshapen back until they were above his head and he was hanging from them, arms rotated backward. He screamed again. The marble snake turned its head and looked at him with its heavy-lidded vertical-slitted yellow eyes and flicked out its silvery double tongue. He screamed—and they hung the first of the weights from his feet.

He stretched, and screamed. The snake struck, sinking its fangs into his stomach, pumping him full of silver venom. He felt his right shoulder go, the collarbone that had broken the year before snapping like a glass rod, like a beaker dropped on the floor and spilling silvery slime that slithers off into the gaps between the flagstones....

They added another weight. He stretched. There were two loud pops right in his ears as his shoulders dislocated, and his body lengthened again. He screamed, and a cloud of silver moths spewed from his mouth, fluttered, flew, and settled all over his face, flapping in his nose, his mouth, his eyes and ears. "Visualize divinity, Monsieur de Fontrailles!" a voice called. "Visualize divinity!"

Twisted ropes of silver venom emerged from his stomach and laced themselves across his whole body in a web. Then they jerked taut, and the convulsions began. His body curled spasmodically forward, he *lifted* the weights attached to his feet, and then his body curled backward and the weights swung out behind him like a pendulum. There were more popping sounds, and he screamed through the moths.

And.

They.
Added.
Another.
Weight.

CHAPTER LIV
THE THIRD DAY OF CATHARSIS

I must be dead, Louis thought. *I couldn't have survived what I remember going through.* But the more he thought about it, the more confused his memories became. Some of them rang true, but some were horrific visions, and most were some mixture of the two.

He seemed to be lying on his back, on something soft. *Probably an upholstered coffin.* But not soft enough: even lying still, everything hurt: arms, shoulders, neck, hips, knees, ankles. It hurt simply to breathe. With every heartbeat even his pulse inflamed the agony in his joints.

However, pain and Louis d'Astarac were old acquaintances. Ever since his father had locked him in his corrective iron corselet at age eight, he'd known how to objectify pain. He began to do that now, settling himself, concentrating to take the agony and distance himself from it, until the pain stood apart from him, an object in his mind's eye that he could turn round and round as if it were a curious stone, or a songbird's egg.

He heard something like a muffled sob. A drop struck his face and broke his concentration. He gasped and opened his eyes.

Isabeau. Weeping.

"Ah," he croaked. His throat was raw—from the elixir? Or from screaming?

"Louis," Isabeau gasped. He was in the queen's big bed; there were candles behind Isabeau; her face was in shadow. Another drop struck his cheek. "Louis," she said, "it's Isabeau."

Time to talk. He steeled himself for the pain. "Good—that settles it," he rasped.

"Wh-what?"

"Whether I've gone to heaven or hell." He tried to turn his head toward her and his eyes widened at the pain—from his neck, and worse, his shattered right shoulder.

"Oh, Louis," she sobbed. "What have they done to you?"

"On the whole ... I think I'd rather avoid that subject." He swallowed; he had a taste in his mouth like blood and metal. "How are you?"

"I'm all right." Her hands fluttered. "But there's nothing for me to do, nothing but pray for you and ... and worry. It's worse even than La Rochelle! At least there I could help Éric."

"You can help me, too, Isabeau," he said.

"How?" she said. "Tell me how!"

"First, you must stop worrying about me." For reply, she merely sobbed. "Second, tell me: have they allowed Vidou to wait on you?"

Isabeau wiped her eyes. "Yes. I also have a *grisette*."

"She'll be a spy," Fontrailles said.

"Louis," said Isabeau. She nodded her head slightly—over her shoulder.

"Joseph?"

She nodded again.

"Lean closer, so I can whisper," he said. "If Joseph asks what I was saying to you, tell him it was words of ... affection." He paused; he wished he could see her expression, but it was in shadow. "Does Vidou consort with the other servants?"

"Yes," she whispered back, "though he can't leave the *hôtel*."

"But the other servants can?"

"I believe so. They buy food, and other things."

"*Bien*. Now," he continued, "here's what I want you to tell Vidou...."

After Father Joseph had escorted Isabeau to the door, the monk returned to the bed and bent over Fontrailles, his hands buried in his sleeves. Des Cartes hovered somewhere behind him. Joseph looked at Fontrailles with hungry eyes and said, "Do you … suffer, my son?"

The only replies that came to Louis were acid, so he curbed them and only nodded, which made him gasp and swallow. Father Joseph nodded in return. "It is as I thought it would be. I granted your request for a visit from the woman. Was it agreeable to you?"

Louis wanted to spit at him, but instead he closed his eyes for a moment to set aside his anger. When he had hold of himself, he opened them again. "Monseigneur," he said, "she cannot understand."

"No," whispered Joseph. "Few women can. You are on a path she cannot follow."

The dark door at the back of the room opened, and with a bustle Doctor Kircher and Père Míkmaq entered the royal bedchamber, the priest pushing a wooden chair mounted on large, squeaking wheels. "God watch over you, Father Joseph," Kircher said. He glanced at Fontrailles, and then averted his eyes. "How is our initiate this morning?" he continued, with palpably false cheeriness.

"You have spared him no pains on his path to enlightenment," Joseph said, an edge in his whisper. "But he lives."

"*Sehr gut,*" Kircher said. He turned to Louis, tried an embarrassed smile, and then gave it up. "Tell me, Monsieur: can you move?"

Fontrailles twitched his limbs a little, gasped, and made a face. "No."

Père Míkmaq, who looked as if he disapproved of the entire world and all its history, drew a vial from a pocket somewhere inside his white robe and thrust it toward Fontrailles. "Drink this," he said.

"Dare I ask what's in it?"

"Lambe said it was an abated tincture of poppy." Míkmaq shrugged. "He said you should drink it, and after a few minutes it will mitigate the pain of moving you."

"Once we get you up to the platform," Kircher said, "today's rites will not be so hard on you."

"Less torture, more witchcraft?" Fontrailles said.

"Please, Monsieur de Fontrailles! Put such bitter feelings aside; they could compromise your exaltation and reformation! And you know perfectly well," Kircher added in a minatory tone, "that our undertaking is a blessed pursuit that can in no way be categorized as witchcraft. No member of the Society of Jesus would condone such prohibited activities."

"Certainly not," said Father Joseph, with what Louis could have sworn was a touch of irony, "especially since it was a Jesuit, your Martin Del Rio, who gave us the definitive denunciation of witchcraft in his *Disquisitionum Magicarum*."

"And a Capuchin, Hannibal Rosseli," Kircher sniffed, "whose six-volume exegesis on the *Corpus Hermetica* expounds the ancient wisdom upon which our procedures are based, and endorses it as holy revelation."

"I've read Rosseli too," Père Míkmaq said. "He warns sternly against the use of Black Arts."

"Quite so, Père Crozat," Joseph said. "The Capuchin Order is rightly known for its abhorrence of heresy."

"Oh, yes," sneered Míkmaq. "That's why Bernardino Ochino, Vicar of the Jesuits, turned Calvinist in 1543 and fled to England to escape the Inquisition."

"Please, Messieurs!" Fontrailles wheezed. "This is most unseemly! Doctor Kircher, I apologize for my derisive comment about witchcraft. I spoke from my flesh rather than my mind."

"Accepted, Monsieur," Kircher said, with a little formal bow. "Now as to today's agenda...."

"As to that," interrupted Fontrailles, "on the whole, I would rather not know beforehand what we will be about. It, um, interferes with my concentrating on exaltation."

"Very well," said Kircher. "By now the tincture should have taken effect. Shall we go?"

Tincture or no, Fontrailles nearly fainted when Kircher and Míkmaq lifted him from the bed and placed him in the wheeled chair. His dislocated limbs flopped at random like the arms and legs of a broken marionette, and every motion felt like a knife in his flesh. He cried out several times despite his resolve to control himself, and by the time they got him strapped in place he was bathed in sweat. "Water," he said.

Kircher nodded. "Very well; a little."

"Here," said des Cartes, emerging from the background with a cup of water—more, probably, than the doctor would have allowed him, but at a glare from Père Míkmaq the German made no objection.

Louis felt every bump in the floor as they wheeled him to the Column. "How are you going to get me up the stairs?" he asked Père Míkmaq. "Are you going to carry me on your back?"

Míkmaq snorted. "No. We have a better idea. You'll see."

There were a half dozen people waiting in the Column's pedestal chamber, a squad of men-at-arms under the command of Bernajoux, gathered at the foot of several long ropes dangling from a pulley fixed in the tower ceiling high above. Louis saw that one of the ropes ended in an iron hook and began to tremble. They were going to strappado him again, this time all the way to the top of the tower!

Míkmaq gave a grim chuckle. "No stretching today, Monsieur de Fontrailles; these soldiers are going to hoist to the top, chair and all."

"Oh," Fontrailles said. "Oh. Yes, I see that. Of course." He swallowed. "Should be fun."

"All right, hook that chair on," commanded Bernajoux. "Now haul, you worms—and don't let him drop, or you'll have to clean up the mess."

Fontrailles was strapped into place, so he had no fear of falling out, but as the *gens d'armes* heaved on the rope the chair spun and swung alarmingly. Louis screwed his eyes shut and tried not to remember the time he and Éric had dropped a melon from the top of Château de Fontrailles to watch it burst on the garden steps far below. How they'd laughed! Louis wanted to vomit.

Doctor Lambe was waiting at the top of the steps. "Here comes our initiate, lofted toward the sun like Icarus!" he said cheerily. Louis thought savagely about dropping Lambe from the top of a château: it helped, a bit.

Lambe was joined by Kircher and Mikmaq, who had hustled up the spiral stairs, and together the three managed to swing the wheeled chair onto the landing and bump it up through the trap door onto the platform. Outside, the morning was sunny, cooler and less humid than the day before, and despite the effluvia of abattoirs, open sewers, and countless chimneys, the air over Paris was almost fresh.

Fontrailles was removed from his chair and laid on the *monas*-table, naked under a white sheet, his limbs arranged over the painted designs with excruciating care. By the time they were finished Fontrailles was shaking and bathed in sweat. He asked for another dose of the tincture of poppy, but Lambe refused. "It might put you to sleep, and we need you awake so you can participate in the rituals," he said.

"I won't be much good to you if I pass out from pain," Fontrailles replied.

"You'll wake up again if I swivel one of your joints," Lambe said blithely.

"We begin," Kircher announced from behind the bookstand, "with a prayer to the angel Bynepor, who rules Thursday, and upon whose exalted power resteth and dependeth the general state and condition of all things. When he comes thou art magnified by his coming, and are sanctified, world without end."

"Amen," said Lambe and Mikmaq, joined a little late by Fontrailles, whose mind was wandering. Perhaps it was the poppy, perhaps the pain of his mistreated body, but he had a hard time following the subsequent rites, which involved more computations and repetition of nonsense-syllables, then a prolonged orison to the angel Michael, whom Kircher in an aside said was identified as the Sol-angel in the *Steganographia* of the Abbot of Sponheim. "Sponheim," Louis repeated, a name that suddenly seemed indescribably funny. "Sponheim, Sponheim, Sponheim!"

"Monsieur!" Kircher said sharply. "Get hold of yourself! You must retain your focus."

Lambe gave Louis's right wrist a twenty-degree twist, and suddenly nothing seemed funny at all. "God damn your soul," he hissed, at which

Lambe merely raised an eyebrow.

"Positive thoughts, Monsieur de Fontrailles," said Kircher. "We are going to sing the Ogdoadic Song of Gratitude while Père Crozat plucks out today's harmonic note on the golden harp. The refrain goes—no, *fa*, Père Crozat, *fa*; *mi* was yesterday—the refrain goes as follows...."

Fontrailles followed Kircher's lead, moaning his way through the song, while Lambe assembled his alchemical kitchen on a nearby trestle table. Louis watched apprehensively out of the corner of his eye as the Englishman, whistling tunelessly, set out his vials, beakers, pelicans and alembics, mortars and mixing bowls and many-colored bottles. From a hinged wooden box he drew forth a long, twisted object that Louis recognized. "*Ohé!*" he burst out. "That's Breedlove's leg! Where did you get that?"

"Hmm?" said Lambe distractedly. "Oh, the unicorn's horn! That's right—that old sailor-man who brought it to me *had* been attached to you, hadn't he? I'd forgotten that."

"He was attached to his leg, too!"

"And quite a fuss he made about giving it up! But such a treasure couldn't be left where it was, of course. Act of Providence, really, that brought it to my attention." Lambe smiled at the memory as he gazed reverently at the horn.

"The song, Monsieur—the Ogdoadic Song!" Kircher said impatiently.

"Just a moment," Fontrailles said. "I want to know what he's planning to do with Breedlove's leg."

"I'm going to abrade some powder from it for enrichment of today's elixir," Lambe said proudly. "Wonderful stuff, unicorn's horn—so very many uses."

An acerbic remark sprang to Louis's lips. He suppressed it, but it was getting harder every time.

By the time they finished the Song of Gratitude the alchemist was ready; Lambe declared that today he would concoct an Elixir of Copper, enhanced by powdered unicorn's horn and a potation of Virgin's Milk. Louis swallowed a sarcastic query about this only by a supreme act of will. He

195

tried to pay attention, mainly because he wanted to make sure no cockspur of rye was involved this time, but as Doctor Lambe ground, heated, poured, and mixed, Louis's mind kept wandering toward what was coming next. So far, today's rites had been all too easy.

Père Míkmaq was setting a dozen or so fat, white candles into place on the *monas*-table around Fontrailles, lighting them, and then re-lighting them as they were blown out time and again by the freshening breeze. He muttered un-churchly curses under his breath as he plied his flint and steel. "What's coming next, Father?" Fontrailles asked, during a pause while Lambe was boiling the Virgin's Milk.

"Thought you didn't want to know," the Jesuit said. "Probably a wise policy. But if you can't stand the suspense, look at what Doctor Kircher is preparing for you."

Fontrailles turned toward the bookstand, where Kircher was fumbling in a satin-lined box with something shiny.

Needles: gleaming metallic needles, thick and nearly a foot long. A lot of them.

Louis suddenly felt dizzy. He laid his head back and closed his eyes.

"Focus, Monsieur, focus!" Lambe called. "Our elixir is almost complete! Now watch this: we stir in the precipitate, and *voilà*, as you say here: enhanced Elixir of Copper!" Doctor Lambe held up a beaker of a ruddy liquid. "It will open you to celestial influences, and facilitate your connection with the Third Domain through the *acus electron*. That's the...."

"I know," Fontrailles said. "The electrum needles."

"Ah," said Lambe. "Exactly." He poured the elixir into a pewter goblet and handed it to Míkmaq. "If you would be so kind as to administer this to the initiate, Father...?"

"Of course," Père Míkmaq said, taking the goblet from Doctor Lambe and returning to Fontrailles's side. Then he did something very curious: he glanced at Lambe and Kircher, both of whom were engaged with their equipment, looked at Fontrailles, and touched a finger to his lips to enjoin silence. Then he drew the tincture of poppy from within his robe and added a dose to the elixir—a large dose. He returned the vial to his pocket, held the goblet to Fontrailles's lips, and said, "Slowly ... but drink it all—you must be open to the celestial influences."

Fontrailles obeyed, though the hot liquid burned his throat, all the while gazing into Père Míkmaq's narrow, scarred face. What was brewing behind those angry eyes?

"Excellent, excellent," said Kircher. "I've prepared the electrum needles—you'll note, Doctor Lambe, that I have affixed an amber bead to the butt of each one, the better to concentrate the reception of the astral flow and conduct it into the shaft. I think, if you are ready, we may immediately commence inserting them into the initiate's joints."

"Not just yet, if you please," said Père Míkmaq. "I believe it would be best for me to first lead the initiate in a few prayers for a successful outcome of our blessed endeavors. There are some appropriate ones here in Canisius...."

Kircher spluttered in mild protest, but Míkmaq held up a firm hand, and as he began to page through his prayer book Louis realized that the Jesuit was stalling to give the poppy a chance to work on him. So he did his best to follow Père Míkmaq's prayers, and the Jesuit kept him at it until Fontrailles began slurring the Latin and the white-robed forms around him began to blur. Then Míkmaq thumped his book shut and nodded to Kircher, who picked up the first of the needles.

He started with the left ankle. Abruptly what had become a warm poppy dream for Louis became a nightmare, and he found that he still had the strength to scream. As Lambe held him down, Kircher pushed the needles deep into his joints, tapping them in with a mallet when they encountered resistance.

It seemed to take hours. Eventually Louis, flopping like a fish, was studded with shining amber-headed needles like an animate pincushion. Then, in a shaky voice, Kircher invoked the Sephiroth and the agency of the Empyrean, summoning the dynamic celestial forces to flow down to the inner world and concentrate in Fontrailles's disjointed skeleton, preparing it for reformation in sympathy with the ideal. And all the while Louis twitched, and moaned, and howled whenever one of the long needles was touched.

Finally, one by one, Kircher drew the needles out. At first the shaft fixed in Louis's left elbow wouldn't come; Lambe joked that if they couldn't pull it out, they might have to push it through. No one laughed. Using pincers to hold the needle, Kircher and Lambe together were finally able to work it out of the joint by rocking it back and forth, though the soft electrum bent almost double in the act. With the final yank that freed the needle, Louis screamed his last scream and passed out.

Whatever the rest of the day's rituals were, Louis missed them. When he returned to his senses he was strapped once more in the wheeled chair, and Père Míkmaq was pushing him down the corridor that led from the Column to his bedchamber.

"Come around at last, have you?" the Jesuit said.

"It seems so," Fontrailles said thickly. "I want to thank you."

"For what? Assisting at your torment?" Père Míkmaq stopped and turned the chair around, pulled back one of Louis's eyelids and looked thoughtfully into his eye.

"For giving me the poppy," Fontrailles said. "Otherwise, the needles—I'd have gone mad."

"Then you could be like the rest of us." Míkmaq squatted back on his haunches and regarded him.

Louis collected his thoughts. "You know, Father," he said, "why Father Joseph has enabled this, don't you?"

Míkmaq narrowed his eyes. "Of course I do." He paused, and then said, "Why?"

"Because he hopes to implicate Jesuits in acts of witchcraft so he can denounce them to the Vatican," Fontrailles said. "The Society of Jesus has too much influence for him, in both Rome and Paris, and he would like to see you disgraced."

"Hmmp," Míkmaq said. "I'll see that doesn't happen."

"I know that's supposed to be your rôle," Fontrailles said. "You're more than Kircher's assistant—you report to the General of your Order in Rome, don't you? You're assigned to make sure Kircher doesn't stray too far from orthodoxy."

Míkmaq shrugged. "And I will."

"But that's not how it's going to look," Fontrailles said, with effort. He felt a wave of unconsciousness rising to engulf him, but he had to keep talking. "It's Lambe. Don't you see? He's an English heretic, Buckingham's personal sorcerer, in France entirely on the sufferance of the State—which means he's beholden to Father Joseph, and the cardinal. Lambe will testify to anything they tell him to, say whatever they want him to say, or he'll disappear into the Bastille and never be seen again. You and Kircher are already as good as tied to the stake."

Míkmaq gazed at him coldly for a moment, then said, "Why should I believe you? You're in the same situation as Lambe—or worse. And it was your man who did *this*." He touched his ruined nose.

Fontrailles was ready for that one. "My man? You think Cocodril was my man? He's Joseph's man, and always has been. He played the same part you do with Kircher: keeping an eye on me for my superiors. When I went out of circulation for a while, he was assigned to the same rôle with Milady de Winter. You knew he'd been attached to her, didn't you?"

"Yes …" Père Míkmaq said slowly. "But I saw Cocodril leave with your friend Longvilliers when we trapped you on the bridge at Tours."

"That's right—and Father Joseph let him pass, didn't he? He's Joseph's man, not mine. I don't have my men slice off people's noses."

"Then it was Joseph…." Míkmaq touched his nose again. His face was flushed; the scar made by Cocodril's knife was livid. "Bah!" he burst out. "Poppy dreams."

And Jean-Marie Crozat, known as Père Míkmaq, would say nothing more.

CHAPTER LV
THE FOURTH DAY OF CATHARSIS

The next morning Fontrailles had a high fever and was drifting in and out of delirium. Des Cartes, awakened by his ravings, pounded on the door until the guards brought Lambe and Kircher. The doctors agreed that the fever was an excellent sign, an indication that the energies of the Holy Spirit, received through the electrum needles, were circulating within Monsieur de Fontrailles's *corpus*. But des Cartes insisted they do something to help his suffering friend, and Lambe and Kircher finally decided to administer a soothing infusion of herbs and honey.

Louis's later memories of the next phase of the Catharsis were distorted and fragmentary. He was brought once more to the platform atop the Column of Destiny, though he couldn't remember how. Kircher announced that this would be the phase of Illumination, which would culminate in the final stage of corporeal disassembly. There were more elaborate invocations, followed by some sort of sympathetic magic ritual involving his collection of clockwork automata, all wound up and activated at once: tiny lion roaring, miniature fountain bubbling, wind-organ moaning.

Louis was only intermittently aware of what was happening, but it seemed to him that the accord between his three tormentors was fraying, and there were frequent disagreements.

When the sun reached its zenith Fontrailles was bound to the *monas-table*, which had been converted to a rack, using a system of ropes, ratchets, and pulleys, with weights suspended over the side of the tower. Then, slowly, they racked him. He was delirious through most of this, and passed out when the strain on his spine became too much to bear.

When he came to he was back in his bed, and the fever was gone—which was unfortunate, because it meant that he could feel the full effects of what had been done to him. He tried to begin his mental routine of distancing himself from the pain, but with agony lancing from so many parts of his body it was extremely difficult.

Eventually des Cartes noticed he was awake and asked if there was anything he could do to help. "There is," Fontrailles replied. "I've been trying ... a trick of meditation to mitigate the pain, but it's not ... working particularly well. Distract me. Talk to me."

Des Cartes sat next to Fontrailles and looked down at him, concern shadowing his dark, deep-set eyes. "Very well," he said. "Let me see ... I had an interesting conversation with Doctor Kircher after he brought you back from today's ... operations. The man has a wide-ranging and original mind; he seems fascinated by everything, and is quick to see connections between different branches of knowledge where none have been seen before. But I fear he allows enthusiasm to get the better of his critical faculties."

Louis tried to concentrate on what des Cartes was saying. "How do you mean?"

"From what he told me, I believe that as a youth he started with some of the same questions about generally accepted philosophy that I had, questions that led both of us to investigate Rosicrucian thought and principles. But whereas I concluded that Rosicrucian syncretism was too broad and based on unproven, and unprovable, foundations, Kircher found in it the synthesis of science and theology for which he'd been searching. The Hermetic tradition has become the basis of his entire approach to thought—and now everything he learns serves only to confirm his cherished beliefs. All contradictions are blithely ignored. It is," des Cartes said ruefully, "a way of thinking all too common to scholars of every discipline."

"Give me ... an example of where he's gone astray."

"Our conversation this evening provides a perfect illustration. Who is the primal authority of the tradition upon which all Rosicrucian wisdom is based?"

"Hermes Trismegistus," Fontrailles said, focusing his eyes on des Cartes's. "The ancient Egyptian prophet, whose revelations pre-date Moses."

"Exactly. Now, do you know the work of Isaac Casaubon?"

"Casaubon?" A stabbing pain from his right elbow made Louis gasp. "The ... name is familiar. Wait. Classicist, wasn't he? At Cambridge?"

Des Cartes nodded. "That's the man. His *De Rebus Sacris,* published over a decade ago, includes a textual analysis of the original Greek *Corpus Hermeticum,* the manuscript upon which the entire reputation of Hermes Trismegistus as an ancient prophet is based. And Casaubon proves, conclusively, that the *Corpus* could not have been written before the Fourth Century A.D. ... after Christ, and over a thousand years after Moses."

"Heh. Do you say so? Well ... well, well. Didn't know that."

"The *Rebus Sacris* has not been widely read outside England. But Kircher has read it. I know, because I asked him."

"And what did Kircher have to say about this ... conclusive dating of the *Corpus?*"

Des Cartes waved as if shooing a fly. "He dismissed it out of hand. It was too contrary to his beliefs for him to accept it. He said that if Augustine, Reuchlin, Sponheim, and Candale all accepted that the *Corpus Hermeticum* was of ancient provenance, then that was enough for him."

"I see your point, then. What else did you talk about?"

"Not much. Father Joseph came in to observe your condition, and Kircher suddenly remembered that he had business elsewhere. Are you sure there's nothing else I can do for you?"

"Just talk. Have you heard anything ... about Isabeau?"

Des Cartes looked uncomfortable. "Mademoiselle de Bonnefont? No. I should have asked Father Joseph about her, but I did not—it didn't occur to me. I apologize."

"I ... understand, Monsieur des Cartes." Louis made what he hoped was a smile. "You have other things on your mind, I'm sure. Such as why they are continuing to hold you."

"Indeed." The scholar nodded. "I am confounded by an acute lack of information. If I only knew why Father Joseph...."

He was interrupted by the sound of the bolt being slid back on the inner door. It opened to admit Père Míkmaq, garbed not in white linen but in the severe black robe of a Jesuit priest. Ignoring des Cartes, he strode directly to the side of Catherine de Médicis's massive bed and glared down at Louis. "Monsieur de Fontrailles," he said. "I am glad to see you have regained your wits, for I have something to say to you. When you spoke to me last night, you told me things that ... that...." He raised his chin and glared down his ruined nose. "Things that I cannot believe! I will not accept them. In short, Monsieur, I believe you are a liar. You can look for no further goodwill from me."

With that, Père Míkmaq turned on his heel and marched from the room.

"*Pardieu*," said des Cartes. Then, in a whisper: "I don't know what you were up to with him, but it seems to have failed."

"Ah," said Fontrailles. "Is that what you think?"

CHAPTER LVI
THE FIFTH DAY OF CATHARSIS

Fontrailles was weak and weary when he awoke on Saturday morning—the fifth, and last, day of his Catharsis. Though des Cartes had been warned not to feed the initiate, he thinned some of his porridge with water and fed it to Fontrailles in slow spoonfuls. It seemed to help: afterward Louis, though physically drained, felt more alert than he had in days.

He was also more alert to the pain; even swallowing the thin gruel was an ordeal. But his breakfast was cut short when Kircher and Lambe entered abruptly from the inner door. "Monsieur des Cartes!" Kircher cried, raising his hands from the handles of the wheeled chair in horror. "Are you trying to ruin all our careful work?"

Des Cartes was defiant. "I confess to having no great opinion of your 'careful work.' Monsieur de Fontrailles needed sustenance. I fed him."

"And I have no great opinion of your prospects if the operation fails because of your meddling!" Doctor Lambe growled, looming over the smaller des Cartes. "Perhaps *you* will be our next subject!"

"No threats, if you please, Doctor Lambe," said Kircher. "I will not countenance threats."

"Indeed?" said Lambe. But he said no more, and he and Kircher commenced the excruciating task of transferring Fontrailles from the bed to the wheeled chair.

By the time they reached the chamber at the base of the great column Kircher's good humor was somewhat restored. *"Regardez,* Monsieur de Fontrailles! I have improved the chair-lift by adding another pulley and some counterweights, increasing its ratio of mechanical advantage. Now a single man can raise you unaided to the top of the tower!"

"Well, well. A mechanist, too," Fontrailles said, sweating from the agony of movement. "Salomon de Caus would be proud."

"Do you think so?" asked Kircher, entirely missing the irony. "Doctor Lambe, you're by far the strongest of us. Would you mind...?"

"Why don't you add another pulley?" Lambe said. "Oh, very well, very well."

As Lambe hauled on the rope, Kircher paced Fontrailles's ascent by circling him on the spiral stairs as the chair slowly rose. "It is a grand day, Monsieur de Fontrailles," he said, "the Day of Union! We shall commence with prayers unto luminous Bnapsen, who casteth out the power of all wicked spirits. Then we will open the celestial portals to capture and focus the flow of harmonious energies. You will feel your body almost *glowing* with astral radiance!"

Fontrailles clamped his eyes shut as the chair suddenly spun in a full circle. "I look forward to it eagerly. Are we there yet?"

"We are!" Kircher said. "Tie it off, Doctor Lambe—I've got him!"

A minute later Lambe, blowing out his cheeks, joined them on the landing, and the two doctors began working the chair up through the trap door and onto the platform. "This would be a lot easier with your Père Míkmaq helping us," Lambe complained. "Where the devil is he, anyway?"

"I'm certain he'll be here any minute," Kircher said, sounding not at all certain.

"He was up till all hours last night, praying aloud," said Lambe. "I could hear him."

"Oh?" Kircher sniffed. "Is that why you stayed up drinking your own potions and reading proscribed literature?"

"You know perfectly well the *Clavis Salomonis* is not on the Index of forbidden works."

"Only because it circulates in manuscript and has never been formally published!"

By this time they were outside and atop the Column. Low, dark clouds filled the sky from horizon to horizon, and the stone floor of the platform glistened with recent rain. Lambe said, "My esteemed colleague: if we are going to complete our grand operation, we had better leave off bickering. And it might be best if you went to find your associate—we will need him."

"No need," said Pére Míkmaq, ascending through the trap door. "I am here."

For a fact, Louis thought, the priest did look as if he hadn't slept. His robe was badly wrinkled, soiled and frayed at the knees, and there was a haunted look behind his eyes. Kircher welcomed him as if nothing was wrong, but Louis could tell the German was worried.

Lambe began to loosen the straps on the wheeled chair. "Before we begin," Fontrailles said, with as much authority as he could muster, "let me tell you what I require."

Lambe stood back. "What you *require?*"

"That's right—so that I will cooperate whole-heartedly with your rituals, which I believe is what you need. Is it not?" He looked at the three white-robed men; after a moment, Kircher nodded. "Very well," Fontrailles continued. "I am in … considerable pain, Messieurs. I will need regular administration of that tincture of poppy—though not enough to make me bleary, if I'm going to attend to the rites. Second, and most important, I want your binding oaths, on the Bible, that regardless of the outcome of today's procedure you will work to secure the liberty of Mademoiselle de Bonnefont."

"Ha!" sneered Lambe. "You must think you're…."

"Be silent, Doctor," said Míkmaq. "We will do as he says. It is no more than we have already agreed to."

"Quite so, quite so," Kircher said hurriedly. "Come, gentlemen, let's be about it! Doctor Lambe, do you have that tincture for Monsieur de

Fontrailles?"

The three men swore their oaths, and then Kircher and Fontrailles began another lengthy series of prayers and invocations. Père Míkmaq gazed on with dull eyes, plucking out the same note over and over on the golden harp. Lambe set up his alchemical apparatus and commenced a long, complex procedure, involving distillations, desiccations, precipitations, and dissolutions.

The morning wore on; the clouds darkened and rolled, but the rain remained only a threat. As Fontrailles was completing his repetition of an inverted series of summoning syllables, he saw Lambe set out some equipment he hadn't seen before: hollow tubes, pointed at one end, made of what looked like silver. "Ethamz, ozol, ialpor, aldon," Fontrailles said. "What are those for?"

"Well done, Monsieur," Kircher said. "Those tubes? Ah, well you may ask! Those are for use in the final act of our Catharsis, an operation drawn directly from the Third Legacy of *The Three Mystic Heirs*! In order to ensure your internal system is pervaded with the humors that will enable your grand reformation, we shall undertake an alchemical transfusion of your blood!"

"I beg your pardon?"

"It's just as he says, Monsieur," Lambe said, warming an alembic over a spirit lamp. "The base of the *philtrum transfusorium* is this Elixir of Iron I've been preparing, a concoction that rubifies and constringes the flesh and knits together bone. It will be combined with a solution of your own blood, drawn from you on previous days, augmented—and this, in my opinion, is the single most brilliant contribution from *The Three Mystic Heirs*—augmented by the active ichor of umbilicus, which will receive the effulgent ideal of the Empyrean and infuse it throughout your skeleton. Your bones and joints, in short, will be born anew, re-knit into the forms they should have taken at birth! It will be a conclusive vindication of the theories of the great Rosicrucian Andre Libavius."

"Wha...." Louis's thoughts were confused—he was almost sorry he'd asked for the poppy. He seized upon the only part of Lambe's speech he could understand. "Libavius, a Rosicrucian? But he wrote a tract attacking the Brotherhood! I used to have a copy of it."

"Oh, that was mere protective coloration," said Kircher. "Libavius didn't want to be identified as a Rosicrucian any more than your friend des Cartes. But there's no doubt about it: Libavius had his laboratory laid out in the shape of a monad, the very symbol you're lying on now! And he was known to be a friend of Johannes Andraeaus, author of *The Three Mystic Heirs*. Why, the material on transfusion in the Third Legacy is a virtual paraphrase of Libavius's own *Chirurgia Transfusoria*, albeit couched in more allegorical language."

Fontrailles glanced at Père Míkmaq, who seemed even more perplexed than he was. He said, "I don't know ... swallowing draughts and tinctures seems acceptable—that's taking medicine the way God intended. But to sully my very blood through direct pollution? How can that be permissible?"

Père Míkmaq stood up from the golden harp and came to the center of the platform. "You will do it," he said. "You have agreed." He paused, and then continued, "But I will pray."

"Thank you, Père Crozat," Kircher said. "If you will pray to the side there, Doctor Lambe and I will complete our preparations."

Louis began to feel desperate. "But, Herr Doctor! This sounds extremely risky! Aren't you concerned that this, this *transfusion* might kill me before the Catharsis could be completed?"

"Not really," Kircher said. "The description in the book is very encouraging. The greatest danger is probably *mors osculi*, the mortal kiss of heaven—the possibility that the ecstasy of your reformation will be so intense that your soul will actually leave its body and be assumed directly into the Empyrean." He smiled. "In that case, of course, the Catharsis will have been successful."

"I'll be dead."

"But your soul will be among the angels!"

Louis couldn't think of anything to say to that, so he laid back and watched with anxiety verging on panic as Lambe and Kircher continued their preparations. They completed the miscegenation of the elixir with a pelican full of Louis's own blood, and Lambe began assembling the silver tubes that would convey the mixture into Louis's bloodstream.

And then, Louis knew, he would die.

Kircher approached Louis where he lay helpless on the table and asked, "Louis d'Astarac, Vicomte de Fontrailles, do you readily and of your own free will accept the holy gift of Catharsis?"

"I ... I...."

Père Míkmaq, still holding his book and praying loudly, joined Kircher and looked down at Fontrailles. Kircher said, "Do you commit yourself, body and soul, to the will of God?" He pulled back the sheet to expose Louis's arm, tapped the vein on the inside of his elbow. "Do you open your heart and mind to the influx of the Holy Spirit?"

"Answer!" growled Père Míkmaq.

Fontrailles looked around wildly, and his eyes lighted on Lambe: the alchemist was drawing a small glass bottle from his sleeve.

"Is ... is the transfusion elixir c-complete?" Fontrailles sputtered.

"It is," said Kircher.

"Then what's Lambe adding to it? *What does he have in his hand?*"

Kircher and Míkmaq both pivoted to look at Lambe. The alchemist smiled, but held his right hand behind his back. "He's raving," Lambe said. "We gave him too much poppy."

"You're holding something behind you," Père Míkmaq said. "What is it?"

"Nothing, really," Lambe said. "Just a little tincture I thought we might use. But I wasn't going to. Use it."

"You said the transfusion elixir was complete," Kircher said.

Père Míkmaq put down his prayer book "Whatever is in your hand," he said, "give it to Herr Kircher."

Lambe shrugged, drew his hand from behind him and handed Kircher the bottle. Kircher drew out the stopper, sniffed the contents and recoiled. Carefully, he touched the stopper's insert lightly to the end of his finger, and then touched the finger to his tongue. "Hellebore, distilled into concentrate," he said, amazed. "Poison."

"I was only going to add a drop," Lambe said. "In small amounts it can be quite beneficial."

"No," said Père Míkmaq. "You were going to poison Fontrailles."

"In God's name!" cried Lambe. "Why would I do that?"

"Because you wanted him to die before the Catharsis was complete," Míkmaq said grimly. "You wanted the operation to fail—spectacularly— and you wanted the blame to fall on the Society of Jesus."

"That's *absurd*," Lambe said in a voice of reason, but he suddenly thrust Míkmaq and Kircher aside and dashed for the trap door. Kircher just stared after him, but Míkmaq leapt in pursuit, drawing a sort of hatchet from within his robe. He caught Lambe by the collar as the alchemist started down the stairs, turned the hatchet to reverse it, and struck the Englishman savagely on the back of his head. Lambe slumped and slid out of sight; Père Míkmaq tilted back his head, gave an ululating howl and disappeared after him.

"Herr Kircher," Fontrailles said. "Help me."

"I...." Kircher's round face was blank as a dinner plate. "I don't know what to do."

He looked toward the trap door. Père Míkmaq reappeared—incredibly, though he was much smaller than Lambe, dragging the limp form of the alchemist back up the stairs. He dropped the body onto the floor of the platform, and Fontrailles and Kircher saw with shock that it was bleeding from the top of the skull where a long, ragged piece of scalp had been torn away. Míkmaq stood before them, holding a swatch of bloody hair in one hand and his hatchet in the other. The hatchet's haft was decorated with colorful, tinkling beads.

"What ... what...." Kircher looked down at Lambe, shuddered, looked back at Père Míkmaq. "What happens now?"

"Now we go," Míkmaq said, breathing hard, "before the Capuchin gets wind of this."

"Are you leaving me here?" Fontrailles said.

"No. We need your testimony." Père Míkmaq gestured toward Kircher with the hatchet; drops of blood flew through the air. "We must get him into the chair, Doctor."

The Jesuits strapped Fontrailles into the wheeled chair. Míkmaq removed his white robe, now stained with red, thrust both hatchet and scalp into his belt, then helped Kircher bump the chair down the stairs, hook it onto the pulley and lower Fontrailles to the base of the tower. Kircher seemed terrified of Père Míkmaq and kept flinching away from him. Míkmaq kept close watch over Kircher and kept the hatchet handy, as if he suspected the German would run if he thought he could get away.

Louis just concentrated on managing the pain and trying to keep his head. When the chair was unhooked from the ropes and Père Míkmaq indicated that Kircher was to push it toward the door, Fontrailles said, "Isabeau. You promised to help free Mademoiselle."

"Things have changed," said Míkmaq.

"Not that," said Fontrailles. "Without Isabeau, I will tell anyone who asks that you, at the orders of your General, have used forbidden Black Arts and invoked demons."

Míkmaq glared at him and hefted the hatchet; Louis felt his scalp tingle, but the priest nodded and said, "Very well. We collect her on our way out."

When they entered the rear door of Queen Catherine's bedchamber des Cartes put down his book and rushed toward them. "Monsieur de Fontrailles! What happened? Are you all right?"

Père Míkmaq displayed the bloody hatchet. "We go. If you wish, you may follow. Now be quiet." He strode to the outer door, struck it, and called, "Guard! It's Père Crozat. Open up; we're coming out."

The bar slid back; the door opened; the hatchet struck, and the guard fell to the floor. Míkmaq gestured. "Follow."

The guard outside Isabeau's room gazed curiously at Père Míkmaq and his group as they approached, but the priest walked calmly up to him and said, "We are here to visit the lady. Open up." When the guard turned to draw back the bar, Míkmaq felled him with the hatchet.

Míkmaq unbarred the door and the party entered Isabeau's grand bedchamber, des Cartes now pushing his friend Fontrailles's chair. When they were all inside, the door abruptly slammed behind them and armed men stepped from the shadows.

"You come at last," said Father Joseph, appearing from behind the bed on which Isabeau sat, pale and trembling. "I am bound to say, Monsieur de Fontrailles, that I expected you to contrive your escape somewhat sooner than this."

CHAPTER LVII
A SCENE FROM JACOBEAN FARCE

Though he was helpless, strapped in his wheeled chair, Louis automatically tallied the opposition: three men-at-arms commanded by Bernajoux, a notable duelist. To fight would be futile: they were caught.

"Oh, Monsieur!" Vidou ran from behind Father Joseph and fell to his knees before Louis. "Oh, Monsieur! What misery!" He began to weep.

Isabeau came up behind him and placed a hand on his shoulder. "Come, Vidou," she said gently, "crying is no use. You have your master back; we must do what we can to help him."

"That is so, Mademoiselle," Father Joseph said as he approached. "I fear he has been most cruelly used." The cowl turned right and left, the pop eyes blinking myopically. "It is dim in here, but I think I do not see Doctor Lambe. Has he suffered a misfortune?" He looked at Père Míkmaq. "There has been no ... *violence*, I hope?"

The Jesuit priest glared back. "You are a devil."

"I?" whispered Father Joseph. "But I have tortured no one. I have trafficked with no dark powers. And I have no fresh blood still glistening on my hands."

"Perhaps not," said Míkmaq. "But now you die."

He whipped the hatchet from his sash and raised it. Joseph swiftly backpedaled, bare feet slapping on the floor. Míkmaq howled and charged, and everyone recoiled—except Bernajoux, who calmly placed himself between the Jesuit and the Capuchin, smiling beneath his perfectly curled black mustache. Míkmaq veered and swung his hatchet at the Cardinal's Guard, but Bernajoux simply stepped inside the swing, grabbed Míkmaq's arm, turned him on his hip and twisted the priest's wrist. The beaded hatchet flew away in a glittering arc, and Míkmaq landed on the floor on his back. When he tried to rise, he found Bernajoux's boot on his chest.

"I fear you are going to regret that, my son," Father Joseph said sadly. "It is bound to be held against you at the trial in the ecclesiastical court. *À propos* of which, let us go find dear Doctor Lambe. It seems probable that he is in need of medical assistance—and we will have need of his testimony."

"But what is this talk of trial and testimonies, Monseigneur?" protested Kircher. "All our researches were approved in advance, and we have done nothing to transgress the sanctions!"

"With all my heart, and for the good of your eternal soul," Father Joseph replied, "I hope that is the truth."

"It is!" said Kircher.

"Then you have nothing to fear, do you?" Joseph approached Fontrailles. "You have suffered badly, Monsieur de Fontrailles," the Capuchin said, "but others have suffered more and still gone on to achieve great things. I look forward to many long conversations with you during your convalescence."

"And Isabeau?" Fontrailles said. "She goes free?"

"Yes. I believe Mademoiselle de Bonnefont will be much happier back at her home in Armagnac."

"Louis, what does he mean?" Isabeau said. "I won't be sent away!"

"You will do as God wills, as we all must," Joseph said. "Now, come."

Bernajoux gestured to his men. Two of them jerked Père Míkmaq to his feet and held him by the arms, while the third went to collect his curious weapon. Then Father Joseph led them all out into the dark, echoing halls of the Hôtel de Soissons.

As the strangely mixed band marched through the empty chambers, Louis thought he heard a sound behind them. He perked up and listened more intently, but it was hard to hear over the creaking of the chair wheels and the *sotto voce* muttering of Vidou, now pushing behind him. But then Louis heard it again: a low rustle and murmur.

As they entered the queen's antechamber the rear guardsman heard it, too. *"Monsieur l'Officier,"* he called, "I hear something behind us!"

Then they all heard it: the rising rustle of rags and the mutter of toothless mouths. They turned to see a gang of filthy gray figures blocking the doorway behind them. Only Fontrailles and Father Joseph looked ahead, where another mob of mendicants appeared in the doorway before them.

Joseph turned on Fontrailles in sudden fury and hissed, "This is your doing, isn't it?"

"Mayn't I have some of the credit?" rang a voice from the doorway in front of them. The gray mob parted to allow a tall figure in shining finery to pass through: Commander de Longvilliers, looking as if he'd just stepped from a painting depicting the martial glories of the Order of Malta, a naked rapier in one hand and a lace handkerchief in the other. He was followed by Beaune and Gitane, looking grimly efficient rather than glorious, each bearing a brace of pistols.

"Vidou, roll me forward," Fontrailles said. "Welcome, Sir Knight! I was expecting to see my friends, the renowned Beggars of Paris—Vidou, here, smuggled out a message to them—but to find you among them, Monseigneur, is an unexpected delight."

Longvilliers bowed slightly, with a flourish of the handkerchief. "It was but...." His eyes widened. *"Mon Dieu!* Is that really you, Monsieur? What have they done to you?" He glared around the room, knightly nostrils flaring. "Someone will pay for this!"

"The Chevalier is prudent," said Bernajoux, stepping forward. "He makes his threats while backed up by bullies with pistols." He gave his mustache an insolent twist.

"By God, you'll answer for that, if you have the honor to be a gentleman," Longvilliers said hotly. "Draw your sword, and my men will put up their pistols!"

"Enough!" said Father Joseph. "Bernajoux, I forbid you to fight. Put down your weapon, and have your men do the same." He turned to Longvilliers. "I must advise Monsieur le Chevalier to think well before he involves himself further in this matter. It is no longer criminal, or even political—it involves acts of heresy and witchcraft, and is now in the hands of the Church. I know you for a devout man, a member of a Holy Order, and one who will not lightly oppose himself to God's emissaries on earth."

Longvilliers sheathed his sword. "You are right, Your Gray Eminence— so they call you, do they not? When I draw my blade, it is in service of honor and loyalty, never against the holy Church—but I am compelled to say that I see nothing of the divine going on here." He waved the handkerchief. "This whole affair stinks of corruption. I advise *you*, Father, to drop the matter before your reputation is hopelessly soiled. And besides," he added with the twitch of a smile, "what *would* my knightly brother Soissons say if I told him what you'd been doing with his hôtel?"

Father Joseph glared balefully from under his cowl, but before he could reply Fontrailles interrupted. "Well said, Commander! But please explain how you come to be here in company with the beggars."

"Why, I remembered you said they know everything that goes on in Paris, so I sent Gitane to talk to them," Longvilliers replied, "hoping they might know something of your whereabouts. He returned with a Monsieur Montfaucon, who took me to meet their leader."

"Their leader?" said Fontrailles. "And who, these days, is that?"

"Why, Great Caesar, o' course," called a voice from the rear, and all turned as the mob in the doorway behind parted to admit a man with one eye, a wooden leg, and a hook for a hand. "Him what is the *new* Great Caesar, that is."

"Sobriety Breedlove!" cried Fontrailles. "We thought you were killed on the Pont Neuf."

"Not ... quite," said the old sailor, rubbing his neck with a hand half-hidden by a billowing lace cuff. "A comely lass took pity on me, an' nursed me gentle-like back to health." He gestured. "Come in, sweetling, come in!"

The ragged mob parted again, and Proserpine entered the room. She seemed even taller and broader than Louis remembered, but radiant, her eyes nearly eclipsed by her glowing cheeks. Breedlove took her hand and patted it fondly. "Drew me back from the brink o' death, she did, and as she tended me, I told her tales o' me voyages wi' Drake an' Hawkins. Her heart were moved an'—well, I lived up to me name. Monsieur, I married her!"

There was a little ripple of applause from the assembled *mendigots*. Bernajoux rolled his eyes theatrically, and Father Joseph actually tapped one bare foot impatiently on the tile floor. "Cannot these human interest stories wait?" he said, addressing Longvilliers. "Weighty matters impend! You have the upper hand, it is clear: what do you intend to do with us?"

"Why, as to that," Longvilliers replied, "let's hear what Monsieur de Fontrailles has to say."

The first thing that occurred to Louis—*Get me a doctor, a bed, and more tincture of poppy!*—he knew would never do, but before he could think of anything else there was an interruption. "I got one! I got one!" cried a voice from the chamber beyond Longvilliers. "Let me through! I got one!"

Ragged beggars were thrust aside, cursing vilely, as the great dim lout known as Shit-for-Brains pushed his way through the doorway, dragging behind him the struggling, bloody-headed form of Doctor John Lambe. "I was watching for sneakers, I was, like you told me, Great Caesar," babbled Shit-for-Brains, "and I caught one! Hur, hur!"

"May God blind me!" said Caesar, stumping forward. "It's Doctor Lambe, as I live and breed! Shit-fer-Brains, ye've performed a noble service—aye, that you have! Ye're promoted, and from now on will be known as ... Porridge-fer-Brains!"

"Oh, *merci*," said the lout, knuckling his forehead. "*Merci beaucoup,* Your Majesty!"

Lambe, scalp still dripping blood, was clutching a burlap sack and a long wooden box to his chest. He looked around desperately, as if seeking an escape route.

Caesar stumped over to the alchemist and looked up into his wild eyes. "Lambe, ye scut!" he said. "D'ye remember me?"

"No, why should I? Father Joseph—Monseigneur—what's happening here?"

The commander, who had drawn his sword when the commotion began, now placed its point beneath Lambe's chin. "*I* say what happens here, Englishman. Great Caesar has asked you a question. Answer it."

"Aye, answer it," said Caesar. "D'ye know me, Lambe?"

Lambe peered at the bizarre figure before him, blinked, and said, "Why, it's the sailor-man! From the duke's summer house!"

"Ha-*ha!*" Caesar grinned and placed hand-and-hook on his hips. "He-he! Ye can't know, Doctor, how I've longed to meet you again! What a great an' unexpected pleasure!"

"Your Majesty," said Fontrailles, enjoying himself despite the pain of his wounds, "make him open that wooden box."

"My box? No!" Lambe clutched it tighter. "There's nothing in it—just some personal items I didn't want to leave behind."

"Open it," said Longvilliers, waving his blade for emphasis.

Lambe looked around again—still no escape. His chin quivered. He carefully set the burlap sack on the floor, placed the long box atop it, and opened it.

"Oi!" cried Caesar. "That's my leg!"

"It's mine!" Lambe said. "It's a unicorn's horn!"

"Unicorn's horn, my eye!" Caesar growled. "It's me leg, an' I'll have it back!"

"The Duke of Buckingham gave it to me!"

"I had it first, I say—won it fair, I did, off a dying whaler, at primero."

"Fight for it," called Bernajoux. "Trial by combat!"

"Eh?" said Lambe.

"Now, there's an idea!" said Caesar. "Aye, we'll fight for it!"

"Darling, no!" bugled Proserpine, billowing forward. "You can't risk it, not...."

"Not when a little emperor's on the way?" Caesar patted her abdomen familiarly; Proserpine blushed and looked down. "Never fear, chuck. A'sides, ye can't expect a sea-dog what sailed with Drake to back down from a challenge—especially when it's o'er his own leg!"

"*Fight* you? An aged cripple half my size?" Lambe said. "Well ... yes, I suppose I could do that. And if I win?"

"Ha! If ye win, I'll be dead, so ye can keep me leg an' go free, for all of me." Caesar grinned, beard bristling. "Choose yer weapon, ye reptile."

"Why, I'll have a rapier, I believe," Lambe said, gaining confidence. "But I must warn you, I'm rather good with it."

"Take mine, Monsieur," said Bernajoux, picking up his sword and handing it to Lambe. The alchemist drew the rapier from its scabbard, balanced it in his hand, made a couple of trial passes, and nodded his satisfaction.

"Yer form an't bad," said Caesar. "It's many years since I held a sword...."

"Ha!" said Lambe.

Caesar raised his hook. "...And the hand I used to hold it with, ye took in the fight over me leg...."

"Ha?" said Lambe.

"...So if that sword's your arm, I b'lieve *I'll* use ... me leg." He reached down into the long box and picked up the unicorn's horn. He held it by the thick end and waggled its point at the alchemist.

"You can't use that!" Lambe cried. "It might be damaged!"

"I'll try to stick it only in yer soft parts, so's it won't get nicked," Caesar said, with a grin that showed all his remaining teeth.

"Monseigneur, I implore you, this is most irregular," Lambe said to the Commander de Longvilliers.

"Are you sure, Great Caesar?" Longvilliers asked. Caesar nodded; Longvilliers shrugged. "He has the right," he told Lambe.

"Very well," Lambe said grimly. "Then let's finish this farce." He stood erect and saluted Caesar with the long rapier. Caesar saluted him in return with the spiral horn, and then both dropped into a crouch, weapons held at guard position.

Lambe, facing a left-handed opponent armed with a weapon he didn't want to damage, seemed at a loss for a moment, especially when Caesar suddenly flipped the horn in his hand so that he was gripping the narrow end. Lambe gritted his teeth, then passed forward with an outside cut that he turned into a lunge. Caesar half-stepped back and parried—not with the horn, but with his hook. He twisted the hook around the blade in a bind and pushed forward, bending Lambe's wrist painfully back, then raised the horn and struck Lambe on his already-wounded head.

With a wordless cry, the alchemist fell to his knees. Caesar, keeping his enemy's sword bound within his hook, raised the horn again and brought it down on Lambe's skull—once, twice, three times, each blow harder than the last. Blood spattered, then bone, then brain. Isabeau turned away; Louis, who'd thought he couldn't feel any worse, felt his own gorge rise.

When he was finished, Caesar looked down at Lambe's corpse with satisfaction, and then tucked the dripping horn under his arm. "Now *there's* a good day's work, an' no mistake," he said.

"Filthy scoundrel," Father Joseph hissed. "I'll see that you scum are swept from the streets of Paris."

"D'ye say so?" said Caesar, unperturbed.

"Well, then," said Longvilliers, rather embarrassed that the joke-combat had turned out less droll than he'd anticipated. "I think it's best we were on our way."

"Aye, that it is," said Caesar. He turned to Fontrailles. "Ye said we could take anything that weren't nailed down. But there an't much in the place."

"If you look atop the astrologer's column you'll find quite a few valuable items, some made of precious metals," Fontrailles said. "But warn your people not to drink anything from the bottles."

"Then we may go?" said Father Joseph.

"Of course," said Longvilliers. He nodded at Fontrailles and Isabeau. "We have what we came for. What do you take me for, a kidnapper?"

"Wait!" Doctor Kircher piped up. "We don't want to go with Father Joseph!"

"They are prisoners of the Church," said Joseph. "They go with me."

"Monsieur de Fontrailles?" asked Longvilliers.

Louis looked at Kircher and Míkmaq for a long moment, remembering the strappado; the needles; the rack. He said, "If you could suffer even a small part of the pain you inflicted on me...." He gnawed at his lip, and then shook his head. "Ah, the devil with it. Let them go."

Père Míkmaq shrugged off the grip of the two soldiers who'd been holding him and marched up to the third. "Give me my otamahuk," he said.

"Your *what?*" said the soldier.

"My hatchet," Míkmaq said. "Give it to me."

"Heh. *I'll* give it to you...."

"Bernajoux!" said Joseph. "Order your man to give Père Crozat his weapon. We will have no more fighting today."

Père Míkmaq held out his hand; the soldier gave him the hatchet, then the two Jesuits pushed their way out through the beggars and left.

Father Joseph gestured to Bernajoux and made as if to follow. "Wait, Monseigneur," said Fontrailles. "Let's give them enough time to find their way out without the help of you and your men. And in the meantime," he added, "let's see what the late Doctor Lambe had in that burlap sack."

"But of course," said Father Joseph. "Where are my wits? It must be...."

"*The Three Mystic Heirs,*" said Longvilliers, drawing the heavy book from the sack. "This is luck, indeed! I've been chasing this thing, off and on, since the sack of Prague eight years ago. And it occurs to me that if I brought it to dear Lucy, she might very well be happy to see me again."

"Commander!" said Father Joseph. "You would give that cursed book—to a *woman?* Do not even think it! It must disappear, forever!"

"Must it?" Longvilliers said. The commander flipped through the book Louis d'Astarac had coveted so long, and Louis, watching, found that he no longer cared what happened to it. Longvilliers noticed his expression and turned back to Joseph. "But perhaps you are right, Father. In fact, considering the ill luck and catastrophe it's brought to all who've possessed it," Longvilliers said, "I do believe that I *want* you to have it."

CHAPTER LVIII
EXCURSION

It was the jolting that brought Louis back to his senses; it was relentless, and hurt like the devil. He opened his eyes and said, "Where am I?"

"Oh, Louis!" said a blurry Isabeau, leaning over him. "You say that *every* time you come to."

"It's only because I want to know." Louis tried to focus his eyes.

"You are in Monseigneur de Longvilliers's carriage." Des Cartes's voice came from somewhere near at hand. "We left Paris just an hour ago."

"We did?" The carriage struck a rut in the road, hard. "Arhh! God's *teeth,* that hurt." But it wasn't agonizing, merely excruciating. Fontrailles tried to move his left arm, and found he could, a little. "What's happened? I'm bound up, but my joints are working, somewhat." He tried to move his right arm. "*Oww!* But the broken bones are still broken. Is this bandaging your work, Monsieur des Cartes?"

"*Please* don't try to move, Louis," Isabeau said.

"You were treated by the physician who tends the prisoners at the Bastille," des Cartes said, "assisted by your man Beaune, who apparently has some experience with victims of the rack. Together they—would re-located be the proper term? Let's just say put back in place your dislocated joints, treated your puncture wounds, and bound or splinted your broken bones. It was a rather horrific procedure—I could force myself to observe only the first hour of it—and you made a great deal of noise throughout."

"Perhaps it's as well I don't remember it," Fontrailles said. He blinked and looked about. The interior of the carriage was beginning to come into focus: functional rather than opulent, probably a hired vehicle. "Did the physician say anything about my prospects for recovery?"

"He said that, if you don't die from putrefaction of your wounds, you should be moving around more-or-less normally in about a year."

"A year? *Merdieu*! Now I wish I hadn't let Kircher and Míkmaq off so easily." The carriage struck something in the road with a jarring thud. "Agh! Did the physician happen to give you any more of that tincture of poppy?"

"I asked, but he refused," des Cartes said. "He spoke quite vehemently against it. He said that if you were in pain you should take a little *eau-de-vie*."

"Do you have any?"

Des Cartes nodded, produced a bottle, and poured Fontrailles a small glass. Hand shaking slightly, Fontrailles drank it down. "That will help. I must say, I'm surprised to hear that the physician for the Bastille is available to treat private citizens."

"His services were not formally engaged," des Cartes said dryly. "The transaction was more in the nature of a brief abduction."

Fontrailles smiled. "The Knights of Malta do seem to prefer the direct approach. Ouch! Curse it! But can't we ask him to slow down a bit? This pace is killing me!"

"But, Louis," Isabeau said, "you agreed that we should leave immediately and make all the speed we could."

"I did?" Fontrailles said. "Well, I'm sure I knew what I was talking about. Umm ... where are we going?"

"North to Béthune, in Artois," said des Cartes.

"To save Éric," said Isabeau.

"To save him? From what? He's going to be exchanged for French prisoners the English are holding, and then set free."

"But, Louis," Isabeau said patiently, "you said that since he was still in the hands of Father Joseph's intelligence service that Joseph would probably take his revenge on Éric."

"I said that? I have a fine, logical mind, I must say." Louis considered for a moment. "Why did I think he was in Béthune?"

"That English spy, Blakeney, told Monsieur de Longvilliers that he was negotiating the prisoner exchange, and was returning to Béthune," Isabeau said. "But we don't know where to look for Éric once we get there."

"You don't?" Fontrailles smiled. "I do. Have you ever been to Béthune? There's a Carmelite convent just outside the town. And Éric was spirited away by a bravo wearing a friar's robe—an all-white *Carmelite* friar's robe."

"Louis!" Isabeau leaned over and kissed him on the nose. "Sometimes I think you know everything."

"Hardly," he said, grinning like a fool. "But I did go to seminary, after all. So ... we're racing to reach Éric ahead of Father Joseph's vengeance."

"And, not incidentally, to get ourselves beyond the reach of His Gray Eminence as rapidly as possible," added des Cartes.

"You're leaving Paris for good?" Fontrailles asked. He could see des Cartes clearly now: the scholar's deepset eyes were sunken even deeper with sleeplessness, and his face was lined with fatigue.

"I believe so," des Cartes said. "Having my work closely scrutinized by Richelieu's chief intelligencer has made me distinctly uncomfortable about remaining in France." He sighed. "I think a relocation to the United Provinces is indicated."

"And the sooner the better, eh?" said Fontrailles. "Very well, that explains your haste. But," he looked at Isabeau, "*chérie,* considering what Éric ... *did* to you in La Rochelle, it escapes me why I should be in such a hurry to save his misbegotten life—especially in my current condition."

"Oh, Louis." She looked down at her hands, which were clenched tightly in her lap. "Must I tell you all over again?"

"Well...." He searched his memory, came up with nothing. "It seems so."

Without meeting his eyes, she leaned forward to whisper into his ear. "Because, Louis ... I'm with child," she said. "Éric's child."

CHAPTER LIX
WHAT HAPPENED IN PARKS ON
22 AUGUST 1628

In the moldy study of the shabby house on Rue Garancière, the man called Cocodril was groveling before the naked feet of Father Joseph. "Pardon, Monseigneur Eminence, pardon!" he said to the feet. "How could I have known that the bastard knight Longvilliers would leave the address I reported before you could snare him?"

"Get up, Jean Reynon," whispered Father Joseph. "When I speak to you, I want to see your eyes. Perhaps you could not have known when he would leave, my son—but you could have determined in advance where he would go when he did leave."

"You are right, Your Holiness." Cocodril rose to his feet, stooping a bit so as not to tower quite so much over the Capuchin. "I have disappointed you. But I am resolved that it shall not happen again!"

"That is correct," said Father Joseph. "I have no more use for you."

"Oh, but you cannot mean it, Monseigneur! You will find no servant more highly motivated than I." Cocodril was fervent. "I must have my revenge on Longvilliers, and on those miserable swine who took my place."

"Our service does not offer revenge as a benefit," said Joseph. "How is it that you came to leave Monsieur de Longvilliers so abruptly?"

"It was those two rogues of the hunchback's that he brought in, Beaune and Gitane." Cocodril almost spat, but then apparently thought better of it. "Especially Gitane. Why, the man is practically a criminal! He said that he didn't trust me—can you imagine it, Monseigneur?—and that if I didn't shift off, I might wake up to find my throat had been cut while I was sleeping."

"Most distressing," said Father Joseph. "I know these men: they were given an opportunity to make amends for their misbehavior by serving the State, and have repaid us by returning to their former habits. I'm afraid their souls are lost to evil, and the next time they are caught they will be shown no more mercy. Now, as to you...." Joseph looked intently at Cocodril for a moment, and then sighed very slightly. "We are sadly short-handed just at present; perhaps I do have a task which will enable you to prove your worth. You are known to the Comte de Rochefort, I believe."

"I had the honor of meeting His Excellency while in Milady de Winter's service, Monseigneur. And I think I can say that he does not hold me in low esteem!"

"As long as he won't shoot you on sight, I am content," said Joseph. "Monsieur de Rochefort has left on an urgent mission to Béthune, in Artois—but conditions have changed, and I have new orders for him."

Bernajoux, who had been leaning on the mantel of the cold fireplace idly cleaning his nails with the point of a long dagger, broke in. "I thought I was going to carry that message."

"I have other work for you," said Father Joseph. "Wait a moment, Reynon, while I write a brief note."

"I am patience incarnate!" said Cocodril, assuming a posture of zealous attentiveness.

Father Joseph sat at the writing table that was the room's sole furniture, scribbled a short letter, folded and sealed it. "You will ride as rapidly as you can in hopes of catching Monsieur de Rochefort before he reaches Béthune. When you do, you will give him this," Joseph said, handing Cocodril the letter. "He must stop first at Liller to deliver other orders, so you may find him there."

"It is as good as done, Your Holiness!" Cocodril bowed nearly to the floor, backed across the chamber, still bowing, to the main door, then turned and departed.

"That's a rogue I wouldn't trust with anything important, Monseigneur," said Bernajoux.

"Of course not," Father Joseph said mildly. "That's why you are being sent to Montferrat instead of him. The Hapsburgs are drawing their web tighter around the Duc de Nevers in Mantua, and I need up-to-date intelligence on the passes over the Alps. Now approach. It's late; I'm expecting no one else this evening, so I can afford to spend some time going over the maps with you."

The pair had spent several minutes with their heads bent over the parchment sheets when there came a thump from the hall outside the door, followed by what might have been a gasp. Both looked up, and Bernajoux put his hand on the hilt of his sword. "Conceal yourself behind the side door," Joseph hissed. "Go quickly—and draw your weapon."

There was another thud from beyond the main door. Joseph placed himself on the far side of the table; Bernajoux ducked out the side door and closed it almost to behind him, just as the main door was pushed open.

Into the Capuchin's study stepped Père Míkmaq. His cheekbones were daubed with crimson crosses, his eyes were wide, and he was breathing heavily. In his hand was the beaded hatchet, its edge red with blood.

"Stop right there, Père Crozat," said Joseph, in a tone louder than usual, though just as mild. "That is close enough for us to talk."

"I do not come to talk," said the Jesuit.

"But you would be wise to do so—and to keep your distance."

"Ha. Why?"

"Perhaps I have a small firearm concealed in the capacious sleeves of my habit," Father Joseph said reasonably. "If you threaten me, I might have no choice but to shoot you."

"You have no firearm."

"What have you done with Philippe and Nadeau?"

"They resisted," Míkmaq said. "They are dead."

"More deaths on your conscience," Joseph said sadly. "How will you atone?"

"With another death: yours."

Joseph shook his head. "That is just sin upon sin."

"You have led my soul to perdition!" Míkmaq cried.

"Not I, my son."

"*You* enticed Kircher into performing that evil Catharsis!" Míkmaq said. "You planned the entire thing! You were behind our degradation!"

"Oh, my son," Father Joseph said gently. "What pain you are in! You were tempted by the forces of darkness, tried … and found wanting. You knew in your heart that what you were doing was wrong, evil, corrupt, and now your spirit is in agony."

"Be silent!"

"It is true; you know it's true," Father Joseph whispered. "And there is only one answer. You must beg forgiveness, my son."

"I?"

"Pray for forgiveness, Père Crozat. You know it is the only way. Pray to God for forgiveness. Fall on your knees, my son, and pray."

"I … I.…" The priest wavered; the hand with the hatchet drooped; the other hand fumbled at a crucifix at his throat.

The side door moved slightly, no more than half an inch. But Père Míkmaq saw it. "Deceiver!" he cried. "Die!" He raised the hatchet and stepped forward.

Bernajoux burst into the room, sword in hand. Míkmaq paused, cocked back his arm, and whipped the hatchet at Father Joseph. As it spun through the air the Capuchin shrieked and fell back; the hatchet gashed his left shoulder, then clattered off into a corner. With an ululating cry, Père Míkmaq charged toward Joseph—and ran full onto the point of Bernajoux's rapier.

Bernajoux pulled the blade, with some effort, from the Jesuit's chest, and kicked him to make sure he was dead. Then he turned to inspect Father Joseph's wound.

"You were slow," said Joseph. "Is it bad?"

"I didn't know that thing could be thrown like that," Bernajoux said. "You will live, Monseigneur, though if it had struck two more inches to the left you'd be dead already."

"It hurts," Father Joseph said, and his voice was not at all mild. "Ahh! But I must remember our Lord suffered much worse on Calvary."

Bernajoux took a handkerchief from his sleeve and pressed it into the wound, then began to bind it in place. He said, "This isn't the first time someone has tried to kill you, and it won't be the last. Perhaps you *should* carry a small firearm in your sleeve."

"And perhaps," said Father Joseph, his breathing ragged, "I should simply get more skillful guards." And His Gray Eminence closed his eyes and fainted.

CHAPTER LX
AT THE FRANCE INN

At the Auberge La France, the best inn in Montdidier, Isabeau wheeled Fontrailles's chair a little closer to the fire. Then she knelt down in front of him and tucked a coarse wool blanket around his body and legs. "Are you sure you'll be all right here in the common room?" she asked, for the third time.

"I'll be fine in my chair. I'm glad you thought to bring it." Fontrailles smiled wearily. "Believe me, anything is better than being bumped up the stairs to the private chambers."

"Won't you be uncomfortable?"

"To be frank, *chérie,* I won't be comfortable no matter where I sleep. This will do."

She touched him lightly on the cheek, looked at him for a moment and then silently took her leave, climbing the stairs to one of the tiny private chambers above. Des Cartes, who loved his sleep, had gone to his room a half-hour earlier. Of Fontrailles's party that left only Commander de Longvilliers still in the common room, along with a half-dozen pilgrims and commercial travelers who were all keeping to themselves. Longvilliers had drawn discreetly aside while Isabeau had been saying goodnight to

Fontrailles, but now he approached, swirling the wine in his wineglass. "The farther north we go, the worse the wine," he said. "Soon we'll have to switch entirely to ale."

Fontrailles stirred uncomfortably in the chair, which despite what he'd said to Isabeau was already poking him in various tender places. "Personally," he said, "I'm beginning to wish I hadn't decided to limit my intake of *eau-de-vie*."

"If it helps, why deny yourself its aid?"

"It's bad enough being lame and halt; I don't care to become a sodden drunkard into the bargain."

"I suppose I may be badly wounded someday," Longvilliers mused. "I wonder how I will deal with it?" He smiled. "I hope, Monsieur de Fontrailles, I will have as charming a nurse as you. Have you noticed how she rather resembles Lucy Hay?" He continued to smile, while stroking his mustache with a finger.

Uh-oh, thought Louis. *The gallant knight casts his eye on the maid from Armagnac and finds her fair.* "Monseigneur," he said slowly, "the Demoiselle de Bonnefont...."

"A moment, Monsieur," interrupted Longvilliers. "Those two rascals of yours have come in, and it looks as if they have something to tell us."

It was, indeed, Beaune and Gitane, crossing the room toward them with an air of urgency. One-eyed Gitane ducked his head and said, "Begging your pardon, Monseigneur, Monsieur, but we thought you should know: we've seen that Englishman who used to call himself Parrott in the stable, checking on some horses. We watched him; he went up the outside stairs of the inn to one of the rooms on the first floor."

"Blakeney," said Fontrailles. "Did he see you?"

"I don't think so, Monsieur."

"Well done, both of you," Fontrailles said. "Blakeney was involved in the prisoner exchange negotiations that included Éric. I think we should find out what he's doing here."

"What if he won't talk?" said Gitane.

"He's a canny fellow, from what I've seen," said Longvilliers. "We won't take him easily."

"May I make a suggestion?" said a dry English voice.

"Blakeney!" said Fontrailles. "How the devil did you do that?"

"Trade secret, old fellow." Sir Percy Blakeney stepped out of the shadow of a smoke-darkened pillar. He was dressed in a travel-stained buff jacket and tall, worn leather boots, an outfit he somehow wore as if bedecked in Court finery. "Good evening, Sir Knight—and to you, Fontrailles. I must say, you're not looking at all well. Are you traveling to Forges to take the waters? You know," he said confidentially, "you all just looked so *furtive,* gathered around the fire speaking in low voices, that I simply had to find out if you were talking about me. And, sink me, you *were!* Immensely gratifying, don't you know. And now, if I didn't know better, I'd almost say that your men were maneuvering to surround me." He tapped Longvilliers's glass and said, "What are you drinking?"

"Blakeney," Fontrailles said, "has anyone ever told you that you blather?"

"Alas," Blakeney sighed. "It's my only failing. Dear Lucy said that's why she was returning to England; she couldn't stand it any more. You know, before your men get any more intimate with me, I feel I should point out that the ever-efficient Enfield is standing behind that post there, and he has simply all sorts of weapons about him. So do please ask these charming fellows to back off, and let's all have a nice, polite chat without any disagreeable attempts at intimidation."

Gitane looked at Fontrailles, who nodded. After noting the location of Enfield, he and Beaune sat at a nearby table where they could keep an eye on everyone. At a nod from Blakeney, Enfield sat at another table. Blakeney watched all these evolutions with a pleasant smile while warming his hands behind him over the fire. "Satisfied?" Fontrailles asked.

"Eminently," said Blakeney. "I'm extremely curious, Fontrailles, to find out what's brought you to this low estate—more than a fall down the stairs? I thought so. But perhaps we'd better address business first. Why were you all devising nefarious schemes against me just now? I thought we were such good friends."

Fontrailles looked at Longvilliers, who made a gesture of deference to indicate that Fontrailles should take the lead. Louis said, "We really just wanted a talk with you, Sir Percy. We're very interested in one of the prisoners you've been negotiating for."

"Ah, yes—you must mean Gimous, that fellow who came out of La Rochelle with you. If you were hoping to be reunited with him once he was freed, I'm afraid I have bad news for you: the negotiations are off."

"What?"

"Cold fact. Your friend was going to be traded for Richelieu's man Boisloré, but the word from across the Channel is that Buckingham was in a nasty mood one morning and had him beheaded." He shrugged as if to say, *Prime Ministers: what can one do?* "In response, your cardinal broke off the negotiations, and I wouldn't be a bit surprised if he doesn't have your friend Gimous beheaded in retaliation. Bad news all around."

"Your mission here is over, it seems," Fontrailles said. "What are you going to do now?"

"I?" Blakeney cocked an eyebrow. "I'm not best pleased about having the rug pulled out from under me like that, and it's not the first time. Milord Buckingham is increasingly arrogant and capricious; I believe it's time to return to England and hand in my resignation from his service. Then, perhaps I'll retire to a cottage in the country and cultivate roses."

"What should we do about this?" Longvilliers asked Fontrailles.

Louis tapped his teeth, shrugged, and said, "Ow! That hurt, curse it. Commander, I think we're just going to have to go discover where they're holding Monsieur de Gimous and find a way to free him before they lop off his head."

"My thought as well!" said Longvilliers. "If that lovely girl wants that young man saved, you can count on me."

"Do you know," said Blakeney, "you're both as mad as hares in March. You probably don't have the vaguest idea where Gimous is being held...."

"The Carmelite convent at Béthune," Fontrailles said.

"A point for you, Fontrailles: that's *almost* right," Blakeney said. "But you don't know the set-up there, how your man is guarded, or what would be the best escape route. Whereas *I*," he raised a finger, "have already thoroughly scouted it out."

"Well, are you going to tell us what you know," Fontrailles said, "or are we going to have to resort to disagreeable attempts at intimidation?"

"*Tell* you? My dear fellow, I'm going to *show* you," Blakeney said. "Gimous is an allied prisoner, one of the men whose freedom I was sent here to obtain. Buckingham, alas, mucked up my mission—but I do believe," he said with a smile, "that I shall complete it anyway. Just to spite him."

CHAPTER LXI
CONVERSATION ON THE
MIND-BODY PROBLEM

Bouncing over the rutted roads of Picardy was hard on Fontrailles, but he really would rather have been nowhere else, as he was spending hours with Isabeau, more than at any time since leaving Armagnac. It was pure pleasure to talk with her, and when talking was done, simply to gaze at her. More and more often, when she looked back at him, she blushed and looked down. "I do wish you'd stop looking at me that way, Louis," she finally said, "as if I were a painting, or one of your ivory cameos."

"Oh, you're far better than a painting or cameo; your face is so alive, so different from moment to moment," Fontrailles said. "I won't stop looking, and you can't make me."

She smiled and shook her head. "You idiot," she said gently.

Des Cartes was staring pointedly out the window at the passing countryside.

"Louis," Isabeau said, "I have no experience of Paris and the Court, and of such exalted folk as dukes and Knights of Malta, so tell me...." She hesitated. "Is the Commander de Longvilliers like other high-ranking nobles, or is he ... different?"

"Different? Ha!" Fontrailles said. "They're *all* different so far as I can tell. They're as different from us as we are from the peasants who work our lands." Des Cartes raised a skeptical eyebrow. "All right, perhaps not *that* different. But with nobles of high rank, there's nothing to rein in their eccentricities but their peers' disapproval. Why do you, um, ask?"

"Oh, I've just been thinking about the Lord Commander." Isabeau knit her brow, lines appearing where none had been before La Rochelle. "In some ways he reminds me of ... oh, forgive me, Louis, but of your late brother Raoul. The commander's still kind of a boy, playing with horses and soldiers. Raoul was like that."

And you almost married him, Louis thought with a chill.

The sound of hoofbeats, and then Longvilliers's smiling, handsome face, bouncing up and down, appeared at the left window. "It's a glorious late summer day, Mademoiselle, and we have a spare horse," he said. "Won't you come ride with me?"

"Alone?" Isabeau said. "I think I'd better not."

"Ah, Mademoiselle is wise," said Sir Percy Blakeney, bouncing up and down at the opposite window. "She's heard something of the habits of noble knights."

Isabeau laughed, and Longvilliers said, "That, Monsieur, is uncalled for!"

"So much of what I say is," replied Blakeney. "But if Mademoiselle is in need of a chaperone, I'd be proud to serve in that capacity."

Isabeau looked at Fontrailles, in his splints and double arm sling. "Louis?"

"Go ahead," he said. "Enjoy the day."

It's time I got used to parting from her, Louis thought. *I'm going to lose her forever once we liberate Éric-the-rapist.* He sighed. *She's bearing his child; there's nothing to be done about it. Longvilliers and I are both wasting our time.*

Once Isabeau had ridden off ahead, laughing, between the two cavaliers, Fontrailles said, "Monsieur des Cartes, is there anything in your *Rules for the Direction of the Mind* of use in solving an ethical dilemma?"

Des Cartes raised his soft dark eyebrows. "Nothing that will help a man whose dilemma is a woman. My rules apply only to the mind, not the heart."

"What makes you think my problem is a romantic one?"

"I'm far from blind, Monsieur," des Cartes sniffed. "You must think me an oblivious pedant."

"Pardon me, Monsieur!" Fontrailles said. "Distress made me thoughtless."

Des Cartes shook his head. "No, it is I who must apologize. I confess I was vexed that you have preferred to spend your time talking with the young lady rather than conversing about intellectual matters. Foolish of me."

"Not at all; the fault is mine," Fontrailles said. "I've been preoccupied with my ethical—all right, *romantic*—dilemma. Frankly, I'm at a loss as to how to resolve it."

Des Cartes nodded. "I have long observed that strong emotion is the enemy of clear thought."

"Mind and body must be kept separate, eh?" said Fontrailles. "Not easily done."

"Few have found it so. But a mind—a soul, if you will—is the gift we have from God that makes us different from the animals, which are mere mechanisms of instinct. The responses of your heart are instinctual, but fortunately you are endowed with a mind that can rise above the base urgings of your physical person."

"So, cultivate a life of the mind and set my feelings aside," Fontrailles said. "I hope you'll pardon my saying so, but that's uncomfortably like the advice I got from Father Joseph."

"Father Joseph is a *mystic*," des Cartes said with asperity, "not to mention a sanctimonious hypocrite."

"Now that's something we *can* agree upon."

The carriage stopped at a shallow ford. Beaune and Gitane, who were driving, allowed the horses to drink while they hopped off the box to check the traces and the baggage on the rear platform. A cramp hit Louis below the stomach; his guts were still feeling the effects of Doctor Lambe's elixirs. He slid himself to the window and called, "Beaune! Best bring me the chamberpot."

He was about to lie back on the seat again when a drumming of hooves from behind caught his attention. He craned his neck and watched as a horseman passed the carriage at a gallop, splashing through the stream.

"*Merdieu!*" he cried. "That *can't* be a coincidence!"

"Why?" said des Cartes. "Was it someone you recognized?"

Fontrailles nodded. "Cocodril."

CHAPTER LXII
TWO SORTS OF REPTILES

Changing horses at Arras, Cocodril had asked about the town of Lillers and been told there wasn't much to it: Lillers was just a market town, a stop on the road between Béthune and Boulogne, barely large enough to have a post-stable. A cavalier like the Comte de Rochefort would cast a long shadow in such a place, so Cocodril didn't doubt that if Rochefort was there, he'd be able to find him.

Lillers was a blocky church and a cluster of houses sprouting from the fertile farmland of the Pas de Calais, and as Cocodril trotted into town from the south he whistled a sprightly tune he'd learned in a Paris cabaret. Opposite the church he found the travelers' inn, where he paused to inspect himself multiply reflected in the inn's diamond-paned bayfront window. He cocked his cap to a jauntier angle, straightened its cock-feather, brushed some of the road-dust from his tunic, and practiced an expression of respectful zeal, leavened by a slight but knowing smile. Pleased with the effect, he resumed whistling his tune and turned his horse toward the post-stable behind the inn.

There he found his man: the Comte de Rochefort, cursing at a pair of louts who were trying to repair the broken axle of a sadly tilting carriage.

And who could blame him for cursing, Cocodril thought, afflicted as he must be with servants so far inferior in wit and *savoir faire* to the standard that he, Cocodril, embodied. Assuming the expression he'd practiced in the window, Cocodril dismounted, approached the count, and bowed with the correct measure of deference. "Jean Reynon, at your service, Monsieur le Comte," he said, doffing his cap. "May I offer my condolences on the state of your equipage?"

"Eh? Who the devil are you?" snapped Rochefort. "Hold, I know you— one of Milady's men, Cocodril I think she called you. Are you looking for her?"

"In happy fact, Your Lordship, I'm looking for *you*! I have an urgent message for you," he said, lowering his voice, "from the Capuchin."

Rochefort now turned his full attention on Cocodril—which was highly gratifying! "Indeed?" he said. "Give it to me."

This seemed a trifle cold, but Cocodril thought it prudent to maintain his respectful demeanor. He reached into his tunic and, with a little flourish, produced the note from Father Joseph.

Rochefort took it without so much as a thank you. Cocodril's feelings might have been bruised if he hadn't been taking admiring note of the count's haughty manner, for later emulation in his own dealings with inferiors. Rochefort read the letter and snarled, "*Corbleu*! Have you been lounging by the roadside, you lazy dog? If you'd caught up with me sooner I wouldn't have to undo what's already been done."

"But no, Monseigneur! I have ridden from Paris like the wind itself!" Cocodril cried. This was so unfair! "It's true that I was given a winded horse at Montdidier, but the hostler is to blame, not I. In fact," Cocodril added, "it may have been a deliberate act of sabotage. I didn't like that hostler's looks...."

"Carriage is fixed, Monsieur," interrupted one of the louts, saluting the count with what Cocodril considered greasy over-familiarity.

"Good, Malafer," said Rochefort, "because now I have work for you. You must go to the priory at Béthune and pick up one of the prisoners, a Sieur de Gimous, and escort him back to the Bastille in Paris. I'll give you a note for his release."

"Then who will drive the carriage to pick up Milady de Winter?" Malafer asked.

"This rascal will," Rochefort replied, turning to Cocodril. "Attend me, rogue. It's convenient that you are known to Milady, because I need you to drive to the Carmelite convent in Béthune to pick her up. Milady will inform you of what to do thereafter; you are to follow her orders."

"An excellent plan, Monseigneur," Cocodril said, "but in the interest of its success, permit me to offer a slight emendation! Regrettably, Milady and I did not part on the best of terms, and she may be strongly disinclined to accept my services again, willing though I may be to offer them. Fortunately, a solution is at hand! I am also known to Monsieur de Gimous, who has no reason to regard me with disesteem."

"So?" said Rochefort.

"So, if I inform him surreptitiously that this transfer to the Bastille is really a ruse on the part of his friends to liberate him, he will accompany me eagerly!"

Cocodril looked expectantly at the count, but Rochefort's grim face lacked the appropriate enthusiasm. "Hmph," the cavalier said, regarding Cocodril much as a snake considers a rodent. "Very well—we will do it that way. But hear me: you will take Gimous directly to the Bastille, with none of your follies, or I will find you and personally cut your throat."

Cocodril gulped, but stood at attention and said, "You may count on me, Monseigneur! Death before dishonor!"

"Exactly," Rochefort said. "Wait a moment while I write you a short note. Then you must hurry—I was just at the priory, where I gave them word to prepare the English prisoners to go to Boulogne for the exchange. You must catch them before they leave. The others are to stay, but Gimous goes with you. Got it?"

"Indubitably, Monseigneur!"

The priory, Rochefort had said while writing his order, was on the extensive lands owned by the Carmelites near Béthune, though separate, of course, from the convent. It housed the priest who attended to the pastoral needs of the nuns and novices, as well as a few friars who oversaw such masculine activities as butchering and brewing. But the priory also served another function: it was a northern station of Father Joseph's intelligence service, and currently housed three prisoners awaiting exchange for French agents held by the English.

When the note was ready Cocodril vaulted into the saddle of a fresh horse and took off at a gallop, leaving, he was certain, a favorable impression on the haughty count. Outside Lillers he caught up with Rochefort's carriage, lumbering along the same road, and passed it with a rallying cry and a jaunty wave of his cap.

In less than an hour he was in Béthune. He rode past the Carmelite convent and followed the Festubert road, which curved around a small wood before turning east. A league farther, on a small hillock north of the road, Cocodril found the priory: an ancient edifice built of stone blocks the color of pale ale, overgrown with thick dark ivy. The heavy front door was set deep in a vaulted doorway; Cocodril leapt from the saddle and pounded on the dark wood. "Hello, the priory!" he called. "An urgent message!"

"Hey, you! Stop that noise!" came a voice from off to the side. Cocodril stepped from the embrasure and saw a white-robed friar at the corner of the building, who gestured and said, "This way, you fool!"

"Fool, yourself!" Cocodril replied, leading his horse after the man. "A little courtesy, please! I'm an official messenger."

"An official fool, if you go around drawing attention to yourself like that," said the friar. He was an ugly fellow, thought Cocodril, with a face rather like a dog, and his looks were not improved by a shaggy tonsure that had not been tended to recently. He led Cocodril into a stable yard behind the priory and said, "I'm Frère Heureux. Now who are you?"

"I," said Cocodril, adopting something of the manner of the Comte de Rochefort, "am Jean Reynon, in the service of His Eminence. This is for you," he said, thrusting Rochefort's note at the man, who stubbornly refused to look impressed. "See that you act upon it immediately."

The friar took the note and read it, lips moving, then snorted disgustedly. "Bloody fools. Why can't they make up their minds?" He turned toward the stables and called, "Pieux!"

Another friar came out of the stables and said, "What?" His white robe was filthy, he was unshaven, and his tonsure was even more ragged than Heureux's.

"We need only one horse. Two of the guests are staying; Gimous goes with him." Heureux jerked a thumb toward Cocodril.

"I got the other horses ready for nothing?" Frère Pieux growled. "All right, then. They get old Splayfoot."

"Do I care?" said Frère Heureux. He turned to Cocodril and said, "Wait here. I'll go get your Sieur de Gimous."

"Be quick about it," said Cocodril, "or His Eminence will hear of it."

Heureux just shook his head and slouched off toward the priory. Frère Pieux came out of the stables leading a horse that could only be old Splayfoot. He handed the reins to Cocodril and turned to leave.

"Wait," Cocodril said. "Aren't you going to help with the prisoner?"

"That's your problem," Pieux said, wiping his nose with the back of his sleeve. "Big fellow like you should be able to handle it." And he disappeared back into the stables.

After what seemed to Cocodril entirely too long Frère Heureux emerged from the priory leading Éric de Gimous, whose hands were bound in front of him with a length of rough rope. "Here's your man," said Heureux, "and good riddance. He makes us crazy with his continual praying."

"Cocodril!" Gimous said, blinking in the sunlight. He looked wan and sallow. "Is that you?"

"Indeed it is, Monsieur—and as always, discharging my duty to the cardinal with stern severity!" Cocodril spoke harshly, but at the same time gave Gimous a broad wink with the eye away from Frère Heureux.

This just seemed to confuse the young Huguenot nobleman. "I don't understand," he said.

"Just get up on this horse and follow the loudmouth," said Heureux. "You can pray for enlightenment while you ride."

Cocodril gave the friar what he firmly believed was a devastating glare, then said to Gimous, "Yes, come, Monsieur—we must hurry. I must take you back to Paris for incarceration." He gave the young man another surreptitious wink, and was pleased to note it was received with dawning comprehension.

"Ah … yes," said Gimous, struggling into the saddle with bound hands. "Alas for me—I go to meet an evil fate."

"Oh, for God's sake," Frère Heureux said, and slouched back into the priory.

As they rode along the road to Béthune, Gimous chattered happily in the sunshine. "The Commander de Longvilliers sent you, didn't he? And Isabeau," he said. "How did they learn where I was being held? No, I know—Louis figured it out, didn't he? He was always clever." He held up his hands. "Can you cut these ropes off now?"

Cocodril looked around. They were at a bend in the road just before it reached the wood; the road was deserted, and he could see no one in the fields to the right. "But of course!" he said cheerily. He dismounted, drew his long knife, and said, "Hold still, Monsieur."

Gimous held his hands out, but Cocodril seized his right foot, pulled it from the stirrup and slashed across the back of the ankle with his blade, severing the hamstring. Blood spurted and Gimous howled with pain, falling forward onto his mount's neck. The old horse, smelling blood, shied, stamped, and rolled its eye. Cocodril grabbed the bridles of both horses before either could panic and run. He took a few moments to calm them, then turned to Gimous, who was gasping and crying.

Cocodril bound the wound with a rag. "Why, Cocodril?" the young man asked. "I thought you were saving me!"

"Oh, but I am, Monsieur!" Cocodril said. "I fully intend to return you to your friends—after they have provided me with appropriate remuneration. In the meantime, I can't have you running off and getting yourself into trouble. Come, don't take it so hard! What would your noble ancestors think to see the last of their line blubbering like a babe in arms?"

They resumed their ride toward Béthune, Cocodril holding the reins of Gimous's mount. Cocodril tried whistling his cabaret tune but Gimous kept interrupting, moaning about his ankle despite Cocodril's exhortations to shut up and act like a nobleman. But Gimous's laments continued until Cocodril, irritated by such arrant selfishness, slapped him hard in the face and ordered him to be quiet. Only then was he able to resume his whistling.

They were rounding the wood that stood between the convent and the priory when they came upon Rochefort's carriage, parked on a grassy verge near the edge of the trees. The driver, Malafer, had dismounted, and seemed to be binding a wound on his arm. Cocodril pulled up and cried, "*Holà*! What a coincidence, meeting you here like this! Have you encountered some trouble?"

Malafer, a burly blond Norman with a thick face and neck, said, "More than I care for. If you're smart, you won't go through Béthune; there are King's Musketeers in town." He held up his arm. "One of them winged me."

"Why stop here, then?" Cocodril asked. "They might catch up with you."

"We're waiting for Milady," Malafer said. "She told us to meet her here."

There was a rustling from the woods, then out into the fading sunlight stepped Milady de Winter. A strand of blonde hair at her temple was out of place, and there was a tear in the left sleeve of her deep blue dress, but otherwise she looked as if she'd just stepped from a Paris salon. She nodded toward Malafer, and then narrowed her eyes at the sight of Cocodril.

"Milady de Winter!" cried Cocodril in delight. He leapt from the saddle and bowed, his peaked cap sweeping the greensward. "It is I, Cocodril, returned to your service! And," he added, gesturing toward the Sieur de Gimous, "I come with a valuable gift!"

CHAPTER LXIII
THE DROP ON MILADY

"Explain yourself, Cocodril," said Milady de Winter, "and make it brief. I had to kill a woman at the convent, and the musketeers are after me. I have no time for taradiddle."

"I shall be concise—even terse!" Cocodril said. "Because I knew him to be the friend of your enemy the Vicomte de Fontrailles, I've detained the Sieur de Gimous so you can wreak your vengeance upon him—or even better, hold him for ransom! Fontrailles is allied with the Commander de Longvilliers, who has substantial funds at his disposal."

Milady, looking up the road toward Béthune, said, "Where did you get him?"

"He was about to be exchanged to the English for a Frenchman, a clear waste of a valuable resource! So I liberated him myself."

"What's that?" said Milady, now at full attention. "You're telling me you've disrupted one of Richelieu's operations? *Imbécile!* His Eminence's favor is my only hope!" She turned to Malafer. "Can you drive with that arm?"

"Not as well as you may need me to, Milady."

"Cocodril, I require you to drive my carriage," she said. "Gimous is a liability. Take him into the woods and dispatch him."

Both Gimous and Cocodril cried out in protest. "Can't we bring him along so *I* can ransom him, Your Ladyship?" Cocodril asked. "I'll take full responsibility!"

"No. Do as I say." Milady climbed into the carriage. "And be quick about it."

Cocodril shrugged philosophically. One must adapt to circumstance! Gimous, to Cocodril's irritation, did not take the turn of events at all well. He was noisy and disposed to be troublesome; pulling him from the saddle and dragging him into the woods was thoroughly vexing! At the end, the stripling even managed to give Cocodril a shrewd clout over the eyes, which induced Cocodril to employ his knife with rather more savagery than was strictly necessary.

Cocodril, winded, emerged from the wood and paused, blinking at the scene before him. For a moment he thought the blow on his head had made him see double, for now there were two carriages, one parked on the road beyond Milady's. Then he saw who was getting out of the second carriage and turned to flee.

"If you run, Cocodril," called the Vicomte de Fontrailles, "you'll be shot!"

He stopped. It was true; that ox Beaune and the vile Gitane were close at hand and armed with long pistols. Beyond them the Commander de Longvilliers and the Englishman, Blakeney, guarded Milady and her men. Vidou and the Bonnefont girl were helping Fontrailles, who had something badly wrong with him, into a sort of wheeled chair that another man had brought from the rear of their carriage.

Cocodril clasped his hands before him. "Thank the good God you've arrived, Monsieur de Fontrailles! Your dear friend, the Sieur de Gimous, is imprisoned in a priory just up the road, but he's to be taken from there almost immediately! Make haste! I will stay here and guard the Comtesse de Winter."

The Bonnefont girl turned to Fontrailles and said, "Louis?"

"No," Fontrailles said. "He's lying."

"How do you know?" said Longvilliers.

"If he speaks, he lies," said Fontrailles. "Would you oblige me by rolling me forward, Monsieur des Cartes?"

"Do but listen, Your Lordship!" Cocodril cried. "I have just pursued Milady from the convent, where...."

"Your knife drips blood, Cocodril," Fontrailles said. "Drop it. Beaune, keep him covered. Gitane, check the woods."

The dark man ducked under the branches. After a moment he returned. "The Sieur de Gimous, Monsieur," he said. "I'm sorry, but ... he's dead."

The Bonnefont girl shrieked, and Beaune's eyes flickered toward her. Cocodril knocked the pistol from his hand, then darted toward Fontrailles while drawing a second knife from his boot-top. He shouldered aside the unarmed man who'd been pushing the chair, jerked back the hunchback's head, laid the knife at his throat, and shouted at Gitane, "Drop the pistol or he dies!"

"Do it," said Longvilliers. Gitane laid his pistol carefully on the moss at his feet.

"Now," said Cocodril, "I desire some privacy with my old employer, here. We have important matters to discuss. The rest of you are to get on your horses or into the carriages and drive away—far away."

"You'll just kill him as soon as we're out of sight," protested Longvilliers.

"Perhaps," said Cocodril, "or perhaps not. I am whimsical."

Longvilliers cursed. The Bonnefont chit said, "We have to do what he says! He'll kill Louis!"

"Cocodril," Fontrailles said from beneath the blade. "I have a better idea, one that will get both of us away from here alive. Will you listen?"

Cocodril considered; the *bossu* was clever, and he was certainly motivated to think of an alternative, as he must know that Cocodril planned to kill him, no matter what happened. "Speak," he said.

"It's hard," the hunchback said. "So weak—losing my voice. Lean over."

Cocodril looked suspiciously at Beaune and Gitane. "You two: move farther away." They backed off, and Cocodril leaned over to hear what Fontrailles had to say.

There was a bright flash and a very, very loud noise.

When Fontrailles blew off the top of Cocodril's head with the pistol concealed under the blanket in his lap, everyone started, and Isabeau screamed. Milady de Winter did not scream; she was right behind Beaune and Gitane as they dashed forward and grabbed the rogue's falling body, where she knelt at Fontrailles's feet and cried, "Monsieur de Fontrailles! Are you all right? Oh, thank heaven!"

"Get her away from me!" Fontrailles said. "Hold her, and search her for weapons! How many times do you think I want to be taken hostage?"

Beaune grabbed her arms from behind; Milady struggled for a moment, then glared as Gitane searched her, drawing a slim stiletto from a sheath between her breasts. He displayed it to Fontrailles, who said, "Well done, Gitane. How did you know to look there?"

The one-eyed man smiled. "I had this woman once, who...."

Milady interrupted. "If you're through humiliating me, Monsieur de Fontrailles, there are things you must know. Listen, and quickly! There is a dead woman at the convent, a Madame Bonacieux. Cocodril killed her, kidnapped me, and dragged me through the woods to where he knew I was to meet my men after they'd liberated Monsieur de Gimous."

Louis was fascinated; her voice compelled belief, her beautiful eyes were radiant with sincerity. "Cocodril was a thorough criminal, worse than any of us ever knew!" she continued. "He hated you, Monsieur, and everyone associated with you—he murdered Monsieur de Gimous, and was planning to carry me off and hold me for ransom. Thank God you came in time! But now...."

"Stop, Milady, please," Fontrailles said. "You're a remarkable liar—I particularly liked that little throb in your voice when you thanked God for our timely arrival—but we know far too much to accept your story. Even if we did, those musketeers who passed us on the road to Béthune are bound to have opinions of their own."

Milady shook off Beaune's arms and looked down at Fontrailles with icy hauteur. "You, Monsieur," she said, "are far out of your depth. There are matters of State at question here." She pointed at Cocodril's body. "You already have here the murderer of Sieur de Gimous. Allow me to go on my way, immediately, and I believe I can persuade the cardinal to overlook your interference in his affairs."

"No, I don't think so." Fontrailles shook his head. "Isabeau?"

Isabeau de Bonnefont stepped forward, chin trembling slightly, and looked the Comtesse de Winter in the eye. "You murdered my father," she said.

"An accident," said Milady.

"It was murder," Isabeau said. She choked, then continued: "You must pay for it."

Beaune and Gitane closed in again. Milady drew herself up. "What do you think you're doing, *canailles*? You have no right!"

Fontrailles shrugged.

"No," declared René des Cartes. "She's right. It would be a criminal act of revenge."

Louis sighed. "*Merdieu.* Very well, Monsieur des Cartes: what do you suggest?"

"You accuse her of a crime?"

"We do."

"Then," said des Cartes, "she must be tried."

CHAPTER LXIV
THE MAN IN THE MAGISTRATE'S MANTLE

"Tried, me?" said Milady de Winter. "In what court? And on whose authority would you arrest me? I could make a more compelling case for having *you* detained."

The Commander de Longvilliers, looking down his impressive hawk nose, said, "As a Knight Commander of a Holy Order, I have the authority to arrest you, if not legal, then certainly moral. In the name of my sacred oath, I arrest you in the name of holy justice."

"And I can act as judge," said Monsieur des Cartes. "I was trained to the law, and my father and brothers are all magistrates. Indeed, I sorely disappointed my father by not becoming a judge myself. Perhaps, in a small way, I can make amends to him."

"I do not know you, Monsieur," said Milady, "but you came here with my enemies. How can you be my judge?"

"I bear you no animus, Madame," replied des Cartes, "and my intellectual integrity will not allow me to act with other than fairness and justice."

Milady glanced up the road toward Béthune. "What you propose is

251

farce," she said, "and this is no time for theatrics. If you intend to be so foolish as to detain me, so be it. But we must not stay here any longer."

"No, Milady—we'll conduct the trial here and now," said Fontrailles. "It was sheer luck that we caught up with you when we did. If we delay, fortune will favor you again and somehow you'll contrive an escape, I know it. Gitane, keep an eye on her driver. Beaune, stay near Milady." He turned in his chair. "Sir Percy? Will you object, or join the proceedings?"

"Neither, Monsieur, if it's all the same to you," said Blakeney. "I've no place in a French judicial proceeding, however extemporaneous. No, I believe Enfield and I will ride on ahead and make sure you're not disturbed from that direction."

And scout out the priory while you're at it, Louis thought, *in preparation for freeing the English prisoners*. He gave a nod in place of a bow and said, "Thank you. And good luck.

"And now," Fontrailles said, "Monsieur Magistrate, if you would assume the mantle of justice and call the court to order?"

"No!" Milady cried. "Sir Percy! I'm an Englishwoman! You can't leave me here! Take me with you!"

"You, Madame—English?" said Blakeney. "Whatever has England done to deserve that?" He swung into his saddle and rode off, followed closely by Enfield.

"This is an outrage!" cried Milady. "It is … it is dishonorable!"

"Very well, Milady, since you're so opposed to this trial," Fontrailles said, "I'll offer you an alternative."

"Ah, you think better of it?" Milady said coldly. "That's wise."

"Perhaps. Here are your options: we try you, here and now, for the murder of the Seigneur de Bonnefont, or … we take you back to Béthune and turn you over to the musketeers."

Milady turned pale. "To … d'Artagnan? And, and … Athos?" She swallowed, then steeled herself. "In that event, Monsieur … I accept the trial."

"*Monsieur le Magistrat?*"

Des Cartes assumed a solemn and impassive expression, looking, Louis thought, every inch the judge. "This court is convened," he intoned. "Madame la Comtesse de Winter is accused of the willful murder of the Seigneur de Bonnefont. Where is her accuser?"

"Here," said Isabeau. "On the night of April 20th, 1627, on the Pont Neuf in Paris, before my own eyes, this woman shot and killed my father."

"Madame la Comtesse," said des Cartes, "how do you plead?"

"Innocent," said Milady, with all the hauteur of a *grande dame* of the high nobility. "I was armed, but purely for self defense. When we were attacked by an army of beggars, allies of Monsieur de Fontrailles here, I flinched and my pistol went off. The ball struck the Seigneur de Bonnefont." She shrugged. "It was unfortunate, but entirely accidental. I am a lady, not a murderer."

"Witnesses?" said des Cartes.

"I was a witness," said the Commander de Longvilliers. "I attest that before the beggars attacked, Milady threatened to shoot Mademoiselle de Bonnefont unless Monsieur de Fontrailles gave her a certain book. I testify that she fired deliberately, and the ball was intended for mademoiselle. Her father sacrificed his life to save her."

"I was a witness as well," said Fontrailles. "I saw Milady's face when she fired the shot: it was a face of fury and hatred. It was, in fact, the same expression she wore when she shot me in London."

"She shot you in London?" said Longvilliers. "I never knew that! How did it happen?"

"Later, Monseigneur," said Fontrailles.

"Madame, you have heard the witnesses," des Cartes said. "What is your response?"

"I demand that their testimony be disqualified!" Milady said. "Surely you can see that they both have eyes for the little demoiselle? They'll say whatever they think she wants to hear."

"You hell-bitch!" Isabeau cried, tears starting from her eyes.

"Mademoiselle, you are out of order," des Cartes said gently. To Milady he said, "Madame, your objection to the witnesses is not without merit, but there is still the personal testimony of your accuser, and you yourself have admitted to firing the shot that slew Monsieur de Bonnefont. I must rule that you have not shown conclusively that the act was not deliberate. I therefore find you guilty of willful murder."

"What?" cried Milady. "You must be mad! You'll all end up in the Bastille!"

Ignoring her, Des Cartes turned to Isabeau. "Mademoiselle, you are the accuser. What sentence do you demand?"

Isabeau, almost sobbing, fists clenched, glared at Milady de Winter. Her nostrils flared, and she opened her mouth to speak.

"Isabeau," said Fontrailles. "Wait. May I talk to you for a moment? Privately?"

Isabeau blinked, tore her eyes from Milady and looked at Fontrailles. "Louis," she said. "What is it?"

"A word with you," he said. "Please."

Slowly, she nodded. Des Cartes said, "Beaune, please remove the prisoner to a distance of twenty paces so the witness and accuser may talk."

Once Milady had been taken away—Louis noted that she was already whispering furiously to the mountainous Beaune—he looked at Isabeau. She was pale and trembling, but appeared resolute. "Isabeau," Fontrailles said, "hear me: you can't ask for Milady's death."

"How can you say that?" Isabeau almost hissed. "She killed my father! She almost killed you, more than once! She *deserves* to die."

"Perhaps so," Fontrailles said, "but she's right about one thing: if we have her put to death we will be executed for it, or spend the rest of our lives in the Bastille. She belongs to the cardinal, *chérie*, and he doesn't allow people to interfere with what belongs to him."

"We'll go to the United Provinces! Or England!"

"Not I; I'm at the end of my strength. I can travel no further until I recover."

"But ... what are you saying? We can't just let her go! She'll murder again!"

"Well, we can't kill her—but perhaps we can disarm her. Isabeau, do you trust me?"

Her amber eyes warmed. "Of course, Louis."

"Then will you leave this to me?"

She hesitated, then looked down and nodded.

Fontrailles gestured to des Cartes. "Beaune," called the temporary magistrate, "bring the prisoner back before the bench."

Returning, Milady looked sullen, but Beaune wore a broad grin. "What has she been telling you, Beaune?" Fontrailles asked.

"She tried to buy me, with money ... and herself," Beaune replied in his incongruous tenor. "But I used to be an inquisitor, so I've been offered everything there is to offer."

"The daylight fades; we must conclude this," said des Cartes. "Mademoiselle, what sentence do you ask?"

"Monsieur de Fontrailles speaks for me," Isabeau said in a small voice.

"Ah," said Milady de Winter. "Then, Monsieur, I take it there is something you want?"

"Mademoiselle had intended to ask for your death," Fontrailles said, "and rightly so. However, I have prevailed upon her to show clemency in return for your voluntary exile—and a signed confession of your crimes."

Milady laughed, a surprisingly beautiful sound, shockingly so in the presence of two newly dead men. "You are always so surprising, Monsieur de Fontrailles—it would be a shame to bury you in the Bastille. The exile I accept, and the sooner the better. I've had enough of France and the border is near at hand. But a confession? Sheer nonsense. And what good would it do you?"

"A confession of murder, Milady, especially one witnessed by a Knight of the Order..." Fontrailles looked at Longvilliers, who nodded, "will *keep* you in exile, for if you return it will be used to send you to the headsman. But if you refuse to write it, well ... there are always the musketeers. I'm sure they'd be delighted to escort you across the river."

Milady shuddered in spite of herself. "Very well," she said. "I concede. Bring me pen and paper."

In the last light of day, as Milady's carriage clattered off down the road,

Fontrailles, Isabeau, and des Cartes looked at the letter she had written to purchase her escape:

I hereby admit responsibility for the death of the Seigneur de Bonnefont, and the attempted death of the Vicomte de Fontrailles.

26 August 1628
Comtesse de WINTER

Witnessed: Philippe de LONGVILLIERS

"Oh, Louis," Isabeau said. "I hope what we did was right."

"To be honest, I just don't know," Fontrailles said. "It was the only thing I could come up with."

"All ready, Monsieur," said Gitane, coming from the carriage. "Both bodies are stowed securely."

"I'd like to see Éric ... for the last time," said Isabeau.

"Better not, Mademoiselle," Gitane said. "He's pretty torn up."

She began to weep. "Éric ... Éric...."

"Come, Isabeau," Louis said. "We'd better go and ... see to arranging the burial." He took one of her hands and patted it gently, but no more words of consolation came to him. Longvilliers approached and put an arm around her shoulder; she turned her face into his chest and wept.

Louis stared blankly down at his crooked, black-powder-stained hands. "Come, Monsieur," René des Cartes said quietly. "Allow me to help you back into the carriage."

CHAPTER LXV
INTERMENT

A chilly day in Béthune: a violent rainstorm the night before had brought summer to a sudden end, and the weather had turned cold. In the cemetery of the Church of Saint-Vaast a half-dozen people clustered around an open grave as the dirt fell in muddy clumps on the coffin of Éric de Gimous. The white-robed priest from the Carmelite priory, standing in for the priest of Saint Vaast who had left on a sudden journey, stood at the head of the grave. He pronounced the last words of the burial ceremony, closed his book and, with a final blessing, took his leave.

Kissing Isabeau's hand, the Commander de Longvilliers left immediately thereafter to settle accounts with the deacon of the church, where the mass for the dead had been held. Isabeau, des Cartes, and Fontrailles, in his wheeled chair, lingered by the graveside, Louis and Isabeau reminiscing about the Éric they had known as a youth.

"We were lucky, as children," Isabeau said, her voice rough from crying. "The religious wars mostly passed by our remote hills, and our families all managed to stay friendly despite our differences of faith. But poor Éric ... nothing prepared him for what he'd find outside the hills of Armagnac. He tried, but..." a sob caught in her throat. "He just wasn't strong enough."

"Was your childhood so different from his?" asked des Cartes.

"No."

"But you have endured, Mademoiselle," des Cartes said. "Where does your strength come from?"

Fontrailles, watching the gravediggers fill in the pit that contained what remained of Éric de Gimous, saw a shadow fall across the grave and looked up. "Sir Percy," he said. "You missed both mass and burial."

"Regrettably, I had a conflict," Blakeney said, voice more solemn than usual. "Pressing business that had to be attended to while the priest from the priory was here with you."

"Ah," said Fontrailles. "Now I see who made the travel plans for the priest of Saint-Vaast. Did your business go well?"

"As smoothly as such affairs usually do—which is to say, not very." Blakeney walked around the grave, and Fontrailles noticed that he was favoring his left leg. The Englishman smiled wryly. "There were a couple of friars who just wouldn't see reason."

"And their, ah, guests?"

"Enfield has them in temporary lodging outside town. I believe they prefer it to their cells at the priory," Blakeney said. "You know one of them, I think: a certain Balthasar Gerbier."

"Gerbier!" said Isabeau. "Louis, wasn't that the man...?"

Fontrailles nodded. "The Duke of Buckingham's art agent. It was his appearance at my château that launched me into this whole mad affair."

"So I'd heard," said Blakeney. "He had the bad luck to be on this side of the Channel when the war broke out and was interned."

"You think it was luck? I'll wager he was up to something more than just buying art," Fontrailles said. "Well, I'm sure Milord Buckingham will be glad to get him back, and without having to exchange anyone for him."

"The Duke of Buckingham will never be glad of anything again," said Blakeney. "He's dead—assassinated."

"Indeed!" said des Cartes, showing interest for the first time.

"The devil!" said Fontrailles.

"The devil: exactly," said Blakeney. "The duke's assassin was driven to the deed by Milady Winter."

"Who told you this?"

"Lord Winter, her brother-in-law. I ran into him at the inn here, which was a bit of a shocker. He's in Béthune in pursuit of Milady—incognito, of course, so don't nose it about. "

"Milady de Winter!" Isabeau said bitterly. "There've been three funerals in the last two days because of her: that Madame Bonacieux at the convent, Cocodril at the potter's field, and now Éric's...." She turned away, dabbing her eyes with an already-damp handkerchief.

"The death of a friend comes hard," said Blakeney.

"The Commander de Longvilliers has sworn vengeance, despite our agreement to let Milady go," said Fontrailles, and added, "he held Isabeau's hand throughout the funeral mass."

"He's been a dear," Isabeau said, sniffling.

"Has he?" said Blakeney. "And if he tries to hold more than your hand, what then?"

"Monsieur!" said Isabeau, brown eyes flashing. "Louis, I think I have had quite enough of your English friend for the time being. I'm going into the church to find Philippe ... I mean, Monseigneur de Longvilliers. He should be told the news about the Duke of Buckingham."

"I believe I'll go with you; it will be interesting to view his reaction," said des Cartes. "May I offer you my arm, Mademoiselle?"

Fontrailles pivoted his chair to face Blakeney. "That," he said, "was uncalled-for."

"If that's what you think, then you haven't been paying attention," said Blakeney, "though it was, I concede, somewhat indelicate. But it's becoming increasingly clear that mademoiselle is in a somewhat delicate condition herself. I can't believe *that* has escaped your attention."

"It hasn't," Fontrailles said sourly. "And what, exactly, is your reason for drawing attention to it?"

"Nothing, really—except that knights commander are rather good at providing for children, born in or out of wedlock. Longvilliers took care of his first son, didn't he?"

"You obviously know more than I do in that regard, but that's a point I hadn't previously considered," Fontrailles said. He sat musing for a moment, then said, "Blakeney, I have to thank you: you've given me a reason to suppress my jealousy of Longvilliers."

"Not at all, old fellow, not at all. I'm never indelicate without cause."

The gravediggers had finished their grim labor and departed. Fontrailles said, "Sir Percy, would you be so kind as to help me over to that tavern on the square? It's time for another medicinal dose of *eau-de-vie*."

They sat at an outdoor table despite the chill—the chair wouldn't fit through the taproom door—and the barmaid brought them two glasses of the local brandy. "This should warm us up," Fontrailles said.

"*Santé*," said Blakeney, raising his glass. "I must confess that I had another motive for coming back to chat with you before leaving France. Longvilliers told me that the *Three Mystic Heirs* book Buckingham was so keen on is now in the possession of Cardinal Richelieu. Buckingham is dead, but in the interest of England, I have to ask: should I be concerned?"

"Take a good look at me, Sir Percy. There's your answer," Fontrailles said. "One of Europe's leading scholars attempted to prove the virtues of *The Three Mystic Heirs* by healing me with its arts. Instead Athanasius Kircher nearly killed me—multiple times—without, so far as I can tell, doing me the least bit of good. So much for the Rosicrucians and their grand attempt to combine all art, science, and religion."

"Well, that's a relief. If it turned out you could explain everything with natural philosophy, we'd all have to go back to school, wouldn't we? Now we can return to simply having faith and praying to the Good Lord."

"Faith." Fontrailles shook his head. "You can have faith in anything, can't you? It doesn't make it true. Kircher, I'll wager, still has faith in the Hermetic wisdom, despite his failures atop the Column of Destiny."

"What you say may be true, but what does it get you?" said Blakeney, serious for once. "What's the alternative? General disbelief in everything?"

"I don't know," Fontrailles said. "My friend des Cartes has an idea that you should only believe in what can be proved from observation and logic, but even he takes as a given the existence and primacy of the Christian

God. To me, it seems that contradicts his entire approach. Not," he quickly added, "that I question the existence of God, praise his name!"

"Certainly not," said Blakeney. "Atheism being, after all, a capital crime."

"As well it should be!" Both men raised their glasses and drank, then smiled at each other across the table—Fontrailles a little uncomfortably, Blakeney a little too broadly. Fontrailles snorted. "What was it you said your friends used to call you?"

"Diogenes."

"I'd say you've earned it. You certainly excel at discovering others' truths without revealing your own. Well, Master Diogenes, now that Buckingham is dead, what will you do with yourself?"

"I think it's time I returned to England. I'd like to see if there's anything I can do to keep things from going as wrong as they did under Buckingham. King Charles is bound to pick a new favorite, but favorites can be influenced."

"And Lady Carlisle? What of her?"

"Darling Lucy!" Blakeney's broad smile returned. "She's become a sort of favorite herself—not of King Charles, but of Queen Henriette, your king's sister. Restored to favor, and with Buckingham dead, Lucy will go back to breaking hearts at Court nineteen to the dozen." He smiled to himself for a moment, and then said, "But speaking of the ladies, what was that you said about an agreement to let Milady Winter go? I wondered how that little chess-match came out."

Fontrailles drained his glass of eau-de-vie, closing his eyes for a moment as he felt the warmth spread through him. "Ah. Dear Milady," he said. "We released her in exchange for her promise to leave the country, and for a signed confession of her murder of old de Bonnefont. *Peste,* but I wish we'd known about her complicity in the assassination of Buckingham! It must have been done at Richelieu's order—if we'd had that on the document as well, it would protect us against both Milady and the cardinal."

Blakeney drained his own glass and asked, "Do you have this remarkable confession?"

"Right here."

"Let me see it."

Fontrailles drew the paper from under his cloak and passed it to Blakeney. The Englishman automatically glanced around to make sure no one was too close, then opened and read it.

"Why, this will be no problem at all, old friend," Blakeney said. "There's plenty of room between Milady's confession and her signature."

Fontrailles snorted. "What are you going to do, track her down and ask her to add an extra confession or two as a favor?"

"Come, now, Monsieur Master Mind," Blakeney said, shaking a finger. "Think. Do you recall when I first entered your employ under the rather silly name of Mister Parrott?"

"Yes, of course. You said you were ... a forger. Oh." Fontrailles whistled, three descending notes.

Blakeney smiled. "You wouldn't happen to have the pen Milady used to write this note, would you?"

"In fact, I do."

"Lend it to me, won't you?" Blakeney asked cheerily. "Now, some paper, some ink, and a few minutes to practice, and I think I can make it up to you for missing poor Gimous's funeral."

Fontrailles called for paper, ink, and more brandy, then watched, fascinated, as Blakeney went to work. His wide face with its tawny, tufted mustache and eyebrows took on an inward expression, a look of concentration that Fontrailles had never seen on the man before. After working for a while on the blank sheets brought by the barmaid he turned his attention to Milady's actual letter, and his concentration intensified. With eyes only inches from the paper, he traced careful looping lines across it. Finally he set the pen aside, blew on the ink to dry it, and handed the paper back across the table. Fontrailles read:

I hereby admit responsibility for the death of the Seigneur de Bonnefont, and the attempted death of the Vicomte de Fontrailles.

Moreover, I confess to having arranged the assassination of His Grace the Duke of

Buckingham upon the orders of Cardinal Richelieu of France.
   26 August 1628
   Comtesse de WINTER

Witnessed: Philippe de LONGVILLIERS

The new writing, though it still glistened a bit where the ink had not fully dried, was otherwise identical to the old.

"Blakeney," Fontrailles said wonderingly, "you are a true artist."

"Extremely good of you to say so," Blakeney replied. "Another brandy?"

CHAPTER LXVI
EXCULPATION

The next day Fontrailles awoke with a fever once more, and Isabeau ordered him to stay in bed. She was serving him a warm infusion in his room in the Béthune inn when the Commander de Longvilliers burst in. "Milady de Winter is dead!" he said. "Executed by a headsman hired by your friends the musketeers!"

Fontrailles sat up despite his fever. "Where did you hear this?"

"Blakeney just told me. He's leaving town immediately, heading north over the border into Flanders. Your Monsieur des Cartes is going with him." Longvilliers paced back and forth. "We should leave as well—and soon. Once the cardinal is informed, this region will buzz like a nest of hornets."

"Louis's in no condition to travel!" Isabeau protested.

"His condition won't improve in a prison cell," said the commander. "And you're a Protestant—they'll arrest you on mere suspicion. No, my dear: we need to go someplace far enough, and populous enough, that we'll be overlooked."

Fontrailles sighed. "I suppose I can make it to Arras."

"Are you sure?" said Isabeau.

"If I must," he said. "Just don't forget to lay in a couple of bottles of brandy."

They left Béthune that afternoon, arriving at the busy mercantile town of Arras on the evening of the following day. There, next to a tapestry works, the commander rented a sizable house, a place where the Vicomte de Fontrailles could convalesce, the Demoiselle de Bonnefont could complete her pregnancy—and the commander could pay his attentions to the demoiselle. Isabeau was one of those women whom pregnancy makes radiant, and her unfashionably slim figure was ripening into fullness. She seemed happy with her condition, and flattered by the knight's attentions.

Fontrailles spent as much time as he could with Isabeau, but as the weeks passed she was more and more with Longvilliers and he was left to his own devices. The commander had engaged the leading physician of Arras to tend him, but when the doctor prescribed bleedings and purgatives Fontrailles had sent him packing. "I'm not taking any treatments that remind me of what happened on that column in Paris," he told Isabeau. "No more enemas for me, *merci beaucoup.*"

After that, whenever he wasn't reading or writing letters, he was exercising. Beaune, who had seen a lot of torture victims, had recommended that Fontrailles work his muscles rather than let them atrophy. Fontrailles hated exercise, but he was grimly determined not to be a cripple, and had resolved to restore his maltreated body to its former vigor. So he spent hours lifting brocaded cushions with trembling legs, or wheeling himself back and forth across his little study until his arms quivered with fatigue. But it was working: he was young, his body had been strong, and soon, he knew, it would be strong again.

On a morning at the end of September Fontrailles was sitting in his wheeled chair, absently raising a cushion balanced on his calves—up, hold for an eight-count, down—while reading a letter from René des Cartes dated two weeks earlier. The scholar had reached Middelburg in Holland, where he intended to stay for a while with his friend Isaac Beeckman. Blakeney, Lord Winter, and Balthasar Gerbier had gone on to England, which was fine with des Cartes; the Englishmen chattered too much about trifles and interfered with his thinking.

The latter part of the letter related some of des Cartes's recent thoughts about symbolic logic and fourth-order equations, and Louis was just starting to puzzle it out when a knock came at his door. "Isabeau?" he called. "Are you back from your ride?"

The door slowly opened, revealing not Isabeau de Bonnefont, but the tall, erect figure of the Comte de Rochefort, holding a gleaming, naked rapier. "*Bonjour,* Monsieur de Fontrailles," he said, teeth gleaming like his rapier. "I took the liberty of letting myself in."

Louis's pulse pounded in his ears, and not from the exercise. "N-not at all," he said. "Make yourself at home. We're informal here; you can sheath your sword."

Rochefort was orbiting the room, checking behind screens and furnishings. He didn't sheath his sword. His eyes kept flickering back toward Fontrailles. "Why don't you put that cushion down?" he asked.

Louis realized he was holding his legs straight out, frozen in the position they'd been in when Rochefort had entered. He lowered them, expelled his breath, and tried to control his thoughts. "What are you doing here?" he asked.

"I came for my pistol—the Spät," Rochefort said, completing his circuit. "You wouldn't have it at hand, would you? Say, under that blanket on your lap?"

"Sorry—I lost it in the salt marsh at La Rochelle," Fontrailles said. "I felt bad about it, though."

Rochefort called out through the doorway, "The room is safe," then turned back to Fontrailles. "If you were really sorry, Fontrailles, you would have ordered me a new one from Herr Spät. So far Munich has survived the German wars, so I presume he's still in business."

"In fact, I've ordered t-two—one for each of us," Fontrailles began, but he was interrupted by the sound of bare feet on the parquet floor. Father Joseph came into the study, cowled as always, his arms hidden in his wide woolen sleeves.

Calm as a tree, the Capuchin surveyed Fontrailles. "God bless you, my son," he said quietly. "How do you fare?"

"As well as can be expected, *mon Père*," Fontrailles said nervously. "You will pardon me if I don't rise to greet you?"

"*Mais bien sûr*," said Father Joseph in his accustomed whisper. "You have my entire sympathy. You may not be aware of it, but like you I suffered injury at the hands of that poor Père Crozat. I have only recently recovered enough to travel—so I, too, will sit." He placed himself in a chair with carved, curving arms, sitting somewhat gingerly. Rochefort sheathed his rapier at last and stood behind Father Joseph, glowering.

Calm, Louis, he told himself. *You knew a confrontation like this was inevitable.* He said, "I've been expecting an emissary such as Monsieur de Rochefort, but I didn't think to see you personally, Monseigneur. To what do I owe the honor?"

"I've come to Arras primarily to meet with Monseigneur de Longvilliers," the Capuchin said. "But I wanted to speak with you first."

"Then I fear you will have to be brief," Fontrailles said. "The commander went for a morning carriage ride with Mademoiselle de Bonnefont and should be returning at any moment."

"I think we will have time to talk," said Joseph. "The knight will probably be delayed by repairs. It was imprudent of him to take out a carriage with a rear wheel in such precarious condition."

"There was nothing wrong with it yesterday," Fontrailles said.

"Indeed? Then perhaps I am ill-informed," said Joseph.

"What do you want with Monsieur de Longvilliers?"

Father Joseph frowned slightly. "The question is presumptuous, but as I hold you in high esteem, Monsieur, I will answer," he said. "The siege of La Rochelle is nearly over; once the city falls it will effectively end internal dissension in France and the king will be able to turn to the threat of Spain and her allies. With war in the offing, it is time for the Commander de Longvilliers to set aside his frivolous personal pursuits and cleave to the Crown. The Hapsburgs are numerous and powerful; France will need all its strength to oppose them."

"An appeal to patriotism," Fontrailles said. "It may work. The commander, if I may be so presumptuous as to comment, has talent and energy but lacks purpose."

"That is how the cardinal sees it," said Joseph, "as do I. I am not surprised to find that you share our perception; it shows I was correct to make time to speak with you. I am here to ask you once again, my son, to join us in our holy labors on behalf of the Most Christian Kingdom of France."

"Another appeal to patriotism?" Fontrailles said. "Speaking as a French nobleman, the House of Bourbon has my entire allegiance, and I have never done anything to injure it. Louis, the Thirteenth of the Name, is my king. But what you ask me to do is serve the House of Richelieu—and that is a different thing entirely."

"You object to our purpose?"

"I object to your methods. They are too harsh, and in the end they will be self-defeating. My current state is an example of their results."

"I fear your personal suffering has narrowed your vision," Joseph said. "There is no great achievement without risk; and sometimes, to test or chasten us, the Lord permits innocents to suffer. But we must never lose faith, or conviction in doing what is right."

"I'm not so sure doing what is right includes torture and murder," Fontrailles said acidly.

"I see you have fallen under the sway of the ideas of that person des Cartes," Father Joseph said. "He should have been charged with heresy."

"You are mistaken, Monseigneur; I am not at all persuaded that Monsieur des Cartes is on the right path. In truth, I'm not entirely sure what to believe. But these days I have a lot of time to think—and perhaps, by the time I recover, I'll know."

"You already know what to believe, my son. The Word of the Lord is written in your heart, your mind, and in the world around you. Devote your efforts during your convalescence to thinking of Him."

Fontrailles shook his head. "I can see I must speak plainly: I will not join you, Father Joseph, not now or ever."

Joseph sighed. "Then, Monsieur de Fontrailles, I must speak plainly as well. You are a tool that has been forged for the hand of the Lord—and it is the hand, not the hammer, that decides when to strike. If you will not serve from conviction, you will serve from self-interest."

"Monseigneur is obscure," Fontrailles said. "What do you mean?"

"The warrant, please, Monsieur de Rochefort," said Father Joseph. Rochefort slid a gauntleted hand into his violet doublet, drew out a folded sheet and handed it to the Capuchin. "We know from Monsieur de Rochefort's servant that you were involved in the destruction of Milady de Winter," whispered Joseph. "This is an order signed by the cardinal for your arrest and detention in that matter. Whether or not to exercise the warrant has been left to my judgment. So why be obstinate, Monsieur de Fontrailles? It will do you no good. You see, you *must* join us."

"No; this time, you are wrong, *mon Père*."

Joseph said sadly, "You will suffer for it, my son."

"On the contrary, I don't think I will—and with Monseigneur's permission, I will show you why." Fontrailles turned his chair toward his writing desk and reached into a stack of papers. Rochefort went as tense as a hound that sights a hare. "Don't worry, Count," Fontrailles said. "Our Späts haven't come from Munich yet; I'm merely getting a letter I'd like Father Joseph to see."

He wheeled himself toward the Capuchin and handed him the paper. Father Joseph, who had been looking skeptical, read Milady's confession and sat bolt upright. "Where did you get this?" he hissed. "It is patently false."

"It is not," Fontrailles said. "Milady de Winter wrote it herself. Rochefort's servant was there; he saw her do it."

"And why shouldn't I simply tear it to pieces?"

"Go ahead, if it will make you feel better," Fontrailles said, "but that's only a copy. The original is safely in the hands of a disinterested third party. If anything untoward happens to me, it will be published in London, Amsterdam, and Geneva. It will make a great noise, *mon Père*. What would *you* do if you were His Majesty and your prime minister was implicated in such a scandal?"

"Blackmail." Joseph was grim. "You will burn in hell, my son."

"Not at all; I've already confessed my sin and been forgiven."

"Mockery on top of it," Joseph said bitterly. "I had thought you above such practices, Monsieur."

"If that were true, I wouldn't have been much use to you and the cardinal, would I?" Fontrailles said. A clatter of hooves came from the *cour de cheval.* "Ah, there's the commander now. It was a pleasure to see you again, Father Joseph. Help Monseigneur out of his chair, Rochefort—I believe his wound is bothering him."

Joseph stood, leaned on Rochefort for a couple of steps, and then shook him off irritably. "This is not the end, Monsieur de Fontrailles," he said.

"Of course not," Fontrailles said. "You and the cardinal still have to save us all from the Hapsburgs. *Bonne chance!*"

Rochefort slammed the door.

Louis sat, staring at nothing, pivoting his chair absently left and right. *I gloated, curse it all,* he thought. *I swore I'd maintain a dignified reticence, but I couldn't do it. I gloated.* His ugly face broke into a smile. "How the Spook's eyes popped!" he murmured.

The door flung open and Isabeau hurtled into the room. "Louis!" she said breathlessly. "There you are! Listen!"

"I know all about it," he said.

"Know about what?"

"Father Joseph."

"Father Joseph?" Isabeau said. "*Fry* Father Joseph! Louis, I'm talking about Philippe—the Commander de Longvilliers! He's *proposed* to me!"

CHAPTER LXVII
CONJUGATION

"Proposed?" Fontrailles said weakly. "Marriage?"

"No, of course not," said Isabeau, the words tumbling out. She was flushed, her voice almost shrill. "You know our social ranks are too different for that. He's offered to make me his *maîtresse en titre*, and to legitimize my child on his fifth birthday as his own."

"Official Mistress of the Commander de Longvilliers," Fontrailles mused. "In noble households they often wield more power than the wives. And your child will have his name—Isabeau, that's ... wonderful news!"

"Wonderful news? You *idiot!* This is all your fault!"

"My fault? How is it my fault?"

"How? Because, porridge-for-brains, Éric has been dead for over a month, and you haven't said a *word* to me about marriage! And now I have to find a way to refuse a Knight of the Order of Malta who's been nothing but kind and considerate to us! Oh, *Louis!*"

Isabeau stamped her booted foot and glared at him, furious to her fingertips. She had never looked more beautiful.

Louis's mind was an utter blank. He said, "What?"

"You...!" She trembled with rage. "You...!"

"Isabeau, I … I don't.…"

"Oh, *damn* you, Louis d'Astarac!" She spun, marched from the room, and slammed the door—much as Rochefort had.

Fontrailles stared at the panel, still quivering in its frame, and began to realize what had just happened. "Dear God," he said.

"Ahem," came a voice from the garden window.

Fontrailles turned his chair. "*Bonjour,* dear d'Astarac," said Aramis, from the window. "Mind if I come in?"

Without waiting for an answer, the lithe musketeer hopped nimbly into the room, straightened his half-cape and smiled.

Louis, still preoccupied with Isabeau, could only say, "Aramis! Why are you coming in my window?"

"I can't very well come in the front door," said his friend, "with Rochefort and his bullies watching it."

Fontrailles put his hand to his head, which throbbed like a kettledrum. "You know, Aramis, I'm really *very busy* right now, what with Father Joseph and … and Isabeau. What do you want with me?"

"Well, it's *always* a pleasure to see you, dear d'Astarac," said Aramis, all charm, "but really I'm here to have a talk with the Commander de Longvilliers."

"On the same day as Father Joseph? You can't convince me that's a coincidence."

"I won't even try, *mon ami.* I came on behalf of a … *friend* of mine, who wants to persuade the commander not to join the cardinal's party."

Fontrailles shook his throbbing head. "You never stop intriguing, do you? Are you sure the commander will listen to you? He can be rather high-handed toward, uh.…"

"Toward those of lower rank, like mere musketeers?" Aramis smiled his crooked smile. "I have reason to believe he'll condescend to hear me. Don't waste your energy worrying about that, d'Astarac. I think you have worries enough of your own." He made a small, elegant gesture toward the door Isabeau had slammed behind her.

"Ah. Yes," said Fontrailles. "How much did you hear, d'Herblay?"

"As an aspiring man of the Church, I must make confession: I've been listening at your window for quite some time. And while I was impressed by the way you handled Father Joseph—I particularly enjoyed your gloating at the end—I'm afraid you entirely bungled your interview with the lady."

"I did, didn't I?" Fontrailles said. "But what can I do? She was so angry that by now she's probably gotten back into that carriage and driven off."

"Not a bit of it! Right now she is in her chamber waiting for you to come to her."

"How do you know that?"

"Really," Aramis said earnestly, "you must trust me on this. When it comes to the workings of a woman's heart, I know what I'm talking about."

"But what can I say to her? The entire situation is a disaster."

"Oh, d'Astarac," said Aramis. "How can a smart man be so stupid? You must go to her, you dolt, beg her forgiveness, and ask her to marry you."

"What? Are you mocking me?"

"Never in life!" Aramis protested. "Some matters are sacred—even to me."

"But she said she could never be my wife because she wanted to be certain she'd have children who didn't look like me."

"Well, I hope you will pardon me for alluding to it, but from what I heard I gather your lady friend is already bearing another man's child." Aramis said. "Which means...."

"Oh," Fontrailles said. "*Sacre nom.*" He shook his head. "You're right: I *am* a fool."

"Quite so, *mon vieux*. Now, do you need a push to get that chair moving, or can you get there on your own?"

"No, I can do it," Louis said. *If I can find the courage.*

"Then I'll take my leave, if you don't mind," said Aramis. "I must go back to lurking in your garden until Father Joseph leaves. Good luck, d'Astarac!"

"Good luck, d'Herblay."

Aramis slipped out the window.

Louis wheeled his chair to the door and opened it. *I must do it now,* he thought. *I must do it now or I'll never do it at all.*

Don't think. Roll.

Out in the corridor he could hear voices from the salon, where Joseph was having his conversation with Longvilliers, as well as laughter from the front hall, presumably the guards Aramis had mentioned. But the corridor was empty, so Louis wheeled himself, hubs squeaking, toward Isabeau's bedchamber.

He stopped outside her door, gnawed his lip for a minute, and then knocked, three light raps.

"Isabeau?" he called. "May I come in?"

The End

AUTHOR'S NOTE

The author had a grand time writing this novel, and has dozens of fascinating historical notes that he would love to share with its readers ... but this book is long enough as is. For those who are interested, historical notes and many other fine features can be found at the author's website, **swashbucklingadventures.com**.

The early adventures of the first Sir Percy Blakeney are chronicled in two novels by his creator, Baroness Emmuska Orczy: *The Laughing Cavalier* (1914) and *The First Sir Percy* (1921).

OTHER BOOKS YOU MAY ENJOY

The Three Musketeers

The First Book of the Musketeers Cycle

By Alexandre Dumas

Translated by Lawrence Ellsworth

The Red Sphinx

The Second Book of the Musketeers Cycle

By Alexandre Dumas

Translated by Lawrence Ellsworth

The Big Book of Swashbuckling Adventure

Stories and Poems

Selected and Introduced by Lawrence Ellsworth

The above are published by

Pegasus Books of New York and London

9 780999 815267